Praise for *The Secrets of Married Women*

'Carol Mason unlocks life behind a marriage in this strong debut' *Heat*

'There is a fresh and vital edge to this superior debut novel . . . A bittersweet narrative and ambiguous outcomes make this much grittier and more substantial than standard chick-lit fare.' *Financial Times*

'An eye-opener to those of us unmarrieds who see the grass as greener on the other side. Realistic and entertaining.' *New Books*

'The story is full of realistic emotional twists. The characters' reactions to the challenges they face are frank and unmelo-dramatic; there is a refreshing honesty about the numbness that comes from discovering an infidelity, and the shame that comes with perpetrating one. Equally affecting are the coun-terpoised sources of sadness in Jill's life. Her marriage has faltered because she and her husband can't have children, and yet she must be a mother to her own parents in their old age; it's a poignant combination.' *Telegraph*

'There's a big buzz around this tale of three Newcastle wives tempted to cheat on their husbands and I can see why. Lots of bitchy, cackling sex talk – you've been warned!' *Eve*

'There's dark stuff here. But it's the kind of story that promises you a happy ending. It's got the raw realism of someone writing about a world she knows.' *Dublin Evening Telegraph*

'This poignant novel deals with honesty, forgiveness, love and the realities of modern-day marriage'. *Notebook* (Australia)

SEND ME A LOVER

Carol Mason

HODDER

First published in Great Britain in 2008 by Hodder & Stoughton
An Hachette Livre UK company

2

Copyright © Carol Mason 2008

A CIP catalogue record for this title
is available from the British Library

ISBN 978 0 340 979150

Typeset by Hewer Text UK Ltd, Edinburgh

Printed and bound in the UK by CPI Mackays, Chatham ME5 8TD

Hodder Headline's policy is to use papers that are natural, renewable
and recyclable products and made from wood grown in sustainable
forests. The logging and manufacturing processes are expected to
conform to the environmental regulations of the country of origin.

Hodder and Stoughton Ltd
A division of Hodder Headline
338 Euston Road
London NW1 3BH

www.hodder.co.uk

For Tony

ACKNOWLEDGEMENTS

To my husband, Tony, who never stops being proud of me, no matter how irritating I might get, and who has an annoying habit of always giving the right advice. For, among other things, your support and endless faith, and for being as excited as I am watching the whole process of being published unfold.

To my great friends and family – my lovely brother, and especially my mam, who is as close a mother and friend to me as a girl could hope to have (and who is only a little bit like Vivien in this book!)

To everyone at Hodder, and Jane and the team at Gregory and Company, who work so hard on behalf of my novels – thanks for all you have done. To Emma Dunford, Isobel Akenhead and Carolyn Mays for all the ways you helped make the book stronger.

To Lisa Stratford, Gail Holst-Warhaft, Peter Prontzos, Ed Emery and Matt Barrett (and his brilliant website about Greece).

And thanks to all the booksellers, and everyone who bought my first novel. Hope you enjoy this one!

Death leaves a heartache no one can heal.
Love leaves a memory no one can steal.

From a headstone in Ireland

I

It's a steady face, this Roger's; craggy like a seaman's. The eyes have softly changing colour depths, like bottomless wells of Harveys Bristol Cream, and they rarely leave my face, only when they need to, when the waitress brings the wine, or he orders pizza for us. There's something easygoing, too, in the way he listens to me, with his chin resting on his upturned hand. Yep, this Roger looks like a man who could take anything on board.

Even me.

He hasn't exactly dressed to impress. Which is good, because these days, I couldn't care less about clothes. In the navy windbreaker over grey crewneck sweater and jeans, which somehow go with the salt and pepper hair, you could mistake him for a soccer coach.

'You know, you're my first proper date, since my husband . . .'

He nods before I finish. I get the feeling that this Roger knows a lot of things without my having to tell him.

'Well, second date,' he corrects me, and there's a twinkle of entertainment in his eyes.

He's referring to last week. It was his idea to do pot luck at the Vancouver Film Festival. We walked into the only show that wasn't sold out. The movie turned out to be about a young widow whose grief manifested itself in a kinky fixation on her neighbour. She'd spy on him making love to his wife, then wee on their rhododendron to mark her territory. When we came out, I needed one of us to laugh about it, but neither of us did. I thought for sure I'd seen the last of him as he stood there on the kerb, fog circling his head, and said, 'Well, goodnight, Angela. It's been . . . different,' and he offered me a handshake.

'Pizza?' he said, when he rang me this morning, out of the blue. 'Safer this time.'

'Actually, you're not technically the first man I've gone out with since Jonathan.' I take a glug of thin red wine that comes in a yellow jug with a red rooster on the handle. 'There has actually been one far worse than you.' I feel the need to be funny. I don't do widowed very well.

'Worse? Than me?' His eyes twinkle again. 'Tell me about this freak of nature.' Maybe he's trying extra hard to be light, too, because he doesn't do widows very well either.

I twiddle with my wineglass stem, the tightness back in my chest. 'Well, I met him in Stanley Park while I was power-walking the seawall. Then the next day I was in Safeway and he was right beside me at the checkout. It was weird. Flukey . . . He seemed nice. Not shy. Not pushy.'

Not overly horny.

I knot my fingers in my lap, go for my wedding ring to play with, but realise, with a queer, recently accepting feeling, that it's not there. 'Anyway, well, we went to Milestones for dinner, and right off the bat he made it known that he wanted to be a father before he was forty.'

'You gotta love an honest guy!' When he smiles he has holes up near his cheekbones – dimples, really – only dimples is too cute a description for his weathered, life-beaten face.

'Oh, it gets worse! There we were, sharing a piece of banana cream pie, and then he suddenly changes the subject, looks at me very seriously, and says, "There's something I have to tell you about my family." And then he tells me his brother's a dwarf!'

His brownish, nondescript eyebrows shoot up; he needs nondescript eyebrows on that descriptive face. The mellow Harveys Bristol eyes flare in amusement. 'You're kidding? Good God! What did you say to that?' He sits back, slides down the seat a bit, puts his hands in his jeans' pockets.

'Well, I said, "Oh, boy, did I really have to know that on a first date?"'

He laughs: a staggeringly loud belly-laugh that turns heads at the next table. 'You didn't!'

'I did. It really pissed him off actually. He said, "You are *clearly* a person with a lot of issues." Then he said he'd bet I believed that blacks should sit at the back of the bus. Then he got up and walked out.'

His head shoots back this time and he roars, and the couple at the next table look at us again.

He's nice. My old client, Denise, who set us up, said he was. He's got it all going on. Everything the Second Time Around Club would consider a catch. Attractive. Decent. Divorced. No children. No dwarves. A prominent city planner and university lecturer. A PhD in his field. He has nice hands. They're craggy and steady and sure, just like his face. He'd be a boyfriend a girl could take anywhere.

Boyfriend?

'Did he at least pay the bill?' he asks me.

'Hm? What?'

'The bill?' He studies the small change in me. 'Did he pay?'

'Erm . . . Actually, no. He didn't.'

'So I take it you didn't get an invitation to his family's for dinner?'

I smirk. 'One hasn't been forthcoming so far, no.'

'My brother's seven feet tall,' he says.

'Is he? My gosh, that's massive!'

'Not really. I don't have a brother. Only one very normal-sized sister in Manitoba, with size nine feet. She's married to a podiatrist.'

He sees my sceptical look.

'No, I swear, she really does have big feet. And she is married to a podiatrist. But the two have absolutely no connection. Unfortunately.'

I slap a hand over my smile. He holds my eyes. His face is covered with affectionate kindness. The expression, the gaze, lingers.

He would be a keeper.

'What does it feel like?' Roger asks me now, after this bit of ice-breaking humour has evaporated into the pizzeria smells of bologna charring in a wood-burning oven, calamari roasting on the grill.

'What does what?'

'Dating again.' His eyes scrutinise my face.

A startling crash of glass comes from the kitchen. Every head turns, except his. There's something about that word 'dating' that doesn't sit right. Echoes of Jonathan ride in the air, as though he's watching me with a mix of frustration, goodwill, jealousy and regret.

'I suppose, a bit like being unfaithful.' Denise will have told him it's been eighteen months. He's bound to think I'm a freak.

'How do you know? Were you ever unfaithful?'

'No. Were you?'

'No, but I probably would have been if I'd stayed married. Or one of us would have been.'

I meet his eye. 'I'm not sure I'm ready to compare baggage, Roger . . .' I don't have the heart to have divorce laid beside widowhood as though they're somehow equal, because they're not. If you get divorced you can at least tell yourself, *well, he obviously wasn't the right one; better fish in the sea* . . . A picture of Jonathan arrives in my mind's eye. One of my favourites:

that devilishly good-humoured, slightly teasing expression that would appear whenever something I'd said had just amused him and reaffirmed why it was that he loved me. I don't think there'll ever be any other fish. No matter how many oceans I might swim.

It's back. That hollowed-out, disabling feeling I thought I'd managed to shake.

'You're right,' he says. 'And the very last thing I want to talk about on a first date is my ex-marriage.' His eyes drop to my pizza lying almost untouched. 'You have a tiny appetite.'

'Is there something wrong with that?' It comes out a bit snappy. The chip on the shoulder that came with sudden widowhood. I lost over a stone when Jonathan died. Lost my curves. My boobs went from a C-cup to a smallish B. No matter how I've tried, the weight's not gone back on. I don't feel womanly any more. Padded bras make me feel a bit like I've been given false teeth after a lifetime of having a good set of real ones.

He blanches. Something in his unflappably nice face falters for a moment. 'I didn't mean anything by it. I'm sorry. It was a pathetic attempt at a compliment.' His fingers go to the base of his glass, clumsily, sloshing wine all over the place.

'I'm not very good with compliments,' I tell him, watching him mop away at the tablecloth with his napkin. How could I possibly go out with someone called Roger? It's a geezer's name. The thing is, I've just quickly asked myself if I could kiss him, and the answer is yes. My scalp suddenly feels sore in my scraped-back ponytail. I tug on the elastic band, wishing I could pull it out and give my head a good scratch.

'Doesn't it feel weird to you? Being set up?' I throw this at him. My eyes dart around the room, looking for a means of escape.

He rests his chin on his upturned hand again. 'No. Not at all. I'm actually quite curious about this person that a good friend of mine thinks I have a lot in common with. After a year of going on dates only to find I never want to see the women again in my life, I quite welcome a bit of divine intervention from a friend.' He studies me closely. 'How about you? How do you feel?'

I tug on the end of my ponytail. 'Socially challenged. Can't find a man myself, so I need the help of others who are better at it than I am.'

He smiles. He's not rising to my bait. Perhaps I have to try harder to put him off. Maybe if I pick my nose, or hawk up phlegm. No. I have a feeling he'd still look at me with this face that tells me he's ripe for taking on a head-case girlfriend like me.

Girlfriend.

Why's he interested in a thirty-two-year-old widow anyway? What's wrong with him?

'My problem is,' he says, his eyes swiftly dropping to his wineglass that he twiddles with again, 'I'm not very good with dating. I never was at twenty-two and I'm not much better at forty-two. Small-talk, tiptoeing around things . . . I get impatient for something substantial. It's a failing of mine.' Then, of all things, he reaches in his pocket, pulls out a small comb and runs it through his dishevelled salt and pepper hair.

There. See? He's completely off his trolley.

His eyes, and the way he looks at me, his entire comfortable-with-me, understanding being, it's all more than any girl in my shoes could hope for. Only I don't do grateful very well. I certainly never did with Jonathan.

Jonathan.

He visits me again with a sharp, bleak smack to my senses.

I grab a pint glass of water and gulp the lot down. In the background, some romantic Italian music plays beneath the din of voices in this packed-out pizzeria. 'Tell me about your children,' I say, in desperation.

'I can't. I don't have any.'

'Oh.' I lay the back of my hand quickly on my hot cheek. There's a fire exit beside the toilets. I could make out I'm going to the loo and flee.

'Do you have any pets?' he asks me, and reads my blank expression. 'Dogs? Cats? Parakeets? In case you hadn't noticed, I'm trying to get the small-talk over with fast.'

A sped-up film track flashes across my mind now. Goodnight kisses. Hands roving over bodies for the first time. First time having to do a number two in their bathroom. First person you call when you have something good to tell, or something bad. There are potential-to-be-the-man-who-ends-up-replacing-the-only-man-I-have-ever-loved moments coming out of this, and I am scared shitless. Sweat pours out of my hands, my back, the soles of my feet. A panic attack. I thought I'd stopped having them.

'Have you ever thought that maybe some people aren't meant to try so hard to find somebody to love them, Roger? Maybe they're just meant to be alone.'

He just studies me, holds up his hands. 'That's a pretty negative way of looking at things, Angela. I like to believe that there's somebody totally right for us out there. And that we eventually find them, even if we don't find them the first time.'

It suddenly reminds me of something Jonathan once said. Strange how I'm remembering it now . . . We were larking around, talking about death in the way you do when you assume you're going to live to a ripe old age. We were in bed. We had made love. Satisfying and warm, and extremely horny, as was our style. Particularly after we'd fought, which we did, often. He was explosive. I am. Or was, when I had something to get me going.

'If I died, I would want you to marry again,' he said to me, his finger absently massaging those two dimples at the base of my spine.

'I'd never marry again if you died,' I told him, still feeling a white heat for this man who I'd signed up to spend the rest of my life with. The thought of kissing someone other than him was actually quite yucky.

He ran his hand appreciatively over the curve of my well-exercised rear. 'You would, you know. I'd see to it that you did.'

I propped both elbows on his chest and looked at him, his dark, sharp eyes, the slightly receding hairline that he hated you to make fun of. 'Oh? And how would you do that, then, Mr Hotshot Lawyer Who Thinks He Knows Everything?' I was feeling very turned on again. Just my breasts against his chest hair almost hurt with excitement.

He ran a finger along my collar-bones, looking deep and distracted – lawyerly: the look that was very Jonathan. The look that very often I only had to catch sight of to want really badly to screw him. 'I'd send somebody for you,' he said.

I thought about this for a moment. 'Yeah? You mean a carbon copy of you, right? Because you think you're so damned perfect for me, don't you?' I couldn't take him seriously because I couldn't ever see either of our lives ending.

He scowled. 'God, no. Nobody like me. I'm thinking Elephant Man with a big heart.'

I play-punched him. 'Would he at least be good in bed?'

'Terrible.' He kissed the hollow of my throat, flicked the tip of his tongue across the indentation there. 'Completely hope-less, with the tiniest dick you've ever seen.'

'Thanks. He sounds like a real treat.'

'No, seriously, I'd send you somebody . . . somebody totally right for you. Somebody better for you than I've been, Ange. Honestly, once I got up there, I'd make it my entire reason for being. That is, if you can have a reason for being once you're dead.'

That was Jonathan: my high-achieving husband. Even in the afterlife he'd have to have a mission, some accomplishment to strive for. 'You think I'm joking, but I'm really quite serious.'

Daft as it sounded, I could tell he was. 'I'll hold you to it,' I told him, and then he flipped me onto my back and rolled on top of me.

'But don't think I'm going anywhere any time soon, Angela Chapman.' He sank his fingers into my bum cheeks.

But you did, Jonathan, didn't you?

The din of music and voices and chinking dishes comes back to me now, and the memory slips away, leaving a dull absence in me, as though Jonathan has just been here and has left me, but left me temporarily. Maybe just to step aside and watch me now with this Roger, and to say, *What are you doing here, Ange? With him? When you've got me?*

Roger is studying me. 'What are you thinking?' he asks.

I open my mouth to say something, but the words won't come. I'm like a dyslexic trying to read for an audience.

'Help me out, Angela. I'm trying, here.' When I don't reply, he says, 'Shit. I've got a feeling I'm going the same way the dwarf guy went.'

I give him a look that says, sorry, I can't correct you there.

He studies me with that affectionate kindness again. 'All I was doing, or trying to do – badly, obviously – was to find out about you. I want to know all the little things that make you the person who a very good man fell in love with.'

A pain builds in the bridge of my nose, along with the distant urge to vomit. 'How do you know he was a very good man?'

'Well, I've a feeling there's a reason why he's so very hard to forget.'

He scours my face. His tone is different now, serious. 'You know, Angela, a friend of a friend of mine was married to a man who died in the World Trade Center. All these years later, she still hasn't moved on. She still keeps his toothbrush in the bathroom. She still leaves the alarm clock set for five thirty every morning. She says she still regularly walks into the house convinced she's going to find him there, that he somehow got buried deep in a long tunnel where he was disconnected from the world, but he dug through, he fought his way back to her –'

The scraping noise of my chair along the floor feels like fingernails on a blackboard. When I get my foot caught in the strap of my handbag, and trip, and practically lurch into the bowl of spaghetti on the next table, and other heads turn and look at me, it's his gaze I want to strip myself of. I feel it clinging to my back like a fever as I hurtle towards the door.

He doesn't follow.

Not that a girl could exactly blame him for that.

When I get outside, it feels remarkably like I've had my head held under water but somehow I've managed to fight my way up for air, and the air feels fantastic, and I will never let myself come so close to drowning again.

2

'Do you think it's weird if a hunky Australian sheep-shearer from Perth invites you over to his house to watch *Brokeback Mountain*, which he tells you he's seen seven times, then wants to have anal sex with you?'

I light up when I hear my friend Sherrie's voice on the phone. I take one more look at myself in the bathroom mirror – my pale face and longish, lank blonde hair with about two inches of dark roots showing, making it look permanently in need of a wash.

'Weird?' I switch the bathroom light off. 'Well, if he's from Perth, yes. I mean, if you'd said Canberra or Sydney, that'd be different.'

There's a silence where I feel she's smiling. My four-feet-eleven, carrot-haired Jewish friend is a cotton trader. She spends eighty per cent of the year travelling to the middle of nowhere in China, Egypt, India or West Africa, to buy or sell the bales of cotton that become yarn, that become fabrics, that become our clothes – racking up peculiar sexual conquests in the process.

'What time is it there, anyway?' I ask her, wishing she were here, then we might go out. I'm not starved of friends, but Sherrie's my first pick every time.

'The exact opposite of whatever time it is there, I guess. We're upside down, remember? In case you hadn't noticed,

I'm currently standing on your head. Urgh, but then you'd see right up my skirt . . . Not a pretty sight, especially after –'

'Urgh!'

'Or I could be standing on the soles of your feet. Damned if I know.'

Sherrie will always say that between constantly living in different time zones, and being a slave to her mobile phone around the clock, the world has no boundaries any more. Even light and dark don't mean anything to her, which I find hard to fathom. But some days it sounds like quite a nice problem.

'What you up to, girl, anyway?' she asks me.

I take the phone over to the chair, half abandoning my idea to go out for a walk now. 'Oh, just another rocking Saturday night, you know . . . I'm sitting in my small Ikea love-seat, with my feet up on my small Ikea coffee table, in my small Ikea life that I'm supposed to assemble myself, only it doesn't come with any instructions.'

'Well, it's better than being given a large throbbing enema by a hunky outback guy who's secretly wishing you were Jake Gyllenhaal.'

'Want to bet?'

My friend laughs as though I'm hilarious. 'Well, it was just a quick hello. My cell's about to die on me, so I'm probably gonna jump him one last time before I gotta leave here, if he's up for it. Think I'll put the movie on again! I'll be home tomorrow. Man, do I need a vacation!'

'You're on one!'

'This is work, honey. They don't pay me the big bucks to do nothing, you know. Actually, they kinda do! Anyway, give me a few days to get my schlep together, then I shall take you out and we'll work on getting you laid.'

'You could pack your Aussie in your suitcase for me.' Not that I'd probably remember what to do any more. A fortune-teller once told me that I'd never go a long time without sex. She also said that when I married, it would be for life.

'No, you can't have him! He's all mine! And he's all man. Or maybe he isn't. Damned if I care! Delusion is a great side effect of the drugs!' She blows a string of deliberately British air-kissing 'mwa!'s.

When I put the phone down, I instantly miss her. My friend, Sherrie – who I met quite randomly crossing a road when a driver almost ran her over – is a lover of life. If she has a serious side, she rarely lets it out. If she ever feels down, she compensates by acting up. She's never wanted kids. She doesn't care if she's got nobody to grow old with. If she makes an idiot of herself, she's the first one to laugh. And if she laughs hard and loud, she's the last one to think she's making an idiot of herself. I love Sherrie. Nobody could do anything but love Sherrie, unless they had a thing against small, loud, Jewish people who love life. After Jonathan died, Sherrie and Jonathan's best friend, Richard, who he opened the law firm with – and my mother, who came over from England for two months – were nothing but rocks to me. Many of our friends had become scarce after the funeral. People generally don't know how to behave around sudden loss. With cancer, they've got time to prepare themselves to have you fall apart on them. But not Sherrie and Richard. Sherrie would phone me daily from whichever plantation she was wheeling and dealing on, and listen patiently while I did a very good job of talking about everything except how I was doing or how I was feeling, and she'd always manage to uplift me with some story about a disastrous date she'd had with a megalomaniac, polygamist, spear-chucking pygmy who kept a wild boar. After one phone call with Sherrie I can smile for days.

After we hang up, I decide I do want to go out after all. I stick my hair in a ponytail and pinch my cheeks. I'm always pale lately, which makes my dark brown eyes look almost too intense for my face. And being thinner now, my nose looks bigger. It's the one thing I would change about myself if I dared have cosmetic surgery. It's bad enough that it's aquiline like my mother's, but, unlike hers, it's got a slight cleft at the end, like a nose cut in two. Jonathan used to say it was cute. But then again, he had quite a hooter on him too. In terms of noses we were really quite well-matched.

As I step outside my apartment door I'm still grinning over Sherrie's call, and the man coming out of the suite opposite smiles back at me, then looks to see who's with me. Nobody but the people I carry with me in my thoughts.

Down at English Bay the sand is custard yellow and the water silvery with the sun on it. Vancouver is one of those charming, laid-back cities where you can live and work, yet still manage to feel like you're on holiday. I sit on a bench beside a giant palm tree and colourful blossoms, and con-template the pro-bono speech I'm supposed to be writing for the director of Raise the Roof, a non-profit agency that shelters the homeless: my first real assignment at the peculiar little advertising agency where I recently started working.

The world and his wife are out this evening. I'm just taking in the sailboats that glide past the oil tankers on the horizon when I see them, just a few feet away from me: the black couple I saw earlier today in a café down at Coal Harbour. They have to be tourists. He's a big man, well put together in indigo jeans and a funky waistcoat. She's like a middle-aged Beyoncé, in a clingy, colourful dress. They stop almost right in front of me. She knots her hands around his neck and arches up on her high lime-green sling-backs to pop kisses on his mouth. She has a full mouth and, as she kisses him, before her lips move away, his lips claim her lower one in a big suck, which makes her smile into his kiss. His hands go from cupping her hip-bones to travelling slowly up and down her sides, like he's reading braille, feeling out a language.

Then, surprising me, he starts to sing Percy Sledge's 'Warm and Tender Love'. It's a good voice. It's a good song. He does it unselfconsciously without any display, and, oh, she's in seventh heaven. She curls her arms around his neck, and his hands go to her bum, and he knows all the words, and he sings them, and he doesn't care who's watching.

I can't take my eyes off them, the way they look against this background cinema of mountains and glittery ocean. I realise, and then flood with shame, that I must be wearing a queer, smitten smile.

How easily it takes me back to Jonathan and me in Barbados. It was the last night of our holiday. Just two days before the knock on my door with the news that changed my life. A steel band was doing a very good version of Bob Marley's 'Is This Love?' An older American couple had just asked us if we were newly-weds. Granted, they'd had a few drinks, and the bloke kept asking the palm tree behind me if it planned on having children, but they were sincere. 'No,' Jonathan said, pulling me into a hug. 'Five years married, us.'

When we got up to dance, I got hit with the last night blues. We must come back here, I thought. But Jonathan hated going back to places; like Cat Stevens said, he'd say, we only get to dance on this earth for a very short time. The girl at the next table watched us. I felt her gaze, a quiet heat on top of the heat of a Barbadian evening. I remember realising I was happy. The feeling just visited me, like you might suddenly be aware you feel tipsy or over-full. More than that, I was content, which felt bigger and better than happiness.

'Why do you have goose-bumps?' Jonathan asked, pulling me closer to him, his big hand accidentally finding the burn I'd got from a day spent bingeing on my last dose of sun while he'd been out water-skiing. Jonathan always had to be doing things or he'd get twitchy. It was quite funny. Sometimes it drove me mad.

'Ow!' I said, not realising I'd burnt my shoulders so badly. I didn't know why I felt a chill. I just remember not wanting the night to end. I wanted to keep him there, on that dance floor.

'Take your top off,' he said. 'The straps are irritating your burn.' His eyes took on that ragingly turned-on look.

'Yeah, right. Me, the girl who won't go in the sea because of the jellyfish, and won't have sex on a dark beach because I'm too scared of the crabs in the sand. Yep, that's exactly something I'm going to do.'

Jonathan always had a knack for making me feel boring. Although, next to him, I was. Jonathan was one of those rare people who dared to do, or say, what others would have liked to. The sort of bloke you want at your party, and you really want in your corner if there's a fight. Sometimes you'd wonder if he was a bit off his rocker. Other times you'd dazzle in the knowledge that the most fun, sexy man in the whole world was with you, loved you, wanted to spend his life with you. And you'd want to possess every inch of him, and rip his clothes off at peculiar times, in peculiar places, and straddle him and nail him to the bed and make him promise he'd never leave you, and say that we'd always be this crazy for one another.

He cupped the back of my head and gave me a devouring kiss. Jonathan was like that: an exhibitionist in his love for me. Then he did a sudden departure from the dance floor and swiped a fuchsia cloth off a table. Then, wafting the fabric in the air, he sent it around me like an enchanted cape. And, so nobody could see, he proceeded to remove my sun-top and bra – copping a feel in the process, of course – then finished by tying it at my nape like a sarong, and clamping a kiss on my burn.

Someone in the audience clapped. A bloke said, 'Way-hey!' I hid my face in his neck. His skin smelt warm and so alive, with that hint of showered-off sunscreen. 'Let's go up to our room,' I said. I was as horny as a harlot in June.

The bed had been wonky from the start. We put the mattress through the frame. Jonathan thought it a brilliant testament to his prowess. 'Next time I'm going to put you through the wall,' he said.

But there wasn't to be a next time.

When I come out of my daydream, the black couple have gone. I see them walking off, hand in hand in the distance. I suddenly hope with a passion that neither of them ever finds themselves sitting alone on a bench on a Saturday night, gazing at a couple in love and remembering their last dance, their last kiss with their lover who would leave them. I send silent mental good wishes to them. *Go safely and happily into the night.*

I walk home, feeling a bit like an extra in a one-person play. The speech I have to write floats through my head again, but the words feel like they're in a strait-jacket; I can't seem to animate them, to set them free. I take a short cut past a new ritzy town house development. The Vancouver skyline has shot up dramatically in the few years we've lived here, making it resemble a mini New York. Yet it's not a big, pulsing city. Beautiful, yes. But, as I once read in a guidebook, 'it's beauty in search of a city'. Vancouver and I have a fair bit in common: we both could use a life.

Back in the apartment, I open a cheap bottle of red wine and scoff Melba toasts straight from the packet as I stare at my view of other people's living rooms in the neighbouring buildings. A new day will swirl overhead in just a few hours, and I should be happy about that. But my head is full of the black couple again, and life, and love. Today has been one of those Jonathan-filled days, where I see him and feel him everywhere. When I clue in again, I realise I've sunk the entire bottle and I'm sitting there in a tipsy fug of happy-sadness, with an acid stomach, wishing I'd eaten a proper dinner. I dial Sherrie's mobile. No matter what time of the day or night I call her, she always answers.

'Sherrie, do you think that the dead can intervene in the lives of the living, to, you know, to bring us happiness?'

For some crazy reason I've been thinking about Jonathan's promise, and whether or not he could possibly swing it from up there. Whether he'd even remember. Do you still have a memory when you die? Sometimes I wonder if he watches me, thinking, *come on, get it together*, and if he's up there hatching a plan to sort me out.

There's a pause. 'Angela, my friend, do you know what colour North American black bears are?'

This catches me off guard. 'You what? Black, aren't they? What's your point?'

'My point is – honey – no need to ask a question when the answer's as obvious as the fact that your ass is farther down your body than your ribcage.'

I try not to smile. 'I was being serious.'

'Oh! Well, if we're being SERIOUS and you want my HONEST OPINION.' She pauses. 'Then no. God, no! Dead people intervening in the lives of the living? That's a load of serious crapology! When you're dead, you're dead. It sounds simplistic, but that, my friend, is because it is.'

'So you're pretty certain about that?' I tease. 'I mean, feel free to be blunt. I can take it. I'm tough.'

'Why are you asking me these retarded questions, anyway?'

I hesitate, not sure whether to tell her, in case, like a wish, the telling will stop it from coming true. 'Okay, well . . . I know it sounds a teeny bit mad – and I'm probably only telling you this because I'm a bit pissed – but Jonathan once promised me that if he died, he would send me a lover, and I was thinking of calling him on his promise.'

Another pause. 'In Xambidny, in the far reaches of Africa, the Pogs believe that if they eat the tail off a hippo they'll grow a massive penis overnight.'

I grin my face off. 'But hang on, I didn't think hippos had tails. Only funny little stumps.'

'And now you know why.'

I chuckle. She chuckles. 'And, again, your point would be . . .?' I ask her.

'That, my friend, I suppose there's no harm in believing something if it makes you feel good. Even if it is a serious load of crapology.'

I shake my head. 'Goodnight, Sherrie. Whenever I need a bit of perspective on things, I always know where to turn.'

In bed, I try, but fail, to fall asleep, a restless ache running down my legs, the speech going through my head again, sounding even more hopeless than before. I'm trying to care about the people of Vancouver who don't have a bed for the night, but I can't quite feel it; at least, not enough to make it sound like it's coming from the heart. I sigh and snow-angel my arms and legs out, my feet and hands reaching to the far side of the mattress. Sometimes I'll do this, and I'm convinced I'm going to touch him.

'All right then,' I say, feeling a plonker speaking to ghosts, especially as I don't believe in them. It's the wine, I tell myself. The wine.

'Paging heaven . . .' This really does sound mad, like I'm a pointer short of a Ouija board. 'If you're listening up there, Jonathan, and if you're so damned sure of yourself . . . Here's your chance to prove it. Do what you promised. Send me a lover.'

My eyes search the ceiling.

While I'm waiting to see if he's going to answer, I fall asleep.

3

When I open my door the next morning, I'm surprised to see Richard hovering there, looking very awkward.

'So this is where you live,' he says, gazing past me at the view. He's being facetious. He knows where I live because he helped me move in here after I had to sell my house. What he means is, in the three months since I've been here, I've never asked him round, even though Richard and Jessica still have me over to their place for dinner virtually every second Friday night.

'Neat view,' he says, walking over to my window and standing with his back to me.

'Not really.'

'You can see the mountains.' He looks at me over his shoulder.

'Is that what they are? I'd wondered.'

He turns fully now, looking mildly entertained. 'You love it here, really, don't you?'

'Love isn't quite the word, Richard.'

He stares at all the boxes piled in the corner. 'You still haven't unpacked!'

'Yes I have! I'm in the process of unpacking. I emptied one yesterday! And I plan on doing another one today!'

No I don't. Because I hate this place and I'm moving out. I just have to work out where I'm going and how I can afford more rent.

'How's the neighbourhood treating you?'

'Fine. I love living among gay men, and I've discovered I've got a particular affection for transvestites. I love seeing them with their tongues down each other's throats in the lift. Especially first thing in the morning. I really like listening to the two above me humping away seven hours a night. It's like white noise. Soothes me to sleep.' When I had to sell our lovely home because I couldn't afford the mortgage on my own, the gay district was about the only area of the city where I could find cheap rent. It's really not that bad. Just makes me feel even lonelier sometimes.

He smiles, like he knows that under my bravado I'm a wounded bird. 'You've got to unpack, Angie. Start making this place . . . comfortable.' He looks caught out because we both know he was going to say 'home'.

'Baby steps, Richard.' I brush over his clanger. 'Baby steps.'

'Speaking of steps . . .' he stares at my feet in my one red ladybird slipper, because the other one's been missing since the move.

'You should try seeing what I look like when I go out in only one shoe.'

Yet I know exactly where I keep Jonathan's blue T-shirt that he'd go running in, Jonathan's wedding ring and Tag watch that they gave me straight from his dead body, Jonathan's well-worn sandals with his toe-prints marked indelibly on the leather.

'I'll make us a cup of tea. Just don't expect a teapot.' I fish in my cutlery drawer. 'Actually, even a teaspoon could be stretching it.'

'I have something for you,' he says as he watches me put the kettle on. 'Or, rather, *we* have something for you' – meaning he and Jessica.

Jessica is Richard's 'hot' wife who disproves the myth that you can't be blonde, beautiful, have size E breast implants and still have a brain. Although for a while I had wondered. For starters, she's never worked or gone to college. All she ever talks about is beauty stuff and exercise. But two years ago she started up a blog, called 'Goddess Girl'. It was a hobby – just her blabbing on about beauty products she likes and dislikes. But now, much to everybody's surprise, it's morphed into one of the biggest Internet sites of its kind, attracting several thousand hits a day! Aside from receiving free products to review that would fill a warehouse, she's now raking in dollars from businesses advertising on her site. *Business in Canada* magazine recently did a two-page feature on her, and her new spin-off charity, Powder Power, that helps underprivileged women get into the workforce by 'making them up' for their interviews and giving them stash-loads of products. Yet when you talk to her, you feel you're talking to a moron. It's very weird.

Richard hands me a shiny British Airways envelope, then he runs his hand through his dark auburn-chestnut hair, pushing back the piece that always tends to flop forward over his eyebrows. When Jonathan first introduced me to Richard at a house party, I thought he was quite attractive. Something about the unusual colour of his hair that seemed to perfectly complement his hazel eyes. Not quite ginger, he doesn't have a single freckle. Then I noticed his very odd habit: when he sits, he wraps his feet around the front legs of the chair, so his knees look primly glued together. This small detail made me realise I could never fancy Richard. But then again, I was so busy fancying Jonathan that Richard could have been Richard Gere and it probably wouldn't have made one iota of difference.

'A return ticket to the UK!' I slap a hand over my mouth. 'Richard! What's this for?'

'For you,' he says, softly.

'But why? I mean, how did you know I've been thinking of going back?'

'Haven't you been thinking of going back for ten years?'

'No – well, yes – but, I mean, just for a visit. I was actually just thinking of it yesterday, as it happens, and wondering how I could possibly afford to go . . .' And now Richard walks in bearing a ticket.

In my low moments I've thought of going back for good. My mother's on her own over there. I'm on my own over here. We're the only family each other has. But after living in Canada for so long, I don't quite know where I belong any more. I'm not Canadian, because I constantly remind every body I'm British. But I'm not quite British either. I don't know the new names for the old institutions like British Gas and British Rail. I wouldn't know who to ring to set up the Internet. I call a toilet a washroom, and I have an annoying habit of saying hello to strangers and asking how they are. Going back would be a bit like moving to a foreign country, and that would be depressing, because I'd be expecting it to feel like going home.

'I didn't know you were seriously thinking of going back, Angie. I just thought – Jessica and I thought – that it might be a good idea for you to get away from here. You haven't had a vacation since—'

Jonathan died. I drag my ponytail over my shoulder and look at my feet. I somehow can't imagine this being Jessica's idea. Not that I've anything against her, just we've never really clicked. Which is just another reason why I have to say, 'I'm sorry, Richard. It's marvellous of you both, but I can't accept this.'

This isn't the first time Richard has been a bit of a fairy godfather to me. When I was going into default on my mortgage, Richard bought Jonathan's partnership interest in the law firm they'd started up together three years ago. I suspect that what he paid me was over-generous. I didn't have a job at the time, because I'd recently got fired from the advertising agency where I was a senior executive, and I was taking time – Jonathan's idea – to think what I might want to do next. Plus we had debts, and I'd discovered, much to my surprise, that Jonathan and I had very little saved. I knew we spent a lot, but I didn't think we were *that* bad. Richard knew how much I didn't want to lose our house – the fabulously dilapidated Cape Cod-style home Jonathan and I were renovating together, with its hazardous wraparound deck overlooking the ocean, its springy floorboards, its mysterious musty smell in the airing cupboard, and the cathedral ceiling in the bedroom that somehow echoed all of our sexy moans and laughter, and every petty scrap we ever had. So much of Jonathan was in that house, and I worried that maybe if you took me out of that house, you took Jonathan out of me. I wasn't ready to lose the house as though it were a shell that contained Jonathan's soul, even though his body had moved on somewhere else.

But then again, I wasn't ready to have him die either, was I? So being ready for things really means very little in this life, I have found.

I sat for hours calculating how much I'd have to earn to keep our home if I went back to my high-flying career in another big agency, hoping each time I ran the numbers that they'd turn up a different figure. But it was hopeless. So the real estate agent dug the 'For Sale' sign into the lawn. Old Ms Elmtree, our neighbour across the street, who Jonathan had helped out with a legal problem, even offered to loan me five thousand dollars. But I couldn't take her money, not that five grand would have done any good.

'You've got to take the ticket,' he says now as I stand there in a fug of wanting to take the ticket, yet my pride has a problem with the whole idea. 'You don't have a choice in the matter. It's in your name. It's not much use to anybody else.'

Some people will always feel they owe you something, even when they don't.

'But Richard . . . I have my job . . .'

'That you don't like, in an industry you hate, working for a goof. England or that . . . Hard choice.'

'My mother or my boss . . . It might be.'

Despite my saying I'd never work in another advertising agency, I am back doing just that. Only this one's much smaller and run by a middle-aged British man who lost his wife to cancer six months ago. David hardly has any clients, which makes me wonder why he hired me. As a substitute for dealing with his grief, he sits for eight hours a day telling me all about how fantastic his career once was. I see him as one of those helpless, befuddled Brits who falls apart when their wives aren't there to give them a daily purpose, so they walk around with urine stains on their trousers, covered in their own drool.

'It's not the job. I could leave there tomorrow if I wanted.' Even though I have developed a good bit of affection for my pathetic, entertainingly self-congratulating boss. 'It's . . . well, I've been thinking about Write Strategies again . . .'

Thinking, not doing, Jonathan would have reminded me. And I'd have probably said *back off, bossy clogs; I'll get there in my own time.*

It was Jonathan's idea that I start a business as a writing consultant. Originally I'd wanted to be the person in the advertising agency who wrote the clever adverts. But in an interview they asked me to come up with a tag-line for Imodium. The best I could say was *Stop the Diarrhoea*, which went down like a lead balloon. Then, when I came up with my other piece of brilliance: *Walk, don't Run*, I was quickly shown the door. So I ended up as a 'suit', taking care of the clients. And the job somehow got under my skin, as jobs do, and I acquired the sort of goals that were expected of me. And for a while there, it felt like that thing called life. But it all boiled down to a career I gave my blood to, that wasn't as loyal to me as I was to it.

We decided I was going to farm myself out to corporations whose staff might need to improve how they communicated in proposals, reports, presentations and speeches. I'd do small groups, or one-on-one coaching. I'd give seminars, whatever was needed. I was going to call my company 'Write Strategies'. I even got the business cards done.

Then two policemen stood on my step in the sunshine and told me that Jonathan had crashed his BMW Z4. He'd suffered an epileptic seizure, I later learned. And that was the end of any desire I might have had to start my own business.

But lately, Write Strategies has been back on my mind again.

'Can't you think about all that after you have a vacation?' Richard smiles at me. If Jonathan were the edgy, type 'A' lawyer, Richard is the patient, I'd like to say happy-go-lucky one, but Richard never looks deliriously happy about anything. Then again, I've rarely met a lawyer who does.

'I'm getting desperate, though.'

'For money?'

'Not just money.' *A move forward.*

'Is there anything I can—?'

'You've already done so much.'

He drops his eyes to the ground and stays like that for a moment, and I think, *what's come over him?* But then he looks up, smiles nicely, and says, 'You might come back recharged. Go take your mother somewhere. Jonathan would have wanted—'

Me to start living again. The things we don't say. Because talking about my husband, even all this time later, might mean I will have to cry in front of people, and I don't do tears. I am best off when I'm not being hugged, made to feel better, or told I am loved. Not by anybody but Jonathan. From everybody else it just tends to embarrass me.

'Anyway, I have to rush. I'm supposed to be taking Emma swimming.' He looks like he badly has to get out of here all of a sudden. Emma is his lovely nine-year-old daughter.

I remember I'm still holding the ticket. 'Oh, God, Richard . . . I'm not good with charity.'

He turns when he gets to the door, pushes back that mop of chestnut hair. 'I'm not good with a lot of things myself,' he says. He holds my gaze for a few moments, then does a leave-taking salute, and then he's gone.

Ms Elmtree's house is directly across the street from where Jonathan and I used to live. It's my first time in our old neighbourhood since I moved. Walking down the street makes me feel a bit like I've been regressed and I'm discovering I've lived a previous life.

Ms Elmtree came with me in the taxi to the hospital the day I fancied comfort food and made mashed potatoes because I hadn't eaten anything for about a week after the news. Using my electric whisk, I somehow managed to break my finger in two places. The doctor who saw me was young and handsome and kind and wore a wedding ring, and I ran out of the treatment room before I broke down in tears.

'I'm sorry I've not been to see you in so long.' I perch on the edge of her sofa, trying hard not to look a couple of inches past her head at where I used to live. I'm curious about what it looks like in there now, but I'd not take a million bucks to go in. Memories detonate in me like little land-mines. I'd tread on them everywhere and they'd blow me apart.

'It hasn't been all that long, honey.' She studies me, watch-fully; she's really not much of a talker and is a bit of an odd duck, but I've always felt sorry for her because she has no family. Ms Elmtree is from the Caribbean, the product of a Jamaican mother and a British expatriate father. She never married, and her twin brother was suffocated when a cat went to sleep on him when he lay in his crib. You might call her eccentric, with her shocking pink lipstick and aquamarine eye-shadow, badly applied (my mother looks at her like she's got two heads). And then there's the other thing: Ms Elmtree has some weird theory about how she's a direct descendant of the artist Paul Gauguin. I tend to believe people and was convinced she had to be. After all, she's an artist herself (not a very successful one; she paints rip-off Gauguins – portraits done in feverishly tropical styles and colours). But Jonathan said, well, if she is, where's the money? I did a bit of research on the Net once, and Gauguin certainly didn't die rich, but another thing Jonathan said: if the Vancouver art community doesn't think she is who she says she is, then she probably isn't. Fair point.

Nevertheless, she was very fond of my husband. When a developer built a duplex next door to her that sent all its drainage into her backyard, Jonathan sued for compensation on her behalf and he didn't take a penny when he won. Jonathan might have been driven to make money, but he was large-hearted and had a heightened sense of right and wrong.

'Are you working on any new paintings?' I ask her.

She smiles, hot-pink lips framing slightly yellowing teeth. She's hard to age, given she hasn't a single wrinkle, but I'm guessing early seventies. 'I don't paint any more,' she says. 'I haven't painted in a long time.'

'Oh?' I look around the room at the garish portraits on her wall. 'Why not? I thought you loved it.'

She briefly moves her eyes to where I've just been looking. Then she says, 'I saw him once.' For a moment I worry we might be talking about Gauguin, but then she says, 'Jonathan.'

I feel sick. 'Jonathan?'

'Before he died,' she adds, as though she senses clarification's necessary. The shock passes. Of course before he died. What was I thinking? 'He was sitting in his car, right there,' she points across the street. 'Just sitting, and sitting . . . As though he didn't want to go inside that house.'

I gaze across the street. 'Our house?' Why would he not want to come in our house? 'Well, maybe he was listening to something on the radio . . .'

'No. Something very bad was on his mind,' she says. 'I could see the demon in his face.'

I push away that disturbing image of him. 'It was probably just his work. His mind was always on his work.'

She doesn't answer, just watches me closely again. I wait for her to say more, but she doesn't. I get out of there pretty fast.

'Hello, blossom.'

It's my mam's bright little voice somewhere a world away in England.

'Mam! I was just going to ring you after I went and put a load of laundry in.'

Just yesterday I went into Safeway and there was an elderly lady lying on the floor. A checkout girl was holding her hand while the manager looked out for the ambulance. All I could do was think, what if that were my mother, passed out on a supermarket floor in Sunderland, with a stranger instead of her daughter holding her hand? Sometimes I think morbidity's been grafted onto my personality since Jonathan died.

'Crabs,' she says. 'You can get them from communal washing machines. And I don't mean the ones that walk sideways on the beach. Oh, hang on, I'm just watching . . . Ooh, you know . . . Irish chappie? Oily, rather prattish . . . Does the sing-along with all the old snowies?'

'Daniel O'Donnell?'

She makes a vomiting noise, then chortles. 'It's not his voice, you know. It's him. Watching him. Urrrrrhhhh.'

'Mam! He's a very pleasing-looking boy. He'd make some mother a lovely son.'

'Hide your mothers, that's all I have to say. And your grannies. And maybe even your pet poodle.'

'I think you're tiddled.'

'Excuse me?' she says in that dignity-affronted tone.

'You've been on the happy fluid.'

'Eeh, girl, no I have not! I've just had a small glass of wine and I thought I'd give my only daughter-child a call.' Another groan. 'Urgh, he's back on again. Hang on till I switch his . . . There. I can talk now. How are you, baby daughter?'

Baby daughter. She's tiddled. 'Well, I'm fine,' I tell her. It's not quite true. I've been unsettled since yesterday. 'But how are you, more to the point?'

Just a few weeks ago my mam turned sixty. My mam is one of those rare women who has somehow become sexier and more head-turning as she's grown older – the Helen Mirren of mothers – so she's taking the big six-oh hard. On top of that, she's just found out she's got high blood pressure and has to go on medication. Lately I've had a heightened sense of my mother's time left on this earth. I'll think, if she lives another fifteen years, and I go back to England once a year, that's only fifteen more times I'm going to see her. I can go to the corner shop more than that in a week. How do you make fifteen times count, when you know they're the last you're ever going to get?

'Eeh, mind, you're a cheerful Charlie!' she said to me, when I told her this. 'I'm only fifty. I could have forty years in me yet!'

Here's the other thing. Since she turned sixty she's started knocking ten years off her age. I never know how she can say it to me seriously, but she can.

She might bluff, as she generally does, but I know, deep down, that she feels abandoned. Since I moved to Canada, Mam and I have been largely telephone callers in each other's lives, except for my yearly trip home, where we try to squeeze all the bonding into two weeks. It's never good enough, long enough, or eases my guilt enough. Every time I get on that plane to come back to Canada I shove that blanket over my head and silently bawl my eyes out underneath. Even when my dad died, I couldn't be there because of work. I'm sure my mam knows I've let the side down, although she'd never say anything. Because my mam is one of life's martyrs, which is convenient for me: she never lets you feel truly shit about the decisions you've made, even though we both know that sometimes she has to restrain the urge.

'Well, weren't you going to look up the side-effects of my Beautiful Pretty medication?' she chirps.

That's her other name for her blood pressure pills. There's a part of my mother that I sometimes think is a bit deranged.

'Oh, yeah.' I find my piece of paper with the weird name scribbled on it. 'I'm right on the computer now. Hang on.'

I clack away at the keys. 'Okey-dokey . . . side effects . . . shortness of breath, hives, swelling of the face or tongue.'

She groans after each word, each groan getting progressively deeper and more groany, which is sort of funny.

'Headache.'

Groan.

'Depression.'

Double groan.

'Erectile dysfunction –'

I hear a muffled grunt. 'Well, that last one's got me very worried, Angela. How am I going to please all my fancy men now, then?'

'With great difficulty, probably.'

'Does it say anything about dizziness, though?'

I scour the list. 'Why, like? Are you feeling dizzy?'

'No.'

I tut and stop scanning. 'Well why d'you ask, then?' I click off the Net. 'Anyway, I have some good news for you.' I'm pretty sure she must be thinking I'm seeing a fella, so I quickly add, 'I'm coming home.' Then I add, 'Just for a visit, obviously.' Just in case she gets the wrong idea there, too.

There's a brief silence. 'You can't come home! What about work?' My mother loves having a 'career girl' for a daughter. She only ever worked as a make-up girl in a department store. She was a pretty, well-brought-up, working-class young lady, who might have gone somewhere, only she married my dad. My dad was going nowhere except to the pub. As she'll say, 'All our marriage, he was having an affair. His mistress was the Olde Fiddle.' Even now, there's a disappointment and a bewilderment in her that runs high, because the life she got wasn't the life she wanted. And now that my dad's dead and she can't blame him any more, she's got nobody to blame but herself, and that's not sitting too well with her.

'I'm going to tell him I need a leave of absence. It's not like he's really got any work for me as it is. Sometimes I think he's just paying me to listen to him rant.'

'You can't do that! You had so much time off when Jonathan died.'

If that's what you call confining yourself to the house, moving in a silent world between the armchair and the bed, listening to people intellectualise loss by telling you that there was a reason why Jonathan died at the age of thirty-six, or that God had plans for my husband that didn't include a long life. Yet you're just dealing with the soft, speechless things, like the towel he used after his last shower; the smell of his T-shirt he last went running in.

'I didn't have a job to take time off from! I'd been fired, remember? I was trying to work out what to do with my life.' Is this her way of telling me she thinks I've come to a standstill or I'm going all to pot? 'Anyway, it almost sounds like you don't want me to come, Mam . . .' This hurts. Maybe she doesn't. Maybe it's easier for her to believe I'm doing okay if she doesn't have to sit there face to face with the evidence to the contrary.

'Why would I not want you to come? Do you want to come?'

'I think so.'

'Well, don't go rabbit with delirium!'

I picture ecstatic bunnies hopping all over the garden. 'You mean rabid, Mam.' My mam comes out with the oddest things. I remember when she'd play her John Lennon record and she thought he really was singing, Give *Peas* a Chance.

'What?' she says, haughtily. She's taking my lack of enthusiasm as a personal slight. I know these things because I know my mother, because in many ways I am my mother. This is not just conversation, it's subtext; it's loaded with all kinds of weird business that we're both aware of but won't talk about because it all comes down to feelings, and we are both bad at expressing them. She loves me. I love her. We need one another. But neither one of us wants to admit it too much because she feels she lost me years ago, and I am too busy worrying about losing her now.

'Whatever you do, don't come on my account, Angela. When have I ever asked you to put yourself out for me? Sometimes you disappoint me. You of all people should know me better. I don't think anybody in this world really understands me.' Nobody has ever understood my mother. 'You, your father, you're both mad as marsh hares,' she says.

'Right, if I'm a bloody March hare, then it's best I don't come, isn't it?'

Sometimes she's got this knack for pressing my buttons.

'Don't swear, Angela! And don't shout. I'm not at the North Pole. I've not got Plasticine for ears. Maybe you're the one that's deaf! I'm just saying,' she goes *sotto voce* to prove that people can make a point without shouting, 'do what's going to make you happy, don't worry about me.'

I feel a ridiculous urge to cry because I've somehow affronted her dignity and she's stuck a big knife in me in return, and she doesn't realise she's doing it – she never realises; she never seems to understand that hurting can be a two-way street. Because I don't want to fight with her. I have a new litmus test for life. If I'm going to fight with anybody I love, I'm going to ask myself, Angela, if this were your last day on this earth, is this how you would spend it? Hurting each other's feelings, breaking each other's hearts? Sometimes the regrets mount up in me and they are truly back-breaking; I almost can't take their weight.

'Just because I'm old and my body's breaking down . . .' she adds, for dramatic effect.

'You're sixty, Mam. And you've got high blood pressure, just like the rest of the world. And I *do* want to see you. I really do. I mean, don't you know *me* better?' There, I fling a good one right between the shoulder-blades.

She sighs, but it's a tiddled, partially entertained sigh because she loves me and would rather have a daft argument with me than have nothing. 'Well, how very nice of you. Hang on while I fall on the floor and prostate myself with gratitude.' Then she adds, 'babsy', which means she knows she's been over-sensitive, and she doesn't want to fight either.

Can I really go to England? What if we end up killing each other? I'm not exaggerating. Dismembered bits of my mother lying all over the carpet are a distinct possibility.

The flight is delayed by three hours. I'm in the middle seat of the middle row, right by the toilets. The man to my left has horrid breath. To my right is a teenage boy who keeps sticking toothpicks up his nose to impress his brother. He's aggravating as hell. But if he were mine, I'd love him to bits. I watch him out of the corner of my eye, wondering what our lad might have looked like, if we'd had one.

Even with the delay, I still have three hours before my connecting flight up to Newcastle. The alternative was chugging through central London to King's Cross to then take the train for four hours. Or there's always the other joy of seven hours on the Victoria to Sunderland coach. I often wonder why my mother couldn't have moved away and married somebody who lived closer to everything. She still could have found one that tripped off to the pub every night and never brought her flowers on her birthday, only they could have been London pubs he went to, and London flowers he never sent. It would have made my life so much easier.

I roll out of the taxi at my mother's front door coughing and wheezing like a bag o' drowning kittens. See, the rest of the world has moved with the times, but not Sunderland. The taxi-drivers aren't supposed to smoke, but there's always one who will try to get away with it, and I have to get him. When I bleat, 'I have asthma!' he promptly pulls out a can of lavender air-freshener and tries to simultaneously blind me and gas me, either for my benefit, or to hide the smell of freshly hatched fart that was potent when I climbed in. On top of everything, it's raining again, and rain in the summer makes me uptight.

'You're looking uptight,' my mam greets me at the garden gate, getting seriously drenched, her arms wide open for a hug.

'I'm fine!' I growl.

Something about the constancy of her always being here, the same old mother, just triggers a silent sob in me, but I have to mask it by being stroppy.

'You look pale, Mam!' And older than when I last saw her, nine months ago. 'Have you lost weight? You seem a bit thinner.'

'You look like a skeleton on diet pills, so put that in your pipe and smoke it!' She pinches my cheeks. 'Where did your little face go? Your little chubby cheekies?'

I peel her hands off me. 'I never had chubby cheekies, Mam. And if you're just going to pick holes in me, I'm going back on the next flight.' I drag my suitcase up the garden path, secretly trying not to be too happy that I'm back here.

'My sour-puss daughter's home,' she says. 'All's well with my world.'

Coming into the home where I grew up always fills me with a confused nostalgia. Everything is as it has been for thirty years. Same withered carpet. Same knackered chairs. The random addition of a new photograph with me in it, or the essential replacement fridge. Same mother. My initial reaction was wrong; she doesn't really look older. She's every bit the Vivien Smith she always was. Hair the same style it's been for as long as I can remember – a jaw-length, fringed, ash-blonde bob with wild, untameable bits kinking up at the ears 'like a duck's backside' (her words). Her face is not conventionally beautiful, yet it just is, with its fine mix of femininity in the soft, unusual, almost topaz eyes, and strength, in the aquiline nose ('my beak', as she calls it; 'all the better to peck you with', then she'll dip her nose rapidly to your face and pop a fat kiss right on your lips, making you go, 'Ergh!' and wipe your mouth – something I remember doing a lot of when I was little, and she was always attacking me with kisses). Perhaps the chin is too long, the mouth too wide, the cheekbones too low and the eyebrows too dark against her porcelain skin, but it all adds up to a face you would look twice at, a face you would remember. Other than pronounced laughter lines around her eyes, her skin hasn't a wrinkle. Other than a slight softening in the elasticity of her upper arms, my mother's body could be that of any woman of indeterminate age who takes good care of herself. People do double takes of appreciation when they look at her – and not just men. Her dress sense is shamelessly modern. Like today – she's wearing a knee-length, slim-fitting denim skirt, with a low-rise waistband that coasts over a nicely rounded bottom and pair of hips, nipping in at an hourglass waist. And the rest of the package is a pair of large, high-sitting boobs that are still, unfairly, perfect. You really would never think she was sixty. 'I'm not sixty! I was fifty-nine two minutes ago!' is another thing she'll say, when she's not trying to kid herself she's really fifty.

'Hello?' she snaps, when the phone rings and interrupts our catching up. She's ready to ward off strange telemarketers with the Venom of Vivien. 'Hello, Stan. Yes . . . Very well . . .' She makes a talking-mouth with her hands and rolls her eyes at me. 'Yes, well, I have my daughter here at the moment . . . Angela, yes. Is there any other daughter I have that I should know about? Yes, she's fine, but she really has just arrived, so . . .' She makes a garrotting gesture, then covers the mouthpiece and says to me, 'They get all drippy when they've been on the beer, don't they? Slavering on . . . It's a pity they couldn't swallow their false teeth in the process, then we'd be spared the ordeal of having to listen to them. We'd only have to hear them choke, which could be quite enjoyable.'

She takes her hand off the mouthpiece. 'Yes, Stan. Fine, Stan. Very nice of you, Stan. I love you too, now be off with you, Stan. Very good of you to ring.'

She hangs up and says, 'Die!' and I'm not sure whether she means that for the phone or for poor Stan.

Stan is one of my mam's admirers. My mam refuses to admit that she's the sex siren of the senior citizens' community. Half the widowers in Sunderland get an extra kick in their

leg just thinking of her. 'I'll give them a kick,' she'll say. 'My
ankle right up their anus.'

I've actually witnessed her telling one of them: 'I have lots of
friends. But they are all *lady-friends*,' which is a Vivien way of
telling them that they're not going to get laid.

'No more men for me,' she'll say to me. 'Your dad put me
off for life.'

Three days after I arrive, I wake up feeling crabby. For one
thing, it's still raining, and feels more like February than early
June. The trees droop in the garden. The rhododendrons
droop their lovely big heads. I droop looking at it all, and my
mam droops looking at me. Then there's the added cata-
strophe of there only being Nescafé instant in the house, not
my Illy that I'm used to: the one small luxury I couldn't give up
when I had to start living on the cheap. On top of that, I want
to feel happy that I'm home spending quality time with my
mother, but I can't. Sigh.

I tell my mam that I want to pop into town today by myself,
just because I'm feeling one of my 'perverse' moods (as she
calls them) coming on and I don't want to take it out on her.

Could I live here? I ask myself as I wander around the city
centre. Sunderland has changed for the better over the years.
The place has smartened up nicely, but the people haven't
changed. They're still as nice and friendly as ever. Except for
the scary, rough contingent, unique to the North East, who
will confront you with a menacing glower if you catch their eye
on the train. And there really are some evil kids lurking around
the dodgy council-housing estates. I remember getting ac-
costed by a group of tots as I walked home from shopping.
'Giz us yer bags, or else!' one of them hollered. He couldn't
have been more than eight years old but he and his tiny friends
got my heart going like the clappers.

I tried kissing their small bottoms by telling them I liked their bikes, but they saw that as a sign of weakness. Next I tried being stern, but they started circling me on their bikes, preparing – obviously – to move in for the slaughter. I started to seriously panic. I'd just spent two hundred quid in Debenhams and I was damned if I was going to give them my bags! On the one hand, there was my pride: I was the adult; they were the kids. On the other, I decided my best option was to just leg it. So I legged it. When they finally gave up chasing me, I was nearly doubled over in pain. Even now, if I have to pass a group of kids, I walk the other way.

As I walk past the former train station, one of the popular places to stand and have a Geordie tongue down your throat (the highlight of the week) before falling into your taxi home, where if you'd drank nearly all of your fare, you'd let the driver cop a feel in lieu of payment, my mind goes back over old boyfriends. I honestly think I did date the best-looking lads in Sunderland. Even if they were uncouth, they were always handsome. Yet I was never going to marry any of them. I just somehow knew it. I bloated with pride the times I brought my Canadian home. When his accent would get the sales girls in M&S falling over him to find him the polo shirt he liked in a forty-two-inch chest. Or when the single mothers on the train would gawp at us, as though they thought I'd bagged somebody famous.

It's funny, Jonathan only ever came with me to England twice, yet I can't even walk around Sunderland without seeing him here somewhere.

I'm just wondering what the advertising industry is like up north, and whether I could move back here and start up a cracking agency, when I see it. The ad in the travel agent's window. The photo of an azure ocean, cherry-pink bougainvillea and a whitewashed bell-tower perched on a hill. 'Zante,' it reads. 'The third largest island in the Ionian Sea, the green island of poetry, of song and love . . .'

I remember how, several years ago, I told Jonathan I was going to take my mam to Greece when I went back to the UK for my yearly visit. He thought it was a great idea. But we never went. In the end, I wanted to go on holiday with Jonathan, not my mother.

The price is a steal. What did Richard say about how a holiday might recharge me?

'Greece?' My mam glares at me. 'Why didn't you book somewhere like Lake Garda, if you were going to drag me somewhere?'

'Do you even know where Lake Garda is?'

'It's not in Greece! It's in . . .' I see the wheels of her brain turning. 'Italy,' she says.

'Good guess. What have you got against Greece, anyway?'

'Well, for starters, it's full of Greeks.'

'Weird how that works.'

'Plus, haven't you read about it in the *Sunday People*? The hoi polloi and what they get up to in, in Fal-lal-al-a-Fella-Falla –'

'We're not going to Faliraki, Mam. We're going to some quiet scenic island, untouched by the heavy hand of tourism. A gentle place for mothers and daughters to commune in a state of mother–daughterly grace.' I slide the brochure across the kitchen table and she pretends not to look. 'The guidebook says it's the most romantic place . . .'

Although what I'm doing going to a romantic Greek island with my sixty-year-old mother is, admittedly, a good question.

She glances at it, pretends to be unimpressed. 'How much did they hose you for this?'

'Not a lot. Or we'd not be going, trust me. Don't you remember we were going to go there a few years ago?'

'Only you felt silly going on holiday with your mother.'

'No I didn't!' I point out the asymmetrical white villa amid silvery olive groves with cerise bougainvillea climbing the wall. 'This baby is our hotel.'

She steals a glance while pretending not to look again. 'It'll have its own potty, won't it? I hate having to do a Barry in a shared –'

'A what?'

She looks at me like I'm not right in the head. 'A Barry White.'

I think about this for a second. 'Mam, that's disgusting!'

She scowls. 'What d'you mean? It just means go to the toilet for an enormous you know . . .'

I never know how my mother can be so naive. 'It's Cockney rhyming slang, Mam. What rhymes with white?'

She slaps a hand over her mouth. 'Good heavens! I thought it was because Barry White was so big. Oh dear! I've been saying it all the time. I even told the doctor!' She goes pale then quickly changes the topic. 'It's not going to be too hot, is it?' She flaps a hand in front of her face. 'I'm always in a lather lately.'

'The girl said it should only be mid-twenties.' I realise I'm getting excited. 'Imagine a week on a beautiful island, Mam. We get room and breakfast –'

'And drinks?'

'Not drinks.'

She pushes the brochure away in disgust, crosses her arms over those big, unfairly high boobs of hers. 'It's getting more appealing by the minute.'

I've got to pull out all the stops now, do some serious arm-twisting. 'You know Zante is known as "the perfumed isle"? Poets have lived there.'

Her eyes slide in my direction. 'The perfumed isle, hm?'

I know what she's thinking. It'll be *A Room with a View* all over again. She's Maggie Smith and I'm Helena Bonham

Carter, and we're taking turns about the shoreline with our lace parasols.

'Well, I have to admit, it does look nice,' she says, which means she's wooed like a charm. 'Far more refined than I would have thought.'

'Refined,' I parrot. 'It's going to be very refined, Mam. I promise you that.'

'Dinna be stupet, yer fucka!' The young girl hurls this at the lad behind her, whose T-shirt tells the world '*I have nine inches*'. One of his mates is so pissed he nearly drops the boom box he's got propped on his shoulders like a big hip-hop coffin. They're little more than kids – a gang of Geordie lasses clad in tiny denim shorts and matching turquoise T-shirts that have *Geordie Girls Do Zante* printed on the front. When they turn around, each girl has a different name on her back: *Lil Miss Chatty*, *Lil Miss Saucy*, *Lil Miss Anybody's for an Alcopop*.

Welcome to the departure lounge, gate 8, boarding for Zante, at the ridiculous and most unusual hour of 11.20 p.m. on a Sunday night. It all comes flooding back: why I hate the North East.

'I wouldn't spit on them if they were on fire,' my mam says to me, as she sits there looking like a movie star in her big floppy white hat that we just bought for her at Next.

From a quick scan of the three hundred or so people waiting in the 'loading dock,' as my mother calls it, my mother is the oldest by about thirty years – and I, as her daughter, am standing out like a sore thumb with her. A teenage hooligan points to my mam's hat and does a piss-taking caterwaul.

'It'll be fine when we get there and part company with this lot,' I tell her, doubting my words, as she gazes off in a queenly state of dignity.

'You can tell that to the marines, Angela! Methinks little oinkers will fly before I ever come on holiday with you again.'

The flight would have been all right if we hadn't had to sit on the runway for an hour because the airline was denying boarding to three drunken teenage lads who were making inappropriate cracks about being terrorists. The vast arrivals hall in Zante is sterile and white like a Greek temple; it's about the nicest baggage hall I've ever seen. Until I see there's only one baggage carousel which doesn't seem to work properly, and despite all the signs saying, in plain English, 'No Smoking', all the Brits, trembling at the lighter, light up, and very soon you can't see a luggage tag before you and I am wheezing like an old man. 'It says NO SMOKING,' I tell one bloke, but he comes right up to my face and spouts some angry Geordie hieroglyphics at me. Oh, God, come back polite Canadians, all's forgiven!

Having nabbed my mam one of the rare seats, I then wait – for fifty minutes – for our baggage while my mam tries to put on a brave face. I slept on the plane a bit, given that we left so late. My mam, who keeps telling me that these days she can't sleep like she used to, didn't. Her face is vampire white, except for a splash of pink lip-gloss. By the time we're shipped out to the waiting buses, it's about seven in the morning and the sun looks like it's trying to break out from behind a dusty gauze over a hilly, barren landscape.

After mucking around with a faulty microphone, the perky Scottish rep announces that those holidaymakers booked into Pedallo Sands hotel – that's us – are now being moved somewhere else – to an entirely different resort. The bus lets out a collective groan. 'Don'a be like that! You're getting upgraded to the Athena! The Pedallo's under construction.' She thrusts information packs at us.

'If we live to see the place,' my mam adds, because the driver hurtles off the motorway onto a dirt road full of chickens, sending wings and feathers airborne, much to the entertainment of the passengers. As though this isn't enough to wake us all up, he brakes heavily, giving the distinct impression he might not know where he's going; there's a good grind of the gears, and then we suddenly find ourselves doing the same speed backwards.

'Now, Select Travel is pleased to welcome you to the delightful island of Zakynthos, or Zante, as we call it,' the rep chirps. 'Just one thing to warn you about, though: we've been having some unusually scorching weather on Zante these last couple of weeks. Temperatures in the high forties –'

'Whoo!' goes everyone on the bus. Geordies love their suntans.

'Yes, well, sunstroke happens a lot. It's not unusual even for Greeks to fall like olives off the tree when it gets this scorching. So please avoid the sun during the hottest hours of the day, and when you do go out, take lots of bottled water.'

'What's forty in Fahrenheit?' My mam peers at me.

'I'm not sure, Mam.'

'Well, if it's twice twenty, then *beam me up, Scottie!*'

I have an overwhelming urge to go back to Sunderland and commit heinous atrocities on that travel agent.

The hotel looks like something that might be put in an ad for a recruitment drive for the army. The whole area is more like glorified barracks – perfectly ordered rows of flat-roofed, two-storey, square, yellow stucco buildings with swimming pools. 'Everybody off for Athena!' the rep sings.

'But this isn't what we booked!' I tug on her sleeve as she passes. I'm half expecting to see a bunch of skin-headed cadets run past, chanting 'I Wanna Be Your Drill Instructor'. 'There's supposed to be a sea view! And I thought you said we were getting upgraded!' I whine.

'You are.'

'From what?' my mam asks. 'A mud hut?'

'The ocean's just right there.' The rep points. 'About five minutes beyond those bushes.'

We peer over. 'Yes, but who died and made me Robinson Crusoe?' mutters my mam, as the bus driver admires her legs as she climbs off the bus, in her white platforms with her bright red toenails, making her stalwart grand English entrance onto Greek soil.

4

'It's really not that bad,' my mam, who has an enviable ability to know which battles to pick, says, once we've seen our room.

'No.' I dump our suitcase on a bed and look around. 'S'pose not.'

It's not the lap of luxury either, though. More like Motel Five, only with bright ochre wood panelling on the walls, a high beamed ceiling and a stone floor. 'It's cheerful in its own way,' I chirp, then open the balcony doors, pushing away thoughts of how surreal it is to be holidaying with my mam and not Jonathan. I cop the vista of concrete from the window. 'I suppose requesting a "view" was too open-ended.'

'That aeroplane sounds mighty low overhead.' My mam looks up at the ceiling and whistles. 'Good heavens! Somebody needs to give that its walking papers, don't they?'

'Apparently it doesn't go on all night, though. I was reading they shut the airport down between midnight and five a.m. on account of not disturbing the sea turtles. They're an endangered species.'

'Well, hoorah for an endangered species.'

At that point, we lie on top of our beds, fully clothed, and fall asleep.

I wake up and it's nearly 10 a.m. I'm groggy from dreaming I was in World War II and my job was to shoot down enemy planes. I think I'm still in the war, then I realise I'm on holiday, in my not-very-quiet-but-otherwise-not-bad hotel room, in

Greece, and we have an orientation with the rep in about two
minutes, which feels like bad planning given that we really only
just got to bed. Looking across and seeing my mam, when I'm
not used to seeing her when I wake up, is a bit like finding your
favourite jumper in your cupboard years after you forgot you
had it. I lie there and watch her for a while. She sleeps with her
mouth open, her face is slack and missing the winsomeness of
her usual, awake self. I take in the curve of her cheekbone and
the rounded tip of her nose, her ghostly pallor in the sunlight
that streams through the window.

For some reason I think of the time when I broke my arm
when I was eleven and I had to have it put in a sling. How she
accompanied me to school, taking the bus and then walking
the twenty minutes or so to drop me off, then repeating the
whole thing at lunch, and then again at four o'clock. Six trips a
day, she made – there and back. Six times on buses, in the
middle of a gruelling winter. All to make sure no little thug ran
into me and hurt me.

I realise I've been staring at her and her chest appears
completely still. A quick, hot panic comes over me. Why isn't
she breathing? Good God. I'm just about to spring out of bed,
when I see it. The shallow, almost imperceptible rise and fall.
She twitches and makes a tiny sound. I lie back on the pillow
and heave a big sigh of relief.

I've just time to throw on the cute denim shorts and gypsy
top I bought in Topshop's sale, do a quick splash of my face,
and shove my newly blonded hair into a ponytail. Stepping out
of the door into my first taste of a Greek morning feels like
walking into an oven fit to bake a mean baklava.

'*Kalimera!*' says the smiling Greek girl, which I quickly
gather means 'Good morning'. I manage to swipe a couple
of slices of appetising golden bread and a few pats of butter
from her as she clears the buffet counter in the lobby, which
this morning doubles as the dining area. 'Breakfast ends at

nine thirty,' she tells me, with a friendly scold, but offers me a loaded-up bread basket when I ask if I can take something upstairs for my mam. 'Ah! The beautiful English lady in the hat!' she says. I grimace. When you're in the shadow of your dazzling sixty-year-old mother, you sometimes have to ask yourself *what's wrong with this picture?*

I sit at a table by myself, among all the couples who have managed to get up – a few puffy-eyed faces I recognise from the bus. It's a different rep this morning, a hefty girl who talks a mile a minute about car hire, tours, things to do in the area. It feels odd sitting here on my own, getting curious looks from all the holidaying couples, so I take my 'guided tours of the island' package and step outside into a stark white sunshine that glints and shimmers off the mirror-like surface of the swimming pool. Slipping out of my flip-flops, I root each of my white feet onto the hot concrete, enjoying, for a few moments, the masochistic pain.

'You were sleeping.' I put the bread basket and supplies, along with a small glass of orange juice, on my mam's side table.

'I wasn't. I heard you go out.' She's up and dressed now, and she looks so fresh you'd never think she'd had hardly any sleep.

'Ah! So that's why you had your mouth open. I knew it was for a reason.'

She glowers at me. 'I did not have my mouth open!'

'No, you were just doing this.' I cock my head to one side, open my mouth and do a very skilled impression of being dead, or daft, or both.

'You're a real scream,' she says to me. 'Wait while I pick myself off the floor laughing.'

She's wearing an ankle-length white cotton skirt that skims over her hips and settles into a mermaid's tail around her calves. This is teamed with a gold and green forest print cotton

V-necked T-shirt from the Per Una sale that dips to show a fetching bit of lightly freckled cleavage. She looks stunning. 'Come on, Viv, let me take a photo of you,' I tell her. She hates it when I call her Viv.

I've brought Jonathan's megabucks digital camera that I've no idea how to work. I can see him mucking about with it, thumbing buttons and showing me what it does.

My mam fluffs and preens. Then she stands beside the white stone wall, angles her head ever-so, and gazes off serenely into the distance. It's Helen Mirren at the Oscars!

'Put some welly into it!' She grits her teeth behind her frozen smile as I faff on with buttons.

I fire the shutter, then check the pic. 'Oh, you've got no head.' I show it to her. 'My God, it's the best picture I've ever seen of you!' I fire again, catching the playful gleam in her eye, before she has a chance to pull that phoney pose of hers.

We head out before it gets too sweltering. The sun is so intensely white that it's almost painful. Everything appears sharper – the walls of the buildings more yellow, the flowers more pink, the sky more cyan, like a television that's had its colour controls turned up. It's about a ten-minute walk up a steep bank, which, frankly, is a major effort in this heat. But the good thing is we've quickly got used to the sound of aeroplanes and don't really hear them any more. 'So much for being close to everything, Mam! Are you sure you're all right?'

'Soldiering on.'

'You don't have to be sarcastic.'

'You don't have to keep asking me if I'm all right, Angela.' As if to prove how all right she is, she quickens her stride, her dainty feet with their painted toenails going like the clappers. 'You wouldn't ask a person in a wheelchair if his legs got tired when he went for a walk, would you?'

'I don't get the connection.' I hurry after her.

She stops and glares at me, her face clammy-looking. 'Don't mock the afflicted, Angela. It's not kind.'

We reach the main strip and look both ways up the street. 'Oh, God, this is great, isn't it?' I moan. Basically it's a busy road, either side of which are rows of unappealing restaurants, cheesy British pubs and fish and chip shops, tacky souvenir shops and the odd seedy-looking car hire place. 'It's Blackpool meets the Wild West. Was the brochure photographed in a different country? Where's all the wizened grannies dressed in black, making lace?'

'Oh, stop whingeing, will you? Girl, you're such a joy killer!'

'But it's a goddamn dump.'

'You shouldn't use that word.'

'All right then, it's a goddamn shithole.' I try not to smile at her looking all wound up.

'I hate it when you sound so North American sometimes, Angela. You're British. Never forget where you came from and what made you great. You don't have to sound like a damned Yank.'

'Canadians aren't Yanks.'

She mops her cheek with the back of her hand. 'They're tarred with the same brush.'

To her friends, my mother pretends to love Canada. But deep down it'll always be the place that took me away from her. It comes out in little ways. She'll walk into a public loo in Vancouver and if somebody's not flushed, say loudly, 'Were Canadians never taught how to flush a toilet?' In the grocery store: 'Does NOBODY in Canada know how to grow a proper potato?' From her arriving to leaving, it's one big Canada slag-off and I get sick of it.

An English couple tells us we have to go into the corner store to enquire about the times of buses into Zante town, where we'll get a far better taste of the real island than we do here, in package holiday hell. They don't add that last bit –

I do. 'Your problem is,' says my mother, 'you were spoilt with Jonathan.'

I don't need reminding of that. Jonathan and I did have a good life. We had no ties. We didn't even have a cat. We took pretty exotic holidays twice a year and a long weekend away almost every month. After I had to give up our home, it struck me that maybe this was my punishment. Because I'd become too used to the good life and I'd developed an over-keen sense of entitlement. I thought the rest of the world lived like me. When I saw those TV charity commercials about the starving kids in Africa, I'd think, *Oh, that's so sad,* then change channels.

In the store, the Greek man tells us there's only one bus a day into Zante town.

'One bus?' I stare at the top of his head as he thumbs through his newspaper. 'Well, what about coming back?'

'Don't expect to come back,' he talks to his paper.

I get the urge to pull him across the counter by his collar and tell him, listen buddy, tourists keep your economy going, so be nice to them. Instead I slap a hand on the counter, startling his big fat behind. 'But suppose a person, for some quite deluded reason, did get it into their heads that they might like to come back –'

'Never trust the bus,' comes a voice behind us.

I turn, and there is a man there. His gaze is steady on my face, then it drops the length of me, in an appraising, Mr Skirt-Chaser way. Then it shifts to my mam and does the same thing.

'Sisters? Yes?' he says. The eyes roam fast and loose over our hats.

The cheesiness of his line totally appeals to my mother. She bursts into a dirty, tickled-pink cackle. 'Oh, yes! I'm the younger one, of course!'

'I know,' he says, and he smiles at her for a long time, the way a man might do with a younger woman he was attracted to. Then he says something in Greek to the man behind the counter, who sniggers.

'Please, it is not trouble for me to take you into town. I am go there as it is.' He throws a hand in our direction. 'The hats . . . there are two movie stars here.' His English is excellent.

'Eeh, well if your vision's that bad, I wouldn't trust you behind a wheel!' says my mam.

You wouldn't call him handsome. Not in the classical sense. The face is a bit too long, the eyebrows too heavy, the C-brackets at either side of his mouth too deep, like the furrows in his brow. And he needs a good shave. Yet there's something . . . It's his eyes. They have a penetrating expression in them. Soulful eyes. They save him.

I immediately pull my hat off and make a note to give it a slow and painful burial at sea. He makes a point of noticing my self-conscious gesture.

'Well, maybe we should go with the gentleman.' My mam pumps my arm. 'It's awfully nice of him to offer.' Wink, wink.

'*Awfully* nice?'

He looks from my mam to me, then gestures outside. 'My car is just there. Really, I would be happy to have the company.' His eyes briefly alight on my mam's colourful toenails. He seems quite charmed by her.

Now my mam's gone from winking to a wide-eyed, beatific smile. I try to keep the grin off my face and keep her hanging there for a few moments, then say, 'Thanks all the same, but I think we'll pass.'

'Who says we'll pass?' She's practically stopping my circulation now.

'Well, just because your daughter does not want . . . you can,' he says to my mam, which incenses me, the way he's going over my head like that.

'That's because she's a party pooper!' My mam glowers at me. 'Remind me never to come on holiday with her again!'

Then she fawns and flirts to the point where I want to cripple her. 'I personally would love to come with you, but unfortunately I think I probably have to go where the old ball and chain goes. It's a condition of my bail.'

He looks like he might not have understood, but he smiles anyway. Then he looks at me. Is that hostility I see in those soulful eyes? Then he says something that takes me aback. 'You know, sometimes in this life, Angela, you have to take your chance with people. Not all Greek men are like our reputation, you know.' He bows his head to both of us and then he walks out.

I feel like saying, *Hmm, I thought they had the reputation for giving it up the bottom.* But, thankfully, I don't.

My mother's practically legging it after him. I have to restrain her. 'You called me an old ball and chain?'

'If the cap fits!'

If the . . .! I want to kill her. But something suddenly dawns on me, and I feel a strange chill trickle down my spine. 'Hang on . . .' I grab her arm, making her stand still. 'Did you hear what he said?' I stare after him as he walks towards a white Jeep parked right out front. 'He called me Angela.'

'Well, what would you have preferred he call you? Alfred? Or Benjy the three-legged dog?'

'But how did he know my name? You didn't call me by it, I don't think. And I certainly didn't introduce myself.' I watch him climb into the Jeep and glance back at us. He seems to hold my eyes for a few mysterious moments, then he pulls off.

'Well, I reckon I must've,' my mam says. 'Anyway, one option is to run after him and ask him.' She pulls a dirty grin. 'Then maybe we can jump in his car and we can both go for a ride on him. Vivien! Vivien!' She lands a painful smack across her own face. 'You mean, *with* him. *With* him.'

'Oh, you're on your own there, pervert,' I say to her. 'I hate how all these fellas see a couple of English women and think

we've just come on holiday to cop off.' I watch his car
disappear down the road, still thinking *how on earth did he
know my name?*

'No, they don't! What mother and daughter would come on
holiday to – cop off – as you crudely put it? Since you've
moved to that midden of a country, Angela, you've adopted a
very Jerry Springer attitude to life. Besides, I would never
come on holiday with you if I wanted to cop off. Not with your
personality. You'd have 'em running for the hills, clutching
their privates, as fast as they could scamper.'

I glare at her and pretend to be appalled.

'Anyway, I'm sure he didn't think I was fair game. Not at
my age. More's the pity, mind you. I could probably have
given him a good run for his money. And if he thought *you*
were – well, you quickly put him right on that score.' She
scrutinises me. 'You're nothing like your mother, are you?'

'Oh, shame, shame.' I tease her.

'I'm talking about charm. There was nothing wrong with
that era when women weren't afraid to be women and men
weren't ashamed to be men. There were a lot fewer cross-
dressers and homosapiens because of it.' She lets out a slow
whistle. 'If I were young again, I wouldn't let a man like that
cross my path and not do something about it.'

'Come on,' I say, dragging her away.

We truck off to the only restaurant that looks open. An
affable-looking Greek man sits outside and welcomes us
with friendly desperation. We order two Greek salads. 'Oh,
God . . .' I groan when he goes inside to the fridge. 'When
the chef doubles as the waiter and he's only got two
customers at lunchtime, and your Greek salad only costs
three euros, I don't hold out much hope. Notice how he's
not washed his hands. And I'd like to bet he didn't wash
them after he went to the loo, either. Hepatitis, here we
come!'

'Angela,' my mam glares at me. 'Are you going to be in a perverse mood all week, or are you just having a perverse day to get it out of your system in one dose?'

'I'm getting it over in one fell swoop,' I tell her. 'To do you a favour. Bear with me, I'm nearly done.' I smile at her exasperation.

The salads come, along with half a litre of white wine. The vegetables are sweet. The feta is creamy rather than salty. And the olives are worth moving to Greece for. For eight euros we're full, satisfied and ever so slightly pissed. The Greek man's gone back to sitting outside again, from time to time watching the non-events of the street, and occasionally watching us.

'You know, we've never gone on holiday together, have we? Not since you were a little girl.'

'When did we ever go on holiday when I was little? I only remember crap trips to South Shields beach!'

'Don't call them that!'

'Well, they were! Don't you remember? Us having to take three buses to get there because unlike everybody else, we never owned a car, because Dad drank all the money he should have spent on driving lessons.' Or smoked it. I vividly remember him rolling his Old Holborn cigarettes. The cough before breakfast. 'And as soon as we got there he'd make a beeline for the first pub, and we'd have to sit there while he necked back his pints. Always what he wanted to do, never us. Yeah, it was one of life's real joys.'

'Don't say that!' she berates me with a guilty chuckle that tells me she thinks she somehow let me down as a parent because I've only got memories of crap holidays, not good ones. 'Anyway, he only did it because, like all men, he was selfish. He didn't actually mean any harm by it, Angela.'

Jonathan wasn't selfish. But she's right about my dad; he never did mean any harm to anybody. He was just easily pleased and he assumed everybody else was.

The Greek man watches us closely, as though we've pepped up his day. 'Don't you remember Blackpool? When your dad bought you those yellow sunglasses that you never had off your face, and he took you up in the Ferris wheel? And I wore my coral sundress . . .' She smiles coquettishly, remembering herself.

'Yeah, I remember. I've still got that photo of me and him. You must have taken it. He looked quite handsome in it.' He wasn't bad-looking. I can see what she saw in him when he was young, even if he was a waster.

'And I had shoulder-length dark blonde hair back then – like yours – and I used to keep it in soft roller curls, and it was windy and the wind blew my dress up. And there was a man with his wife and little girl . . . And he couldn't take his eyes off my legs. He was just fascinated with them.'

'Oh! That time! Of course. Your legs, and that man! How could I forget?'

'You remember!' she says, thinking I'm being serious. Then she growls, 'Angela! Don't mock the afflicted!'

I shake my head at her and try very hard not to love her so much that it breaks out of my every pore.

'Scoff all you want, but back then there really wasn't much excitement in my life. I was married to a man who couldn't even give the pub a miss the night I brought our new baby home from the hospital.'

'Why did you stay, Mam?' It's something I've always wanted to ask her.

'Where was I going to go? I had you. You loved him. He was your dad.'

It saddens me now to think that my mother never had what Jonathan and I did. And that she stayed with my dad because of me, when she wasn't happy.

'Why didn't you have an affair?'

'I had lots of them.'

'Eh?' I just about swallow my tongue.

'All in my mind, I mean. They'd have different faces on different days. Or they'd be so-and-so's body with so-and-so's face on. Your dad's friend, or Bill the policeman across the street. Bill with the thick thighs . . .' She sees my face. 'Angela, it's my *fantasy* world we're talking about here!'

'I think I've heard enough!' But in some ways I am curious; I've never heard her talk like this. 'Really, though, why didn't you find somebody else? You could have.' I remember the Rington's Tea delivery man, the catalogue delivery man, the window-cleaner . . . how they'd always look at her – a tiny bit pervily – every time they came to the door.

'I was too kind. And I worried about what would happen if I got found out.' She screws up her nose. 'Mud sticks, Angela. I didn't want people knowing that sort of thing about me.' Her face turns quite serious again. 'Now, though . . . I'd take my chances.'

I feel sad for her. I don't want her to have had a crap life.

She polishes off the last of the wine now. A tiny lizard walks along the railing past our table, its bright little eyes seeming to look right at me. 'It's funny how you can lie in bed next to the same person for years and he'll never know you're longing for somebody else, or that you don't long for him. That you've never longed for him,' she says.

'But you didn't long for somebody else, did you?'

'No one in particular. Just some*thing* else, I suppose . . .' She looks at me matter-of-factly. 'I was in love with somebody who didn't exist. Maybe I even still am.'

'This is depressing,' I tell her.

'Not really. Life's only depressing if you let it be.'

'Let's go,' I tell her. We pay up and leave. The Greek man says a polite, 'Thank you,' on our way out.

'Perhaps we'll go back there for dinner,' my mam links her arm through mine and hiccups – a slightly tiddled hiccup – as we cross the road to go back to our hotel.

'You're wasted.'

She bumps into me a bit. 'Don't talk out of your bottom.'

We pass that corner shop again, and I think how there was something beguiling about the man who knew my name. 'I wonder what he does for a living,' I say.

'Who?'

'Santa Claus.'

She stops and looks at me, knowing damn well who I'm talking about. 'He's a chimney-sweep. He dusts the flue with his big bottom as he slides down it.' Then she beams a devilish smile. 'Oh, you mean him! The full-blood! Shag grannies, with a bit of luck. Now I could ensure he's never in the unemployment line.'

We start walking again, and she sighs a slightly tiddled sigh.

The beach, as the rep said, is closer than it looks. I venture down there on my own. I'm pleased to see long stretches of pebble-free sand and gently shelving emerald water. I claim an empty lounge chair under an umbrella, take a few photos, then strip down to my white string bikini. I bought this when Jonathan and I went to Barbados. It's even still got sand in it, because it would never wash out properly, making it look grubby. He wanted to see if you could see through it when it was wet. 'Christ!' he said, when I came out of the swimming pool. 'No!' I cried, and slapped a hand over my groin. He beamed. I knew he was only having me on.

The heat feels like total therapy on my body. Behind my sunglasses I watch a young couple wrapped around each other in the water. He keeps slowly glancing around with a look that's both gratified and shifty. Jonathan wanted to screw in the sea, but I wouldn't. I watched him go in on his own – his causal strength as he dove in – watched him for ages, then eventually lost sight of him. Never for a moment did I worry about him swimming so far out, because it was unthinkable that anything bad would ever happen to Jonathan. Jonathan was so vibrant and thoroughly able to take care of himself. Nonetheless, my eyes studied every head in that sea. Then I saw him, and a smile broke out inside me. I watched him swim all the way to shore, looking forward to admiring his lovely body as he walked up the sand, and to him throwing himself down on the towel beside me, dripping wet, and kissing me with cool, salty lips.

Jonathan sometimes had a way of looking at me, right into my eyes, as though he was thinking things that only his eyes could communicate. I noticed it the first time we made love. I'd had good sex before. But not quite this good. And I'd never had this feeling. As a kid, I used to look at the parents of my best friend, Heather, who seemed to be in a permanent state of heat for each other. I wanted that. I wanted a marriage where the passion wouldn't fizzle out. Maybe it was rare. But I'd seen it wasn't impossible. Was I onto something here with this guy?

'My heart's pounding,' I remember telling him. 'Here,' I pointed to the jumping pulse just above my clavicle. He'd pulled his eyes away from mine then stared at the spot with genuine fascination. He brought his head down, and instead of kissing it, just lay his lips there, as though his lips were feeling the beating of my heart.

That day on the beach, when he came out of the water, he threw himself down on the sand and latched onto my eyes in that same way, gave me that same look. 'Why are you looking at me like that?' I said, when he'd propped himself on an elbow and just lay like that, his gaze heavily on mine, as though there was a part of me that only his eyes could speak to.

I boffed him with my book. 'Stop it. It's unnerving. Go watch somebody else.' I saw that slightly impish expression of his. Then, slowly, undergoing an easy transference of concentration, he slid his index finger underneath one of my bra triangles, moving the material away from my skin so he could see my nipple. Then, with his eyes fixed there, he circled it until it stood up like a raisin. I was mortified. 'God, what if people see!'

'Oh, here we go . . .' He groaned and stopped what he was doing. 'Let them see us, Ange! Who cares? It's not like you know them, or are ever going to see them again.' He flopped onto his back and left me alone.

I'd ruined the moment. Poor Jonathan. Sometimes I think I was so busy trying to prove to him that I was who I was, and he shouldn't ever bother trying to change me, that I sabotaged not just his good time, but my own too.

The couple in the water are still wrapped in a floating embrace. For some reason I feel turned on now. I think back to that promise he made me in bed. Does he know that if he did send me somebody it would be fruitless? I couldn't feel the same. I would always compare.

I slide my hands behind my back, and without thinking too much about it, undo the strings of my bikini and whip the top off over my head. The breeze on my nipples feels lovely. I lie back and enjoy the novel, ticklish sensation, imagining Jonathan is here and the tingling feeling is of him circling my nipple with his tongue, in public; to hell with whoever might watch.

When I come in the door, my mam quickly picks up the book that's lying on her chest and pretends she hasn't just been napping.

'Hello, blossom.' She's got 'bed head' down her left side. Her features look softened with sleep. 'Is the beach nice?' She's wearing one of her full-length 1950s cream slips that she's always slept in. I used to think it made her look so glamorous. Sometimes, as a kid, when she went out shopping I'd try one on, and lounge there on her bed pretending to be alluring, pretending to be her.

'Yeah.' I flop onto my bed and suddenly feel quite wiped out.

'Did you bare your little buzzums?'

'No! And less of the little!' I stretch out my arms and legs like a starfish, depositing sand on the crisp white bedspread, and gaze at the high white ceiling, still feeling a bit horny and unsettled. I wonder if Jonathan could possibly have heard me that night a few weeks ago, when I asked him to keep his promise and send me a lover. Are the dead always in tune with the living? Or do they have to make a point of switching on, like you'd put on a radio and find your favourite station? Because I'm thinking of changing my request. Rather than send me somebody to replace him, perhaps he could just send me a holiday romance. My mind flicks to the attractive Greek man from the store. How did he get on my dial?

'What's the matter?' My mam peers at me over the top of her hardcover.

'Nothing.'

'Pull the other one. I can tell by your face.'

I look away.

'You're missing him, aren't you?' Her voice is a soft whisper. 'I know these things because I'm your mammy. And mammies know when they have a sad baba on their hands.'

Her tender perception makes my eyes burn with tears. 'I wish we'd never come.'

'Don't say that. It was your idea.'

'It doesn't matter whose idea it was.' I catch myself enjoying snapping at her, and hating myself for it.

'Don't be a spoilsport! We're here now. We have to have a good time.'

'No we don't. Who said we do?'

She looks at me sadly. But it's a steel-edged sadness, as though she's not going to be my whipping boy. 'Why don't you go and find a boyfriend? Have a bit of the rumpy. Do something productive.'

'I don't want to find a boyfriend. You go find one.' I try to keep my voice light, as though I'm really not picking a fight with my own mother; this is just a peculiar form of conversation.

'Maybe I will.'

'Good.'

'Maybe it would be.'

She goes back to reading her book. I wait for her to say something else but she doesn't. I kick my flip-flops off and stare at my bare toes, etched with sand. The fuzzy sound of young male voices and mocking laughter comes from the room next door.

'I don't know how you can be so damned happy!'

She pretends to continue to read. 'I'm strange like that.' I watch her for a few moments while she keeps up the act of ignoring me, annoying myself with my self-pity. Eventually she puts her bookmark in the page, claps her novel closed and lays it beside her on the bed. 'You don't have to be like this with yourself, you know.'

'Like what?'

'Guilty. That you're alive and he's dead.'

The words rip me open. Sometimes just *Jonathan* and *dead* in the same sentence sends this staggering blow of disbelief into me. I'll want to curl over and blare for the wrongness of it. Still.

'You can't let yourself be happy because you think you're being disloyal to his memory.'

That choking sensation. The build-up of pain in my nose. 'That's unfair! Aren't I allowed to have my off moments? I thought you were supposed to be my mother and I didn't have to put on an act for you. You make it sound like I'm en route to the funny farm.' Maybe I am.

'Don't be mad. Of course you don't have to put on an act with me! Nobody's saying you shouldn't have your off days. But you have to remember something, too, Angela: Jonathan was robbed of a life. But you weren't. He'd have wanted you to accept his death. You don't have to go on being angry to prove that you still love him.'

I think about this for a while. 'Anyway, what would you know?' I used to ask that of her a lot when I was a kid. When she used to push me to do the things that were supposed to be good for me: things that she never did. It was a question I knew she didn't really have a good answer for. It was my exercise in having the last word.

'What would *I* know? I lost my mother. I lost my father. My sister. I lost *your* father, didn't I? There was a point in my life when I felt I was always losing everybody.'

'But you weren't my age when my dad died. And you said yourself you were never happy. He was never right for you.' She always looked happy. My dad was a good man. They rarely fought. Maybe he wasn't ambitious, and his idea of celebrating her birthday was to have an extra pint for her down at the pub, but he meant well, even if he never quite put his intentions into action. Yet she always said she wanted *more*. She had a house. She had clothes – even if they weren't always new ones, she looked better than anybody else's mam because she was so pretty. Yet sometimes there was a far-off expression in her eyes. Presumably when she was thinking of more. I couldn't imagine what more meant.

'Your father was in my life for nearly thirty years. I still get days when I can't believe that he's not here any more. I still dream the same dream, where I know he's got lung cancer, but instead of him getting worse he just stays the same. Somehow we go on living on borrowed time. I'll wake up relieved that he didn't die. And then, of course, I realise it was just a dream.'

The pain in the bridge of my nose moves swiftly around my head. I didn't know she had dreams like these. Because whenever I'm with my mother I always feel I have to try hard not to get too close.

'Do you ever dream of Jonathan?'

'No,' I lie.

Or rather not as much as I used to. The things I'd have thought had the least place in my heart would always come back to me the strongest. The tiny bald spot on his jaw that was the pink colour of newly healed skin. The 'zzz' sound of him shaving in the bathroom. The details would be so strong that my breathing would become scarily shallow. I'd force myself to stay awake because the alternative was something that scared me, almost literally, to death.

'You know, maybe there's going to be somebody just as good for you as Jonathan was, waiting around the corner. Somebody who is supposed to follow Jonathan.'

I can't have this conversation.

She turns onto her side, props her head on her hand. The colour of her petticoat lies somewhere between the porcelain of her skin and the amber of her freckles: the only true colour on her is those luminous almost Tiffany-blue eyes. 'Angela, the thirties and forties are a magical time for a woman. Because at that age, you're at your wisest, yet you can still make men go weak at the knees. Whereas when you get to my age, you only make their legs go because they were probably going to collapse anyway.'

She studies my unchanging face.

'You've still got a lot of life to look forward to. But you can't see the road. You can only see the roadblocks.'

I turn my head away sharply, meaning, *enough now*.

'Do you want to know something?' she says after a while, and I don't, but I have a feeling it won't make a difference. 'I wish I were in your shoes, because you have a life ahead of you,

you're not just at the end of it.' She looks frustrated and sad for a while. 'I don't want you to turn out just like me, Angela. I'm a very unhappy, messed-up old fruit cake!'

'I thought you said life was only depressing if you let it be.'

'I've changed my mind.' She glares – not really at me, more at life in general. 'I don't want to grow old gracefully. I want to grow old disgracefully. I want to rock the walls of this life until the house falls down . . . When next door's nineteen-year-old is lifting his dumbbells in the garden, I'm peeking from behind that curtain going, "Corr!" But oh no, it's wrong and distasteful. I'm supposed to behave myself. But I don't want to behave myself! Suddenly I've stopped being a woman and become a senior citizen. I'm a member of this club that grants me all these privileges, yet there's no glamour to being in it. Young people aren't lining up to get in. The paparazzi aren't hiding out in the bushes . . .' She shakes her head angrily. Tiny thread veins bloom on her cheeks. 'You know, the best thing they can say about Tony Bennett is that he's eighty?' She laughs humourlessly and throws her hands in the air. Her face looks staggeringly young. Like I always remember her, and I hope I always will.

'What's Tony Bennett got to do with anything?'

'I'm trying to make a point! That when you get older, your age becomes your achievement. It's pathetic. It's a damned crime against humanity.'

'Mam, you're not eighty like he is!'

'No, but I'm a whisker away from being seventy.'

'Give over! You've just turned sixty!' I try not to laugh, because I know she won't see the funny side.

'What's ten measly years? I know how quickly the last ten have gone.'

She really is serious. I feel for her because she looks all steeled into a corner, and I'm just across from her in mine, but there's a massive divide between us, because I can't help her out of hers any more than she can help me out of mine. 'Don't get so het up! Think of your blood pressure!' I tell her. But it's the worst thing to say.

She glares at me. 'Did you HAVE to say that right now? Something OLD like that! Could you not have said something like . . . like . . . keep calm. Mind you don't go into an early labour?'

We lock eyes. She seems momentarily taken aback by her own wackiness. 'Angela . . . all I'm saying is that life goes by frighteningly fast. And I don't want you regretting wasting yours, like I regret wasting mine.' Her voice softens and goes very quiet. 'Just remember one thing, Angela, and then I promise I'll shut up.'

I hope she means that.

'You will outlive your worst pain. Dogs die of a broken heart. People don't.'

I turn my head away from her and gaze at the balcony doors so she can't see my eyes fill up. The problem with us is we're each other's Advil that we're trying not to take.

She goes back to reading her book. In my peripheral vision I see her give a tiny, exasperated little shake of her head. A voice warns me that one day I'm going to regret keeping my guard up with her; it'll seem like such a wasted battle with myself. I sneak a peek at the impossibly young-looking hand that holds her novel, the long, elegant fingers with the splashes of red polish on the nails. The tender sight of her chokes me.

I get up quickly, push open the balcony door for air, and an oven blast of heat comes at me.

'Aye-up, sexy!' A young lad appears on the balcony next to ours. He's wearing leopard-print trunks and nothing else. He looks like he just woke up at three in the afternoon. His breakfast is a can of Stella. 'What's your name, then? Is there two of you in there, then? What's the other one like?' he wiggles his eyebrows. 'Them your Bridget Jones knickers?' He points to a pair of my mam's big knickers drying on the back of a chair.

Why's she done laundry? We've barely been here a day!

'I'm Steve-o,' he raises his can in greeting. Then three bleary heads shoot around the door. 'And this is Cock-head, Lil Bill, and Jimmy Gonads.' Bleary eyes trail a path from my chest to my crotch.

I run back inside and crash the doors shut. 'Good God!'

'Who-head, and Jimmy what?' my mam slaps a hand over her mouth while her cheeks flood red and she tries hard not to laugh.

'It's not funny! It's disgusting! What was I thinking of, coming here with you of all people? It's a bloody cesspit, this place!' Such a far cry from my previous five-star travel.

I hear the faintest escape of a titter. Her shoulders jag up and down.

I can't believe she's got the gall to find it funny! I glare at her. 'And in future, don't hang your great big dirty drawers on our balcony. Those buggers think they're mine.'

A laugh bursts out of her so hard that she nearly cracks a rib.

5

Last night I had a dream. I got off a train because I was going to meet somebody. It was foggy and there was nobody on the platform. As the train pulled away, the fog lifted. A man was standing there. At first I thought it was Jonathan, but then I saw that he was broader than Jonathan, darker with soulful, penetrating eyes, and he looked like he could use a good shave.

'*Kalimera*!' the young Greek tour guide welcomes me off the boat onto mainland Greece. 'Pretty lady. I'm Costas. You travel alone, yes?' Today is predicted to hit a whopping forty-six degrees. Mam wasn't feeling up to it, but as we'd booked the trip, it made sense that at least one of us came.

This Costas takes off his 1970s aviator reflector sunglasses, as though to deliberately show me his eyes, and his intent in them, which in a strange way is vaguely amusing and quite flattering. He puts them in the back pocket of his stonewashed Levi's and his gaze, all laid bare like open-heart surgery, fixes itself optimistically on mine. 'Let me see your ticket. Ah, the pretty lady is travelling alone!'

Is it my imagination, or does he say it pointedly loudly for the benefit of the three Englishmen who board the bus ahead of me?

It's about an hour's drive to the site of Ancient Olympia. I get chatting to a friendly British couple and their fifteen-year-old son who boarded the tour from another hotel. The son excitedly tells me that he only came on the holiday for this particular day-trip. It registers, with a near paralytic clang of my heart, that Jonathan – the former All-Ontario 400m Champion in Track and Field – would have loved this, even with his indifference to anything old.

As we stand in line to collect our passes for the archaeological museum, I observe, more closely, the three Englishmen at the top of the queue who are having a good bit of banter with Costas. There's a nondescript ginger fellow and a blond. But it's the other guy I'm surprised I'm only just properly noticing now. A tall, tanned man with light brown hair and clear-looking green eyes, who is, by anybody's standards, a hunk, but wholesomely so.

We enter the museum for a tour given by Cathy, who Costas tells us is our guide to the site. But I pay scant attention, because having now noticed the Englishman, I can't quite keep my eyes off him. The statue of the Goddess Nike might be fascinating, but when I discreetly swing my gaze over my shoulder to the tall, well-built figure of a man at the back of the crowd, Cathy's gentle voice becomes like sound that's had a blanket laid over it: faint and indistinct.

Stepping outside the museum and taking my last glug of bottled water, the heat is breathtaking. The Englishmen are laughing at something and I notice the good-looking one's yellow T-shirt has something about surfing written on the front. I wonder if they're here on a team. He looks fit and outdoorsy.

I debate whether to go in search of a vendor to buy more bottled water before we embark on the tour of the site, but decide there's not time.

'The first official games were declared open in 776 BC, and held in honor of Zeus, God of men and God of gods,' Cathy tells us. 'During the games, participating city-states were bound by a sacred truce to stop beating the hell out of one another and compete in sports instead!' Cathy's exuberance makes me think I'm going to find Olympia far more interesting than I was expecting. As she talks us through a tour of the Temple of Zeus and the Altar of Hera where the Olympic flame is still lit every four years, I see the Englishmen talking between themselves, the ginger one's voice and laughter occasionally rising above that of the crowd. At one point, when I look over, I think the nice one might have just been looking at me, but our gazes slide past each other, his a little too quick, mine a little too slow, so I'm not even sure it really happened.

When Cathy gives us fifteen minutes to go off on our own and explore, I wander in the opposite direction to the crowd and find myself in the Byzantine Church, with its crumbling walls, where competitors used to pray for victory. I perch on what's left of a stone altar, enjoying the serenity and feeling, strangely, less widowed today – like there are two me's – the single me and the widowed me, and we're somehow hinged, but the widowed me has just become unattached and drifted away a bit. I wonder if it has anything to do with this man.

By the time I head back to the meeting point, I realise I'm going to pass out if I don't get some water. I abandon any intentions of joining the tour and wander back out the way we came in. At a mobile shop selling food and drink, I buy a Greek yoghurt and a bottle of water, and down them while sitting on a bench, listening to a middle-aged American couple complaining about the heat. I deliberately wore my flowery tankini top, along with a denim mini, because I thought I'd breathe more easily in it. But it feels a bit underdressed, now, for such a reverent place. The back of my neck is hot and sweaty, but when I look down at my feet and slip my flip-flops off, I can see attractive tan lines. Then, of course, there's the toenails. When I woke up this morning, I thought my eyes were playing tricks. Mam was hovering at the end of my bed in her petticoat, carefully applying red varnish to my toenails that were sticking out of the covers. I felt the little tickle of the brush.

I'm still sitting there when I see the three Englishmen walking over this way. I feel a dart of pleasurable panic. Behind them are a raunchy-looking couple, maybe Turkish or Spanish. She's got an enormous boob job, and a big jiggly bum that hangs out of tiny white terry-towelling shorts. Her boyfriend, draped in gold chains, is all over her like Godzilla on Viagra. It's interesting because, with the built-in radar that men have for these things, the three Englishmen, who come and sit on the bench adjacent to mine, cop her, and their gazes follow her as she passes them.

I find myself watching the nice one watch the girl. I don't know if their quiet comments and grins mean they think she's hot or not, but for some stupid reason I feel the teeniest bit envious of her. I notice he wears a wedding ring. They all do. *He's married.* Of course he would be.

Their fascination with the girl goes on too long, though. And as if that weren't bad enough, the ginger one pulls out his digital camera and aims it at her bum. Then they pass the camera between them, the blond one mucking around with the zoom. 'Here, mate . . .' The ginger one waves Costas over. 'Come and look at this, then!' And I think, *oh, for heaven's sake, grow up!* Costas studies the camera and smiles. Then he must say something to them because they all turn and stare at me. I quickly snap my gaze away, but I feel the nice one's eyes on me moments longer after the other two have looked away. But when I glance back, they're all fixed on the camera again.

Oh, I've seen enough of this now! I get up, and as I feel too self-conscious to pass them, I take off in the opposite direction, across a lawn. There's a payphone, and I just bought a phonecard this morning. It's the middle of the night in Vancouver, so rather than ring Richard at home, I ring his

office and leave a message on his voicemail, asking him if he'll
go by my apartment, pick up my mail and deposit a cheque for
me. Then I call Sherrie. Predictably, she picks up.

'I can't believe you had the nerve to go to Greece and not
invite me along, you witch! I have to go to Bangladesh on a
sales trip. It wouldn't have been that far off!'

'Yeah, they're practically neighbours, Bangladesh and
Greece.'

I hear her titter.

'You wouldn't care for it here, Sher. It's full of very
attractive married men, and slimy, randy tour guides. Plus
it's, like, three hundred degrees. My mam's pegged out in our
room. I was just on a tour of the ancient ruins of Olympia but I
nearly became an ancient ruin myself.'

'Slimy, randy tour guides? I'm logging on to Air Canada as
we speak . . .' She squeals with joy. 'But you're having a good
time, my friend? That's what I really want to hear you say.
That you're having a great time with your mom, and you're
happy.'

'Funnily enough, Sherrie, I am having an okay time. Mam
and I have nearly killed each other a couple of times, but we're
licking our war wounds today.' I miss her suddenly and regret
my testiness with her yesterday. The toenail-painting episode,
I sense, was her way of making amends.

'Has Jonathan sent you a lover yet?'

The question comes as a bolt out of the blue. I'd almost
forgotten I told her that night. Just as I'm about to reply, I see
the Englishman walking my way with his friends.

I follow him with my gaze. 'No. Not yet, Sherrie. Still
waiting.'

How likely would it be that Jonathan would send me a
married Englishman? Not very. Pity. Maybe my life could use
the drama. I lean back against the wall, propping a foot up
behind me, listening to Sherrie's patter. As the Englishman

approaches, I close my eyes and do a very good job of tilting my face, indifferently, to the sun.

Costas wants to sit beside me for lunch.

Oh, give over! Must he? I've snagged a nice table for two under an arbour, and I'm just reaching for the wine list. Now I've become somebody's charity case. Or their fair game.

'Actually, if you don't mind, I really would like to just sit on my own.' I pull a slightly desperate pleading smile, trying not to be rude. The last thing I want is everybody on the tour thinking the single English girl is copping off with the cheesy guide.

He says something in Greek to the middle-aged mama, whose restaurant this clearly is. I try to go back to my wine list, but then the Greek mama speaks to me. 'You please join another table.'

Just when I think it's nice of her to care that I have company, Costas explains: 'This restaurant, it gets busy . . . full. Another tour bus expected in ten minutes. One person cannot occupy table alone, when a couple may come along who will want it.'

So my good time doesn't count because I've got nobody to share it with? 'Well, where am I supposed to sit, then?' My churlish tone gets looks.

'Here!' Big mama indicates a long picnic table-type bench that's empty except for the three Englishmen seated at one end.

They look up from their bottled beers to see me hovering there. Not sure what else to do, I sit down, making a point of pulling out the chair farthest away from them. It strikes me how odd I'm being. Why can't I just sit and talk to them, like a normal person?

When I glance over, the fair-headed guy smiles and says a cautious, 'Hiya.'

I nod, then bury my cringing embarrassment in the menu. The nice one couldn't seem to care less about my arrival at the table. And why would he? He's a married lad enjoying a guys' day out. She's probably back at the pool, frying herself in factor 8. She'll have one of those lean bodies that still manages to have fair-sized boobs, a funky hairstyle and a belly-ring. And she'll worship the ground he walks on. And despite the fact that he might casually observe a femme fatale in hot pants, or a thin blonde who doesn't look like she has much of a personality, the feeling will be mutual.

I stand up abruptly. The three Englishmen look up and say something to each other as I leave the table: something disparaging, no doubt.

I walk up into the town, embarrassment dragging after me. On an inconspicuous patio, in the shade of a tree, I wolf down a spinach pie and a baklava, then rather wish I hadn't.

It's a blustery ferry ride home. The five o'clock sun is kinder than it's been all day, and I brave sitting outside on the top deck, my head tilted up to its rays. When I go inside to the toilets, I'm not even bothered that the Englishmen are sitting on the seats right outside the toilet door. I feel them watch me. When I come back out again, the three of them stare right at my face.

'Jesus,' I hear one of them mutter once I'm past.

Large shots of Greek brandy are only three euros. I buy myself a couple.

Jesus. I wonder what that was supposed to mean.

Boarding the double-decker coach that collects us off the ferry to deliver us back to our resorts, after saying goodbye to Costas and leaving a scant tip, I stay downstairs, and, by chance, find myself across the aisle from my three fellow day-trippers. The one who has the strange effect on me is directly opposite. At one point I tune in and hear the ginger chappie say to him, 'It's all going to be different, though, isn't it? When you move away.'

I look at my guy for his reaction. 'How so?' he says. 'Why does it have to be that much different? It's a small world.' The accent almost sounds Irish. I wonder where he's moving to.

I sneak a few looks at him and note how the golden tan makes the whites of his eyes look fabulously bright. Even his hair has flecks of gold among the brown. He must sense me looking, because he glances over. When I look away before our eyes connect, I feel there's something uncivil between us. The die's been cast, though. It's too late now to show that I actually am a nice person after all.

I stare out of the window, not knowing why I feel so spiritless. Maybe it's because in a different set of circumstances, I'd have gone for him; he'd have been my type. He's still alive, for one thing. I could have been the one who waits for him now, with fresh new tan lines, wondering how his day out with his mates was. I bet she's potty about him. I bet they make a lovely couple. I bet that could make a still broken-hearted widow really envious. If there were one around.

They talk quietly now, below the level of the droning bus engine. I try to look out of my window at the view, but I just keep seeing snatches of my desperate face. How did I come to be sitting here on my own, on a bus in Greece, admiring a married man and feeling discombobulated, stricken, that I'm never going to see him again? The absurdity of it almost makes me scream out in bewilderment.

'Kalamaki,' the driver announces the name of the resort as the bus pulls to a stop and I recognise the fruit and magazine stall where a few of us joined the bus this morning. The friendly couple who boarded with me, and their son, come clunking down the stairs.

'Phew!' the father says to me. 'Another one bites the dust. Are you going on the Athens trip tomorrow?'

I tell him I'm not. As I get up out of my seat, the Englishman's head moves ever so slightly over his shoulder as I pass him.

The family and I step off the bus into the early evening sunshine. The bus doesn't pull away immediately and I feel my heart quicken, knowing he's still there.

'Glad you put Costas in his place,' the husband says. 'Smarmy git. And that was a downright disgrace in that restaurant! Them not letting you sit where you wanted! We were going to ask you to sit with us. But then you sat with them fellas, and next time we looked, you were gone.'

The bus is going to pull away. I feel anxious. I bumble some sort of smiling explanation that I sense they're waiting for, and my eyes go back inside the bus again.

The Englishman is watching me, as though he has been all the time. Our eyes lock, and neither of us looks away. And it surprises me what I see in his face: a long, unsuppressed look of attraction. The sort you can give to a strange woman in Greece when you're married, when you know you'll never see her again.

6

There are no real paths to the Kiritsakis Olive Oil Company. Only very rocky, dry soil that looks well furrowed by enormous tyres. Mam and I get off the tour bus, relieved that it's cooler today.

This day-trip sounded like it'd be a good one – a visit to a real olive grove and a chance to see some of the true Zante. Given that Mam ended up staying in the hotel most of yesterday, it seemed vital to get her out today.

We all pile off the bus and find we're in the middle of a hilly, olive-treed, barren-earthed nowhere that has a single, fairly large apricot-coloured stone house that dominates the landscape with its sense of peeling, decrepit unlived-in-ness. Instead of weathered Greek men hauling in olives in sackfuls, there are about three charmless tanker trucks parked outside the house.

But it's who is talking to the three charmless tanker truck drivers that makes our jaws drop and some very peculiar noise come out of both of us. Just as we notice him, he notices us. It must be the hats; we're about the only two wearing them. My mam gives me three sharp digs with her elbow. 'Be still my beating heart.'

'Give over,' I tell her. But I'm wondering why my own heart is ticking fast now.

Within moments he is walking over to us, then he drops two kisses on our pretty tour guide's cheeks, and they exchange a few words in Greek, his eyes going from me to my mam.

'Do you think he ever shaves?' I ask my mam, while he chats to Stella. He's sexier than I remember him. Riskier-looking. More Greek. 'Do you even think they have razors in Greece?'

As though he hears that, he rubs a hand over his jaw and looks at me playfully. 'The ladies with the hats,' he says.

'We don't always wear them,' my mam says. 'Not the same ones, I mean. We have different ones for different occasions. If I'd known you had a thing for hats, we'd have packed the lot.'

His eyes coast over her, like a man who appreciates anything this feminine, no matter what age. But then he says, 'Well, I hope you enjoy the tour. There is much to see.' And then he turns and looks like he's going to walk away. No sooner do my mam and I exchange *don't let him leave!* looks, than he stops, mid-step, and turns around again. I wonder if he's playing with us. When he says, 'Or, there is always another option,' I'm pretty certain he is. 'I could ask Stella if I could steal two ladies from her and I could show you around myself. Give you a private tour.' He says it matter-of-factly, and there's something very appealing about his casual demeanour.

'Corr!' my mother leans into me. 'I'd like the private tour.'

He studies me with a hint of wickedness in his eyes, like he might have heard her.

'How do we know to trust you? You might be a mad Greek rapist,' I tell him.

My mam gives my arm a tweak that means, *Oh, I hope!*

'I promise I am to be trusted.' He looks from my mam to our tour guide. 'Ask Stella.'

Stella flirts with him a bit too cosily. And I bet that, whatever they're saying, it's to do with the fact that he most certainly isn't to be trusted.

He extends a hand to my mam and then to me. 'Georgios! Your personal tour guide for the day.' His hand is big and warm and leaves an imprint on mine that sends pleasant little waves through me.

'I hope we can afford you,' my mam flirts from under the brim of her enormous hat. 'And you might as well know, we're English so we don't leave very generous tips.'

Those dark eyes seem to sparkle now.

'Vivien,' she says. 'Or Viv, if you'd like to call me that. And this is –'

'Angela,' he supplies. He looks at me cryptically.

'Don't you have work to do?' I ask him. 'Won't your boss be a little peeved if you just decide to take the day off?'

Before he can answer, Stella says, 'One of the perks of *owning* Greece's fifth largest olive oil export business is this type of thing.'

My mam's jaw drops, and of course I feel like a right wally.

'Give me a moment.' He holds up a hand, walks backwards. 'Don't go anywhere.' Then he strides off purposefully in the direction of the truckers, and I notice he's really only average height, but being lean and long-legged, he appears taller.

'*Today I met the man you're going to marry!*' My mam quietly sings in my ear.

'Get out! Why on earth would you say something like that?'

'I feel it. Just like I did when you brought Jonathan home that first time.'

I roll my eyes. 'Yeah! But Jonathan and I got engaged during that visit, didn't we?'

'Are you scoffing at me again?'

I narrow my eyes at her. 'What? Mocking the afflicted, you mean? Me? Never.'

She gives me a withering look, and goes back to marvelling at Georgios as he talks to the men. 'Be still my beating heart!'

'Oh, shut up, you've said that ten times already.'

Stella tells us that Georgios will have to have us back here, in front of the house, no later than five, if we are to join the rest of the group for the scenic ride back to the hotel. I must say, we get some very curious looks from the other day-trippers as we step out of the crowd and follow Georgios.

'I'm having a good gloat, personally. I don't know about you . . .' My mam squeezes my arm. 'I love a good gloat. There's nothing like it.' She plants a kiss on my cheek. 'I'm having a very nice holiday now. Are you?'

I swat her off. 'What? You mean because of him?'

'No, girl!' She sends an elbow through my ribs. 'Because of you, dear. All because of you.' She digs in her handbag, takes out her compact mirror, peers in it, and twists her hat round to a more coquettish angle.

Georgios Kiritsakis knows a thing or two about olive trees. 'In Greek legend, Athena – is goddess of wisdom, and Poseidon – is god of the sea – they two claim a city as theirs. There is big fight . . . The gods said that the deity who could leave behind the most important thing for the people would win.' He looks at us to see if we're following him. We are. It's like a melody to our ears. He smiles, a touch vainly, like he knows we're really not listening to a word he's saying. 'Athena, well, she produce the olive tree, symbol of peace and plenty. Poseidon, he produce a horse, symbol of strength and courage. So who win? The gods gave the city to Athena. They think that the olive would be of more longer use to humans than war.' Georgios's white Suzuki Grand Vitara navigates its way through dense terraces of olive groves, climbing higher and higher. He drives like a man who could feel his way blindfold through these hills, swinging his gaze from the road, to my mother, to me in the back, as he talks. My mother chuckles skittishly and hangs onto her hat as we hurtle over bumps so big they make your teeth chatter. From time to time she sends me that cock-a-hoop, conspiratorial look over her shoulder, and I snap a photo, catching the exhilaration and young-womanliness in her eyes.

'I've heard that story before,' I tell him. Not that I have. 'About how Athens got its name. It's in all the tourist guide-books.' The old unimpressible me. Like when I met Jonathan, and my friend who introduced us said he was a lawyer. Maybe that might have made other girls throw themselves at him, but not me. I was playing it ever so cool. The act didn't last long.

'Speak for yourself!' My mam glares at me. 'I haven't heard that story before.' Her gaze goes back to eating up Georgios. 'I think it's a charming story. It's incredible to imagine that, thousands of years ago, the big powers of the day had the sense to see that war is a poor solution to any problem, which really does make you wonder if we have evolved or just got more stupid.'

He looks at her and smiles. 'I think we've definitely got more stupid.' Then he looks at me again in the back seat, and there are touches of handsomeness about him, even though his face is too tanned and rugged to be called anything as boring as good-looking. He comes to a sudden halt and swivels round so he can talk to us both more easily. The sun on his stubbly jaw makes it even more dark and shadowy, giving him a danger-ous, prison-break quality that contradicts his gentlemanliness and reserve.

'You know, the ancient Greeks, they always think that the olive tree is immortal. It can survive almost any weather, and even if it dies, you will see new shoots quickly grow. The olive tree never lets go of life. It clings to the soil, to eternity, to its instinct to keep growing to the sun.'

'Where did you learn such great English?' I ask him. He has a big bump just below the bridge of his nose, as though it was once broken. I can see him as a boy: the first in there, starting the scraps.

'In school. And then I learn in travel. I work in America. I go often to London. All in business, you know. The business of olive oil.'

'That's wonderful.' My mother is oblivious to the temptress looks she's sending him. 'I mean, your story about the olive tree. Maybe immortality of the olive tree was the gods' gift to this earth.'

'I think it was.' His eyes hold my mam's for a long, charmed while, and I'm thinking, *Yeah, ma, where did you get this sudden brilliance about immortality and the gods from?* Then he shifts the Jeep into gear again. There's a violent scratch on his hand that runs almost the length of his index finger, which looks like it must have been painful, and I wonder how he got it.

'How on earth do you collect all these olives?' I ask him, astonished by the chaotic tangle of trees. 'Do you have special machines?'

'Machines?' He waves the scratched hand out over his pride and joy. 'No. This is all the work of hard-working men and women who have olives in their blood.'

'Of course they don't have machines!' My mam throws a scathing glance over her shoulder at me. 'Machines!' she says, like it's a dirty word.

I think I see Georgios smile.

'But surely a machine would make harvesting more efficient? Then if you harvested more olives, you could sell more oil and then people would make more money.' I sound so practical, so North American. The words don't belong here, in this place. It strikes me, with a surprising disappointment, that neither do I.

'We harvest what the trees yield. But machines don't make people more efficient. People make people efficient. People work hard when others work hard, when it is in their blood. Machines make people not able to appreciate. That is all.'

My mam's gaze steals over his profile once his attention's back on the road. He glances affectionately at her, as though he feels he's being watched, and I take a quick photo, capturing their profiles, and her smitten eyes over him. I do believe my mother's in love!

They go on talking between themselves – Georgios seems to find her conversation scintillating – and I'm happy to tune out and just look at the view: the true Zante. But if I lived here, wouldn't I get fed up with this rhythm of life? Wouldn't I pine for Vancouver traffic and frustrating one-way streets? Lattes at Artigiano's? Speeches to write, and rain, lots of rain, and falling apple blossoms that litter Granville Street in the spring? I suddenly feel a bit homesick for the city that contained my life, whereas I've always thought that my life felt contained by the city. 'Isn't Italian olive oil supposed to be the best, though?' I ask him, picking up on their conversation now.

He briefly meets my eyes again through the mirror. 'It is Italian that you find a lot of abroad. But here is fact not well known: seventy-five per cent of Greek oil is exported to Italy – it is tempting for poor farmers to sell to the Italians for quick money. So the Italians buy our excellent oil, and some of it will be packaged as if it comes from Italy.'

'The scheming Eyetics!' spits my mother.

Those C-brackets make way for a broad smile, and he laughs like my mother is the best thing since feta cheese. 'Well, they have a reputation for having the best olives, so they use that. And who can blame them? Everybody has to earn a living. Mediterranean life is not always easy. But when it comes to quality, there is none such better virgin olive oil than Greek virgin olive oil.'

I gaze at the back of his darkly tanned neck, the way the shiny black hair burrows into it, as my mother and him start talking about the euro. And I wonder if he's married, has a girlfriend, had a girl in his bed last night. Another mad thought goes through my head – if Jonathan were to send me a lover, well, he could do worse than pick this one for me.

Come on Jonathan . . . Get sending.

'So, I take it you don't care for the Italians too much, then?' I say to him.

He shrugs. 'But I live and I let them live, as the saying goes.'

'Live and let live,' I repeat for him.

He holds my eyes in the mirror again, and I feel a flutter of something go through me.

'So when does the harvest start?' my mam asks him, running her smitten gaze down the length of his muscular, hairy arm. The Jeep rumbles over rocks and throws us about. My mam hangs on to the handle above the passenger door window, her cheeks and her smile vibrating from the motion.

'Early spring its fruit changing from green to red to black. When the tree is three quarters black, we pick – this in October. Then we press instantly to preserve the freshness and virgin character of the oil.'

We reach the top of the hill and I look back on a carpet of olive trees that glistens a silvery green, and plunges to a pea-green sea that dances with sunlight and rolls its frothy skirt up to a sliver of powder-white sand that's fit only for a lone and lucky shipwrecked man. Where are all the tourists? The beer-bellied Brits, and topless women, and screaming kids? Spectacularly not here. We seem to have turned back the clock to a time when Zante was inhabited only by olive trees and gods.

He stops the car, shuts off the engine, and suddenly everything is motionless, windless, waveless and serene. The sudden temporal stillness and quiet fill me with a sense that I believe in something, although I'm not sure what. High up in this celestial place I feel nearer to the sky than I do to the ground. The sky looks bluer up here, a gleaming painter's palette cyan: bottomless and cloudless. I bet anything's possible in life and death, if you were up there, looking down here.

Georgios shifts in his seat again, rests an arm on the steering wheel and looks at me. 'When you consume olive oil, Angela, it is the place where the olives were born, the climate that nurtured them, the character of the soil, the character of the person who looked over it, and cared how it was handled and pressed.' He grips the top of my arm. 'Olive oil is all about emotion. I tell you this as a passionate Greek who has the olive juice running in his veins.' Completely unsuggestively he runs his thumb along a vein on my arm, and I look at his hand there.

How about a little self-fulfilling prophecy, Angela? Who says I need Jonathan's help?

He gets out of the Jeep and plucks a handful of olives from a branch. 'Try.' He offers his hand out to me, those black-brown eyes all atwinkle.

I pick one and bite into it. 'Ergh!' I spit it past my mam's head.

'Good heavens, Angela!' she says, startled. And he laughs a broad laugh.

'Oh, ha ha ha.' I beam at him. 'If this is so funny, I think you need to get out more.'

He gets back in the vehicle and turns to my mam. 'You have a sarcastic daughter, no?'

'With foul table manners.'

He smiles at her. 'It is not true that these olives are good from the tree. With these we have to cure in oil or brine before they are eaten.'

'Well you've totally spoilt the illusion,' I tell him, and my mother chuckles. 'How come you didn't get one?' I glare at her.

'Maybe it's his way of telling you that you've got too much to say for yourself. So he thought he'd give you something else to push in your cakehole.'

He starts the engine up again. 'What Greek food have you eaten since you got here?'

I think of the meal we had last night: moussaka, from one of the touristy tavernas on the strip. The maitre d' fawning all over my mam and her hat. 'God, it looks like something the dog passed,' I said, when I looked down at my plate.

'Don't say that!' She looked horrified. 'No dog could do something that awful-looking.' She pointed to the grovelling maitre d'. 'I bet it was him.'

'Well, last night we had moussaka that tasted more like dia—'

'Angela!'

He laughs. 'After the harvest, you should see the feast of food we have!' He swings a glance at me. 'Stay for the harvest. Both of you. Stay.'

'We're only in July now! That's quite a long way off,' my mam tells him.

'You know, Angela, there is no better place than Greece to spend some time and reflect on life.' He looks right at me and his words make me shiver.

'What makes you think I need to reflect on life?'

For a moment he hesitates. 'Well . . . doesn't everybody?'

'You love your country.' My mam changes the subject.

'Of course. In Greece there is much to love. But you love your country too, no?'

Oh, no, here we go . . . My mam elongates her proud-to-be-British spine. 'Oh, I do! I love England. Because the English are good at so many things.' She turns and deliberately looks at me. 'They put on fantastic concerts and celebrations. They turn out the best musicians, and they make excellent television programmes!' She cocks another quick glance at me to make sure I'm listening. 'And they have a good sense of style, and good fashion in their stores, and good food in their shops, and they're direct, no-messing people, and when they like you, it can be a wonderful thing, although they're never *so nice and polite* that it's irritating. And they're not afraid to let their hair down, and have a drink at lunchtime.'

There she goes – shitting on Canada again in her roundabout way.

He smiles at her. 'And you?' he says to me, looking over his shoulder again.

'Angela doesn't live in England. She lives in *Canada*.'

'I know,' he says.

I feel myself blanch. 'What do you mean, you know? How can you possibly know that?'

'Because . . .' He seems to stumble here. 'Because you have not the same accent as your mama. You have North American sound in some of your words. And because I travel in America many times with business so I know.'

'But you said I sounded Canadian.' I narrow my eyes at him. 'You were quite specific.'

'No, he didn't!' my mam jumps in. 'I said you lived in Canada and Georgios said he could tell!'

Oh.

He throws the scratched hand in the air. 'But Canada, America – they are one of the same, are they not?'

I grin. 'Ooh! I'd like to hear you say that to a Canadian!'

'They are!' chimes my mother again. 'It's one big melting pot over there. Everybody melting in the mire together.'

He looks at me again, curiously. 'The man you were married to was Canadian, no?'

My stomach lifts and drops. My tongue practically sticks to the roof of my mouth. I can barely speak. He's still studying me. 'What on earth made you say that?' I ask him, determined to find out what's going on here. Even my mam must think this is weird, because her eyes rivet on him, then they rivet on me, as though she's feeling left out of something. She's not the only one.

He stops the car, reaches for my left hand, rubs his thumb over my wedding ring finger below the knuckle. 'This track in your finger. Tell me a man alive who does not look to a woman's hand to see if she is married?'

'Angela is a widow. Her husband was a lawyer and he died two years ago.'

'Thanks for that, Mother.' I glare daggers at her. I finally took off my wedding ring before I went on my date with that Roger, to the pizzeria. Our first date – the disastrous trip to the movies – I'd left it on. I thought I'd jinxed it. I thought taking it off might make our second meeting better, because I wanted it to be. It didn't. The groove still hasn't gone from my finger.

'Two widows, then,' Georgios says.

'That makes us sound like a real barrel of laughs, doesn't it!' my mam chirps. 'Two single girls is how we prefer to think of ourselves.'

And before I dive over the seat and throttle her, Georgios says, 'Would you two single ladies like to have some wine?'

He turns his head one more time to me and his eyes go quickly to my wedding ring hand once more, before he starts up his vehicle again.

7

The mill has an exuberantly earthy reek to it, which is even more pungent to my nose after the several glasses of floral retsina and the *pretza* he's fed us. It's dark in here, and cold. The floor is damp. The walls are damp. The place is like a tomb with olive oil seeping from its pores, or a musty wine cellar, or a cold stone church.

Georgios guides us through the olive-pressing process – mostly talking to my mam because she's the one hanging on his every word. I'm just boggled by the olive press that looks like a medieval torture chamber. 'From our latest harvest. We call the early harvest oil *agoureleo*, or 'unripe' oil. The Greeks believe it is the best.' He reaches into a big drum, and his palm fills with a liquid the colour of dull emeralds that glints and sparkles in the sunlight from a nearby window. 'Taste.' He holds his hand out to me.

I back off. 'You're all right. Some other time.'

He laughs. 'Please. This is not a trick.'

'Yeah. I believe you. Thousands wouldn't.'

'I gave birth to a thoroughly wimpy daughter. I don't know where she gets it from.' My mam ventures an index finger into the oil. Then she sticks her finger in her mouth. 'Delicious! It's . . . I don't know . . . it's almost peppery. Sharp.'

'You have a good palate,' he tells her. 'You should be in the olive business. You want to taste an egg fried in this. It will be the best egg you ever try.'

I stare at the well of oil in his hand, then I dip my finger in. It all feels a bit intimate for my comfort zone. I wonder if I'd find something sexual in something as innocent as him scratching the back of a raggedy-looking kitten. I think I probably would.

'It's good,' I tell him, keen to make sharp work of that.

He licks the rest off his palm, and – there, it's not just me – my mam and I look at one another and think the same thought, share the same smile.

'My grandmother said that a small handful of olives can fill you up as can a large beef steak. When I come to America, I cannot eat in these American steak housing places.'

'No, I know what you mean. The food can be pretty crass. Just honking great portions of things.'

'It's awful!' my mam chimes in. 'Order a piece of beef and you get half the cattle ranch belly-up on your plate. And when you ask for a sandwich, instead of getting one slice of ham you get thirty! No wonder they're all enormous!'

'They're not all enormous, Mam! Canadians aren't enormous.'

'Well, you wouldn't call them svelte.'

'I could never live there, in North America,' he says.

He stops beside the door, with his back to me. His hand reaches out and touches the wall; he runs it appreciatively over the rugged, ancient stone. 'Or maybe it is wrong to say never. Only, I think maybe . . . if I fell in love with a woman who lived there. Then possible.'

My mam sends me that look. I glare at her, meaning, *pack that in!*

There's something promising, though, in the strong white afternoon sunlight as we step outside. The arid heat. The sound of crickets humming like faulty electricity lines. The parched-earth, barren beauty of the place. It's all a bit *Under the Tuscan Sun*. Or how about *Under the Grecian Sun?* I lean against the cold wall, close my eyes and absorb the scents and smells of a very alluring way of life.

'Or maybe . . . if I did fall in love with a woman who lived there, I would do my best to get her to give up what life she has there, and to come here.'

I open one eye and look at him. 'That sounds pretty sexist, if you ask me. Maybe she'll have a life she won't want to give up for a man.'

Or maybe she won't. Maybe she'll just bugger off from all her problems and live like Diane Lane, or Sylvia in La Dolce Vita. *Now there's a thought . . . Angela Chapman in* La Greek Dolce Vita.

'Maybe,' he says.

But he looks at me like he's really not convinced.

'I don't quite know what to make of him,' I tell her.

My mam is flopped out on the top of her bed in her petticoat. Her face has caught the sun. There's a shaft of red running right down her nose, making her look like a rather glam Hiawatha Indian, and a triangle of it on her chest, which makes her look like a burnt English rose. I grab the camera and take a quick photo of her.

'Why do you always have to make things of people, Angela? I don't think there's anything that needs to be made of him. He's nice. He's comfortable to be around.' She looks across at me. 'He's a charming, delicious full-blood and I'd have a bit of the rumpy with him as sure as Bob's your uncle.'

'Do you think he does this with all the tourists?'

'Girl! Put a higher price on yourself than that! Of course he doesn't! It's us! We're irresistible.'

'My backside.'

'Yes. Your backside is too. So's mine.' She bounds off the bed, turns around, bends over and shoves her bum in my face.

'You're a bit disgusting sometimes, for a mother.'

She grins at me over her bum. 'And you're a boring, stick-in-the-mud of a daughter. Gosh, if you were Eve in Adam's garden, we'd never all have got here, would we?'

I stare at the ceiling, feeling a soft exhaustion settle around me. I think of how he absently massaged the vein in my arm, even though his mind was clearly on the subject of his olive trees, not me.

'What are you thinking?' My mam interrupts my thoughts.

'Nothing. Just that he *is* easy to be around. You're right.' Jonathan never was. From the moment I clapped eyes on him at that house party, Jonathan was never easy. I was dating another guy at the time – Paul somebody; I can't even remember. When Paul somebody went to the kitchen to get us another drink, Jonathan took the opportunity to move in on me.

'I'll give you three minutes to tell him it's over,' he said.

I said something like, 'Oh, give me a break! You really think I'd do that? For *you*?' Meaning, *I'm really not that impressed.*

As I walked over to the kitchen to dump Paul faster than he'd ever been dumped, I happened to glance back; Jonathan was deliberately looking from me to his watch. I gave him a look that said, *I'm not really going to do this! I'm just going over there to get a drink.*

But Jonathan knew he had me, right from the start.

Even when he proposed to me, twenty-five dates later – a date for every year I had lived – it was bonkers how he did it. We were in the middle of Tescos in Sunderland. 'Marry me,' he said, getting down on one knee as I picked deodorant off a shelf.

'And have your babies?' I asked him, leaning onto his shoulders.

'And have a great many of our babies.'

'And be with me when I die?' My eyes smiled into his.

He plucked a hair away from my mouth. 'And die with you when you die.'

See, that was Jonathan. He wanted a contract for eternity, not just for life.

'I was just thinking of Jonathan,' I tell her, because she knows I've just been off in space. 'You know, some time ago, Jonathan and I had a strange conversation . . . It's daft, really, but he said that if he died before me, he'd send me somebody from the other side.'

'What? D'you mean a dead person?'

I tut. 'No! Not a bloody dead person! A man . . . A lover. Somebody to follow in his footsteps. The next him.'

Just the concept of there ever being a next him is depressing and encouraging at the same time. I've often wondered if Jonathan will somehow cease to hold primacy with me when he's no longer the last man I've been with. I can't bear the thought that he might diminish in my eyes, because some other man, who I would never have been with had Jonathan lived, might come along and stamp his personality in the place where Jonathan's should have been, stamp it so indelibly and love me so vigorously and for far many more years than Jonathan got to love me, that Jonathan will just be the man I was married to before I met my husband.

She looks sentimental. 'You know, I could see Jonathan doing something like that. He loved you so much, and he knew you so well. He'd want to make it his mission to find you the right person.'

'Actually, those were his words. He said if he could do it, he would do it.'

She studies me softly.

'Do you think it's possible, Mam? That he could do something like that?'

She seems to give this some thought. 'I'm not sure . . . I tend to think that we have to paddle our own canoe. But still, though, it's a nice idea that the dead never truly leave us.'

She doesn't believe it. I feel a stab of a reality check: they put Jonathan in a box and then they burned him. Jonathan can't pull any strings any more.

'What's that look for?' she says. 'I'd love to think that when I die, I can still be not too far away, watching you and looking out for you, and gently steering you away from trouble.'

'Did you ever feel like Dad was watching over you?'

She shakes her head. 'No, after your dad died, I just felt . . . left. Like it was the end of an era.'

She studies my glum face. 'But you know what? I hope that if Jonathan does send you somebody he waits until he's sure you're ready. Because the way things stand now, if somebody came along and was staring you right in the face, I don't think you'd see him, Angela. I don't think you could.'

'See, this is why I prefer not to tell you anything.'

'Well, on another topic . . . I hope you know I'm not coming with you tonight.'

'Where?'

'For dinner.'

'With Georgios? Don't be daft! Of course you are! He invited both of us. I mean, half the time it's you he's talking to in any case.'

'He's respecting his elders. The best way to the daughter is to impress the mother. And I'm certainly not coming. I'm not going to be a spare wheel, or a heel. That's worse than not being a wheel at all, or having no feet.'

'Hang on a minute . . . this doesn't have anything to do with what we've just been talking about, does it?'

'No!' she says, and nods her head manically. 'Everything! I mean NOTHING!' She grins at me, dives off the bed and leaps into the air. 'It's him!'

'Eh?'

'Who Jonathan's sent!'

'Two minutes ago you didn't believe in that!'

She jumps up and down. 'I've just found religion.'

'You better be careful. It's one size fits all, and it shrinks in a hot wash.'

She's on a roll. 'That's why he knew you were called Angela, and he knew you lived in Canada and you didn't have a husband any more, and why I said I knew right away that you were going to marry him.' She's panting. 'It all fits. And Jonathan's sent me along on this holiday to ensure I keep you two on course.'

'Get away! Like you reminded me before, you were the one who told him I lived in Canada. And he didn't know Jonathan had died, just that I used to wear a wedding ring. And as for him knowing my name, he must have heard you call me by it . . . So I don't think there's any mystery. Anyway, all this is great, but you're still coming to dinner!'

She flops back down on the bed looking knackered now. 'But I'm not, though.'

'You can't make me go on my own!'

'Oh, come on! Go and kiss him, and tell me what it's like.'

'I've got no intention of kissing him. I don't even fancy him. He's too short. And too old.'

'He's at least five nine, and he's probably mid-forties. What's wrong with that? He's aligned in your stars, Angela; the rest is just details.'

'I'm not going on my own, so tough tits.'

'Girl!' she says. 'Tough buzzums, if you must use that horrible expression.'

*   *   *

'My mam's not coming,' I tell him when I step outside the lobby into the mid-evening air that dances with the chorus of crickets.

'Oh?' he says. 'Why not?' He looks really disappointed and I try not to take it personally. *No reason in particular – only that she's convinced you're the man I'm to marry, who has been sent for me by my dead husband. No pressure there.*

He's wearing a white short-sleeved shirt, slightly more form-fitting than the one he had on earlier today. 'I don't know,' I tell him. 'I think she's worn out.' *Because her imagination's working overtime.* 'Or she's sick of me . . . It's a mother–daughter thing.'

His eyes travel slowly over my face, then over my hair, which I've washed and left hanging loose, and which somehow feels shinier and fuller than it's ever been with the mineral-heavy Greek water. Then his gaze moves down the front of me.

My GAP T-shirt and I have finally parted company. My self-appointed fashion advisor decided on a white wraparound cotton cap-sleeved dress that's simple and knee-length and shows off my new tan, and too much inner thigh when I walk. I thought I was going to feel ropey in it and look like one of those curtain rods people drape silly bits of fabric over. I'd somehow debunk the myth that thin girls wear clothes better. But I surprised myself and actually looked good.

'You look like a model, but I think you should go back upstairs and try to make her come with us,' he says.

If only he'd left an attractive pause between the words *model* and *but I think* . . .

'It would not be right to leave her alone,' he adds, probably because he sees my face.

'We won't change her mind. You don't know my mother.' In fact, if he hadn't mentioned my mother at all, that would have been fine too.

His gaze falls to my sexy gold strappy sandals (well, not exactly mine; I don't know what she was thinking to buy these tarty cripplers). But he just continues to stand there.

'We don't have to go,' I tell him, desperate to put us both out of our misery. Maybe he wanted an innocent meal out with the two of us and now he feels he's going on a date. Maybe he doesn't want to go on a date with me. Maybe he's got a girlfriend. 'In fact, we could totally abandon the idea if you like . . .'

'You sure we should not phone her from lobby?'

This is getting tiresome! 'Go ahead, if you want to. I'm not stopping you.' I do a sod-it-I've-had-enough about-turn on my heels when he grabs my hand and pulls me back.

'If you think she doesn't want to come . . . we go alone. I would enjoy that too.'

It's not like he's out to get cosy with me, though. He drops my hand the second he's got me walking to his car.

He takes me to Bohali, pulling up outside the rooftop restaurant that has stunning views of Zante port and town, twinkling under a black sky.

'You must be psychic,' I tell him. 'I saw this place this morning on the tour bus, and I thought how fab it would be to come back here and eat.'

'But we're not eating here.'

'Oh.' My heart sinks. 'We're not? Why not?'

'It's bad food.'

When he sees my disappointment, he says, 'We may come out later, for a drink, if I haven't sent you bored over dinner.'

Where he takes us is a place I would never have ventured into without him, that's for sure. From the outside it looks like a house. Apricot walls of ancient crumbling stone, capped with an ochre tiled roof. Knotty vines and hot-pink bougainvillea run rampant up the sides of the doors, across the walls to the roof, then back down a narrow twisting stone path. Outside the front door frolic two scrawny black cats.

We take a set of uneven stone stairs down to a room that buzzes with the din of happily wined and dined Greek patrons. It's white-walled, with one wall a virtual wine cellar of barrels, and an uneven, pock-marked floor painted 'Thalassa,' Georgios tells me when he sees me studying it. 'Greek blue.' There are only about a dozen tables, but each is crammed with convivial Greeks. A handsome boy with a ponytail, dressed in a white T-shirt and jeans – the owner's son, Georgios tells me – moves back and forwards between the tables and a tiny kitchen, keeping plates of food coming in steady waves. I smell garlic and charred aubergine and ouzo and wine and lamb and cigarette smoke and coffee and olives and hot-pink flowers and fresh fish, and somewhere on my anatomy, the perfume that my mam assaulted me with before I disappeared out of the door. 'Want a little squirt of it up your skirt?' she asked me.

'No! You pervy old woman! The only thing that might be getting up my skirt tonight is a mosquito. And even then, it'll have to be lucky.'

She'd cackled.

At the far end of this room is a grubby open window carved, apparently as an afterthought, out of the stone. Beyond it is a view, not of the ocean, or charming Zante town, but of the inner belly of a hacked down cypress tree, and the sky.

It's by this window that Stavros, the son, seats us. Before we can even ask for it, a carafe of red wine lands splashing on our table, along with two glasses of ouzo and a plate of tiny white fish. '*Marides*,' Georgios explains, 'flash-fried, served with extra virgin olive oil, lemon and oregano. Ouzo and fish are a partnership you must try.'

'And Stavros here just happens to know we wanted this?'

'Stavros knows that what I like, you will like.'

'That's pretty arrogant of Stavros.'

'Arrogant Greek men. Are there any other kind?'

'That's why we love you.'

'We are so arrogant to believe you do!'

I gaze at the fish, unable to resist a small tease. 'Pity I'm vegetarian, though.'

He freezes, his fork on the way to his mouth. 'You are?'

'Yep.' He looks devastated. I can't keep up the tease for too long. 'I'm not.'

He narrows those dark, intense eyes. 'Not? You are not vegetarian?'

'No.' I grin. 'Honestly. I love fish. And meat. But especially fish.'

'I suppose this is you get back to me for the olive tasting.'

My face breaks out into another smile. 'I'm paying you back,' I correct his English. 'Yes, I could be.'

'Here,' he rolls up a thin disk of deep-fried aubergine with mint – the newest arrival to our table – dips it in some twinkling honey-coloured liquid, then leans across the table and aims it at my mouth.

'Apparently, since I was about a year old, I've managed to feed myself. I was really advanced that way.'

'Open,' he tells me. So I open, and he pushes it into my mouth.

'You can lick my fingers.' He holds out his fingers.

'You have to be kidding!'

His turn to smile now. 'Is the response I was expecting.'

We get through the appetizers, and the ouzo goes down far too easily, as does the conversation. Then we're served long, strandy fried cheese called *saganaki*, with lemon squeezed on it, followed by a traditional *bourghetto*, which he tells me is a seafood stew of courgettes, potatoes, tomatoes, sea snails, limpets, cuttlefish and octopus, piled high. Every ingredient tells a story for Georgios, reflecting his love for food. 'You know once, as a boy, I spent an entire summer living on the island of Kythira and this is all I ate – *bourghetto*. Every day. I was so sick of it, I couldn't eat it for years. Now, of course, I know that I lived like a god.'

'That's like the kid who gets filet mignon at home but always wants a McDonald's hamburger. That's what my husband used to say about growing up in a well-off Toronto family. He ate like a king, but he wanted to eat like a runaway teen.'

'McDonald's hamburger is shit, no?'

It surprises me to hear him say shit. I laugh. 'You're right there!'

He quickly says, 'Did you love him?'

I peel sticky cheese off my fingers, looking at this table so laden with food that I almost don't know where to start. 'I couldn't have loved him more.'

'Did he know it?'

'Oh . . . I fought with him a lot. Because I always had to have the last word. Jonathan expected it and I'd have hated to let him down.' I roll my eyes at myself. 'Jonathan was very strong-willed and sometimes you had to argue with him or . . . get walked on.'

He ladles seafood stew onto a plate for me. 'Fighting is good. If you fight, it is because you care. But you grieve like how you loved. You loved him with passion and deeply, so you grieve for him deeply, with passion. It seems unfair.'

'Love is unfair.'

'Losing somebody, when you not expect it, is unfair.'

I go very still, can barely swallow the mouthful of food. 'How do you know it was unexpected?'

He seems to contemplate this, and I think, *hang on, why does he always seem a bit puzzled by his own observations?* 'Well, he died young, yes? Unless you married an old man. Anybody who dies young . . . is unexpected.'

Unless it's cancer, I feel like saying. But instead I tell him, 'Well, his death was unexpected. Jonathan was killed in a car accident.' He doesn't react, seems just to wait for me to tell him more. 'We'd just got back from a holiday in Barbados . . . He'd gone out to work, and I was having a lie-in. When the knock came on my door, I just assumed he'd been in work ages ago, and yet there were two people standing there, telling me that Jonathan was dead.' I feel a tension build between my eyes, but just as quickly, it subsides. 'I don't remember much after that, just going back to bed and his side was still warm . . . I didn't know if it was from him, or because I'd rolled over there once he'd got up.' I shake my head, the feeling of tension returning. 'It mattered so much to me whose body heat it was. Because if it was his, I wanted to lie there and save it there . . . I wanted to keep his heat underneath me like that.' I look up at the stars now, thinking how Jonathan once told me that stars are lights from suns that have long since burned out. Jonathan knew things like that. Because Jonathan would have paid attention in all those classes at school, whereas I just sat there rolling my eyes, because school was boring, teachers were boring, and I was just doing time until I could get on with living my life. I wonder, now, if Jonathan's watching me from up there, from among those burned-out suns. Maybe he too is a light that goes on shining, long after the power source has been shut off.

A gentle breeze comes in the window, slightly lifting my hair. Georgios follows my gaze. 'Is it still hard for you to talk about him?'

I shrug. 'Sometimes I still feel it, right here . . .' I dig a fist into my ribcage. He watches the action of my hand. 'Less often than before, of course. But when it hits me, it's still as strong.'

Yet the memory of his face isn't. It's like a portrait done in charcoal that's had the edges rubbed out. Right now, in this starlit restaurant, across from Georgios, it's particularly blurry.

'But it seems to me it's not a pain for the words left unsaid, for wrongs that were not made right. There is no conscience in this pain. Maybe?'

'You put things very well for a foreigner,' I tell him. Stavros glides between tables with plates held over his head, a tea-towel hanging from his belt. Suddenly a strong waft of garlic stings my eyes. 'You're wrong, actually, though. There is a conscience.' I run my hands up my bare arms and look into the belly of the cypress tree, meaning, *no more questions right now*. He doesn't press me.

We eat in silence for a bit, listening to the raucous chatter from other tables, but my mind hangs on what he's just said. 'Jonathan had an epileptic seizure at the wheel of his car,' I tell him.

'And you never got to say goodbye to him.'

'No.'

'And you think it would have been easier if he'd died of cancer, and then you would have had time.'

For a moment the beat of my heart seems to pulse between our gazes. 'How do you know that?'

He doesn't answer.

'We'd been talking about having a baby. We'd ordered hardwood floors for our bedroom because Jonathan was convinced the carpet was making my asthma worse; Jonathan was going to put them in that weekend. The Runner's Room had just rung saying the pair of trainers he'd ordered had finally come in . . .' My voice sounds insistent, on the edge of anger. 'I remember thinking he couldn't be dead. I was convinced I was going to wake up and he'd be beside me, and I'd feel so relieved, and I'd realise how precious he was to me . . . how my life would be unthinkable without him.' I rub my arms again, suddenly feeling cold, even though it's not

cold in here. 'I'll never forget what it was like to have somebody be there, and then not be there, you know . . . so starkly
like that. No more phone calls throughout the day, little check-
ins to see how I was doing, see if I wanted to order in or go out
for dinner, to complain about his secretary . . . He used to say
that sometimes he just wanted to call because he liked to hear
my voice.' I smile, the ordinary groove of married life revived
in me. 'Yet all his things were there, you know. His toothbrush
sitting in a pool of water, his dirty clothes in the laundry bin,
his sandals by the door that had his toe-prints marked on the
leather . . . I thought those prints had to be proof that he was
still alive. But they weren't. They were just the last tracks of
him in my life.'

I look out of the window, distantly, while he pours water
for us. 'Isn't it funny how when you look at the stars,
there's always one that seems to twinkle more than the
rest?'

He follows my gaze again. 'But we all see them differently.
Maybe the one that twinkles most to me isn't the one that
twinkles for you.'

I smile. 'I think I like that idea, somehow – that we each have
our own star that twinkles for us.' I spear a black olive. 'Sorry
to turn the evening bleak. It's odd I'm telling you stuff I've not
even told close personal friends.'

'Normal, no? To tell a stranger.'

'Yet you don't feel like a stranger.' I smile at him. The rest of
the wine in my glass goes down easily and he fills it up, looking
pleased with my comment. 'He could have killed somebody if
there'd been another car involved.'

'But he didn't.'

'He'd only had one other seizure before. It was while he was
writing his exams in law school. He thought it was because
he'd been popping caffeine pills to stay awake all night to
study. The doctors prescribed him Tegretol – it stops you

having seizures . . . Jonathan took the prescription, but never took the pills.'

He listens without reacting.

'But a month or two before he died, he'd complained of having weird *déjà vu* sensations. He described it as doing or saying things he'd done or said before, in the exact same way. He said it was eerie. He said he got a strange metallic taste in his mouth when it happened. I just wondered if he was working too hard. That's why I booked Barbados. I wanted him to see the doctor, but Jonathan had to do everything on his terms . . . I was always on at him to stop being such a mad driver, especially since he'd bought the new sports car.' I shake my head in exasperation. 'When he died, I was angry, even though I knew the accident had nothing to do with speed. But now, I accept this recklessness was who Jonathan was, and I'd probably not have loved him if this one rebellious shade to his personality had been missing.' Georgios listens attentively, seems to understand me, even though I know I'm rabbiting and not really making allowances for the language barrier. 'After the accident, I spent hours on the Internet reading up about epilepsy. It turns out that those weird little sensations he kept getting were actually things called petit mal seizures – a sort of loss of consciousness in their own right.'

'So you go around wishing you'd checked the Internet before. Because you think you should have somehow saved him. This is why you said there was a conscience in your pain. Because you blame yourself.'

We look at one another for a few moments. 'You know, when I'm tinkering around with my computer, if I do something wrong, I can just press the refresh button and go back to a time before the damage. That's what I'd like for life. A refresh button.'

'It would be a good tool to have,' he says.

There's a long-ish pause, then he says, 'It's not easier if they die of cancer. My father did. And there were things I could have said to him when I knew the time was short, but if you are not used to speaking those kind of words, they are no easier to say in the final hours.'

I look at the scratch on his hand. 'How did you get that?'

He glances at the wound. 'I have a friend who is involved in sea turtle rescue. I went to help her . . .' He looks dismissively at the hand again. 'There was a beer bottle in the sand. I had to have a surgery.' He seems faintly embarrassed, and shrugs. 'But now it is nearly healed.'

I wonder if she's his girlfriend. He's obviously not a monk. 'Do you regret not saying things to your father when you had the chance?' I try to peel my attention away from that hand.

He seems comfortable with how our conversation jumps around. 'I don't regret what I never said. I regret more what I never did.' He breaks off a piece of bread and drags it around his plate, cleaning up the tomato sauce. 'I was always too . . . my mind was always on how different we were for me to try to find that we may be similar.'

'It's funny, because the only thing my dad and I had in common was that we both liked to sleep with our feet sticking out the bottom of the duvet.'

He smiles. 'So did you regret not having closeness with your father?'

'I regret not getting to know him better . . . things about his life, when he was growing up. It seems I know so much about my mother's, and nothing of his. And of course now he's gone, I can't ask him, can I? All his stories die with him.'

'You love your mother very much. But you love her with complications.'

'Actually, yes, you're right on the mark.' I wonder how he picked up on that. I turn my face to the breeze coming through the window, welcoming the refreshing feeling.

'May I ask how old your mother is?' he says.

I laugh.

'Why you laugh?'

'Oh, I don't know. I suppose I felt that coming. She's sixty. She'd kill me for telling you, though!' I can hardly say she's fifty, or that she used to be fifty-nine!

His eyebrows shoot up. 'Sixty? I was thinking fifty!'

'You and a lot of other people.' I feel bad for betraying her, even if it is harmless.

'She is stunning,' he says.

'She is. She just had her sixtieth a few weeks ago, actually. It's not a good topic. In England you become a pensioner at that age. It means you're officially old.'

'But she is not old.'

'No. She's younger than me in many ways.'

'She has passion.'

This description of my mother moves blithely around us as we eat, easily, without speaking for a while. 'What about you? Were you ever married, Georgios?'

'No. But I've come close many times.'

'How many times?'

'Well, three. But I am forty-five, and I first was interested in women from eleven. So that is not so terrible.'

I pull the last bit of oil-soaked aubergine off the plate before Stavros removes it. 'What happened? You didn't love them enough to commit?'

'Or maybe they didn't love me.' He says something to Stavros in Greek, I assume a compliment about the food. 'Let me tell you of a true story.' He relaxes back into the chair. 'A man was to marry a girl. On their wedding day, a cousin who had been living in America, he come here. The groom has not seen his cousin in long time. And so, the cousin arrives, and he and Helena . . .' He clicks his fingers.

'I think I like this story already!'

'Well, here they are, strangers, not even live in same country. Yet they know that somehow they have drawn to each other and they cannot be pulled apart.'

I twinkle. 'So, what happened?'

'Well, Helena left her fiancé for his cousin, and a life in a foreign country. And she did it because in her heart and mind there would never be another choice for her.'

'That's quite a story.' I'm suddenly aware I feel tanned, and thin, and blonde, and randy, and very close to this man, and not entirely sober. 'Was the groom very pissed off?'

'Not pissed off.' He looks at me cryptically across the table. The room feels like it's suddenly gone dark, except for the light of the candles on the tables. 'The groom was I.'

'You!'

'It was odd to explain . . . I loved Helena. But it was the love I could have felt for any good person I knew well. Ours was not – how would you say? – an epic love story. I was twenty-eight. I wanted to be the man who fights the shark and kills him, the gladiator who takes down the lion. I wanted that sort of force, as it could apply to love.' He smiles, almost sadly. 'And I haven't found it, even though I have looked everywhere. I am beginning to think that perhaps it is not existing.' He looks for a moment at his hand, at the scratch. 'I was right not to marry Helena. It was the workings of the gods, who some believe never truly gave up their power, and sometimes they come down to earth to play in the lives of mortals. Some people think that Zeus has the power to undo the direction of our fate.'

I think back to that idea again of the dead intervening in the lives of the living. Jonathan's promise to me, lovely and true that is was. 'I'm not sure I believe that. I may really want to, but I'm not sure I can.'

'Well, there is perhaps nowhere else in the world where you can. But let me tell you, when in Greece, you can believe anything you like.'

Stavros brings us desserts – homemade halva, Georgios tells me: Greek semolina pudding. I dig in. 'Do you think people have to have an epic love, though?'

I remember how Jonathan and I felt when we first met. In the few months we'd known one another, we had developed a strange attachment. He went nowhere without me, and if he did, he said he could concentrate on nothing except his desire to be with me again. He said he'd always wondered how he would know when he was in love, but once he felt it, it was like spotting a hole in your socks: it's there and you see it clearly for what it is. He said it was embarrassing how often people told him he looked like he was off in space, or asked him what was he thinking about. Half the time he was just thinking about how happy he was.

It was the same with me. I wanted Jonathan with an almost unhealthy compulsion. I wanted him physically, without drawing breath; I wanted the constancy of him, like a family member, or a true friend. The very idea of wanting to be a free agent forever – another badge I'd worn with pride – went sailing right out of the window. The thought that he might one day be somebody else's made me want to get commitments from him that it wasn't fair for me to ask him to make so soon. That felt pretty epic at the time. But once I got him and stopped idealising him and started to see his faults, the epic-ness wore off.

'Perhaps epic is too big a word,' Georgios says. 'But I do believe that for each and every soul, there is somebody sent for us.'

My heart gives three or four little pulses in my ear, like whispered words.

'What is that look for?' he asks.

My eyes rivet on him, reading new meaning into him. 'I don't know . . . Just something you said.'

He said *sent for us* . . . Interesting choice of words. But why would Jonathan send me a man in another country, where I'm never going to live? To complicate my life? Yes, Jonathan would do that, because a part of him would probably believe that the obstacles might be good for me.

'A soul mate,' he adds. 'Plato said that the two shall be one, and after death you shall be one departed soul, not two.'

'That's lovely.'

He pours more wine into my glass. 'The ancient Greeks believe that when a person is born, their existence is decided by the three goddesses of destiny. Between them, a person's path of life is determined. Clotho is the spinner, who spins the living thread that creates when we breathe air. Lakis decides how long our life will last. And Atropos stands at the end of the thread with her shears, ready to cut the life.'

'That's a frightening picture.'

'But it makes it easy, no? Perhaps if we believe that we were meant to marry the people we choose, then it becomes easier to settle our disagreements, or to forgive.' He looks at my face intently. 'Have you cared for anyone else since your husband died?'

'It hasn't been long enough.'

'How long is long enough?'

'Some happy medium between what feels right for me and what I think will feel right to other people.'

He seems to think about this for a while. 'What do you miss most by not having him?'

I smile. 'His arm lying across me when I sleep. It always would. Even when he got up to the toilet he'd get back into bed and lay that arm across me again.' I try very hard not to just pause and imagine that feeling. 'But really, what do I miss the most? I don't know. There are so many things . . .'

'I'm sure it's the thing you feel the strongest, and the thing you find hardest to say.'

I stare at the stars again, wondering about them. 'I suppose

. . . I miss having somebody to believe in. Somebody who believes in me.'

He nods. 'You will have that again.'

'How can you be so sure?'

He looks right at me, barely missing a beat. 'I am sure.'

We've eaten, we've drunk, but he makes no move to leave. And even though I feel we've exhausted all there is to say, I am in no hurry to go.

He suddenly blows out the small candle that flickers between us, and his face goes into silhouette, and I wonder why he did that, because now nothing in this restaurant seems to exist, except an invisible thread that somehow connects us across the darkness.

'Have you ever asked yourself what it would be like if you could have him back just for one day? One day that would be your last together . . . What would you do? How would you spend it?'

I look down and try not to blink so the tears won't drop. 'I have. So many times. I'd give the world to have one more day with Jonathan. Just a few more fantastic, ordinary hours with him.'

'Well, I told you already, in Greece you can believe in any kind of magic. If somebody made me God, I would make it so that we all get one more day with the departed. Where they come back to us, and they are exactly as we remember them, when they were healthy and full of life.'

I lean across the table, wishing he hadn't blown out that candle, because I can't see him clearly any more. Who is this man who says all the right things and seems to see inside my soul?

'So what are you suggesting, Georgios?' I dab a finger under my eye.

'I'm saying take one day of this holiday and make it yours and his. Give yourself one last day with him. And then say goodbye.'

I force a smile. 'Isn't that a little bit mad in the head?'

'Is it? Why is it? Maybe it's what you have to do to let him go.'

The candle flickers back to life again, even though I thought he'd blown it out. I see his face again.

Could this be the face of an angel?

8

'He's obviously got serious mental health issues.' Sherrie gives her verdict on gorgeous Georgios after I've bounded to a telephone to give her the low-down on my strange night out, eager to hear what she'll make of it.

'I mean, let's not put too fine a point on it, but he's whacked in the head. And the last thing somebody who's bananas needs is to hang out with somebody who's even bigger bananas than they are.'

'Are you making another sexual reference, by any chance?'

'Mm. I wasn't. But I can do if you want me to.'

We titter.

'Seriously though, Ange, let's just take a moment to get some perspective on things, girl. On the one hand you've got your dead husband promising to send you a lover, and then you've got your lover sending you on a date with your dead husband. I mean, I'm an open-minded soul, but there's something a bit kooky about this. And if I were you, I'd either shoot myself or book myself in for some serious electric shock therapy.'

'I'm not loony, Sherrie.'

'Aren't you? Some people might disagree.' She sighs. 'Ange, honey, all I'm saying is, yes he might be gorgeous, and yes he might be well off, and yes he might know all this stuff about olives and gods, and save turtles and be a mind-reader into the bargain. But think about it: of all the good advice somebody could give a person, you going on a date with your dead husband, well, I'm afraid that wouldn't cut it. Some people drink from the fountain of wisdom, but he obviously wasn't very thirsty.'

I sigh hard. 'Erm, the line's going funny,' I play with her. 'We're breaking up. Going . . . Going . . .'

'I think it's you breaking up, not the line. Cracking . . . Cracking . . . *Cracked*, more like.'

I hear her chuckle just as I hang up on her.

'I'd love to have you along,' I tell my mam, 'but I'm going to take the ferry to Kefalonia, maybe rent a moped and tour the island.' I look at her face. 'It's okay. Feel free to have your bottom jaw rejoin your top one any time.'

'You're going on a moped? A two-wheel thing with an engine?'

Jonathan begged me to go on one in Barbados, but of course I wouldn't. We ended up taking ludicrously expensive taxis and service buses that were over-full and didn't have air-conditioning. He kept giving me that look that said, *we could have rented a moped.* And I gave him one back that basically said, *up yours.*

'What makes you think I don't want to go on a moped with you?' she says.

I pause while I climb into my shorts. 'You know, somehow, I knew you'd say that.'

'Look, if you just want rid of me for the day, Angela, you don't have to go and put yourself in traction just to make the point. I mean, a below the neck transplant, while desirable, might be a little far to go just to get rid of your mother. If it's all because you're going on another date with Georgios –'

'I'm not going on another date with Georgios! He never even suggested one.' Pity. I was sure he would.

'Well, if you must go somewhere, why don't you just stay here and explore Zante? Why do you have to go to another island?'

'Because Kefalonia's supposed to be gorgeous. I might as well see it while I'm here. It's where they shot *Captain Corelli's Mandolin*.'

'Why did they have to shoot it? What did it do?'

I grin at her.

'Well, like I say, if you *are* going on a date with Georgios, and you don't want to tell me in case you think I'd be stricken comatose with envy, then all I can say is I'll cope. I really will try.' She haughtily sniffs the air. 'Just don't be a yellow-bellied coward and invent some cockamamie story about how you want to go on a moped around an island, Angela! The Angela I know would *never* go on a moped. Good heavens, you were thirteen before you learned how to ride a tricycle, and even that had disastrous consequences for next-door's tortoise. I'll never forget the sound of that shell crunching.'

'I'm going on a moped! Why does everybody have so little faith in me?'

The ferry gently bumps over bottomless, velvety green water as I sit with my head resting on a railing, giving myself up to the swell and tipping motion, and stare at an isle off in the distance: Kefalonia.

The 'port' is little more than a concrete block that juts out into the ocean. The rep from the hotel recommended a reliable place to hire a scooter from, right in the capital of Argostoli. The Greek man who sells me the twenty-euro-a-day rental generously gives it to me for fifteen when he sees me get off the service bus that brings me up from the dock, looking a whiter shade of my T-shirt from all the twists and turns and the speed at which the driver took them.

When I mount my MBK Ovetto, after a crash course (almost literal) in how to get the thing going, I am overcome with fear, and instantly want to give the thing back. 'Maybe you not so safe,' the Greek man tells me, as he watches me zigzag hazardously and nearly run into a wall when I try to take both feet off the ground at the same time. But I don't listen. I'm giving it as far as the end of the road before I pack it in.

The outer edges of urban Argostoli are at least, thankfully, flat. I wheel around trying to get a feel for the controls and to accustom myself to how uncomfortable it is on my bum. Then I'm off, gingerly at first, then gathering a tiny bit of confidence and speed. Before long I've escaped the blossom-treed boulevards with their swish stores and tavernas, and the hordes of tourists sitting on patios, enjoying metzes and ouzo, street scenery and sunshine, and I'm climbing deep into the Greek countryside. The view is breathtaking, and I struggle to watch it and watch where I'm driving at the same time. To my left is a mountain with a dense, rich carpet of black fir trees. To my right, parched hills are dotted here and there with bulbous church spires, and the odd tiny stucco village. Steep roads that the bike chugs unconfidently along suddenly swoop downwards without warning, sending me into a rapid free-fall that would stop my heart if it weren't for something inside me that automatically gives way to the moment. I feel Jonathan's arms tighten around my ribcage, the hollow of his broad chest against my back, the full weight of his chin settled watchfully on my shoulder, and I see not the danger, only a sparkling Ionian sea that's so beautiful that tears prick my eyes. My stomach lifts and drops again as the bike and I hug the road, and we coast, a little too swiftly, around a sharp downwards turn. The wind rips through my hair, sending it up in snaky strands, plastering it across my face, then whipping it out behind me. My arms and the tops of my legs fry under a scorching sun. I've never felt as free.

Only when I try to negotiate a hairpin curve too slowly, to avoid an oncoming tour bus that seems in danger of taking my kneecap off, and the bike nearly tips, do I falter and remember my limitations again. My foot instinctively goes out to break the fall I'm anticipating, and the smack of concrete sends a quick pain shooting up my leg. For a moment I think I've seriously hurt myself. But then I realise I haven't come flying off, have I? I'm still in one piece. The crisis is over. I have a whole new sense of power. I glance over my shoulder. Elation and pride dance across my husband's face.

It doesn't take long to realise I'm lost. I pull over and try to read the map, but a map's not much cop when you don't know where you are. I try to worry about this, but the miraculous thing is, I can't. Because I'm too busy gawping down the sheer drop of a cliff-side at the beach I've just spotted: a tiny crescent of unpopulated white sand, sheltered by rocks and lapped by turquoise Ionian water that bleeds to an indigo blue. It's a steep climb down, and there's no obvious road there. But I have to put my feet in that water! I venture back the way I came for about three kilometres, because I vaguely remember a fork in the road.

My intuition's right on. It's dodgy getting down there, but the bike and I make it without my taking a header. The engine stutters to a stop and I'm off quickly and doing a buckling run down a pebbled incline, throwing off my shorts and T-shirt, stripping down to my bikini. I romp into the water without thinking twice about it, and right next to me I hear a loud thwack as Jonathan's lean, fit body plunges in, with dolphin-esque expertise, shattering the calm surface. There is a moment of euphoria for both of us when he comes up and we lock eyes and beam at one another. Then he disappears swiftly, and I think *hang on, where did he go?* But he reappears several yards away, that cute puffiness under his eyes when he smiles, as if to say, *fooled you!* I swim towards him but he ventures out deeper, as though this is a game: a game to get me to be brave. I paddle quickly after him, not wanting him to get too far away from me. He treads water for a bit, letting me catch up, his chin floating on the velvety surface, his cheeks rosy against his fair, tanned skin; his smile is brilliant. His in-loveness is written all over his face.

It's not long before my feet can't touch the seabed any more, but I'm okay. More than okay. I'm fantastic. The water keeps me afloat. 'I'm not scared!' I shout, because I'm not.

I roll from my front to my back, close my eyes and feel the sun beat on my face. The water makes a rippling sound in response to my movements, and to Jonathan's as he floats beside me. When I look down I can see my red toenails, and the many coloured pebbles on the seabed, and shoals of fish coming at us and diverting around us. I marvel at the quivering shadow I cast upon the sandy sea floor. But where's Jonathan's? Jonathan doesn't appear to have a shadow.

I close my salt-burned eyes again, to stop my momentary panic, and I feel him put his arms around my bottom, lifting me, then lowering me, so that every part of my body gravitates to his. His arms hug me around the waist. With my legs clasped around him, my knees can feel his lean, straight hips that always fascinate me for their complete lack of hip-bone. When I open my eyes again, his very dark hair, with its widow's peak, has a wet gleam. His chest hair gleams. His skin gleams. His eyelashes look blacker, his eyes and eyebrows darker, and the one freckle on his earlobe cuter. I'd forgotten about it. His freckle.

I don't spare one more thought that my bikini top is now slowly sailing out to sea. It floats on top of the water, four tails of white string, like gangly serpentine limbs. I am too busy adapting to the familiar. His kiss is in living colour, all my senses revived by it, as I lie back and close my eyes, letting the water be a blanket for my head, making extra special note of the feel of his lips as they trail down my throat, committing it to memory, in a way that you would only do when it's the last occasion of something fabulous that you're never going to have again.

I remember the conversation we had once. Not necessarily one of our most profound . . . 'How do you know you love me?' I'd asked him.

He'd thought about it carefully. Jonathan always thought a lot before he answered the serious stuff: it was the lawyer in him. Then he said, 'Because even when we're just hanging out, when we're not really doing anything in particular, I still feel like I'm doing something because I'm doing it with you. In fact, whenever I'm with you, no matter what it is that we're doing, I can never imagine that I could be having a better time doing something else.'

He was completely earnest. I had smiled long and lovingly at him, thinking, *I am so lucky. How did I ever land this guy?* Was it my imagination or had his eyes glassed over with tears?

'So, your turn, tell me . . . how do you know you love me?' he'd asked, with that slight cocky streak of his turning the moment playful again.

I'd pretended to think hard. 'Because you call me a dickhead and yet I've not left you.'

He'd pulled that little smirk on me. 'I never call you dickhead. Mental midget, but never dickhead.'

But for some reason the easy way he loved me filled me with misgivings. I didn't want to love him so much, or to feel he loved me that much. I wanted to leave us both a loophole in case he ever left me and shattered my heart. 'Let's not get serious, Jonathan, and ask heavy questions about why we love one another,' I said.

He scowled at me, as though I'd hurt him, broken the faith: I can picture his disappointment so clearly. 'You started it, egghead.'

In my mind, now, I answer his question without a hint of the old Angela bravado. *I know I loved you, Jonathan, because losing you has hurt so much.*

We stay in the water until the glare of the sun starts to bother me. I swim after my bikini top, which hasn't drifted far, and secure the wet strings around my neck and my back again. It takes ages to chug back up the cliff, but I feel, peculiarly, as though time is small now, in the grand scheme of things. At more than one point the Ovetto strains and I'm convinced I'm going to end up stranded here, and I half hope I will be: stranded here with Jonathan. What did Georgios say about Zeus? Maybe this will be him changing the course of fate.

At the top I buy bread and feta from a street vendor, and find a shady spot among some trees to sit and eat it. The bread is warm and smells like it's just been pulled from a stone oven. The cheese is marinated in oil and herbs and is a combination of soft and sharp, sweet and tangy. A single shaft of sunlight cuts through the trees, and Jonathan sits in it, chewing and looking far off into the distance, all the muscles in his jaw working hard. Jonathan always had a way of eating absently, as though his mind was on something else. He looks thoroughly content, though. I wonder what he's thinking about. Then he looks at me, and that peaceful, good-humoured expression makes me think he might have been thinking about . . . well . . . just, precisely, this.

In the afternoon, I park the bike in Argostoli and sit for half an hour on a patio in the sunshine, satisfying my addiction to really good coffee, beside a small square where a festival is going on. Afterwards I walk around for a bit, then let a woman selling jewellery flatter me inside her store.

'Too flashy.' 'Too big.' 'Too wide.' 'Too plain,' I tell her, as she presents me with one ring after the other, telling me how her brother designs them. Then one does catch my eye: it's white and yellow gold, with a band of what looks to be interlocking 'S's. A motif I've seen before. 'I like this,' I tell her. 'What is it?'

'It is man's ring,' she says. 'No good for you. Only for man.'

I try it on my thumb. 'That's fine. I have a man.' I smile at her. 'He's outside, actually.' We both look out of the window. When I look back at her, she is watching me curiously.

My eyes go back to the ring. There's something about it, even though I normally don't care for jewellery. 'It *is* lovely,' I tell her, holding my hand away and admiring it. 'Does this pattern mean anything?'

She takes my hand in hers and rubs her thumb over the ring. 'It is the *meander*. The Greek symbol for long life.'

'The meander,' I repeat, feeling an unusual bond with the ring. When I look at her again she is smiling. 'I can't afford it, unfortunately,' I tell her.

She reaches into a drawer and pulls out a calculator, starts fiddling with buttons. 'I have a good feeling about you. I am going to give you discount . . . Twenty per cent off.' She wags a finger at me. 'But you must not tell my brother.'

She'd sold it to me even before the discount.

When I come out of the store, something has gone from me. I feel the change flatly.

It's the day. It's Jonathan. I look around for him but I can't see him any more.

I cross the square again, suddenly adrift, rubbing the ring on my thumb with my index finger. Amidst the street performers eating fire, and people dancing with the Greek flag, I see a small stall selling books. I don't know why it draws me, but I wander over and my attention is instantly pulled to a thin, somewhat dog-eared book. I pick it up and it looks like some kind of jotter. Each of the rough pages has something written on it in Greek. Then there are a few blank ones near the back. But on the last page is a verse, handwritten, in English. I read . . .

I search to find you, so I will be found.
I follow footsteps for their sound is yours;
All the places you would walk with me.
I stalk shadows that are but empty impressions of you.
They lead me back to myself.
For you have gone.
I have lost myself.

Underneath the verse is written 'Rebetika. Untitled. By Iannis Mariatos'. For some moments I go quite still; the world seems to become toneless. Nothing happens except for a tear that seems to take a long time forming. Then it lands, onto the page beside my thumb. I don't bother bartering with the Greek lady when she tells me that my strange little find is ten euros. I walk away quickly, as though someone might take it off me if I don't.

When I get back down to the dock, after returning the bike, I'm early for the crossing, so I sit on a bench in the shade and open my book at that page again.

'I love you, Jonathan,' I whisper, after reading it again. I just whisper the words out there; there's really nobody around to hear. I suddenly feel tired, as though all the events of the day have just taken a run at me and made me buckle. I put the book down, tip my head back and close my eyes. Jonathan won't be coming back with me on the ferry, to Zante. I have to leave him here. But in my mind's eye, he's here with me just for a few more moments. He's got his arms around me so I can rest against his chest.

And when you are gone from me, you will never be gone from me. Even when I let you go – if I ever let you go – you will never be gone from me.

I just think the words without saying them, hoping somehow that they'll be carried to him, through our clothes, through our skin, and he'll take them with him.

When I open my eyes, that wonderful feeling of Jonathan's beating heart at my back has left me, and I realise I must have nodded off, because I have a dull head, the kind you get when you've lain down to nap but fallen into a fully-fledged sleep instead.

The line for the ferry is huge now. There's a commotion going on between a small Greek child and his parents – the boy doesn't seem to want to go on the ferry, and keeps attempting to run off as his dad tries to grab hold of his arm. His scream cuts through my fuggy head and I wonder why he wants to stay so badly. I stand up to join the line, not convinced we're all going to get on, looking around one more time for Jonathan, but knowing he won't be here. Jonathan always hated good-byes. As I tag onto the end, I become aware, very strongly, of a strange vibe coming from the front of the queue. I look ahead to see what it can be. Somebody is watching me.

It's the handsome Englishman from the tour to Olympia.

9

Somebody pushes in front of me, blocking my view: the father of the Greek boy, joining the line again, with his son firmly in his grip this time. When he moves out of my way a bit, and I look for the Englishman again, he's gone. I scan every head in the crowd for his, but it's as though he too was never really there in the first place.

The aluminium gangplank springs under the weight of the many feet that clatter up it. I grip the railing to steady myself, and it's wet and shiny from sea-spray. I hesitate there, thinking, *maybe I won't board the ferry.*

I have to board the ferry.

People are moving around me; I'm obstructing them. As I walk on, I'm aware of the unpleasant off-kilter sensation under my feet. I don't go up on deck, just hang back at the stern until everybody is on board, then I watch as the ferry pulls away from the dock. My hands smell salty and metallic from holding the railing. I can still feel the imprint of Jonathan at my back, gradually fading as we slip away from the shore. I look at the ring on my thumb, the Greek symbol for long life; the white and yellow gold sparkles on my tanned hand.

I will have a long life, and a good life. The life that Jonathan would have wanted for me. I will live it for both of us.

I breathe in deeply, feeling the salty spray on my skin. The breeze kicks up in my face, sending my hair up behind me into the air. My T-shirt slaps against my body like a small sail. Goose-pimples break out on my arms, as I watch the wake of water swiftly elongating, taking me farther and farther away from Kefalonia. Eventually, the island becomes a faint and indistinguishable blur.

When there's nothing more to stare at, and I feel quite exposed and wind-burned, I go up onto the main deck. It's then that I remember the Englishman again.

He's not up here, where most of the passengers seem to be sitting – I look up and down each seat aisle for him – nor is he inside the main cabin. I check the bar, keep a lookout at the men's toilets . . . Where can he have gone? I saw him get on, didn't I? Or at least waiting to get on. I think of his fixed but distant gaze on me, as though he'd been watching me for a while. Had he seen me sleeping on the bench? I buy a drink, take it up top and find a seat. But I can't finish it; my stomach feels too queasy.

I manage to put my head on a railing and sleep most of the way home. It's only when I disembark, and my feet touch Zante soil, that I realise I'm missing something.

The book.

I make a quick dive back up the gangplank, pushing through the crowd of people coming down it. It's not where I was sitting. I check the toilets and the bar – all the places I went – but it's not there either. I ask the man standing on the dock as we all get off what happens with lost and found property, where I might go to find it. He just looks at me, disinterestedly, and shrugs.

'I wasn't expecting you'd be back so soon,' my mam grills me, as we have an early evening beer on a patio by another hotel's pool, the entire day now feeling surreal, yet the dim feeling of Jonathan still being there with me, the dim feeling of his touch, the recent bright reminder of his face . . .

We've ditched our hotel for a smarter orange-roofed one a little way down the road, towards the beach; their patio is bigger, greener, brighter, more five-star, and somehow we feel more like we belong. The beer is sharp and ice-cold, and as those first few long sips go down, they cool me and steady me again.

My mam looks striking, her brilliant white T-shirt bringing out the blue of her eyes. That and the grey-blonde of her hair under the wide brim of her white picture hat, and the flush of pink across the low apples of her cheeks, make her look less like a mother and more like a 1950s screen goddess.

'You missed me.' She angles her head coquettishly. She knows there's more to it than that, but she's not going there without some clearer signal from me that she can. Which is good, because I don't feel like telling her that I spent the day with Jonathan and he felt so real to me that I thought he hadn't died.

'I did,' I tell her. 'And I felt bad for you being on your own all day.'

'I wasn't feeling all that chirpy this morning, so I've enjoyed the rest.' She takes a paper napkin, dips it in a glass of iced water, squeezes it out, then presses it to the spot of pink skin at the V of her T-shirt neck; a gesture that's lavishly feminine and very 'her'. My mother is the kind of person who never lets you hear her on the toilet, who can be joyous but never over-excited, peeved but never fit to be tied. Sometimes I wonder, is she the real McCoy, or a living creation of her own imagined self? But then I'll see tiny alternating glimpses of her, by turns vibrant then despairing, and somehow the answer is clear.

'Why weren't you feeling great?' I ask her.

'I feel much better now. Far more like myself.'

'Was it the heat?'

'I don't know. Could be.'

'I shouldn't have left you.'

'Don't be silly.' She studies me for a while with a secretive smile.

'What?'

'Georgios came by.'

'And you're only telling me this now?'

She tuts. 'Well, he came to see you, obviously, but when I told him you'd gone off on your own to kill yourself on a moped, he politely offered to take me to lunch.'

'You went to lunch with him?'

'I wasn't hungry. But we went for a little ride-out and we had an iced fruit drink.'

'And?'

'And then he had to work so he brought me back.'

'So that was a load of crap about you missing me! Seems you were quite busy.'

'I never said I missed you. I said *you* missed *me*.'

'Oh, yeah! Right. You did.' She did, actually.

'You could have stayed as long as you liked if you were having a good time. But, admittedly,' she looks at me like I'm her unspoken passion, 'I'm glad you're back now. Because between you and me, forget Georgios: there's nobody I'd rather spend time with than my daughter.'

'I'll tell her that, if I ever meet her.' I sneak a look at her. *My mother, whose company makes everything right.*

'Something odd happened,' I say, as we split another beer. 'There's a guy . . . an Englishman . . . he was on my trip to Olympia on Tuesday. He was with two other blokes . . . friends.' I decide against telling her he's married. 'Anyway, I saw him again today.'

She seems to bloom, as she always does when we do the girl-talk. I see it in her quiet absorption in me, in the sheen that suddenly comes to her eyes. A *man*, I can imagine her thinking. *Progress at last.* 'Spill your guts. What happened?'

'Nothing happened. He was on the ferry. Or at least, I think he was . . . I saw him as we were about to board. Then when I looked again, he was gone.'

'What's he like?'

'He's . . . nice.' I reflect on his face. 'Handsome. Whole-some. Like the guy next door. He'd have got your vote.' How can I not remember all the times she would vet my boyfriends? 'Too gobby.' 'Too mute.' 'Too common.' 'That laugh's too loopy.' 'His chin'll get around the corner before he does.'

'Did you sit with him? Was he on his own?'

'No. Like I say, he was waiting to get on the ferry, but I never actually saw him once I boarded. I don't know if he was on his own.' Come to think of it, wouldn't he have been with his wife?

I stare off across the swimming pool. The dim feeling of Jonathan and I frolicking in the sea still lives inside me. My gaze lingers for a moment on a busty, topless young woman with jet-black shiny hair floating on a red air mattress; how perfectly glamorous she looks.

My mam pretends to snore. 'That's so exciting. Angela, my chest is collapsing. Whoosh! I've not had this much excite-ment since I found out I didn't win the lottery again.'

I narrow my eyes at her. 'Are you being sarcastic, by any chance?'

'Me? Never.' She drags a long-sleeved blouse across her shoulders and covers her arms from the last spot of sun that we haven't quite escaped by sitting in the shade.

'I bought a ring.' I show her.

She pulls a face. 'It's ugly.'

'It's not. It's Greek.'

She picks up my hand and examines it. 'What is it? The pattern?'

'I don't know,' I say. 'It's just a ring.'

'What's rebetika?' I ask Georgios, feeling sad about my little book. There was a phone message for us when we got back to the hotel, inviting us to dinner. So now we're sitting on the white-tiled patio of a tiny *ouzeri*, which is perched on a razor-sharp cliff-edge, overlooking a flawless bay. Again this place is more like somebody's house than a restaurant. Georgios has brought us here to see the sunset from the island's finest viewpoint. I quickly changed into a floaty black halter-neck frock from H&M that I teamed with a pair of white flip-flops to tone down the dressiness. My skin is sun-kissed and soft, my hair silky and unstyled. Georgios seems to appreciate the dress, which makes me feel good. We drink ice-cold retsina and eat *bekri meze* – 'drunkard's tidbits', apparently – strips of pork marinated in wine and topped with hot salted cheese. A thin grey cat slinks over to our table, and weaves the letter S around my calves.

'Rebetika?' he wipes his hands on a napkin. 'It was a style of music popular between the wars, something like your American blues. The people who made the music came from the hashish dens of the Greek underworld. But it caught on in many of the nightclubs of Athens.' He shrugs. 'Rebetika is not happy music. The words are shocking and passionate. There is always a sad story, a sad theme of romance and bitterness, grief and fate . . .'

I stare, unblinking, at the two inches of wine twinkling in my glass. If it weren't for the ring on my finger, I'd think finding that poem – in fact, the entire trip to Kefalonia – had been a dream. I can't remember all the words of my verse. I can barely remember who wrote it. Iannis somebody.

'Are you all right, Angela?' I hear my mam, distantly. 'You seem on another planet.' The sky is subtly changing from flame red to copper, turning the water to petrol blue. The air smells heavy with flowers, and kitchen aromas, and the scent of the rustling ocean. 'No. I'm okay.' I don't want to start turning things wacky. Talking about flitting around an island with my dead husband, and finding poems that feel like they might be a message from him is just turning things, as Sherrie would say, too kooky. Maybe my friend was right. Maybe I really am losing it.

'Why do you ask?' Georgios says. 'About rebetika?'

When I conspicuously don't reply, Mam says, 'Angela went to go around Kefalonia on a moped today and came back a different person.'

'You did?'

He looks very dark against the shifting palette of night, except for the dazzling white linen of his shirt. There's something about his intense physical presence that suddenly besieges me. It's more than his manliness, or his gritty accent, or the keen eyes. It's more, and yet . . . what is it? Suddenly, the case of the disappearing Englishman and the day with my dead husband cease to trouble me as much. Thoughts of me and Georgios having a good old-fashioned romp sail through my head. Then me going home to – where? England? Vancouver? – and having got it over with: sex with the first man after Jonathan. One task off my mental 'to do' list. But if Jonathan's sending him to me, he sure is taking his time.

I almost forget he's just asked me a question. 'I did go on a moped,' I tell him. 'It was fun. I survived to tell the tale. But I didn't come back a different person.'

'That is good,' he says. 'I wouldn't want you to. I like you as you are.' He lays a foot on his opposite knee, angles himself so his back is no longer fully to the sunset, and gazes far out across the water. He must know I'm staring at him, because his eyes come back to mine. Are we flirting? We could be. If I had vanish dust, I'd sprinkle it on my mam just about now.

The reds of the sun drop away swiftly, replaced with transient saffron, ochre and marmalade, all commingling like silent fireworks. 'It's beautiful,' my mam says. Then Georgios picks up his fork and stabs a few times at the huge salad of rocket, sesame chicken and shaved parmesan, glistening with greeny olive oil, that a young waiter sets down before us. I like how he fills his mouth. Not a thought to his table manners. It's odd how he's never mentioned going out with my mam this morning.

'Rebetika, if you want to know, was very unpopular for a long time. Very often the lyrics were about drugs, and ideas of rebellion, so the music became illegal. Some people believe it died. But others say that no song that is still sung today can be dead.'

I can't see his eyes any more as we're eating in the dark now, but I feel his gaze and it seems to discombobulate me. My mam starts saying something about the early music of Johnny Cash, her favourite singer. 'And then there's my two least favourite songs of all time,' I hear her say. 'You Must Have Been a Beautiful Baby', and 'I'm Hairy'. He laughs, genuinely entertained, when she sings some of the lyrics to the last one.

The chicken is warm and flavourful and goes well with the olive oil, which is unexpectedly fruity and flowery. It feels oddly nice to sit in darkness. But when the maitre d' goes around the low stone wall lighting a series of tiny white candles, there is something ethereal about the mood that's nice too. Food. Wine. The salty, spectral darkness of the sea. Being here with my mother. Her smile is long and warm and motherly, and intermingles with a feeling of sudden, surprising contentment in me. Georgios reaches out to pour some more wine.

'I bought a little book on the island. It had a verse written in it. I think I left it though, on a bench before I got on the ferry.'

'Oh?' he says.

'Have you heard of the poet . . . Iannis . . . Iannis somebody? His last name begins with M, I think.' My day is already fading, like sand slipping through an hourglass. 'He wrote a rebetika verse in English. He just called it Untitled. Maybe you've heard of him?' Iannis M. I'm not giving him much to go on.

The cat slinks around my foot and I take my flip-flop off and stroke her back with my toes, surprised at how coarse her coat is.

He catches my eye across the candlelight as the wine glugs into my glass. 'No, Angelina. I can't say that I have.'

Soon after Jonathan died, two very strange things happened. I had gone to bed convinced that I might finally manage some proper sleep. Just as I was dozing off, I heard something that made me open my eyes and stop breathing. It was the picked-out piano notes of a classical melody tinkling into the air – the first track on a CD I'd brought Jonathan back from England that I'd got free with the *Daily Mail*. At first I thought I was dreaming. But no. The music trespassed surefootedly through the stillness of the darkened house, like a ghostly soundtrack in a movie where the heroine is under siege from something. It was coming from downstairs. Jonathan was here again. He had to be. Hadn't I been convinced that if I wanted it enough, and I willed it enough, I'd magic him back somehow? But I didn't expect he'd come back as a ghost. I didn't want a ghost. I was shit-scared of ghosts, and he knew it. So why would he play this game with me? I quaked my way out of bed and down our stairs towards the source of the music, chanting a series of expletives, furious to think I was Jonathan's prey, or his pawn. When I saw what I saw, I got that quick and awful feeling where you can't fathom why the walls and the floor are moving, and in different directions. In the dark of our family room, our sound system was all lit up, its green and red lights moving like alien code. When I could finally move, I reached out for the *off* button. And then I saw it: the little red 'alarm' light was on. Of course! There'd been a power surge during the day; we were always getting them because with the slightest gust of wind, the massive fir trees in the neighbourhood would drop branches onto the power lines. That's what had happened. I'd had to reset the clock on the stereo in the afternoon, because four red numerals kept blinking at me like a confusing, annoying traffic light that was prompting some kind of reaction from me, when all I wanted to do was to sit in that chair, undisturbed, in a void of memories and sadness. So I'd stabbed at buttons, and I'd obviously accidentally turned on the alarm. The stereo had been programmed to wake me up at 2 a.m. with whatever CD we had in it. I looked at the clock. That's what time it was.

The other episode was a bit more puzzling.

Shortly before I got fired, I was working on a Sunday night on a complex billing matter that was due to the client on Monday and I'd asked Jonathan to make up our bed with the sheets and duvet cover I'd just washed. 'These goddamn buttons!' I heard him say, after he'd had a grumpy wrestling match with the king-size duvet, getting it back into the cover. 'Why does it have to have a million buttons, Ange? What's wrong with a zip?' Jonathan's impatience was legendary. But his constant huffing kept distracting me. 'Just bloody do it and quit whining!' I told him as I jabbed away at the computer keys, resenting my job, resenting his complaining.

'Excuse me, but isn't this why we pay a cleaner?' he hurled at me. I was shocked to see that he was genuinely pissed off.

'Cleaners don't do everything!' I spat back. I'd just asked him to make up the bed, not build one!

'Try finding one that does,' he said. Jonathan could be very high and mighty at times. When he did it with other people, it could be embarrassing, but sometimes effective. But I hated it when he did it with me. Or when he'd play the lawyer and try to outsmart me in an argument, or cross-examine me.

'Oh, piss off, you self-righteous prick,' was my last word and not particularly clever reply. I got up and watched him faffing on with the buttons. It was the first time in our years together that I'd wondered what I was doing with him. The doubt – and its easy, irrational trigger – saddened and disturbed me.

Weeks after his death, after this incident was long forgotten, I had finally got around to stripping the bed and laundering the sheets. Just as I was about to put the cover back on, I noticed something very peculiar. All the buttons were done up. Obviously I'd had to undo them to take the thing off. And they couldn't have just done themselves up in the wash. All I could think was that in my semi-out-of-it state, I must have buttoned them up myself before I threw the thing in the washing machine, without realising what I was doing. There could be no other explanation. However, the next time I washed it, I did wonder if something weird like that was going to happen again.

It didn't, of course.

10

My mam has gone turtle-saving.

Georgios invited us to join his friend down at the beach at 4 a.m. Now while I'm all for preserving nature, to me, 4 a.m. is the middle of the night, and I only do one thing in the middle of the night, and that's sleep. Although with 'The Locomotion' and Wham! belting out from the hotel opposite until 2 a.m., and the lads next door – Jimmy Gonads and crew – ribbing each other and having farting competitions, there hasn't been too much of that.

'*Adios Amigos*,' I said to her, when she stood at the door and asked me one more time if I wouldn't change my mind and come. I pulled the blanket over my head.

After breakfast, she still isn't back. I decide to go down to the beach to try and find them.

It's hot already – must be low eighties – and the sand burns the soles of my feet. They're not here. Not a turtle-saver in sight. I wonder where they've gone . . . I claim one of the few available lounge chairs, strip off to my bikini, then quickly decide to go the whole hog and get the top off too. Two Italian-looking men and a heavily pregnant woman claim the loungers next to me. The woman and the shorter fellow walk into the water. I watch how slim she is from behind and feel a big thump of sadness. Will I ever be pregnant? It's one of those things I am now resigned to just not knowing about myself. Like how long I'll live.

The tall, really handsome one doesn't go into the water. He gets out a book and starts to read, but not before looking me over and giving me a suggestive smile. On that note, quite pleased with myself, I stand up and walk into the water, aware of his gaze on my bum.

The seabed is smooth and pebble-free. The sea is a gentle shelf of warmth, which climbs higher up my body to lap around my ribcage. The sun beats down on my forehead and shoulders. Right this minute, Vancouver, and my non-life at the moment, feel a million worries away. The job. The flat. I should, but I can't, care less. Because right now it all feels remediable. When I dunk myself in and pop up again, the air suddenly feels cool on my skin and I see my nipples are rock hard, which is like I'm looking at a sexy body that's not mine. I roll from my front to my back, enjoying the freedom of being almost nude, realising that since being in the sea in Kefalonia, I'm not frightened of swimming, or what might lurk on the seabed any more.

I am free. The thought just hits me. I don't have to go back to Canada if I don't want to. I could work in London in an ad agency there. I could come here every year for a holiday. Hell, maybe I wouldn't even work in advertising. Maybe I'd do travel writing – push myself to write more creatively. Just because I was having trouble writing a speech doesn't signify the end of my career, and the world, any more. Yes, I could go back to Vancouver, ditch the job, ditch the flat. There's a thrum of excitement inside me at the thought.

I wade out quite far but then the water becomes deep, which is a bit scary, but I can't expect to be totally cured. I float on my back, closing my eyes to the sun, languidly thinking of Georgios. What if he said *Don't go back to Canada. Stay here. Work with me*? I could learn all about the olive oil industry, employ my marketing skills. I could buy a run-down villa like Diane Lane in *Under the Tuscan Sun*. A really small one, made for one, with a double bed, and pots of basil on the step, and maybe I could do travel writing on the side. I push the velvety water away from me, feeling it lap and swash, and imagine this being my life. I could live here. Forget Sunderland, Vancouver, London. This is better.

'Hello, beautiful.' Before I realise it, I've floated far out of my comfort zone. There are two teenage boys swimming behind me, and the good-looking one has his eyes glued on my nipples. I dunk myself under the water so all he can see is my head. He's a real show-off, dipping and diving and disappearing, then coming up like a dolphin. They talk in Greek, their eyes fastened mischievously on me like I'm their free peep-show.

'Leave me alone,' I snap.

'You no like me?' he says brazenly, clearly quite practised at hitting on female tourists.

'You're too young.' I try swimming away, casually.

'Really, it is no problem.' He swims faster, narrowing the distance between us.

'It is for me!' I do a hurried flap of my arms and attempt a fast stroke, thinking, *Oh, God, please don't let me get felt up by two Greek teenagers! That's all I need.* But fortunately, after they pursue me for a moment or two, they give up. Wading out of the water, my bikini bottoms cling to my bum. The two men and the pregnant woman watch me walk up the beach. When I sit down and try nonchalantly to put my bikini top back on again, my heart is thrumming. Not from nerves, I realise, but because I'm really turned on.

It's only when I'm on the lonely dirt path, heading back to the hotel, that I hear them. 'Why you not have fun with me?' the cheeky one says.

Oh no. Have they lain in wait? I turn around and they're on dirty-looking mopeds. There is something hungry and vaguely threatening about them.

'Get lost,' I tell them, like I mean business.

The cocky one smirks. 'Beautiful tits.' He stares at my breasts, where my T-shirt clings to them.

'Seriously,' I say. 'Piss off. Go find yourself a teenager.'

'Beautiful tits,' he says again, but a little less confidently, as though I've found some chink in his teenage armour.

'Can't you think of something more original to say?' I fire back, not feeling quite as laid-back as I'm sounding.

I'm just thinking, *why aren't you here, Jonathan? Then this stuff wouldn't happen,* when I hear a voice: a faintly Irish accent.

'What did you just say to my wife?' the voice says, and the fact that he called me his wife right as I was mentally addressing Jonathan turns me queerly nauseous.

When I look around, I'm stunned to see the Englishman standing there, barefoot, with a glass of beer in his hand. The lads rev their engines and vanish noisily, in a cloud of dirt and sand.

For a few moments I can't speak. 'Thank you,' I eventually manage to say, when my heart rate comes down. 'Although I was handling it fine on my own . . .'

He looks, today, a bit more like he belongs on a package tour, with the beer, the sandals, the sleeveless white muscle shirt with his nicely worked-out, golden arms showing. He's still attractive, though.

There's a few awkward seconds where his eyes very un-deliberately travel down the front of my T-shirt. Then he says, 'Sorry about calling you my wife.'

I smile, recognising how badly I want to correct his earlier impression of me. 'It seemed to do the trick.' His eyes are a greenish-blue in this light. I've never seen such clear whites.

'One of the joys of being a single woman travelling on her own, eh?'

I smile. 'I'm actually not exactly on my own, although I know it would seem that way.'

He gives me a sceptical look. 'It would, yeah. Seem that way, for sure. The ferry, yesterday . . .'

'So that *was* you!'

He looks at me oddly again. Of course it was him. 'It was weird,' I try to explain away my surprise. 'You were there one minute, in the line, and then two seconds later when I looked, you were gone.'

'Cos I realised I'd bought the wrong ticket so I had to go back to the booth.' He says it like there really is no mystery.

I look at my feet. His feet. The dirt path between us. 'I didn't think you were staying in this resort. Coming back from Olympia you didn't get off the bus . . . It seemed like you were going on somewhere else.' I sound like I've given it too much thought. The memory of us locking eyes like that seems to hang there, palpably, between us.

'Argh, yeah, we transferred hotels. We were supposed to be staying in the Pedallo Sands, in Tsilivi, but then they moved us somewhere else nearby and, God, it was a right pit, so we decided to upgrade to here – that one, actually.' He points to the hotel where Mam and I ate yesterday, where the glamorous dark-haired girl floated on the air mattress.

'We were supposed to be at the Pedallo too!' I tell him. How weird. 'They changed it last minute for us as well. For some reason they put us here, in Kalamaki.'

'What's your hotel like?'

'Nothing to write home about.'

'So we could have been in the same hotel,' he says. 'Funny, eh?'

When I don't reply he asks, 'How long have you got left? Before you go home?'

I have to think backwards over each day's events to re-member it's Friday. 'Oh . . . Three more full days, I think . . . Yes. We leave late Tuesday.'

'Are you American? You've got a bit of an accent.'

I push my wet hair off my face, feeling over-sunned and a mess. 'I'm a Brit, actually. From Sunderland. I live in Canada, though. I guess I've picked up a bit of the twang.'

He holds his beer glass out and looks at it, self-consciously, as though he can't imagine how he's come to be carrying it. 'Where in Canada, then?'

'Vancouver, on the West –'

'Yeah! I know Vancouver. I mean, I know where it is. Seattle's not far from there, is it?'

'Two hours.'

'Right. Yeah. That's what I thought. Actually . . . I've got a job offer to go there.'

'Where? Seattle?' I feel the fast throb of my pulse in my neck. That's what I overheard them talking about on the bus – when his friend said something about him moving.

'Yep.'

'Wow. We'll be neighbours.' There's a silence where we both seem to process the likelihood of this. 'What do you do?' I ask him.

He rubs the back of his head, like it's itchy; something Jonathan used to do a lot when he was thinking. 'I develop computer software.'

'You're going to be working for Bill Gates?' I ask, half seriously.

'Yeah. Actually, I am.'

'Really? Are you? I was just joking . . . I didn't really think . . . That sounds impressive.'

'Well, it's not like we're going to be on first-name terms or anything. Not that I'd think, anyway. I mean, I might say *All right there, Billy Boy* to him when I see him at the coffee machine, but I doubt he'll know me.'

His humour – everything – he feels so familiar to me. He's the rare kind of lad I might have met in a bar in Sunderland when I was eighteen, and there'd have been something about his reserve, combined with his good looks, that would have put him at a distance from his environment and his buddies, and made him intriguing and a little bit untouchable, and I wouldn't have been surprised to learn later that he'd amounted to something. 'You're Irish, aren't you?'

He smiles again. How did I ever think he was hung up on himself? 'I was born in Ireland. Lived there till I was nine. Then we moved to England. We live outside Liverpool.'

'You don't have a Liverpool accent.'

'No. My brother does, though. He was four years younger when we moved. My dad, now he's another story. You can't make head nor tail of him. Broad County Antrim.'

He lights up talking about his family. 'So, when are you moving to Seattle?' I'm aware our conversation's going on too long now. *Three more days!* Suddenly the thought of not seeing him again panics me, as though I have some entitlement to see him again.

He shrugs. 'That's the thing, like. I don't know if I am.'

'Oh?'

'My wife's not so keen to go.'

I knew he wore a ring, so it shouldn't surprise me to hear the word 'wife'. But when he says it, it floors my heart. I miss being called that. I miss saying, 'my husband'. Now when I say those words I get frowns and pity. I don't want to be free, like I was thinking earlier. I want those tiny invisible threads that connect me to somebody, that complicate, yet simplify, everything; that hold me there, even when I think I want to go, when I think I don't want them.

'Where's he hiding, then?' he asks, looking like he's ready to get going now. 'You said you weren't exactly here on your own. You said "we" go back on Tuesday.'

I try to hide my bleakness with a smile. 'It's not a he. It's a woman, as it happens'

'Well now, I wouldn't have said you're that sort of girl.'

I smile. 'It's okay. She's my mother. Last I checked I wasn't in the least bit attracted to her.'

Those magnificent greenish-blue eyes smile at me. 'Your mother, eh?' He seems to process this, and slowly nods, still standing there looking awkward with his glass of beer. 'Look after yourself,' he says. 'I'm sure I'll bump into you before you leave. Seems I keep seeing you everywhere I go . . .'

'Where did you go?' My mam looks very happy about something. 'We came back here to find you, thinking we'd all have breakfast, but you weren't here!'

'I went to the beach looking for you.'

She hovers over my bed as I lie there with a book on my chest, pretending I've been reading.

'Are you cross?' she asks. 'You are! You're cross with me! I don't believe it.'

'I'm not! Just, well . . . it's four in the afternoon, for God's sake, and you're only just coming back now! Didn't you think I'd worry?'

She laughs, aghast. 'No! I didn't realise there was a curfew on me.' She bends over, sticking her bum out at me. 'Here. Give me the strap.'

'Don't be a child. Where were you, anyway?'

She looks tanned. Her eyes are the bluest of blue: true Tiffany gems, set off by the cornflower colour of her form-fitting, zip-up hooded top that strains slightly over the eye-catching shelf of her big boobs. Her fitted, white linen pants sit low on her hips, showing just the teeniest band of tanned midriff – I don't know why she doesn't just get a belly-ring and be done with it. Even in this thrown-on-at-four-o'clock-this-morning little ensemble, she looks fantastic, and brimming with sex appeal. I feel a relic by comparison.

'He rowed us out to Marathonisi Island to see the turtles.' She claps her hands together. 'Oh! It was fascinating. Their big heavy bodies . . . these gigantic, lumbering shadows in the water . . . I've never seen anything like it. It was magic.' She sits down on the end of my bed and pats my leg. 'Georgios is magic . . . We wanted you to come. That's why we came back for you.' She slips off her white thong flats that leave tan lines, making even her feet look glamorous. 'Georgios wanted you to come.'

'Yeah. That's why he buggered off with you.' I realise I'm jealous, which is odd, given I've spent the last few hours lying on my bed, staring at the ceiling, thinking of the Irishman. Whose name I didn't even ask. Who knows I'm leaving in three days, and didn't seem to care, even though, in my mind, I've mentally married him, and therefore he damned well should have some opinion on the fact that I'm leaving in three days.

'You're jealous!'

'Get serious.'

'Is that another one of your eloquent American turns of phrase? Get serious? Very nice. Jerry Springer would be proud of you.'

'How about get knotted? Or get stuffed?'

'That's not a very nice thing to say to your mother. But while we're at it, get knotted and get stuffed back! There!' She blows a raspberry at me then goes over to her bed, unzips her hooded top and peels off her trousers to reveal her Bridget Jones' knickers, which makes me hide my smile. Her bum, peeking out of the sides, looks lily white, like a baby's. But young! Even her backside looks young. It's not fair!

I get up and dig in my make-up bag to get the remover to take off my chipped toenail polish, because suddenly I'm feeling very self-conscious about my toes.

'He only took me because when you weren't there, it would have looked very ungracious of him to back out. All he talked about was you.'

'Yeah, that's really believable.'

'We only went to see the turtles!'

'To see my backside!'

'I don't want to see your backside. Certainly not if it's half as sour as your face.'

I tut. 'Anyway, what's his girlfriend like?'

'You mean Eleni? She's not his girlfriend. They're just friends. She's very nice. She's dying to meet you.'

'Why?'

'I wondered that myself. Obviously she's got a persecution complex.'

I tut at her again. 'We're not seeing him tonight,' I tell her.

She plonks down on the bed, suddenly looking drained of colour. 'You're right, as it happens. We're not.'

'We're not?' My heart sinks. 'What d'you mean? Why aren't we?'

She starfishes her arms and legs and blows a content, partially tired sigh. 'Because he's got a date.'

'A date? What? With another granny?'

She turns her face to mine. There are shadows under her eyes that weren't there when she came in. For a second I think she doesn't look very well. 'That's really not very nice . . . It's a sad reflection on you, Angela, if you've got to keep making disparaging remarks to your mother like that. A sad reflection.'

I feel bad that I've hurt her.

And she's right. It is.

Rather than use the payphone in the hotel lobby, where I can be seen and heard, I find one up on the main street and ring Sherrie and bawl tears. 'I don't know what my problem is, Sher! One minute I'm fine, like I've passed some hump in the road. Then my life's gone back down the drain again.' I gasp for breath. 'I'm so mean! I dragged my mam on a holiday she really didn't want to come on, only to get her here and all I do is make her life a misery!' I rub the pain in my head. 'I'm so screwed up. Here I am leaving in three days, and I'm pining because there's a very happily married Irishman who I'm never going to see again! Tell me I'm not certifiable! And then on top of that there's Georgios . . .'

'Errr . . . hang on. Is that the really rational one that sent you on a date with your dead husband?'

In spite of myself, I smile. 'The very same.' I sniff and scrounge in my bag, looking for a tissue to blow my nose.

There's a long pause, where, for a moment, I think she's gone off the line. 'Christ. You're desperately searching for a man, Ange . . . Why?'

'I – I don't know,' I stammer, vaguely insulted now. 'Anyway, Sherrie, you do it all the time. Maybe it's the popular pastime of singles and widows.'

'But the difference is there's an odour of desperation to you. I can smell it from here, and we're not even in the same country.'

'There is?'

'Uh-huh. Hang on . . . I'm whiffing up . . .' She pretends to cough. 'Let me get out the Febreze.'

'I'm not desperately searching for somebody, Sherrie, I'm really not.'

Am I, though? It feels horribly un-feminist, yet a tiny bit like progress. 'In any case, I don't believe you find people just by looking. After all, it never works for you. My belief is that the right people show up when you least expect them.' I think of Roger who I went for pizza with. He could have been the right person. Only I wasn't expecting him and I didn't know what to do with him. Sad.

'Hang on, Ange, all this talk of people finding their way to you – this isn't a round about way of you getting back to being convinced that Jonathan's going to send you a lover, is it?'

I think about this 'No! I mean, I don't *think* so.'

She groans. 'Oh, you had to add that last bit!'

'But Sher, you have to consider that . . . well, it *is* possible that Jonathan has sent me Georgios. I mean, a teeny weeny little bit possible –'

'He has a teeny weeny? Oh, sorry. It's a bad connection.'

'Can you be serious, just for a minute? I'm just trying to say that I know you think the idea's ridiculous, but there's something about Georgios that's different from anybody I've ever met . . .'

'But there is another possibility too. Isn't there?'

'There is?' I brighten. I'm glad she's finally adopting the idea.

'There is. The other possibility is that maybe Jonathan has sent you nobody, Ange, because Jonathan can't send you anybody. Because Jonathan is dead!' She has that triple-exclamation exasperation in her voice by the end.

'You have to keep harping on that point, don't you?'

There's a frustrated pause. 'In Ouch-ya-eet-ma-arma, off the coast of Papua New Guinea—'

'Oh, not another penis-eating story!'

Pause. 'Could it possibly be?' Disgusted tone.

I sigh. 'Go on, then.'

'The Nibbils tribe perform a nightly ritual of beating their drums and dancing to ward off unseen spirits. They do this from the day they are old enough to stand, to the day they die.'

'And?'

'And nothing. That's it. The point I'm making is that even people who can't read, can't write, and go around eating each other, still have enough common sense to want to keep a sizeable distance between themselves and the afterlife. Because there's something damned spooky about it, man! So I wish you'd get the whole idea outta your head!' She shudders noisily. 'Ange.' Her voice turns serious now. 'I'm just saying that maybe you'd be better off believing that nobody is gonna send you anybody. Maybe if you're waiting around for Jonathan to send you somebody, you're using that as an excuse to not go out and find somebody yourself.'

I don't know what to say. Which is okay, because she's still talking.

'Angela, baby. I have some serious, one-time-only, take-it-or-leave-it advice for you. Here it is. Are you ready? Drum roll . . . Maybe you should give yourself a bit of a break, hon.'

'What do you mean?'

'Well, stop thinking in terms of soul mates and lost loves and happy ever afters, and allow yourself to have a bit of fun. You are allowed, and furthermore, what you've been through means you're entitled to it. So . . . if you're so convinced that Jonathan has sent you a lover, and Georgios is that lover, then my advice is go for it.'

'And?'

'Screw him senseless. There's not much time left.'

11

There's not!

When I get back, my mam says that Georgios rang and invited us to his house for dinner tonight, which feels like telepathy to me. Another definite sign. I find that once you tune yourself into this cosmic forces business, it's really quite good.

'Hang on, though, I thought you said earlier that he had a date,' I remind her.

'I think he cancelled it to spend time with us – or more like with you, because he never got to see you earlier.' She watches me closely. 'I told him I was exhausted after being up so early. So I said you'd go on your own.'

'Is this some sort of scheme?' The Vivien I know would rather chew her own toes off than admit she's too tired to go out for dinner with somebody like gorgeous Georgios.

'Scheme? Actually, if the truth be told, I really am feeling tired.'

'Are you okay?' I stop tarting myself up in the mirror and scrutinise her.

'Just tired.'

She seems it. Her eyes look sore and almost puffy.

'Should I not go?' I ask her.

'If you don't, I will!'

Okay, so here I am. The hair casually pinned up with a clear plastic clip. The skirt: short, colourful, a bit eighties ra-ra, not really me. Something Mam picked for me at Topshop. The tiny little white tank top – sexy when you wear it bra-less. Which I don't. Then I do. Don't. Do.

'Get them out!' my mam growls.

'I think not! You're a disgusting mother.'

The sandals – the tarty cripplers – are about to make an appearance again. I look in the mirror and deflate. 'Gawd, I look like a tiny-titted hooker now!'

She glares at me. 'Don't call them tits! Call them buzzums. You look like a tiny-buzzumed hooker. What's wrong with that?'

I throw my arms across my chest. 'Okay, that does it. You can have your hooker shoes back. They look better on you.' I put on my new hot-pink H&M diamante flip-flops. Far more me.

'Make-up?' my mam reminds me, watching me hurriedly bung bright pink polish onto my toenails with a shaky hand, making a right botch-job of it in the process.

I look in the mirror, and miraculously I don't look like I've been crying to Sherrie at all. I decide on only a dab of clear lip-gloss and the teeniest sweep of black mascara. There.

'Maybe there's a shop you can go by, on your way,' she says.

'What for?'

'You know.'

'I don't.'

'You know . . . some . . .' She widens her eyes and nods rapidly. 'Dulux,' she whispers. 'Just a little packet.'

For a moment I have to think what she can possibly mean. Then I get her gaffe. Only my mother could confuse Durex condoms with Dulux paint. 'And while I'm at it, I'll pick up a roller and a pot of turpentine.' I wag a finger at her and she scowls at me, clueless.

I pick my bag off the bed, look once more at her bemused face, and drop a kiss on her brow before heading nervously out of the door.

'There's something else I never told you about Jonathan,' I tell Georgios, as he and I sit in a tiny vine-covered terrace at the back of his house, drinking amber Metaxa. The chances of us having sex might be improved if I could have one conversation with him that doesn't bring up my dead husband.

'Jonathan had bought some stocks without my knowing. It was . . . do you know what I mean by an insider tip?'

'Of course,' he says, sitting casually beside me, his eyes on the foot that I've got dangling across my other leg.

'He put a lot of money into a copper mining venture. Nearly all our savings. He even re-mortgaged our house.'

I hold up my glass and stare through it, watching the amber liquid glint in the sun. The air hangs hot and heavy, and is alive with the sound of crickets. 'He never told me a thing about it. I had no idea until after he died that he lost nearly a quarter of a million dollars of our money.'

'And you've been thinking about this today and that's why you have depression.'

'Depression?'

'Vivien said you feel not good today. She suggest I bring you here to . . . make you smile again.'

'She said you had a date!'

'With you.' His eyes look playful.

My damned mother! 'Do you own a shotgun? And can I borrow it?'

We laugh.

We finish off the brandies, then go inside the house for the dinner he's going to make us. It's cool in here, with the stone walls, bare floors and minimal furnishings. I like the rustic kitchen; it makes me feel like I could suddenly be transformed from a crap cook into someone who could concoct delicious culinary wonders made with simple ingredients and olive oil. I like the red brick arch that leads from here to an area with a couch right in front of a wood-burning stove. It makes me think of romantic, television-free winters by candlelight.

I pull out a chair and sit at the table.

'Have you forgiven him?' he asks me.

I run my fingers over the rough grain of the wood. 'I was furious at first . . . I mean, first I lose him, then I realise I'm penniless. Well, not quite, but close. But obviously I can't keep being annoyed at him, because ultimately he lost a lot more than I did, didn't he?'

I think now of what old Ms Elmtree said about Jonathan sitting in his car. I wonder if it was the day he realised he'd lost the money. Maybe he dreaded facing me, even if he knew I had no idea. Or had he had one of his seizures, right as he'd pulled up at our house?

Georgios opens the Metaxa bottle to give me a splash more, but I put my hand over the rim. 'You're supposed to be a team when you're married. No secrets. You don't just do things without telling the other.' It was that reckless, devil-may-care, law-unto-himself thing that drove me mad about him, because it was a part of him that I had no influence over. It was the one part of him I couldn't own. 'I'm sure, though, he'd be pleased that I had something to hold against him.'

Georgios sits at my side. 'A house is just a thing, Angelina. Before I was born, we had the great earthquake of 1953. Almost everybody lose everything they ever own, including the roof over their heads. And look now. Almost everything you see on this island is rebuilt. Those who lived took the only path. The path of survival.'

I look around the four walls of this room, with ancient history seeping from every pore. 'What happened to this place?'

'As I say, most everything was destroyed on this island. But not the olive grove. Not my family home. This place miraculously survived when very little did.'

I hold out my empty glass. 'I think I would like another brandy.'

The candle on the kitchen table is the only light in the room. We've moved on to red wine, only it's mostly me doing the drinking. I slump across the knotty wood surface after we've eaten a simple meal of marinated vegetables and grilled chicken in oil and herbs. I don't know what we've been talking about. I've been far too preoccupied with thinking about kissing him.

I've missed kissing. More than sex, or even a good old cuddle. I've missed having the back of my head cupped when a man is devouring my mouth. Fingers kneading my skull. Fingers knotting in my hair. Laying a hand on a man's rough, warm cheek. Negotiating that sexy place at the back of his neck. His breath going straight into my lungs, nicer than deeply inhaling fresh air.

'Why is there never anyone here, Georgios? In this cold stone house.' *Why, after all those talks, do I still not really feel I know you? Why are you still not quite real to me?* 'Don't you miss family?' I hope he doesn't think I'm putting myself forward for the role.

'There are always people here. Those who work with me. My brother and his wife and sons when it's time for the harvest.' He looks at me as though he knows what I mean. 'When you do not have family of your own – children, a wife – it can feel silent. Life can feel silent sometimes.'

I shiver. 'I think that's what worries me the most, Georgios – my life feeling silent. Sometimes I'll think that if I never marry again, there's going to be nobody around to love me. I'll be old, and I'll never lie there napping and have my granddaughter stand over me and scour the familiar features of my face and be filled with love for me, because I am her blood, her family, the mother of her mother.' I look at him listening closely to me. I love how he does this and can't quite fathom why he'd care to listen to all this soul-searching by a woman he's never going to see again after this week. 'And then when my own mother is gone . . . there'll be no one behind me, and no one in front of me, no one tying me to anyone, and won't that be the loneliest feeling in the world?'

'There are always people, somebody . . .'

'But it's family that really counts. The thing is – and I've really only realised this recently – other people are the point of life, Georgios. We all think we're the point of our own lives, but we're not. Other people are. It's not what we take from this life, it's what we leave, and what others leave us.'

'You are wise.'

'Well, with Jonathan's death I think I grew up by about forty years. But wisdom, just like life, isn't always kind. Sometimes it tells you a few things you wish you didn't know.'

We sit just watching each other for a while.

'Do you not have a mother?' I ask him.

'She died when I was four. I was grown up by my father and my brother, and my grandmother, and an aunt. It was a combined effort. Maybe that explains why they did not get me right.'

'What's not right about you?' The thought of going to bed with him sends a ripple through my body, like a warm tide slowly rolling up a beach.

'Lots of things, or so women have told me.' His eyes smile. 'I should probably get you home.'

He gets up and carries our plates over to the small, ancient, peeling sink. I look at the crusts of bread left lying on the table.

The jar of olives lying open. The bottle of green olive oil. The red wine in the bottom of my glass.

'I don't mind staying up late.' It sounds like a proposition.

He glances over his shoulder at me, then abandons the dishes and comes back to the table. 'Stay, then,' he says. 'There is no hurry.' He sits down, cocks his head, and looks at me enquiringly.

The first time I had sex with Jonathan, he said I almost attacked him. I don't remember any attack, to me it was just that getting naked with him was a high priority. Everything about our meeting had been urgent. He'd given me three minutes to ditch my boyfriend. And I had. I think in two. I wanted Jonathan instantly and more than I'd wanted any other lover. I could pretty much count all of them on one hand. Okay, two hands. But I was sure Jonathan was going to be my last.

We stood in the hallway, the sounds of the house party going on behind us. 'Just because I dumped the guy I came with doesn't mean I'm going home with you,' I told him.

I turned and attempted to walk away. He reached out to pull me back and drew me to him, like a dancer draws his partner into a hold. Only it was into a kiss. And what a kiss! A ravishing, hands plucking at hair, nose-knocking, teeth-knocking, back-of-the-neck-stroking, ravishing, damned hot kiss. There was no point in trying to act unbothered. His mouth blotted out all the pretence. There was to be a future here; I think we both knew it.

I let him walk me home, but I wouldn't allow him to kiss me at the door again. 'I don't sleep with men on the first date.' I gave him a small push when he started moving in on me.

He moved in so close I could see the tiny black lashes on his lower lids. His face stayed there, and he just looked at me for what felt like a very long time. 'We haven't been on a date, though, have we? I met you at a party, two hours ago.'

Carol Mason

'Hmm . . . That should make it worse, shouldn't it?'

I pulled him, ravenously, by his sweater and we practically fell through my door.

I feel Georgios's breath on my face as he bends over me, studying my face. 'What are you thinking now?'

'Nothing,' I tell him.

'I think you're thinking something.' He sits down, rests his chin on the backs of his hands.

I'm thinking that my heart is thrashing, but I don't know whether it's from anticipation of Georgios, or from remembering Jonathan's and my first kiss, which is the last sort of confusion I want right now.

'Come on!' He stands up suddenly and holds out his hand. 'I want to show you something.' He picks up his keys from the countertop and leads me outside.

'Where are we going?' I ask him. But he doesn't answer. I listen to our feet crunching the gravel as he walks to his car.

The white Suzuki Jeep bounces its way through the darkness, as though on a path to the moon. I can smell the olive trees without seeing them. Georgios drives confidently as the rugged ground seems to come at us under the beam of the headlights, making me a bit dizzy. 'How can you even see where we're going?' I ask him.

'You don't have to see things to know they are there, Angelina,' he says.

When we reach the top, it's like that day when he brought me and my mam here, that same feeling of being in the celestial heights. Georgios shuts off the engine and all I hear is the sea, a dim and steady swash below us. The only light is from the crescent moon, like a bright smile lying on its side.

'Let me tell you a story. Do you know who Selene was?'

I shake my head. History was something else I zonked right out of at school.

'Selene was goddess of the moon. One night, as she rides across the sky, she looks down and she sees Endymion, a humble shepherd. Endymion is sleeping there, outside . . .' He looks across at me. 'Of course, she was immediately attracted to him. So she go to him and she kiss him, just lays a kiss on his eyes, on his face . . . Now, Endymion feels this kiss, strongly. So when he wakes up, he realises she came to him only in a dream. But of course, now there is a problem for him. Now he has tasted her kiss, he can think of nothing else. His waking world has no appeal any more. All he desires is sleep, so she may come to him and kiss him again.'

I stare far across the darkness, lost in the charm of his story.

'Selene fell in love with him. She loved him so much that she asked Zeus to give him the most special of gifts – to allow for him to choose his own fate. So Endymion chose to never grow old and to be in eternal sleep, where he would be visited every night by Selene and her rays of light.'

I smile at him. 'Did she do it?'

'Every night. She come. And somehow, even though he stay in everlasting sleep, Selene managed to give birth to fifty daughters from him.'

I look at his scratched hand resting on the wheel. 'Fifty daughters! That's a lot of stretch marks.'

'I think ten might have been good.' His eyes play with me. 'Fifteen is most.'

'I'm glad you're a modern man.'

We smile long and fondly. I wonder if Selene is up there, languishing on the crescent moon, and what she might be making of us.

After a while he says, 'Let us go back,' and he gives one final glance up at the moon. I'm a bit bummed out, because I was thinking one nice moonlit snog might have been in order.

We drive down the mountain in the darkness. Neither of us talks until we get back to the house, where he turns off the engine and seems to just sit there looking awkward.

'Angelina, perhaps you can help me. I have a small problem.' He looks at me candidly. 'I shall put it as a hypothetical question . . .' He clears his throat. 'Say there was a man, and this man was interested in a woman. Only the woman is not travelling alone, and she is here for only short time. Now he can forget about her . . . Or he can find a way to ask her to spend her last days with him, if they both feel that the person who travels with her will understand.' He rubs a hand across his face, and I feel my heart kick into gear again. 'I am wondering, what should he do?'

'Well,' I pretend to think hard, my heartbeat going scatty. 'Is the man so very confident of the woman's attraction to him?'

He hesitates. 'Somewhat.'

'Well, perhaps he needs to find that out first.'

He holds my gaze. 'But under the circumstance . . . How?'

'Well, let me think . . .' I lean across the seat towards him. 'How about if he took a moment when he has her entirely on her own? Something, I don't know, maybe a bit like this.' I try an offhand shrug before meeting his eyes. 'And he should hold her gaze for a few moments – in a way, a bit like we are doing now.' My gaze goes now from his eyes to his mouth. 'And then, well, just maybe he should kiss her, to see how she might respond.'

Those eyes smile at me, the left side of his mouth twitches ever so subtly. 'And you don't think she will mind? If I do that?'

I smile softly at him. 'I don't think she will mind that at all.'

He exhales. 'I am relieved,' he says. His gaze hangs on mine before he puts the vehicle in gear again. For a moment, I'm not sure what's happening. 'Here's to tomorrow, then,' he says.

'Tomorrow,' I repeat.

'Just the two of us.' He smiles at me.

We don't say much as he drives me back to the hotel. I tip my head back, enjoying the warm breeze that the speed of the car sends over my face, already thinking of tomorrow. Is it really going to be fair to abandon my mam for our last three days? Fair? She'll be cock-a-hoop.

When we pull up outside the hotel, he shuts off the engine and angles himself so he can see me better, his scratched hand resting casually across the wheel again.

'It's been wonderful,' I tell him. 'Tonight. It really has.'

The edges of his mouth twitch up into a little pleased smile.

I look at his hand again, wondering if I should say, 'Look, let's kiss tonight, then it won't leave so much to do tomorrow.' But I don't. Because it quickly becomes apparent that he's thinking the same thing. His hand leaves the wheel, and as he moves in on me I close my eyes, my chin tilting up, waiting for his lips.

Then I hear the car door open. I open one eye. Georgios is reaching across my lap.

'Goodnight, Angelina. And thank you.' He gives the door a little push. 'Will you tell your magnificent mother that I will pick her up at ten?'

12

'Bloody Jonathan's sent my bloody lover to the wrong person!' I squeal at Sherrie, on the hotel payphone. 'Can you believe it? It's my mother he's after, not me! He called her magnificent!'

'Uhhhh, wait until I sit down. You mean . . . let me process this . . . Gorgeous Georgios's got the horn for your ma?'

'Stupid cupid needs to get his bloody blindfold off, that's all I can say. He pinged his bloody arrow and it struck the wrong female! They're on a date! The dirty rotten toerags. He picked her up this morning. Wants to spend as much time as he can with her from now until she leaves. He's grateful I understand!'

'Oh, man! That's so sweet!'

'It's not sweet. It's catastrophic.'

'And what does she say about all this? Madame Sexpuss Vivienne?'

'Nearly peed herself with joy! So much for all that claptrap about *you're going to marry him, I can just feel it* . . . She nicked him off me!'

'Sounds to me like she didn't have to do much nickin'.'

I picture those Tiffany gems twinkling, madly and infatuated. 'There was one-upmanship written all over her. Gleeful one-upmanship.'

'Well, I'm not surprised. It is quite an achievement – that he'd pick a woman her age over you. Actually, I'm starting to like him more now.'

'How do you make that out?'

'It makes him more of a human being and less of a man.'

'Hello? Sherrie, are you still there?' I ask her, when she seems to go quiet.

'Oh, sorry . . . I was just wondering something.'

'What?'

'If you know how to say "dad" in Greek.'

I step outside the hotel into the dazzling sun.

The Irishman is standing right there.

My face must register my shock, because he smiles slightly, his expression a mix of awkwardness, confusion and – is that relief?

'I wasn't,' he says, after a long while of us both just standing there, looking at one another.

I scowl. 'You weren't what?'

'So sure I would bump into you again. Before you left. Like I said I was.'

Still he stands there, his hands in his shorts' pockets. His golden tan gleaming against the white of his T-shirt, his hair a golden brown. 'So I came looking for you.'

'I don't know what to say,' I tell him, because I don't.

'Do you want to go for a walk?' he asks, awkwardly.

There's something upright and responsible and honest about him that makes it impossible for me to distrust him. But I still say, 'Maybe I should ask you the obvious question first.'

He cocks his head. 'Go on.'

'Where's your wife?'

He doesn't flinch, just continues to look at me. 'I felt that coming. And, well, you're right to ask, and it's one of the things I can tell you about . . . if you come for a walk. But not if we just stand here . . . obviously.' Some people come out of the hotel behind me and look at us. But I continue to stand there.

'She's gone with the girls to Athens for a couple of nights.
Us blokes didn't want to go,' he says.

'And the other?'

'Other what?'

'Thing you were going to tell me?'

'Oh!' He does a flick of his head in the direction of somewhere away from here. 'Can we? Please? It'll be easier to talk.'

'How did you know where to find me?' I ask, when we start
walking.

He laughs a bit. 'I didn't, did I? I mean, yesterday, when you
walked away, I watched you walk up this way, so I knew your
hotel was up here somewhere.'

'There's a million hotels up this way.'

'Well, not a million, but there's certainly a good few, yeah.
But it's weird . . .' He stops, turns and looks at me. 'The first
hotel I happened to glance in . . . there you were.'

I shake my head, baffled. He stops and looks at me again,
like he too is in a bit of a quandary. 'There's no harm in us
walking, is there?' he says. And I'm not sure whether he's
asking me or telling me, but I say, 'Suppose not,' all the
same.

'My mother has a date with a very attractive Greek man.'

We sit on a dune on the curve of the bay, overlooking the
water dotted with topless women, dads and kids. I give him a
short version of the events of our holiday so far.

'Get out!' he laughs. 'So you had the hots for this fella and it
turns out this fella's had them for your mother?'

I rest back on my hands. 'I wouldn't go as far as calling
them the hots.' I kick off my flip-flops and run my feet over
the coarse grass. 'I liked him, though. I did. He's nice.
Attractive. Decent. Interesting. Single . . .' I flop back on
the grass, feeling him watching me. 'And crazy about my
mother.'

'It's a bit *Shirley Valentine*, isn't it? Coming on holiday and copping off with the Greek? A bit *Mamma Mia*. Have you seen *Mamma Mia?*'

I squint up at him. 'I saw it when it came to Vancouver.' Jonathan hated it. 'But no, it's not really like that, not if you knew Georgios and my mother. It's actually kind of sweet.'

'But it's the thing to do, isn't it? To come on holiday and have a mad, passionate romance with somebody you're only going to know for one week. For some reason the rest of the world thinks that's really appealing. Like that's going to solve a lot of bigger problems in their lives . . .'

I look at him now, sitting there, staring off into space, knees up, elbows resting on them. The long line of muscle that runs down the underside of his arm, the soft golden hair on his legs; his handsome profile, long eyelashes, nice nose. 'I don't think that's the case with my mam,' I tell him, but I don't bother elaborating; I don't really want to just sit here talking about my mother, plus, what he just said makes me wonder something: did I come to Greece secretly hoping I'd have a fling?

'There was that case not so long ago in the newspapers, wasn't there?' He looks at me with lively eyes. 'D'you remember? Some woman went to Africa and came back with a tribal leader who knew no English and shacked up with him in Cornwall or somewhere. And he got frustrated cos he couldn't understand the customs or speak the language, and he didn't even know what a kettle was for, or a toilet, and he ended up bludgeoning her to death.'

We smile.

'Why're we smiling?' he says.

'I don't know.'

'It's not really funny, is it?'

'It shouldn't be, no.' I sit up now, and notice his eyes quietly taking in my legs.

'So I reckon I must look normal after a freak like that, then?' he says. 'Just a normal married lad from England, on holiday, stalking a seemingly very nice and very pretty single lass around the resort while his wife's gone off on a trip to Athens.'

For some reason, he's impossible to take offence at. 'And then there's the taking photos of a girl's bottom at Olympia.' I try not to smile.

'I never did that! Boz took it! I just looked at it.'

'Did you think she was attractive?'

'God, I can hardly remember now.' He grins. 'You're making me sound horrible! A real perv.' He laughs. 'What're you doing here with me? Eh?'

I look at his handsomeness. His hair, his shoulders, his lovely smile. The sincerity in his eyes. 'That's a very good question.'

The lamb *gyros* is spicy. Sloppy – a sloppy bloody mess, quite frankly – and filled with onions, tomatoes, shredded lettuce and loads of tzatziki. 'Yak!' I wipe my face with a napkin. He's got lettuce on his T-shirt, lettuce on his shorts, lettuce stuck to his chin, a piece of lettuce hanging off the end of his nose, which he quickly gets rid of. 'I love these,' he tells me.

'You can't tell.' I gesture to my chin, meaning *wipe yours*. He does. 'I've been eating about ten of 'em a day.'

'That would qualify as loving them, for sure. Or an eating disorder. I'm not sure which.' I look him over. 'How do you stay so fit if you eat this much? You don't go and put your fingers down your throat afterwards, do you?'

He laughs. 'Neh, I got therapy for that a long time ago. God they're good, though. Nothing like the ones you used to get in Liverpool after a night out round the town. Kebabs.' He pulls a face. 'Remember them?'

'I thought they only did that in Sunderland.'

'You know, I keep forgetting you're from Sunderland. You just don't sound it. You don't act like it, either. You're very . . .'

I dunno, cosmopolitan. Are you sure you really grew up there?'

'Hey, don't knock Sunderland. People who live there can, but nobody else! Actually, I've been thinking of moving back.'

'And? Are you going to?'

'Probably not.'

'Can I ask you something?' He turns and looks at me once he's finished chewing, and licked all the runny bits off his broad, tanned fingers. 'Why's a lovely lass like you coming on holiday with her mam, and not her boyfriend?' He must see my face, because he quickly says, 'I've said something wrong. What's the matter? I've gone and put my foot in it, haven't I? Let me guess . . . You've just broken up with somebody. You and him were very close. You were even going to get married. So now you're devastated.'

'No.' I shake my head, trying to be breezy. 'Neither of those, actually. The truth is . . . I was married. My husband died.'

He quickly scours my face, as though for some deeper reaction from me. 'Died?' he says, like he can't fathom such a thing. 'Oh. That's crap. When? How?'

'Two years ago. Car accident.'

He scowls. 'He must have been just a young bloke . . .'

'Thirty-six.'

He rubs a hand across his face. Looks shocked. Visibly troubled. 'Whoah. I'm sorry. I don't know what to say. It must have been awful for you.'

I pull a smile. 'And not so great for him, either.'

When I get back to the room, my mam's got the radio on full throttle and is hula-dancing around the room to U2's 'Mysterious Ways'. She promptly stops, breathless, when I come in. 'I just got back a few minutes ago,' she shouts over the music. 'I wanted to come back and see how you are, babsy.'

'Babsy, my arse. You know what the cuckoo is?' Didn't somebody ask this in a movie? 'It's a bird that goes and lives in another bird's nest.'

She reaches for the deodorant stick, runs it up under her top. 'Cuckoos live in clocks,' she says, and then she chuckles. 'Are you really upset? I'm sorry. It's not right me being off with Georgios and you being left here. You should be with us.'

'Yeah, I'm sure that would be a real party. What was it you said? I don't want to be a spare wheel, or a heel, or somebody with no feet?'

She beams at me. 'Are you mocking the afflicted?'

'Unheard of.' She looks so happy, it's impossible to seriously want to kill her. 'Go and kiss him and tell me what it's like,' I tell her. The very thing she said to me.

She plonks down on the edge of her bed, clasping the deodorant tightly to her chest. 'I want to,' she says quietly. 'Oh, Angela . . . I want to.'

'You're supposed to say you don't! That was supposed to be my job!'

'I know! And I'm supposed to say that he's too old for me and too short!'

My words to her, once.

'But it's not true.' She claps her hands either side of her face. 'It's just not true, Angela.'

'Spare me.' I hold up a hand. 'I don't want to know how your loins are twitching just thinking of him.'

I see her try not to smile.

I whip my glance over her – the long, pale pink T-shirt with the sleeves that come down to her knuckles, and the way she's got two silver bangles over them, napkin-ring style. The pale denim A-line, knee-length skirt. And the cream, peep-toe wedge espadrilles with her snazzy toenails peeking out. 'So, where is he, then?'

'He had some work to do. He wanted me to come with him, but I didn't want to be in the way. He's not on holiday like we are, is he? But he's coming back for me at four.' She stares at me, as though her mind's elsewhere. 'I wanted to see you. I was missing you.'

'Liar. You wanted to come and gloat.'

'No.' She shakes her head and gives me a dirty grin. 'Actually, I'm dying to tell you something.' She's giddy now; it looks like a mix of nervousness and excitement. 'A girlie confession.'

'Hang on . . . er . . . you've bonked him.'

'Don't say that! That's so uncouth, Angela. But along those lines . . . What I wanted to tell you was that . . . I haven't . . . you know. Anything. Not in fifteen years.'

It dawns on me that she's talking about sex. My mam and I don't talk about sex. Even when she taught me about the birds and the bees, she did such a good job of focusing on animal biology that I didn't realise it applied to people as well until about ten years later. 'But Dad's only been gone eight years.'

'Your dad and I . . .' She clutches her hands in her lap, her index fingers making a tense, bent steeple. 'Nothing. Not in a good many years.'

I swallow hard. 'Oh . . . I had no idea.'

She glares at me. 'Don't look at me like the topic's so distasteful!'

'It's not! I mean, I wasn't looking at you in any way. Don't be so touchy.'

She's too happy to fight. 'You know, I've never told you this . . . but a long, long time ago, well before I met your dad, there was a boy . . . I met him at a dance, with my friend Eva. Eva and I both thought he was a bit of scrumptious. But it was me he liked from the start.' She gazes wistfully into the distance. 'He was handsome. Decent. A little bit forward – certainly not boring. And I was potty about him, only I don't think he ever really knew it.'

'Did you go out with him?'

'I did. We went to the pictures. And he kissed me in the back row. It was my first proper kiss . . .' She flushes and tries to hide her embarrassment with a laugh. 'He wasn't shy, let's put it that way. He said he knew I was enjoying it because he could feel the quickening of my heart.' She puts a hand on her chest and draws a sharp breath, like she can feel it all over again. 'And I thought that was normal. I thought every man would make me feel like that. The pitter-pat . . . I suppose that's why I thought I could hold out; if it wasn't him, there would be others.'

I think how Jonathan made me feel like that. And when I went on that date with the city planner – Roger – yes, I felt something like that with him. 'What happened?' I ask her.

'There weren't others.'

'I gathered that, but I mean, what happened with him?'

'Oh, well, he didn't want a girl who held out. It was the swinging sixties, remember? He didn't want to tie himself to about the only girl who, for reasons even she didn't know, wasn't going to be any fun. So he went for Eva. Eva made it obvious she wouldn't disappoint him.'

'She stole your boyfriend?'

'I couldn't totally blame her. He and I had really only gone out once or twice . . . It was a case of the easiest girl winning.'

'Well, he couldn't have been very nice.'

She shakes her head. 'I don't think he was. But forty years later, that kiss lives on inside me. It'll come to me and I have to push it away, pretend it didn't happen. I've had to suppress the part of me that responded to that kiss, to make myself a little more accepting of things.' She looks at me like she's desperate for me to understand. 'Is it wrong, Angela, to go on wanting something that you never had, even when you're as old as I am? To look back on your life and not be able to understand it, or have any idea why you made the choices you made? To feel you should have been swinging from the stars! Not all the time, of course. But at least some of the time. There should have been some times.'

'So my dad . . .' *wasn't much cop in the sack, is what she's really saying.* But I don't think I want to know Dad the man. I was sort of just getting to grips with Dad the dad.

'It wasn't your dad's fault. I married him mainly because he was a good man, and, really, I was too young to know myself. The problem was me, not him. He'd have been fine for somebody else.' She prods a finger in her chest. 'I should have had real love and lust and passion, and had my heart broken a few times. Then your dad would have been a good fall-back position. But instead I spent my married life thinking that somewhere out there was a man who would be my match, who I'd click with and there'd be something explosive between us . . . the kind of passion I'd see in films.' She scowls. 'I always wonder, is all that exaggerated? Or has it just never happened to me?'

'What happened to – what was his name?' I ask her. 'Who sounds like a right toad if ever there was one.'

'Edward.'

'Edward. Did he end up marrying Eva?'

'Good heavens, no! He got his legs over and then he went and married a plain, respectable girl.'

'*Leg* over, Mam. It's usually just the one leg – that goes over – or he'd fall off.'

'Let's not draw diagrams, Angela.' Her expression changes from distaste to a certain dreaminess again. 'Do you remember me telling you about the man I saw when the three of us went to Blackpool and you two were up on the Ferris wheel?'

'Hang on . . . Not the one who was with his wife and kid, and you two locked eyes and he gawped at your legs?'

'It was Edward.'

'*That* Edward?'

'With his big fat, celullitey, spotty-bottomed wife. I hadn't seen him in over twenty years . . .'

'How do you know she had a spotty bottom?'

She's still thinking about Edward. 'I knew him in a second. He hadn't changed. And from the way he looked at me, I imagine he thought I hadn't either . . . It was written all over his face. That word *regret*.'

She's still clutching her deodorant stick.

'So, is Georgios going to be the one who makes up for all those lost years, Mam? Is he the man who you're going to have your . . . rapturous moment with?' I wonder if my mother's ever had an orgasm. It doesn't bear thinking about.

'Go on, you were going to say my last hurrah!'

'I wasn't!'

'You were, though!'

'I was, though.'

She beams at me and starts hula-dancing alongside the bed again. 'We'll have to wait and see, won't we? I mean, I'm only just getting used to the idea that it's not you he fancies . . .' She stops dancing. 'Remember that day in the grocery shop? I naturally thought *it's my beautiful daughter he's besotted with*.' She sits down on the bed again. 'I wouldn't have minded if it had been you, you know. I'd have just been happy that you were going to have what I would have liked.' She looks at me fondly. 'I was pleased that one of us was.'

13

His name is Sean McConnell. And no, I don't know what I'm doing eating dinner with him in a tacky tourist taverna when he's married, but he asked me to and I said yes.

'The *gyros* for lunch was definitely better. That's the thing that always happens when you come to a sit-down restaurant and they try to swank up something you should be buying right off a street vendor. It's never as good.' He shoves the last bit in his mouth and licks his fingers.

'I just can't picture them, you know, going at it,' I tell him, as we've been talking about my mother and Georgios.

'Why not? She's still a person, even though she's your mother.'

'Mothers aren't people. And they're not supposed to want rollicking rapturous sex with men half their age.'

'He's half her age?'

'Not exactly. I guess more like a quarter.'

'He's a fifteen-year-old? Good God, is it one of those lads you picked up at the beach?'

I love his humour. 'Yuck! Don't remind me of those two creeps!'

'You don't like 'em that young? Well, that's a relief. How old are you, anyway? You're just a baby yourself, aren't you? Twenty-eight?'

'As if. But thanks. No, I'm thirty-two. Thirty-three soon. What about you?'

'Thirty,' he says.

'Two years younger than me.'

'Nearly three.' I feel I've know him all my life.

'Is she as pretty as you are?' he asks.

'My mam?' I laugh to hide my embarrassment. 'If I say no, I'd be doing her a disservice. If I say yes, you're going to think I'm hung up on myself.'

'But we both know you are.'

'Cheeky!' I elbow him as he finishes off the last of his beer. 'What's that mean?'

'I could tell the first time I saw you. You had that look that says nobody's good enough for you. The way you stuck your nose in the air. You made it clear you weren't interested in us. You wouldn't even sit on the bench and talk to us.'

'That's not true! And I feel bad about that – about the bench. I felt . . . I don't know . . . conspicuous, as though there was something wrong in my travelling around on my own. Anyway,' I tease him, 'I hate it when people who don't even know me claim they know me! They never conclude anything that's a compliment. It's always an opinion you wouldn't want of yourself.'

'I'm not claiming I know you. I'm just saying that's my perception of you, that's all.'

'Like there's a great big difference there . . . So, want to know what my perception of you is?'

He holds my gaze mischievously. 'Em . . . not really.'

'Just as well then.' I try not to smile.

He smiles now.

'Besides, how could I call myself pretty with this nose?' I turn my face. 'Look at it. It's enormous, and it's got a great big crack down the centre.'

He leans in for a closer look, pretends to scour it with this gaze. 'It does look a bit like a bottom. But it makes your face striking. You look a bit like that American actress . . .'

'I know. Mira Sorvino. I've been told that. So, I'm striking now, am I? With my nose that looks like somebody's arse.'

'Come on. You know you are.' He smiles. 'And by the way, I don't know Mira Sorvino from a hole in the wall, but I'll take your word for it. I was going to say Gwyneth Paltrow. But it's that attitude of yours that's really . . . I dunno, that really makes you somebody of more interest than the rest.'

I'm still grinning from the Gwyneth gross exaggeration. 'The rest of what?'

'Women.'

'Well, that's quite the mother of all compliments. Women. We're quite a big group.'

He laughs now.

'Anyway, you three were all into your own conversation. You weren't exactly very welcoming yourselves. Hostile was the word that sprung to mind at the time.'

'Because of you. You were putting out the back-off signals. Mind you, Costas still thought he was going to score.'

He beams. He's devastating when he smiles. He uses old-fashioned words like 'score'. I could talk to him for hours. He makes me believe there's a chance I won't spend my life sad.

'Poor lad. You led the horse to water but you wouldn't let him drink.'

We leave the restaurant pretty quickly because some live Greek music comes on and it's very noisy, and not particularly good, and we're sitting right beside it. 'D'you want to dance?' he asks me, almost as an afterthought, right after he's thrown some money down before I can even go to get mine out. 'Give over.' He brushes off my quick attempt to contribute to the bill.

'Yes.' I lie, playfully. 'I do want to dance, actually.'

'No you don't,' he says. 'Come on.'

I pretend I'm disappointed. When we get outside, he smacks the side of his head as though he has a bee in his ear. 'Perfect. Chronic deafness. That's all I need.'

'I really did want to dance,' I tell him, pretending to be miffed.

He peers at me. 'Did you?' Then he quickly says, 'No you didn't, you liar. But you're one of those really annoying women who would say something like that, aren't you? Just to be annoying.'

'Yes,' I tell him. 'I've been told I'm annoying before.'

'Why aren't you sure about moving to Seattle?' I venture, when we're walking along a dry-grass ledge that overlooks the water. It's quiet here. Well, except for the sea. Quiet and not quite dark yet. And still baking warm.

He puts his hands in his shorts' pockets. He's head and shoulders taller than me. Jonathan's height. But broader than Jonathan, more naturally muscular, without being bulky or looking like he lives in a gym. 'It's complicated,' he says. 'God, when is life ever not complicated, eh?' He says it as though he's more entertained than frustrated by the fact. 'One of the problems is that my wife is very close to her family and she thinks that Seattle's the other end of the world, and once she gets there she'll hardly ever see them again.'

'Well, she has a point. It is a hell of a distance. I had to make a major effort to get back to England every year. I mean, I wanted to go, but you want to see other parts of the world too, and sometimes going home felt like a chore.' I briefly tell him about the age-old tug-of-war in me about being thousands of miles away from my mother.

'But you're obviously a very independent person,' he tells me. 'And you made a commitment to a man in another country because you loved him and you wanted to be with him. You knew exactly what you wanted. Whereas Jen . . . Jen isn't the most independent person. Not really. She only likes to think she is.' His walking slows. 'She's heard they all live in big houses over there and they've all got swimming pools, so she likes that idea. And I've told her we can always come home . . .'

He starts walking again, then sighs. I fall in step with him. 'Although that's easier than it sounds. I mean, once I give up my job in the UK . . .' He looks at me. 'Then it won't be that easy for me to just leave and come back again.'

'Mm. Yeah. Not that I would have any experience of that feeling.' I quickly remember what it is I'm about to go back to. A job I don't want that I have to ditch very soon. And then what? But I'm not bothered about that right now.

'The other trouble is, though . . . and this is the difficult part.' He stops walking now and looks at his feet again. 'I'm not sure I want her to come with me.' He says it very quietly, and for a moment I wonder if I've misheard.

'You don't want her to come? Why?' I scour him with my gaze. He looks at me frankly; shakes his head as though disbelieving something.

'You know, when you imagine how your life's going to turn out . . . Take this . . . I'd have never seen me in this moment, you know . . . walking in Greece with a woman I've just met, telling her that my wife did something that sometimes makes me never want to set eyes on her again.'

'She did? So what are you doing going on holiday with her, then?' The question's out of me before I can stop it. I quickly add, 'Sorry,' but he just looks at me and says, 'No, it's a good question. Definitely one I'd be asking too, if I were you. But then again, I probably wouldn't be sat here with somebody as screwed up as me . . . The answer is, mainly because the holiday was booked, and, well, she doesn't know I know, and I still haven't worked out what to do . . . so it makes sense to say nothing until I know exactly what it is I want to say, and just go on as normal. Meanwhile I'm still getting used to the idea that our two-year marriage all boils down to very little in her eyes.'

'Was it an affair?'

We reach the end of the bluff and there's a drop down to the sea, with nowhere else to really go except back in a circle.

'D'you want to sit here? On the grass a bit?' he asks me, so we do.

'No, it wasn't an affair. Not exactly. Jen's always been a really fun girl, you know. That's one of the main things that attracted me to her. She's good to be around. Only there's a line, isn't there? Between fun and inappropriate behaviour.' He shakes his head pensively, then looks me right in the eyes. 'She went to a strip club, for a hen night. Tiff – Boz's wife – was there. Boz is the one with the ginger hair, who you saw the other day . . . And Michael is the other one from the trip.'

I nod. Boz. The talkative one.

'She did something with one of the strippers.'

'Did what?'

'Something not very nice.'

'But you weren't there,' I say.

'I didn't have to be. I got enough details as it was. Couldn't have seen it more clearly than if they'd taken photos.' He looks at me. 'Tiff told Boz, who of course told me, even though he wasn't supposed to. So I have to look at all of them knowing they know something I'm not supposed to. It's very weird. I have to decide what I'm going to do, then they'll all stop looking at me like they know something they can't tell.'

'Did she actually bonk him?' I ask.

He hesitates. 'No, it didn't quite get that far.'

'Okay, so they didn't have sex . . . So it wasn't *that* bad. Can't you just try forgetting about it?'

He almost laughs. 'No. I can't forget about it. She's my wife.'

'Well, they probably had loads to drink. So if she was pissed . . . I'm not saying it was a good thing to have happened, but I hardly think it's bad enough to end a marriage over. If that's what you're thinking of doing.'

'That's what Tiff told Boz. That she was really wasted.'

'She probably really regrets it,' is about all I feel I can fairly say about a woman I don't even know, a marriage I know nothing about.

He looks at me directly now. 'Jen's not the kind of girl to go around regretting too much of what she does. She seems to think that that's just the way she is, and it's something we should all accept about her.'

'But we all know hen and stag nights are dirty. Maybe what happens at them should be put down to the occasion. Maybe it's best not to know.'

'It might have been. But I do know, that's the problem.' He looks at me, but like he's only half listening. We walk back almost in silence, yet it's not an uncomfortable silence. 'It's okay,' he finally says. 'I'm bothered, but I'm not destroyed.'

I gaze up at him. He's obviously a lot more bothered than he's making out. I wonder if there's more to the story than he's letting on.

Eventually he says, 'I don't even know you, yet I'm telling you all this stuff.'

'That's all right. I have one of those faces.'

He looks down at my face. 'What? You mean people tell you all their problems?'

'I guess. I don't know. I was really just joking. Trying to be light.'

'You are light. That's what I like about you.' Then he stops walking, and looks at me again. 'Or maybe light's the wrong word.' I can tell he's just remembered I'm a widow. 'Maybe what I mean is . . . easy.'

'Better be careful there,' I tell him, and he laughs a bit.

'God, I'm hopeless with women, aren't I? Easy to talk to,' he adds. 'All that's missing is the portable quack's couch, eh?'

'And my bill. Which would probably make all your other problems feel small.'

He smiles. We walk back as far as the main tourist drag. 'God, it's awful up here, eh?' He stops and looks around at the street life. 'They always like package tours – Tiff, Boz, Michael, Becca, Jen. Eating. Drinking. Sitting on the beach surrounded by a load of Brits. I'm a bit sick of it.'

'You're at a crossroads,' I tell him.

He meets my eye. 'Yeah, I suppose I am.'

'So . . . stay married, stay in England, and forgive her. Or . . . Leave her, leave England, move to Seattle.' I don't know why I'm saying this. It all feels like nosediving off a spring-board when I'm not sure I'm going to make the plunge properly; maybe I'm going to belly-flop and it'll hurt like hell.

'Something like that, yes. Or the obvious other option – stay in England, don't take the job and leave her.'

Forgiving her definitely doesn't sound like an option. 'But the other way sounds a bit easier.'

He looks at me. 'Yeah, but it feels more cowardly. Like running away.'

Didn't I run away from England because I felt I wanted to put distance between me and how close I was to my parents? Aren't I thinking of running away again, to try to forget Jonathan? 'Moving away isn't cowardly, Sean, if you're moving to take a job. Although it's not an easy thing to do, and you can take it from somebody who's done it. But running away is never good, I don't think.'

'Thanks for the input,' he says, tilting his head and looking at me again.

'Has it helped?'

'Erm . . . No. I wish it could be that simple. But it's good you tried.'

'So you don't want me to send you my bill, is that what you mean? The hour hasn't been worth it.'

'No.' He looks at me and smiles. 'It's definitely been worth it.'

We walk back to my hotel. Outside the door, he pauses, looking like he's teetering on the edge of something he wants to say. And then he says it. 'If I asked you to meet me again tomorrow morning, say at ten o'clock – and I absolutely promised you that we wouldn't spend a minute of it talking about me and my messed-up life, we'd just meet and enjoy a good old-fashioned *gyros* off a street vendor in the sun – would that sound vaguely tempting to you at all? You don't have to worry about hurting my feelings if it wouldn't. I'm not going to commit suicide or anything like that. Although if I do, I'll make sure there's a special conscience-screwing note for you.'

The word *rebound* floats vaguely in the back of my mind. But looking at him, this Sean McConnell, with his upright, unaffected, straightforward sense of decency that makes it hard for him to forgive his partying wife, makes it difficult for me to say anything other than, 'Go on, then. It was the *gyros* that sold me.'

He watches me walk inside. When I turn around to see if he's gone, he's still standing there, smiling at me as though I've just entertained him more than he ever thought he could be entertained right now.

14

My mam's bed is empty when I get back to the room, and empty when I get up to pee at two in the morning. I go back to bed and try to sleep but I can't. My head's a mix of my mam, Sean, Jonathan . . . Would Jonathan have left me if he found out I'd got it on with a stripper? Interesting question. I think he'd probably have made me feel really, really small and pathetic, but ultimately, he'd have got over it.

Around three, I hear the door. She creeps in, picks her way around the room so as not to disturb me. I smell a gentle waft of her perfume. I pretend I'm asleep.

He's sitting on the wall when I come out. The sight of him makes my stomach flip over.

'You've got good legs,' he says, looking objectively at them in my short denim skirt. 'Runner's legs.'

'That's what my husband used to call them.'

He smiles, a bit awkward. 'Do you run, then?'

'Only if I'm being chased.'

He gets off the wall. 'By who?'

'Oh . . . wives of Englishmen I meet on holiday in Greece.'

A proper smile now. 'Well, that counts me out. I'm Irish, remember.'

We stand there looking at one another, a bit like we did yesterday, only not half as uncomfortably. 'I've been thinking about everything you told me,' I say to him.

'You and me both.' He holds my look for a while. 'Come on,' he says, leading me out onto the street. 'This is my rental. Well, it's Boz's, really.' He indicates the silver Nissan Micra.

'Where're we going?'

'Away from this pit.'

'Did you tell your friend Boz – is that really his name? – that you're taking me out?'

He pauses, with his hand on the passenger door. 'It's short for Barry, only everybody's called him Boz since he was, like, two. And yeah, I did tell him.'

'Oh.' I can just imagine the tone of that conversation, what they're all going to think.

'Why? Do you care?' He scrutinises me.

I shrug. 'I suppose not. If you don't.'

'He's a good guy, anyway, Boz. No worries there.'

'So what's he make of this, then? This Barry? Boz?' I think of my mam and her daft Barry White gaffe as I get into the car.

'Oh, just that I'm giving myself more problems.'

'And you?'

He gets in and slams the door heavy-handedly. 'He's probably right. But I'm a big boy – I can decide for myself.' He looks at me again. 'Besides, who knows, maybe we were fated to meet.' He starts up the engine. 'Now I'm not going to let Boz and a few more little problems get in the way of that. Am I?'

We drive up to Bohali – the place where Georgios brought me for dinner that made such an impression on me. The restaurant where we ate is closed, as it's still only early morning.

'Did your mam come home last night?' he asks.

'She did. Around three.'

He whistles. 'So what happened with her and the Greek lover? Did she give you the gory details this morning?'

I shake my head. 'She was sleeping when I got up. I didn't want to wake her.' We sit and look at the view. 'How did you meet her? Your wife?' I ask him, after a while.

'Oh, in a bar, in Liverpool. I'd just broken up with a girl I'd been seeing for six years. She was a nice girl. Looking back now, I probably should have stayed with her. Only at the time, it felt like too much too early . . . We met in uni, but then we graduated, got jobs in different cities. When we did get together on weekends, there was too much pressure to have a good time, and somehow all we did was fight. I could tell we were both getting restless to just be rid of each other.' He looks at me now, laughs a bit. 'Anyway, I met Jen, and Jen didn't seem to have a care in the world, or a serious side. It made her very fanciable. She was great to be around. She never really took responsibility for anything. And she still doesn't.' He shakes his head. 'I thought I'd change her, once we got, you know, married, got the house, a life together . . . I thought she'd settle down. Yet it's daft, really, because you can't marry somebody expecting them to change, and I was attracted to her because she was who she was. Maybe I'm the one that's grown up in these last two years – more so than she has. I look at her now and I'm not so sure I see her as the mother of my children.' He knits his brows, looks at me, shakes his head. 'Anyway, let's not talk about all my crap mistakes.'

'Why, are there more?'

He pretends to think. 'Hang on . . . No. Definitely not more, you'll be glad to hear.'

'Phew! Well, that's a relief, then.'

The restaurant where we eat lunch is the exact one I wanted to come to with Georgios. The one that he said had bad food.

'Not a *gyros* in sight,' I tell him, scouring the menu. 'Do you think you can handle it? I wouldn't want you to go into a *gyros* deprivation coma or something.'

He rests his chin on his upturned wrist. 'It's all right. I've got my *gyros* deprivation adrenalin kit at hand. Feel free to give me a jab in the backside if I look like I need it.' He beams at me. 'I have to confess, I brought you here deliberately, because it seems like the sort of posh place you'd bring a girl. The first time we ever talked, as I remember it, I was trotting down the street with bare feet and a pint of beer in my hand. So I don't want you, with all your wordly sophistication, to get the impression that I'm some beer-drinking, *gyros*-eating thug.'

'The thought never once crossed my mind.' I peel off a piece of heavy golden bread and dip it in some olive oil, having just decided on a simple Greek salad, which doesn't sound like something they could screw up. 'Okay. Maybe once.'

He orders a fizzy water. 'You can have a beer, you know,' I tease him.

'I'd better not. Too much booze makes me want to tell everybody I love them.' He grins at me. 'I wouldn't want to scare you off.'

'Oh, it generally happens to me about ten times a day.'

He grins again. 'See, I told you you had an ego.'

My turn to smile now.

He looks around at the view, which feels a lot like being perched on the rim of a ginormous bowl with all sorts of wondrous goodies in it that you might just get to fall into and not be able to climb your way out of. 'It's beautiful here, eh? Look at this. Sea. Mountains. Trees. Crumbling little villages all over the place . . . If I move to Seattle, there'll be none of this, will there?'

'No, but Hawaii's close. And Mexico. And Cuba.'

'And Vancouver. You forgot about Vancouver.' He cocks me a glance.

'Yep, that too.' Could I hurtle headlong into a relationship with a man who has just left his wife? It would be very strange finding out.

'You're not happy there,' he tells me.

'Actually, that's not entirely true. I love Vancouver. It's just that I moved there with Jonathan; I've only ever lived there as a married person, and, well, obviously for a little while as a widow . . . I'm not sure I know how to be single in Vancouver.'

'Have you been on many dates, since . . . ?'

I shake my head. 'I went on one really weird one about eight or nine months ago, with a strange fellow. Then I went on a really weird one shortly after that with a really nice fellow. Then I went on a rather better one with the same guy, but then I scared him off.'

'How?'

'Oh . . . By being me. The widowed me. Something about him made me unable to put the act on. He sort of got to me with his niceness, and his concern . . .' I smile at Sean now. 'He was the one person who was ready to walk barefoot over the shards of a widow's broken heart. But I wasn't ready to have a man do that.' Except Richard, I think. Richard was the one man I could let see my vulnerable side. 'If he'd been a selfish, disinterested asshole who just wanted to get me in the sack, he'd have been just the ticket.'

'Women love a bastard.'

'Actually, I normally don't.' Arrogance, I think, because Jonathan was arrogant. But not a bastard.

'So moving back to England, like you were talking about earlier, would be a whole new start – it'd be easier, is that what you were thinking before?'

I think about this. 'Maybe. I don't know. I spent years thinking I wanted to move back, when I knew I couldn't. But now that I can, I'm not sure I want to. Maybe I'm more Canadian than I've always thought.'

'So we have at least two things in common, then.'

'What's that?'

'We're both thinking of moving across the world, and we're both facing being single again.'

'Well, I think I'm actually living being single, rather than facing it.'

He raises his glass in a toast. 'To getting our bearings,' he says.

'Do you mind if I take your photo?' I ask him.

Before he can answer, I snap one.

'Go on then,' he says. 'If you insist.'

'She gets back early evening. Probably around six,' he tells me, as we walk down a crooked, narrow road past some street vendors selling lace, olive oil, wine and dried herbs.

I sense he's restless because he keeps looking at his watch. 'We can go back now, if you like,' I tell him. 'If you'd prefer.' It's quarter past two. The day's whizzed by. I want to grab on to it and keep it here, stop time.

He looks at his watch again. 'God, is that what the time is? Never mind. Come and try this wine.' He nods over to a man giving out samples from a table under an awning. 'You're a red girl, right?' He taps his nose. 'I have an instinct for these things.'

'White, actually.'

'See, I knew you'd say that.' He picks tiny samples of red and white off a trolley. 'Here, take both. It'll hardly put you over the limit.'

I look at the splashes in the two glasses. 'I don't know . . . too much booze makes me want to tell people things I shouldn't say.'

He grins at me. The white's vinegary and warm. The red, watery and tasteless. 'Gawd, they need a spit bucket for this! I'll buy a crate next time I come back,' I say, sarcastically.

'You're planning on coming back?'

'Probably not. Unless my mother marries Georgios.'

'How likely is that?'

'Unlikely. I hope. Or maybe I don't hope; I'm not sure. I try to picture them as a couple and I can't. But then again, I couldn't really picture my mam with any man who wasn't my dad, even though if you'd seen my mam and dad together you wouldn't exactly have pictured them as a couple. It's very odd.'

'I can't say I'll hurry back here either.' He shrugs. 'This holiday has felt a bit like the end of an era for me. I don't know if that makes any sense . . . No going back for me.'

When I look at him, there's a sad, wistful expression in those crystal clear green eyes.

'I think I know what you mean,' I tell him, and I get the urge to link my arm in his as he stands there with his hands in his pockets; to slide my hand down to his and interlace our fingers. But we won't touch. I'd lay all my bets on that. He's a decent lad. He's got some sense of what's right, and what's probably not right, under the circumstances.

Then the madness of this situation suddenly hits me. 'I don't know what this is!' I tell him. 'You. Me. What we're doing!' I flail my hands. 'I don't know what this is.'

He looks really, really awkward, as though he has absolutely no idea how to respond. Just as I'm thinking of something less dramatic to say, to smooth it over and cover my embarrassment, a withered Greek woman appears from behind a curtain of lace. 'Beautiful couple!' she says, making a lavish gesture from me to him. 'You were made for each other!'

Sean grins and rubs a hand over his face. 'Oh, God! Did somebody pay her to come out here and say that? I think they must have.'

Despite my embarrassment, I smile too.

His eyes hold mine quite seriously now. 'For the record, I don't know what we're doing either.'

It takes us over an hour to drive down the mountain, mainly because we keep stopping to stare at things: church domes, little homes, dilapidated cafés with elderly Greek men sitting outside; an old Greek lady selling honey from a small table in the dappled shade of a tree, in the middle of nowhere, not a customer in sight; a scrawny cat peeking out from under a stone wall; an unusual plant. When we start getting out of the car to look at plants, we know we're getting desperate. We're talking less and less.

It's not fair.

The thought just sails through my head. You can't meet a really great guy – who you get on spectacularly with, who you can see yourself with – spend a couple of days with him, and then never see him again, because maybe he decides not to leave his wife and move to Seattle after all.

'It's all fucked up, this,' I tell him, after we've sat there not speaking for ages. I don't often swear. Why couldn't I have just met him, got on decently with him, and quite liked him? Then I'd not be sitting here feeling like I'm about to lose somebody who is going to leave an empty space in me when he's gone. How do you lose somebody you've never had? I'm as bad as my mother, who's spent her life in love with somebody who has never existed.

'A response might be a good thing right now,' I tell him. But he doesn't say anything. I feel his tension.

'Can I ask you something?' I say. 'How do you just hang out with another woman for two days when you're here with your wife? When your mates know you're here with your wife, yet you're with me? How do you do it? I mean, I know you're a nice bloke and it's not what the rest of the world might make of it . . . The thing is, I know, but I don't know.'

'Neither do I,' he finally says. 'Actually, you've read my mind, because I was just thinking how can it be that I should be looking forward to seeing my wife in a few hours and hearing all about her trip to Athens with the girls, yet all I can think is,

Why does she have to be coming back? Because that means I can't spend any more time with you.'

It suddenly dawns on me what this is. I've got replacement angst. I'm afraid I'll never find another Jonathan, and yet I have to, and clearly, the faster the better, and pretty much anyone will do – whether they're Greek and fancy my mother, or they're Irish and married. Sherrie was right; I am desperate, and this notion I have of Jonathan sending me somebody is really just sugar-coating the desperation. Jonathan will pick somebody for me, decide not just the who, but the when, so it doesn't really appear like desperation at all; meeting somebody else is really being forced on me, so I needn't feel guilty about it. And all this . . . why? Because I can't stand being abandoned.

Life hurts.

It stings like a bloody big slap to the face.

I recognise the road that takes us to the resort. It seems neither of us is speaking because we don't know what to say. We pull up in front of the hotel, a thrum of anticipation beating in my neck. I want him to kiss me. I know he won't. He leaves the engine running but takes his hands off the wheel, crosses his arms, lays his head back on the rest, sighs. I've noticed he sighs a lot. I run my gaze up his arms, to his throat, to his eyes that are closed. Am I being tested to see if I'm ready to care about somebody else? Or is this punishment to remind me that the nice guys are taken? *Why come into my life, if you are going to go and leave me even more hurt than I already was?*

'Angela.' He pauses for a long and complicated while. 'Saying it's been really great meeting you feels a bit like saying the obvious – not to mention the fact that it's ridiculously inadequate – but it has been, and I don't know how else to say it. It's given me a hell of a lot to think about.'

A pain builds in my temples. My head feels like it might explode. I reach for the door handle and am out of the car in a split second. He clamps both his hands on the wheel, and I hear him say, 'God,' through gritted teeth. I let the door close, but don't want to flee like this, to part on these terms. I bend over and look in the window. He turns and meets my eyes, winds the window down. As he exhales, the sad, earnest expression is replaced with something brighter and a touch more optimistic. I think he's going to say something, but I get in there first.

There really is only one thing to say. 'Goodbye, Sean.'

15

The doctor is just leaving the room when I arrive.

When I go in, my mam is lying on top of her bed. She looks ashen.

'I fainted,' she says. 'That's all.'

'Fainted?' I sit down on the bed by her feet, shocked. My first thought is what the hell has Georgios done to her?

'Well, we had sex for five hours straight. I was completely worn out by round four but he just kept on going and going, and—'

'No!' I squeal. I'm going to rip his ears off then castrate him.

'No!' she says. 'No is right! But I knew that's exactly what you were thinking. It was written all over your face.'

'Don't be ridiculous,' I tell her.

'If you must know, I was out all day with Georgios, and I was feeling unusually exhausted. I asked him to drop me off here so I could freshen up, change . . . I came in the lobby, I remember staring at the receptionist and feeling everything go slow, and then I was going down . . . sinking to my knees.'

'Good God, Mam!'

'The next thing, I was being helped into a chair.'

'Mam . . .' I shake my head, put a hand over my mouth.

'I'm fine! It was the hotel manager's idea to call the doctor, not mine.'

'You fainted! You can't be fine!' Why hadn't I taken more notice when she kept telling me she hasn't been feeling herself lately?

'My blood pressure's high, but we knew that already. He said some twaddle about how I should probably get some blood tests done when I get home.'

'Blood tests? This is the first time anything like this has happened, isn't it?'

'Yes,' she says. 'Well, all right then, no.'

'What d'you mean "no"?'

'I had a little episode a few weeks ago. I came round and I was on the kitchen floor. All I remember is that I'd been about to put the kettle on . . .'

'You never told me!'

'I didn't want you to come home! You'd have been on the next plane.'

'Of course I would have!'

'You've got your own problems to deal with.'

'So you dying wouldn't add to them?'

'Nobody's talking about dying. I only fainted. Don't over-react!'

'What did the doctor say? Your doctor?'

'I don't know because I never went.'

'For God's sake, why not?'

She sits up a bit groggily, swings her legs over the edge of the bed, but just stays there instead of getting up, then lowers her chin to her chest. 'I didn't want to find out anything bad about myself. I didn't want to have to tell you.'

She looks over her shoulder at me, sadly.

The restaurant's certainly more cheerful than we are. The waiter is cross-eyed and he brings us the wrong order. Then he grovels around the patio confusedly trying to find the table that ordered the Greek prawns. Then he gives up, and bequeaths them to us.

'He's not exactly the face that launched a thousand ships, is he?' My mam gawps at him.

'He's really annoying. He's a bloody Greek Basil Fawlty.'

'Greek prawns.' She prods them with a fork. 'You'd think they could have come up with a slightly more original name than that. Even if they'd called them Prawns A La Grec.'

She's slurring a bit, because we've seen off a litre of wine and the food has only just arrived. Every time my mam takes a sip, the buzzard appears and tops up her glass. 'I'm not sure you should be drinking,' I tell her.

'I gathered as much from the other ten times you've told me that.' She takes another glug of her wine, a big one, looking at me deviously out of the corner of her eye. And hey presto, here he comes again. 'Scram,' she tells him, before I get the chance to.

She prods another prawn. 'They're rubbery. Like toes off a corpse. I think they want to give the chef his walking papers, don't you?' She pushes the plate at me. 'Don't say I never give you anything.'

I stare at the food, feeling too sick to eat.

'Smile,' she says, after a while of peering at me.

'I'm still too mad.'

'Tell me about Sean,' she says.

'There's nothing to tell. Tell me about Georgios.'

'There's nothing to tell there either. Nothing happened. I wasn't feeling well. Just my luck.'

I rang Georgios and told him my mam had fainted. I suspected she'd never admit that to him, and I was right. All she'd told him was that she was tired and would see him tomorrow – our last full day. She'd kill me if she knew this, of course.

'Are you going to spend tomorrow night with him?' I ask her. Meaning, *sleep with him.*

'Are you going to see Sean when he moves to Seattle?'

'This conversation's going nowhere.'

I feel a perverse mood coming on so instead, trying to fight it, I pick up my digital camera and find the picture of Sean that I took on the Bohali terrace. I zoom right in on him then hold the camera out to her. 'He's not moving to Seattle.'

'How can you be so sure?' She takes it and studies him.

'There was no excitement in him to go. I'm sure he'll leave her, that would be my guess. But he'll stay in England. The two together would be a bit much all at once.'

'He is a bit of all right,' she says, scrutinising the picture of him.

I miss his face. 'Give it back.' I hold out my hand. She passes it to me. I muck about with the zoom some more, then look up and see her observing me. There's something about her private, sentimental expression, the Audrey Hepburnness of the hat, the dainty, effortless poise of her hand by her glass . . . I take a quick picture of her. The camera tells me the card is full. I press the 'back' button to find pictures to delete to clear some space. The waiter creeps up on me, asking if we want dessert. I'm startled, try to click the 'off' button, but accidentally press 'delete' instead. Sean's picture vanishes.

'Oh, shit! He's gone!' I glare at the waiter, pick up a bread bun and pelt it at him.

'Girl!' my mam says, as we become the focus of the entire restaurant. Then she hides a chuckle.

When she sees I'm not laughing, she says, 'Angela, maybe it's for the best. Sean comes with a lot of luggage. The circumstances weren't right.'

The moments tick over, then I feel my annoyance come down. 'No,' I say, staring glumly at my camera. 'He wasn't right.'

She links her arm through mine and we walk back to the hotel. 'Are you still moping?' she asks.

'I'm still mad. At you. For not telling me.'

'Oh, we're not back to that?' She lets go of my arm, and I feel her slightly wobble into me. 'I don't have to tell you anything. You don't own me. I don't know what's wrong with me, but I'm sure it's nothing. But if it's not nothing, we have to accept it. If I croaked tomorrow, Angela, you should have no regrets for me. You should celebrate my life because my life gave me you. You are the main and the best part of me that I leave behind.'

A raw pain cuts through me. 'Who's talking about anybody dying, anyway?' Does she know something she's not telling me?

'Nobody is, daftie! You're the one who's fixated on everybody dying.'

I stop walking, lay the backs of my arms over my eyes, hiding my face. It's very odd behaviour for the middle of the street. 'I don't want you to leave me,' I tell her. Tears burn, so I have to do a sudden dive to make on I'm scratching my foot so she won't see me cry.

I'm down there, scratching, for quite a ridiculous amount of time, and when I look up again, her face is full of the sort of emotion that only a mother could feel and a daughter could understand. 'And I don't want to leave you! Not ever!' Her voice shakes, and whatever colour she gained back over dinner has left her and she's turned quite pale again. 'I hate thinking that one day I'll be gone and I'll not get to see how your life turned out. Whether you marry again, have children, whether you're happy, that you'll stay healthy . . . I feel I have a right to be with you every step of the way because I brought you into this world and I should be with you until you go out of it. I don't want to go anywhere if it means leaving you.'

'Then go see a doctor. Start taking your health seriously.'

Those eyes that moments ago were teary and soft suddenly harden. 'I'll be the one to decide what I do and do not do. All my life I've made my decisions for other people, Angela. If it wasn't for your dad, it was for you . . . Now I'm fifty and I'm going to make my decisions for myself.'

She says it so convincingly, I have to smile. 'Mam . . . you're sixty. Are you a bit tiddled?'

'I know I'm sixty. What are you? My parrot?'

'You said you were fifty.'

'People in glass houses shouldn't throw stones, Angela.' She's getting mad now.

'What's that mean?' I ask her.

'It means I think you're clearly the one that's tiddled, not me.'

The traffic is loud all of a sudden. Cars fly past us, sending up clouds of dust. I feel her small warm hand loop itself through my arm again. Just as we step out to cross the road, a truck comes flying past, and we jump back together to the safety of the kerb.

Now that we've nearly just got ourselves run over, I fill with the need to make everything right with her. 'Oh, Mam, can we be friends again?' I say, thinking, please don't shun my small and pathetic olive branch. 'I'm sorry for always spoiling everything.'

'It's all right,' she says, as though it isn't really, though.

I turn and glance at her face in profile, wondering if I really am forgiven. She glances at me out of the corner of her eye. Then she squeezes my arm with her warm hand. 'Girl!' she says, as we trot quickly across the street, when it looks safe to go. 'Of course we're friends. You're the best friend I've ever had.' She stumbles into me and I grip her to steady her, fearing for a moment that she might be fainting again, but I quickly realise it's only because she's half-cut. 'And you know what? When we get around this corner, I'm going to plop a great big wet kiss on you!'

'Ergh!' I say. 'You female pervert.' And she chuckles.

16

Georgios picks her up in the morning. I take myself out for breakfast, to a little off the beaten track *galatadiko* – a traditional milk and pastry shop – in old Zante town, with ceiling fans, graffitied walls, wooden tables, Greek men smoking and drinking black coffee, and the tastiest Greek yoghurt and *loukamades* – fried dough with honey – that I've ever had.

In the afternoon it's too hot to go to the beach, yet I don't feel like stopping in the room. I change into my bikini and slather on sunscreen; there's not much else to do.

When I get to the beach, I'm right: it's roasting. I try lying there for about half an hour but can't bear much more. I've had enough of the heat and would kill for rain. Back at the room, I start throwing stuff into the suitcase, but that doesn't take too long, then I'm restless again. I plonk down on the bed. Maybe I'll try having a nap.

When I come round, the clock says it's after six. No wonder my stomach is growling, I've slept about three hours, and I'm starved. I pull on my shorts and a fresh T-shirt from out of the case and wander up to the main strip, to the little restaurant where I came with my mam on our first day – where there's never anybody in but a friendly-faced Greek man. I order a pork *gyros*, obviously thinking of Sean as I do. And then as I pass the grocery store where we met Georgios for the first time, I pick up two cans of Heineken.

Back in the room, I finish the *gyros* and one can, take the second out onto the balcony and sit on the only sun chair that doesn't have a pair of my mam's knickers drying on it. There's a couple occupying the room next door now. Their balcony door is open and I can hear their good-natured teasing.

I try to forget his hotel is so close. I pick up my mam's book and start reading. But it's no good. I can't just sit here. I have to go on the snoop.

His hotel has giant palm trees outside it that send fingers of green shooting towards a cerulean sky. Palm trees and bright cherry flowers in giant pots. Hotel Ana Suza. Nerves stir up in my stomach like a flock of tiny birds startled into flight. It crosses my mind that his room might be on this side, so he could easily look out of his window and see me. That would be pathetic. I don't want that, so I keep walking.

I'm past. Good. Now what?

I keep going towards the beach, then park myself on a chair and sit there for a good long while, digging my toes into the cool sand and lifting them out, feeling sand trickle between them. Everybody's out – families, couples enjoying the romantic sunset. I wonder if my mam and Georgios are having sex right now . . .

I get up when I've had enough of sitting, then I walk the shoreline, my feet getting gently lapped by the water. I walk for ages. The sky and water become so dark that I can't see where one ends and the other begins. I don't know where Angela the Widow ends and Angela the Available begins either, but there's a definite horizon where there wasn't one before.

More than one hotel has music blaring out of it. A peculiar medley of cheesiness – Lionel Richie's 'Hello' meets 'Lady in Red'. Couples' music. Jonathan would have run a mile from it. There's something vigorous, though, about the sounds and smells of package-tour Greece. In one bar, a red-faced, beer-bellied Brit is doing a wince-making karaoke version of Robbie

Williams' 'Angels', seriously wobbly and off-key when he hits 'all' and 'water-fall'.

When I walk back the way I came, near the Ana Suza Hotel, it looks like there's a pool party going on. The chairs where my mam and I sat that day when I came back from Kefalonia are occupied by a group of single girls in smock tops and baby doll dresses, drinking orange-coloured cocktails bedecked with fruit. They're chatting and laughing, while behind them, a handful of couples boogie to Toploader's 'Dancing in the Moonlight' that blares out from a sound system behind a lively, colourful bar.

My eyes fasten onto a woman who looks vaguely familiar. Something about the jet-black lustrous hair, and her strikingly lovely body. Yes: the girl in the swimming pool who was floating on the red air mattress the day Mam and I sat here. Her tan is bronze, and now she's wearing a white Marilyn Monroe dress with a halter neck, and glittery flip-flops. She's laughing and talking, and smoking, clearly wasted, and just as she reaches out to accept a drink from one of the men, somebody, who I can't see, pulls her into an embrace. For a few seconds she disappears from sight, but then she emerges again and I freeze. Her hands are knotted around Sean's neck. While I take stock, my mind tries to work out what else this could possibly mean. But it seems to mean only one thing. They're not dancing in time to the music, but rather to their own music, slow and sensual, bodies fitted together, not even room for air between them. His arms hug her like he'd never want to hug anyone else. She rests her chin on his chest and gazes up into his face.

Georgios drives us to the airport.

I sit quietly in the back seat, staring across vast, parched hills, saying goodbye to Greece.

I don't know if I'm ever going to see Georgios again. I listen to my mam and him talking, look at the back of his neck, the way the black hair burrows into it, his hand on the wheel that looks a little more healed now. There, in my gut, I know that Georgios is not the man for me. And it's got nothing to do with the fact that he's crazy about my ma.

I don't know if they have made love. I suppose I don't have the right to ask her, any more than she would, if it were I. And she's certainly not letting on. My guess, though, from the way she languidly moves her gaze from his eyes to his mouth as he talks, and the fact that she no longer looks like something's being held back, is that it would be a thumbs-up.

When we reach the airport, I recognise the Scottish rep who greeted us at the start of the holiday, and a couple who arrived with us, standing in a long line outside. The other rep told us this morning that Zante airport's too small to accommodate the package mob, therefore we have to get there about four hours early. It seemed to make sense to everybody else, but not to me. Nonetheless, I feel impervious to the strains of the airport, as though somebody's just slathered me in a special not-give-a-damn cream. Estée Lauder could package it and make a small fortune. I'm just too busy thinking, *Thank God I'm going home.* Home to Vancouver.

Despite the reps trying to be organised, the line outside the airport has got total chaos written all over it. Georgios stops a good distance away, so we can say our goodbyes in peace, and we get out of the car.

'I have a small problem, Angelina, that I would like to take your advice on,' he says. His eyes have mischief in them.

'Er . . . hang on, I think I've heard this song before.' I wag a finger at him, instantly cheered by something in our exchange, getting a fresh flush of fondness for him. I think of our night out in that restaurant, and can honestly say that it could have been one of the most special evenings of my life.

'The thing is, I've been asking Vivien to extend her holiday, to stay one more week with me, but she doesn't think she can do that. She wants to go back with you, to spend time with you before you go back to Canada.'

I can't read my mother's face, or guess what it is I'm supposed to say. So I just say the truth. 'Mam, I fly back to Vancouver the day after tomorrow. I don't need you to be with me for one day.'

She looks stressed because she's being called upon to make a decision.

'Stay,' I tell her.

'Stay,' Georgios says.

She looks even more flustered now. 'But I have my ticket . . . I have my luggage all packed! Angela, I should go back like I'm supposed to go back.' She turns to Georgios now. 'We're only going to find ourselves in this position in a week's time and it won't be easier, only harder.'

I can't read her. Doesn't she want to be with him?

'But Vivien, we'll have had a week together. That has to be better than just a day, no?' Georgios reaches out and runs a hand up her arm.

'Knock knock,' I cough. 'Am I in the way, here? Would you rather me just go over there and stand with my face to the wall until you've talked?'

'Yes!' my mam says, at the same time as Georgios jokingly says, 'No, not unless you want to.' Then he takes both her hands in his. 'Stay, Vivien, I ask you one more time.'

She stands on her tiptoes and sensually reaches her arms behind his neck. When she looks over her shoulder to smile at me, I feel like I shouldn't be watching.

'One more week,' she says. 'I'll stay.' Georgios lifts her ever so slightly off her feet, and she gives a giddy chuckle.

I go to turn, mainly so they won't see my envy.

'Wait, Angelina,' he says, and lets my mother go. I look at Georgios now and see him just as I did that day in the grocery store. There's something interesting about his face. You wouldn't call him handsome. Not in the classical sense. The face is a bit too long, the eyebrows too heavy and dark, the C-brackets at either side of his mouth too deep, like the furrows in his brow. And he looks like he needs a good shave. Yet there's something in that face. There is something about him that holds me.

'I almost forgot that I have something for you.'

He ducks into the boot of the car, then pulls out a small brown paper bag and hands it to me.

I take it from him, puzzled.

Inside the bag is the little book I bought.

I bring a hand to my mouth, holding his gaze through a softening focus of disbelief, a pain welling in my head.

'I don't understand,' I tell him.

'I have a friend who works for the ferry. I ask her to go look on seat near ferry and she find it . . .' He smiles at me. 'I had her bring it to me.'

I'm too welled up to speak, so I just nod my head. A nod that, hopefully, says everything.

17

Vancouver is like a vibrant colour wheel exploding before my eyes. As the airport bus rolls down Granville Street, past the boulevards of expensive residential Shaughnessy with their canopies of trees, the inky blue-green of the North Shore mountains punches out against a cloudless, duck-egg sky. The ocean twinkles a light steel blue, fringed, in part, by the dense, healthy green valance of Stanley Park. Late-blooming firey pink rhododendrons show off behind the walls of stately gardens. I live in probably the most beautiful city in the world.

My mobile rings just as we pull up to a red light.

'Hey! Where are you?'

Hearing Sherrie's voice, I instantly drop anchor again, and smile. 'What d'you mean, where am I? I'm here, aren't I? I'm home.'

'Where's here?'

'Vancouver, of course! I'm on the airport bus at Granville and Twentieth. Why, where are you?'

'At the airport! I came to get you. You're on a bus on Granville Street? I've stood watching three flights come through the doors, and I asked all these Chinese people if they'd got off the plane from England, and then a stewardess told me the UK flight went through an age ago . . .'

'Oh, God! You're at the airport?' I swell with love for my good friend. 'You came to meet me? I don't even remember telling you which day I was flying back.'

'You didn't. I rang Richard. When I got here, the board said your flight had landed so I went to get a latte figuring you'd be at least half an hour.'

'My bag was the first one out. I zipped through in minutes.'

'Shit! Damn that latte . . . Richard was going to come meet you anyway, but I told him I wanted to.'

'You were fighting over me?' I grin. 'Argh. I'm really touched!' Joking aside, I genuinely am. Now it doesn't seem to matter so much that there was nobody there to meet me when I walked through those double doors, pushing my luggage trolley, searching, stupidly, for Jonathan's face; force of habit. Sherrie was there. She was just buying a latte. And if she hadn't been there, Richard would have.

'Did you buy me one too?'

'What?'

'A latte.'

'Kiss my ass.'

'But you brought me flowers, right?'

'Kiss it twice.'

I smile. The bus is jerking along South Granville, stopping and starting with the familiar clog of traffic. The sharp black façade of a high-end deli has its flower stall spilling summer colours all over the pavement.

'So what are you doing now?' I ask her.

'Paying my parking ticket and getting my car. Without my damned passenger.'

I titter. 'Sorry!'

'Yeah, well. That's the last time I'm gonna try surprising you.'

'Well, come over for a drink, if you'd like. I've nothing in, but we could always order something.'

I hear her grunting and then she screams at a driver. 'Old people,' she says. 'They should only be let out after dark . . . What? Oh, come over? Well, I think I'll pass. I have a date tonight, girl.' I hear her blare her horn. 'Stop straddling the line, you octogenarian! A second date, as it happens. Look, can I just catch you later? I'm getting frustrated talking and driving. Do you mind?'

'I'm heartbroken you'd pick a date over me.'

'No you're not,' she chuckles. 'Cow.'

'Moo.'

I'm ready to hang up when she says. 'Oh, by the way, Ange, I'm glad to have my friend back.'

'Which friend?' I tease. 'Oh, you mean me?'

Back.

I really am.

The same Vancouver streets I've walked many times before. Fashionable Robson Street, with its laid-back, West Coast, California-Rodeo-Drive feel, picturesquely hemmed in by mountains and ocean; where everybody, especially the young and cute, goes to shop. I drag my suitcase on its little wheels, cutting a path through people as though I'm the only one walking against the flow, soaking Vancouver back into my system. How quickly you forget a holiday. If it weren't for my tanned feet, I'm not sure I'd know I'd been away.

Coming into my apartment, I'm hit with the reek of bad recycled air. Sunlight blares through the wall-to-wall windows, paling out my rather dismal navy blue Ikea love-seat. There's a layer of dust on my parquet floors that I could write my name in. The kitchen is barren except for a somewhat stinky tea-towel, a tea plate with crumbs on it – evidence of my last Melba toast supper – and a knife with some rancid butter on it.

I push open a window (one of those boot-box-sized ones that you can't possibly top yourself from; your cat could barely top itself if it got a strong case of apartment-cat blues). A warm breeze wafts in, bringing with it rising street sounds – cars, screaming kids, the chilling crash of glass as the restaurant on the corner dumps its waste into a commercial recycle bin.

I open my fridge for some milk to make tea and find a bag of purplish pulp that may have once been an aubergine, cohabiting with half a can of green-fuzz-covered tomatoes. Of course – no milk.

I pick up my phone, but don't have any messages. I don't bother checking email because I will have a lot of those, but ninety per cent will be junk. There are bills in the handful of mail I've brought upstairs, making me think of my job. But I'm not due back for another two weeks, so the bills may have to wait to be paid.

Normally, the first thing I'd do after getting back from a trip home would be to call my mam and tell her I got back safely. But she's not there, where she always is, at the end of the phone, waiting for my call; she's in Greece, with a man, having a romance.

'I hope you're having fun, Mam.' I say the words out loud, thinking the old post-visit-to-England thoughts: what if that's the last time I ever see her? What if I heard she was ill, and there was a ten-hour flight before I could get to her? Now, on top of this, I'm wondering if she thinks we had a good holiday. I'm regretting that we had to fight so much. It still all feels screwed up: us living at opposite ends of the earth. There's this damned eight-hour time difference. I am never the first person to wish my mother Happy New Year. When I ring her on her birthday, the day is almost over for her.

Sigh.

I spend the next couple of days just getting organised. Filling the fridge. Doing laundry. Answering emails, returning phone calls. Getting rid of dust.

'You didn't return my call,' Richard says to me, when I return his call.

'Isn't that what I'm doing now?' I can hear the smile in my voice. 'Sorry, Richard, I should have called you earlier . . . I've just been . . . Anyway, how are you?'

'How are *you*? How was the holiday?'

'Unusual,' I say, after my mind ping-pongs between Georgios and Sean, then sticks, rather glumly, on a memory of Sean's face.

'Unusual good or unusual bad?'

I switch to Georgios. How he found my book that I now keep in the top drawer of my bedside table. 'Unusual good.'

'I don't have long to talk . . .' He sighs. 'I'm calling with bad news. Hester Elmtree died.'

It takes me a few moments to realise who he's talking about, because I always knew her as Ms Elmtree. 'Died?'

'A week ago, Angie. She had a stroke.'

'How do you know?' Richard had only met her once or twice at gatherings at our house.

'Kevin, your old tenant, phoned me. He was trying to get hold of you but your number's not listed and he didn't know where you'd moved to. So he remembered where Jonathan worked and called here.'

'I'm . . . stunned, Richard. I just went to see her before England . . .' I think of her telling me about seeing Jonathan sitting in his car. 'She seemed fine then.' Or maybe I hadn't noticed she wasn't. What was it she'd said about how she wasn't painting any more? She never did say why. 'I feel bad, Richard.'

'She was ninety-one.'

'Eh? She couldn't have been!' She looked at least fifteen years younger. 'Good God. She was ancient . . .'

'I have to go into a meeting,' he says. 'Can we talk later?' I quickly ask him when the funeral is.

He tells me it was four days ago.

*   *   *

I have a massive case of homesickness. It manifests itself in my reading *Hello!* magazines. Instead of finishing the chores I've started, I call in at the library, take out a year's worth of back copies, and lie around on my sofa flipping through them, soaking British celebrities into my blood, the interiors of British homes, and British recipes, into my every pore. It depresses the hell out of me when there's a new crop of celebrities I don't recognise. Give me Michael Parkinson and newsreaders I know, but when it's fresh, unknown faces and names I've never heard of, I feel a displacement akin to a weird form of early dementia. As though my Englishness and my very identity are somehow bound up in my knowing who Jordan is. Granted, I have bigger things to worry about, but you'd never know it right now.

'It's obvious.' Sherrie wags a fork at me when I let her persuade me to join her at a restaurant for some wine and oysters – particularly as she's paying. 'You're still depressed.'

Sherrie tips an oyster down her throat. Her hair is long and squiggly, and wild, like carrots that have been peeled with a fancy peeler for the purpose of decorating an overpriced salad. Yet every freckle on her face has been bled out with heavy (but expensive and consequently invisible) make-up. 'Depression makes you tired. And the more tired you feel, the more depressed you get. That's for sure what it is. You gotta go talk to somebody about it, Ange.'

'Oh, God, I'm not depressed, Sherrie! I've just been on holiday. I don't have any reason to feel depressed . . .' This can't be about Ms Elmtree dying. Granted, I'm sad about that, but it's not like we were close. 'I suppose I'm just realising that the holiday's gone away, but the problems I had before I went on it haven't.'

'If you talked it through with somebody, you might get some sort of clarity and focus.'

'I don't need clarity and focus!'

'You don't have to be defensive, hon.'

'I'm not being defensive! I'm just stating a fact. And I'm not going to a grief counsellor. Certainly not two years after Jonathan died. They'll commit me.'

I did actually go to a counsellor. Once. Jonathan's mother sent her name to me from Toronto, in a small card. A funeral is a bit like Christmas Day; once it's over, people tend to forget it's ever been and move on with life. The friends had largely stopped calling, and I didn't want to keep phoning to bleed all over my poor mother, when she'd just gone back to England because I'd convinced her I was fine. So I thought, *okay Angela, give it a go* . . .

I have an inbuilt loathing of people who believe that human beings are like cans of baked beans; they only come in so many varieties, and one can either has the sausages in it or it doesn't. But I was prepared to give her the benefit of the doubt. She didn't get off to a good start. For starters, she looked frigid, asexual and intellectual, whereas I was hoping for Lorraine Bracco from *The Sopranos*. She talked to me by looking off to the side of me.

'Grief usually has a time span that is equivalent to half the number of years you were married,' she told me. 'So, what that means is, if you were married twenty years, you'd probably grieve for your partner for ten.'

Her tone made me feel like I was four years old and she was saying, *If Billy has five eggs in the basket and Benny takes away two, Billy will have three left* . . .

'So, if you were married four years, like you and . . . [pause while she forgot my husband's name] Jonathan were, you can be expected to grieve for two.'

I remember thinking it took longer to grow out my red highlights. Needless to say, it was as I'd expected: bollocks. I never went back.

But now I wonder, was she really that far wrong? It's been two years since Jonathan died, and while I have grieved for him every step of the way, I no longer feel that he's the primary reason for my feeling –

'Dislocated.' Sherrie fills in the word, snapping me back to the present.

'You what?'

'That's what I think you are. You're like a limb that's become unattached from your body. You don't work properly any more. To the passing observer, you might look like you're all there, yet when you try to function properly, you can't. You have this disability.'

'Hang on, let me guess . . . In the outer regions of eastern South America, the onyx-jibwies believe that—'

Her grin stops me.

'Seriously, Sherrie, thanks. I'm depressed and I'm going around like a handicapped person. That conjures up a lovely picture. There really is hope for me.'

I wonder, though, now that she's telling me I'm depressed, if a part of me is sad because I am letting go of Jonathan – if letting go is defined as not thinking of him every moment of every day. Maybe grief has become such a habit that I'm actually missing it. Can I possibly be grieving for grief?

'There is hope for you,' Sherrie says, before tipping another oyster down her throat. 'Because I have a solution for you, *ma petite*. Why don't you go and join something? A cause. Do something to help people who've got far worse problems than your own.'

'Join the Peace Corps, you mean? Go build roads in central Africa?'

She narrows her eyes at me.

'You know, Sherrie, me and charity don't really see eye to eye. Did I ever tell you about that doctor I interviewed when I first came to Canada?'

She scowls.

'I got a job reporting for a university rag. I was supposed to write an article on Doctors Without Borders. Some lovely, very overworked, planet-saving MD took two hours out of his busy day to let me interview him. The thing was, when I sat down to write the piece, I was hopeless. I got so frustrated trying to make my article brilliant that I couldn't string two sentences together . . . so I packed it in. I never went back to the paper, and the lovely doctor never got his story published.'

'Come on, that was a century ago! Besides, weren't you supposed to be writing a speech for that homeless charity? What was it called? Raise the Roof?'

I'd almost forgotten my job. The speech. Poor old Raise the Roof – the only 'project' David had given me in the three months I'd worked at his company (mainly because it was the only project David had). I'd had great hope for it. 'Oh, I'm sure it's all written now. David would have pulled something together. He could write, albeit not very well. Raise the Roof was pretty much his one and only client, even if they were pro bono. I'm sure he wouldn't have let them down.'

'Well, why don't you volunteer – say once a week – to feed the homeless, or do something noble and un-self-centred that'll get you outta the house and maybe help you get some perspective on things in your own life?'

'My main concern is paying my bills, Sherrie. That's the only perspective I'm interested in right now. I have about another six months' rent in my bank account, and the ability – if I live very carefully – to exist without a job for that amount of time, then after that . . .' I whistle. 'It'll be me lining up at Raise the Roof, and somebody feeding me slop from a tin can.'

Sherrie looks startled. 'You're not *that* desperate, surely?'

I never told her about how much money Jonathan lost, out of respect for his memory. Only Richard knows. I'm sure she's often wondered how I can be so badly off, when we used to live so well, but she's had the decency not to ask. 'Okay, maybe I have a bit more than six months, but we're not talking much more.'

Her jaw drops. Nobody ever believes it. Not when they think of the life I used to have.

'Well, you gotta turn that crap around, girl!' she says. 'A lot can happen in six months, Ange. But you gotta get started on the right track. Right now, you're not on the track at all. You're completely trackless, my friend.'

I think about this. 'Thanks,' I tell her. 'For your thoughts about volunteering . . . It might not be something I'm going to do, but it was a good idea.' I have to say that; she's buying dinner. Actually, though, I think it's a rather daft idea. I admire crusaders; I'm just not one of them. 'But Sherrie, right now I think my best strategy is to get hired by a big advertising agency again. Then I can earn six figures, maybe buy a place, and – who knows? – maybe even bring my mam over here.' I had a wild thought on the plane – that I should apply to sponsor her to live here, if she'd consider coming.

'Anyway, Sherrie, I certainly can't face going back to that job and sitting on my boss's couch for nine hours a day while he bores my ears off about his fantastic past career, and not a single client ever walks through his door. It's far too depressing. That might have been fine when I needed breaking in gently to the working world again, but I'm just about ready to take life by the horns again. I think.'

'But you hate the big agency life, Ange! It practically put you in a psych ward. Imagine what Jonathan would say if he knew you'd gone back to that again.'

I push my plate across the table and wish I was back on holiday again. 'Yes, but he's not here, is he? And besides, Sherrie, you have to remember something: advertising is all I know how to do.'

She picks up her glass and holds it mid-air before she drinks.

'Well, Ange, the way I see it, that's not a good enough reason to repeat past mistakes.'

'What about the idea you had of starting up your own business? "Write Strategies"?' Richard's hazel eyes fix me with an intent curiosity.

It seems nobody's going to leave me alone to wallow in my own career mess, are they?

'Oh, Richard!' I look from my husband's best friend to his wife, across their reclaimed teak kitchen table. 'That was always more Jonathan's idea than mine . . .'

'Does it matter whose idea it was? It's a good one, isn't it?' Jessica pipes up, sloshing white wine around in her big glass – something she does a lot before she sips. In this case, it's expensive wine, so it's probably worth the somewhat pretentious performance. 'I don't know why you're not going for it,' she adds, pissing me off ever so slightly, because that sentiment is weird coming from somebody who until very recently couldn't even spell the word 'work'.

I like sitting in their old but modernised kitchen, though, with its new granite countertops co-existing with a big, deep, old-fashioned sink where people used to wash their laundry. They've ordered sushi. Something they always do on a Friday night when they have me over. For about a year after Jonathan died, we had a Friday night ritual. It was the 'save Angela from herself' invitation, which neither Jessica nor Richard would let me turn down. Well, Richard, mainly, because it was always he who called to invite me. It was he who began to call me every day soon after Jonathan died. It was he who desperately tried to save me from losing my house. When I think of any point in my rocky road to getting over Jonathan, there was always Richard, propping me up and telling me which decisions were the pressing ones to make, which makes me study him now for a while, then say, 'Let's not talk about Write

Strategies. Not tonight. I mean, let's face it, it's hard to get a business off the ground. I could be at it for a year or two and not make a bean. Plus, it's a tonne of work . . . Networking, building relationships, getting people to actually have confidence in you . . .' I feel lame saying that, given that Jessica managed to get a business off the ground even though previously I wouldn't have thought she'd be capable of it. But then again, she started blogging about something she loves and her hobby somehow miraculously turned into a business, so an unkind part of me thinks it's hardly the same thing.

I pick up a barbecue salmon roll with my chopsticks and dip it in soy sauce and wasabi. 'Once I leave my present job and get a real one, with some real money coming in, well, I could always do it in my spare time. Maybe try to get a business plan together.' Not that I'd know how to start writing a business plan. 'For now, though, guys, I just need a job.'

'I'll do your make-up for you if you get an interview; make you look good,' Jessica offers.

'Thanks,' I tell her, wondering if I've just been insulted. I'd like to think my CV matters more than my lipstick. But then again, her lipstick mattered more than her CV, and now she's one of Vancouver's star businesswomen. So there you go. What do I know?

'You'll never pull off working full-time and launching Write Strategies on the side,' Richard tells me; which is the sort of honest, common-sense thing that Jonathan would have said. 'How much spare time did you have when you worked in your last ad job, Angie?'

'Yes, but back then I had a husband to occupy myself with on weekends. Remember? Anyway, can we not talk about this any more?' I plead. 'Can't we talk about somebody else's problems for a change?'

So we stop talking about it. But it seems nobody else has got problems, so we settle for just eating. Between us we polish off a bin-load of raw fish, Jessica discarding all the rice from the fingers of nigiri sushi because rice is carb and carbs are evil.

'So this is the guy you were crazy over?' Richard scrutinises the pic of Georgios, looking very handsome, on my digital camera.

'I wasn't crazy over him!' I take a glug of the delicious Napa Valley Chardonnay. 'We just hit it off like long-lost friends.' I muse on how convinced I was that Jonathan had sent him. Was it really so absurd?

'I like your thumb ring.' Jessica watches me twiddle with it.

I look down at my thumb. 'I know! I bought it in Greece. It's the meander, the Greek symbol for long life. Or, as I read the other day on the Internet, "the flow of life, eternal life, eternal love".'

Jessica looks glazed over.

We're saved by the arrival of Emma, who comes into the kitchen from the basement where she's watching DVDs with her friend – they're having a sleepover. 'Hi, Emma,' I greet her. Emma walks over to the table in her tiny denim skirt, her long, twig-like legs and silky blonde hair make her look effortlessly model-like. She stands beside Richard's chair. Richard puts his arm around her and pulls her into him. 'Say hello to Angela,' he tells her.

In a motherly gesture, she pushes back the straggly bit of chestnut hair that's flopped onto his brow. She turns and meets my eye, and says a shy 'Hello.' Then she seems suddenly embarrassed, like she's accomplished something that was challenging for her, and flits off to the fridge. 'Mom, can we have some ice-cream?'

I love her. I love her because she's a little girl, yet I can already see the gorgeous woman she's going to be; the tender mother. I love her because I've glimpsed the little shyness in her that she'll soon grow out of, and I hope that one day she might think of me as an aunt.

Jessica swings her gaze over her shoulder at her daughter, who is irrefutably her living image. Their small, heart-shaped faces are, sweetly, carbon copies. The same almond-shaped eyes, neither fully green nor blue. The same groomed, light brown eyebrows, high cheekbones, and slightly-on-the-thin-side lips that act like curly picture frames for teeth that are almost as white as the tips of Jessica's gel nails.

'No, Ems. You've had pie already.' Jessica looks at me excitedly. 'Can you see the colour in her hair? I did her a strawberry rinse, although it's mostly washed out already.'

I scrutinise Emma's head. 'Not really.'

Both Emma and Jessica look at me like I clearly have some missing brain-cells. Maybe aunt status is going to take some working at.

'Please can I have ice-cream?' Emma flicks her hair over her shoulder; a habit picked up from her mother.

'No, Emma!' Jessica is so dramatic in her reply. *Oh, go on*, I think.

'Oh, pleeeeee-aze!' Emma whines. 'It was hours ago when I ate pie!'

'It was only pie,' I say gently to Jessica, knowing I'm looking for Emma's approval.

'Do you want to be fat?' Jessica hurls at her, as though being fat is worse than being what she is – a bit of a dumbo. Oh, I'm being cruel.

I feel like saying, *Look, it's mothers like you who wind up with anorexic daughters. Do you really want to give her a screwed-up attitude towards food?* I would *never* be like that with my daughter. Then I look at Emma and think, why did Jonathan and I wait five years because we wanted to have a life before we had a family? Why didn't we just have a baby right away, when we could have? Then Jonathan would have lived on, and I'd have had a lasting piece of him.

Richard sends me a look of exasperation, which I can't help but share. I've always despaired at how Jessica seems to think that the airbrushed magazine caricatures of womanly perfection are what we all should try to be. Back in the days when I was convinced that her brain was the size of the black on a black-eyed pea, it was very easy to be disparaging, as though putting her down somehow built me up. Making her seem even more of an intellectual blip made me feel like I had a head swollen to bursting point with top-tier brains. But now that 'Goddess Girl' has achieved Internet glory and Powder Power is one of the province's hippest new non-profit support services for underprivileged women – and I don't even have a job – it's hard for me to be smug. Still, though, sometimes you just want to say –

'Christ, Jessica, give her some fucking ice-cream!'

A-ha! It seems I don't have to! Richard does it for me.

Emma giggles when she hears her dad swear, and sends me a look of conspiratorial approval. I'm surprised he did it. It's very un-Richard.

'Richard!' Jessica glares at him. 'There's no point in you saying yes to everything I say no to. Or you might as well just go and be a one-parent family!' She looks at me for sympathy and I try to put on the right face for her, but my reaction isn't fast enough. Her eyes have that moment of truth in them that says, *Well, why would I ever expect you to side with me?*

I often think that without Jonathan or Richard between us, Jessica and I would happily drop the other one from a Boeing 747 with the bum parachute. Our secret incompatibility is the one constant that has existed all these years. It's the only very strong thing we have in common.

Richard gets up, walks over to the kitchen cabinets, pulls out two bowls, plucks the carton of Ben & Jerry's out of the fridge and spoons two good-sized dollops into each bowl – something, again, a bit rebellious that I wouldn't have imagined him doing.

'Thanks, Pops!' Emma snatches the bowls from him and skips back out the way she came.

Jessica stands up, walks through the kitchen doorway, and slams the door.

Richard and I are left looking at one another.

Now I feel bad for her.

'I'm applying for a job,' I tell Sherrie on the phone. This time next week I'm due back at work and if anything has got me off my ass, that thought has. 'I was on Jervais Ladner's website. They're looking for a senior account director. It's packaged goods, minimum five years . . . It was practically written for me.'

'Are they big?'

'They're better than big. Practically every hip billboard campaign or TV commercial out there is JL's. They're the top advertising agency in Vancouver and number two in the entire country.' Just saying the words, I bloat with pride – that same feeling I had whenever I used to tell people that I worked in one of Canada's leading advertising agencies. And look what happened to all that. But I can't let one bad experience scar me for life. 'I'm sure it'll be the same bullshit all over again, but the money will solve a lot of my problems, Sherrie. Oh, the money will be sweet! I *so* want out of this apartment! If I'm to live in high-rise hell, I want it to be a brand new building, with new air. I want it to be in a sane location, a nice family neighbourhood, not partyland. I don't want to see gay men snogging in the lift – I've nothing against gay men snogging, but I just don't need to see it whenever I step out of my door. I want trees outside my window, not concrete and windows and other people's lives. I want grass, mountains, ocean. Isn't that the whole point of living in Vancouver? Because we're supposed to have a better quality of life here than anywhere else in the world?'

There's a long pause. 'Oh? Sorry? You're finished? I thought you were on a long rant. I was about to go put my laundry in and come back on the spin cycle.'

'Oh, Sherrie, I've given it a lot of thought. I actually think I'm ready for the ad agency business again.' *To convince them, you must first, yourself, believe.*

'Angela, darling, any time you want my controversial opinion on the topic, just ask.'

18

Boxes. There are boxes everywhere I look in this apartment. I've got to somehow unpack my life.

Before I moved from the house, I should have just had a big yard sale and got rid of stuff. Instead I hauled it with me – mad, really, when I was going from a four-bedroom house to a place about the size of our former laundry room. I think I was just too muddled to be able to work out what was junk and what I needed to keep, so it was safer just to keep it all.

Opening up boxes now, as I kneel on the floor with a cup of tea beside me, it's pretty obvious what my state of mind was at the time. Shoes thrown in with a watering can and a pair of pasta tongs. Mail bunged in the bread basket. The Visa bill I kicked up a big stink over when they charged me interest after I claimed I'd never received it. Ah! My cosy pink dressing-gown! I thought I was never going to see that again. And last but not least, my other red ladybird slipper, a little bit squashed. I put it on with its mate that I'm already wearing, and I start feeling more like me again.

I notice how everything is mostly my stuff, because Jonathan's I did clear out – an exercise in self-therapy. I'm pleased I did. Moving his things here would have felt like taking him somewhere he didn't belong, because I was too selfish to leave him where he would have most liked to be left.

I did let go, didn't I? The realisation strikes me afresh, as though Jonathan has just given a word of praise in my ear.

I get a few bin-bags and start separating junk from stuff I can give to the charity shop, and stuff I'll decide about later. I'm not far through it when my phone rings.

'How up would you be for going on a blind date?'

I plonk down on top of the bag. 'Ohhhh . . . not up, Sherrie. In fact, down. Very, very down. So down, my chin's polishing the floor.'

'Pessimist.'

'But I've only ever been on one blind date. Remember? The town planner? Roger? About six or eight months ago? That's me and blind dates finished.'

She laughs. 'This one's different. I know him – and you trust me – so I'm your screening process. He's a good guy. His name is Sam. For Samaritan.'

'Don't kid me.'

'I'm not.'

I scowl, not sure if she's serious. I stuff the phone under my chin and continue bunging things in the bags. 'Go on, then. Give me his bio.'

'Well, he's a tiny bit older than you. He's not a real player type or anything, just a down-to-earth guy with a sense of humour. He runs, just like Jonathan used to do. He's in sales. He has a dog called Madison.'

'I hate him already.'

'You won't! I promise you. Okay, so he's not a rugged Greek, or a gorgeous married Irishman who's trying to get a bit of action on the side.'

The gorgeous married Irishman's face floods into my mind's eye and I hold it there for some moments. I've not thought of him since I was on the plane home. But then I thought about him for the whole ten hours, so my mind could use a change of scenery now.

'How did you meet him?' I force Sean's face out of my mind. I have to try really hard once it's arrived, though – really hard – and as his face fades, there's an accompanying disappointment.

She hesitates. 'Speed dating.'

'Good God, it gets worse.'

'No! I went out with him on a proper date – you know, the night I came to meet you at the airport. When I told him I was a cotton trader he looked at me like I was very glamorous. That is, until I said I travel about eighty per cent of the year. That kinda killed it for him. I gotta stop using that line, Angie. I gotta invent some other career. I think I'm gonna start saying I'm a nurse.' She draws breath. 'Everybody loves nurses, because there's something both kinky and caring about them. And kinky and caring is a real edgy combination. They start thinking you're gonna whip them then wipe up their blood. Anyway, I've set you up for Wednesday night. You're gonna meet at Artigiano's, so you won't feel out of your depth. It's just coffee. It's just Wednesday night.'

I've forgotten which bag is which now, and have to think where to stuff a decrepit pink sweatshirt that got bleach on it.

'Earth to Angie. Is there anybody out there?'

'Oh, sorry . . . Erm . . . Well, if I go – and it's a big "if" at this juncture – how will I recognise him?' Anything to shut her up.

'You will. And he'll spot you. I've told him all about you.'

'Thanks. That's sure to mean he'll show up. I'm such a great catch.'

When we hang up, I realise that the next box I have to unpack is one whose contents I'm all too familiar with: the only one I bothered marking 'Handle With Care'.

Stuffed beside his blue shirt are Jonathan's well-worn sandals with the toe-prints inside. On top of the shirt is a little brown envelope containing his wedding ring and his Tag watch. Miraculously, the watch hasn't a scratch on it. Its hands are frozen at eight o'clock. I often wonder if that was the exact moment when his life ended.

I make a nest of my hand and place the jewellery in it. It's still a weird feeling holding something that was removed from his dead body. With each subtle movement of my hand, the watch shifts about, jingling against the ring. I was with him when he bought it. He'd coveted a Tag for ages. I'd catch him lost in gazing at it and would think *you love that watch almost as much as you love me!* But he'd worked hard enough for it. Soon after he died, I found it and held it to my cheek. I was convinced the stainless steel was warm, as though he'd just taken it off.

I put it to my face now.

Of course. I didn't expect it would be.

What was I ever thinking, shoving them in an envelope? What I'm going to do is buy a little velvet jewellery bag and store them in there, so I can keep them safe. I put them back in the envelope and put the envelope on the floor for now.

The sandals and T-shirt though, I'm not sure what to do with. The shirt doesn't smell of him any more. It really only reminds me of the last time he was alive because he wore it to run in that morning. The sandals are different, though. The marks in them that outline his foot identify him, and prove he lived. They feel very precious. I run my fingers over the rounded indentations where his toes were, put them to my nose. They smell of leather and sweaty feet. There's no point in giving them to the charity shop. I can't see anybody wanting to wear somebody else's sweaty old shoes. Besides, I'd feel I was passing on bad karma.

Chuck them, Angie! I can almost hear him saying.

So on an impulse, I put them in the bag that's for the bin.

I get the call from Jervais Ladner on Tuesday, asking me if I can come in for an interview on Friday at four. That was fast. What a time for an interview, though! It'll be hard to feel the interviewer is taking you seriously when you know he's sitting there thinking about what he's going to do with his weekend.

It quickly dawns on me that I've nothing to wear for it. All my old work clothes are about two sizes too big, and if they weren't they wouldn't be in fashion, and that just wouldn't do, not for a power job with a top agency. The good thing is, though, I go for a latte at Artigiano's and while I'm sitting there devouring back copies of *Marketing* magazine, to try to educate myself on what's happened in the ad world since I left it, I see inspiration on legs: a girl a bit like me, wearing a charcoal business suit – a light enough material for a warm day like this, but interesting in the quite un-summery colour choice. It's close-fitting and plain, almost masculine, and she's teamed it with a simple pink and white shirt, wide open at the neck. But it's all set off by about the sexiest pair of black shoes I've ever seen: probably three inches high, with a thick, triangular heel, and a cheeky peep-toe showing her French pedicure. I throw back my coffee, roll up my mags, and hurry like a man on a mission to the mall.

'Have you been to the doctor yet?' I put my mam on speakerphone as I sit on the toilet lid looking in my magnifying mirror, applying a mid-grey shadow to my upper lash line. I can't believe I'm going on a blind date just to make Sherrie happy.

'Why did that have to be the first question out of your mouth?'

'So I take it you haven't?'

'I've really only just got home!'

'I was a bit annoyed you decided to stay longer and not even tell me . . . If you don't go to the doctor they'll never find out what's wrong with you and you'll never get treatment and who knows what might happen then.'

'That's intelligent, Angela. Answer me one question, because you seem to have all the answers: If I ate your brain, would I get your knowledge?'

'Oh, ha ha. Isn't sarcasm the lowest form of a nit?' I remind her of one of her famous expressions.

'You're the only nit round here. Anyway, I only stayed a little while longer. Don't tell me off. Don't spoil what might be my one last chance for happiness.'

I feel like the evil stepsister, or the jealous spinster friend who can't be happy for you. 'I'm sorry. Did you have a good time?' I'm dying to get the skinny on Georgios.

'I had a lovely time.'

'And?'

'And it was lovely.'

'AND?'

'Stop sniffing around my bottom, Angela.'

'I'd never want to sniff around your bottom. I'll leave that to Georgios.'

I hear her titter.

'So you're not going to tell me, then?' *If he rogered you and you enjoyed it.*

'Some people . . . I don't know . . . I have to repeat myself so many times I start to wonder if they're a little bit simple in the head.'

I grin. 'Please just tell me one thing . . .'

'What?' she says, irritably. 'If you're going to put that record back on and tell me to promise I'm going to the doctor, just don't bother saying anything!'

There's a silence. 'Hello?' she enquires, after a few moments.

'I'm not bothering saying anything.'

On my way out to see my 'date', I make a trip down to the garbage chute with the bag of clothes I've been busy filling and all the crap that once lay abandoned in the middle of the floor. Things are looking up. As I step out onto the street and float along with the crowd, I realise I feel good about myself. I've just got back from Greece. In two days' time I have an interview for a great, well-paying job. Now, when I wake up each morning I give myself an exercise in positive thinking. I tell myself that with each day, I'm somehow going to improve myself, and so far . . . well, I think it might be working.

'Holy smokes!' I've just got Sherrie on speed-dial. I peer into Artigiano's window. 'There are two men sitting on their own, Sherrie, and one of them looks like Robin Williams with a toupé on his top lip, and the other's old and orange and he's wearing a shirt the colour of Thai green curry.' I gasp. 'Which one is he, then?'

Of course, I'm waiting for her to say, 'Oh, neither of those two, stupid!' but instead she says, 'He's tanned and weathered-looking because he's a runner, Angie. Duh! Runners have outdoorsy complexions, they're not pale freaks like you and me.'

She clears her throat. 'Ahem! Two more features that the brochure fails to mention . . . He's got a rockin' body on him. And an enormous cock.'

'A what?' I zip away from the window in case I'm seen by the orange man. 'How the hell would you know about his, his, his, penis?'

'How? Cos I slept with him.'

'You slept with the man you're setting me up with?' A couple of latte-drinkers on the patio look up at me in surprise.

'I went on a date with him. What else was I supposed to do?'

She sounds pissed off at my pissed-offness. 'I thought you'd consider it a bonus that I could give him such a good report. How many people do you know have their good friends test the merchandise for them? And if I can call it a whopper, trust me, I've seen plenty. It really is. You got it comin', girl.'

'I got it going, more like.' I trot away from Artigiano's as fast as my legs can carry me. I'm trying to picture an orange man with a huge one coming at me, and it's enough to put me off sex for life.

'Take a maturity pill! You can't stand him up! You've got to at least have a coffee with him! He's a great guy.'

'Yeah, once you get over the fact that he looks like he's been dipped in iodine.'

'You're looks-ist, Angela Chapman. I noticed that about you a long, long time ago. And it's not a good quality in someone your age. You know that song? Something about you might be young and beautiful now, but one day your looks will be bye-bye? Well, that's gonna be you, hon . . . your problem is you're going around measuring everybody against Jonathan. Whereas what you should do is find somebody really ugly and gross, and measure other guys against him. It's called the glass is half full. But with you, if he's not hot or cute, you're not gonna give him a chance, are you?'

'That's not true!' I flee across the grass in front of the art gallery, quickly summoning up the men I've most recently seen myself with on some level, just to disprove her point. But the faces that leap to mind are gorgeous Georgios, gorgeous Sean, and Roger the city planner, who was decent-looking.

'Okay, just because he's not great looking . . . Just because he's quiet, and maybe not the most confident guy in the world . . . That's not a reason to blow him off. Maybe, you know, some people have serious self-esteem issues. There are a lot of lonely single people who suffer from some sort of mental illness—'

'Oh! Mental illness?' I fling my free hand in the air in exasperation. 'That's not a problem for me! I love a little dose of mental illness. It's actually high up on my wish list for a man. Let's think . . . there's knockers first – I love a man with boobs, particularly when they're bigger than my own. Then there's hairy hands. Got to love those . . . Mental illness? Yeah, definitely third.'

'Well, you might think that's funny now, but take it from me, Ange, you've been out of the dating market for quite some time now. Vancouver's a hard city for a single woman to find a man in. You better hope Jonathan's gonna send you some-body, because you're gonna need the help. Everybody's married in this city, because other than mountains and ocean for long romantic walks, there's not that much else to do, so you only come here or settle here if you've got somebody to screw and walk with for the rest of your life. If they're single, they're usually gay or twenty-two. If they're fifty, they're usually divorced, and lookin' for somebody twenty-two – straight or gay. So it's slim pickings . . . And even in general, if you're young and perfect – which you're neither – it's hard finding a man. You got lucky the first time. But you met him in Toronto: totally different scene. But you need to remember an important thing, Angela, my friend: women rarely get the man they really want; they end up having to want what they can get.'

I cross at the lights at the corner of Georgia and Howe, not even heading in the direction of home, just sort of running off at the legs. And the mouth. 'Well, maybe you think like that, Sherrie, but I've never thought like that. That's so lame. Not all of us settle. And some of us never will. If I never meet anybody else, I won't just be with someone because someone will do.'

'I'm sorry if I offended you, Ange. I was really only trying to help. All I'm saying is – or trying to say, subtly – there's an old Yiddish proverb. It goes like this: If you want your dreams to come true, don't sleep.'

I walk home, a little bit furious. I am not a dreamer. I don't think I ever have been. Maybe I no longer believe that

Jonathan is going to send me a lover, but when I do eventually find one, I'd like to think he would be somebody who Jonathan would have approved of.

Coming into my apartment, I see the two green garbage bags in the middle of the floor and step over them. I'm just putting the kettle on, when an awful thought strikes me.

Jonathan's ring and watch.

Weren't they on the floor in an envelope?

I glance at the floor. So where's the envelope?

I dive-bomb the bag marked 'Charity Shop' . . . Not in that one. I pat bags and squeeze bags, tip them up, clothes tumbling into a massive jumble on the floor. But I can't see the little brown envelope with his jewellery in it.

That can only mean one thing: I must have chucked it out with the rubbish.

I don't even wait for the lift. Instead, I gallop down eighteen flights of stairs. I can't have chucked his wedding ring. His watch that he loved so much.

It's not pretty down here: the dump at the back of the building, where the rubbish of two hundred apartments finds itself.

Life as a garbage rat isn't that glamorous, either. With the noise of the door opening, and my arrival, they squeak and scurry away.

The stink is something else, too. A cross between rotten vegetables, the rancid entrails of a million abattoirs, dirty old homeless men, and shit. I cover my nose with a hand but it doesn't help. I already feel contaminated. I can't count how many fastened-up carrier bags, or spewing open carrier bags, or half rat-eaten carrier bags there are down here, but there are a lot. Most of them generic green bags just like mine. With fervid desperation, I pick my way over a heap of stinking squelch and start ripping open bags, searching for something that looks vaguely like my own junk, knowing that it truly will be like finding a needle in a haystack. But I am not deterred. I have to find his jewellery, or I'm never going to forgive myself.

My hands get coated with globs of stinky wet stuff. I retch up a symphony. But I'm on a mission. My tearing becomes more frantic, and I think, *Why did you have to die, Jonathan, and leave me to care so much about the small things that are all I have left of you? Look what you've reduced me to.* I tread over bags, not caring what my feet touch, not caring that the stink is so bad I feel I'm swallowing it; I can taste it. I know I've gone mad, but I am powerless to stop myself. The faster I go, the more hopeless it's getting. I start to cry. A big rush of tears. *Jonathan, why can't you leave me alone? Let me be free of you?* I feel like tears must be cleaning a trail down my grimy, stinky cheeks. I dab at my mouth with the back of my forearm.

Something tells me this is hopeless.

I stand there stock-still, my heart pounding. And I realise something. I'm not crying for me. I'm not even crying for Jonathan. I'm crying for a ring and a broken watch that in no meaningful way affect my memory of him, or my love for him.

I rub one more time at my face. There is a simple truth here. One I will have to accept: Jonathan hasn't gone away. Even though I was convinced, for a short while, that he finally had. And that's both a bad thing, and exactly as it should be.

My heart-rate comes down. My crying stops. A tiny instinct in me says, go on, open one more bag, and if they're not there . . .

But I suddenly feel exhausted to the bone. What's the point? I look down at my hands. They're like the hands of a street person who has forgotten what it's like to have a bath. A black furry creature trips across the top of my foot and I let out a scream. The echo of my own voice breaks through me like a flare going off inside my body.

Give it up, I say to myself. But still that instinct says, *check one more bag . . .*

Okay. There's a bag right at my feet. I sink my fingers into the plastic and rip.

There, on the top, is a little brown envelope.

Inside the little brown envelope is Jonathan's watch and Jonathan's ring.

I pick the watch out and clutch it, looking at its face and rubbing it with my thumb. But what's odd is, the watch doesn't appear to be broken any more. Its hands no longer stick at eight o'clock. The second hand is making a purposeful sweep around the dial.

19

Seagulls swoop off the building tops and soar to a blue sky. I catch my reflection in the window of the Hotel Vancouver – my high (and not particularly comfortable, but devastatingly sexy) black heels, the light, pale grey suit (the closest I could find to that girl's) that's so fitted it gives me a bum when I thought I didn't have one, the baby blue Benetton shirt, gaping open and showing my tan, my hair loose around my shoulders, sunglasses on my head. Jessica rang me and offered to do my make-up again. I suppose my saying yes might have been a good thing for us, but I couldn't bear to be fussed over. Besides, she might get to see that my skin isn't perfect and might never want me in her house again.

Jervais Ladner's building is as 'corporate Vancouver' as it gets: about thirty-five storeys of earthquake-proof, shimmering, floor-to-sky tinted glass – the type of windows you can see out of, but nobody can see in through; three sets of revolving doors; pristine tiled floors that make your shoes clack; a blue-uniformed concierge sitting at a vast desk who will eventually get to call you by your name, because you'll always be the first person in when he comes on early shift, and the last person he shows out before he closes up to catch the last bus home. There are eight elevators. JL is on the thirty-third floor. Nay, JL *owns* the thirty-third floor. The top execs will have the north-facing offices: the best view in the whole damned city – mountains, park, ocean and sky. God of everything up there, you are – the heavens and the earth – only maybe not of yourself. Their windows never open. There'd be far too many suicides.

Progress, I think. That one word just cruises, ironically, through my head.

'Elevator to the right,' the friendly black concierge points out, when he sees me hesitating.

I clack across the tiles, remembering how the sound of my own feet used to make me feel important. Somebody else walks behind me. A man.

But instead of feeling important, like I used to feel, I feel a tightening in the pit of my stomach. Going up. Of course. Literally and metaphorically. The man steps into the lift with me and we stand there, a foot apart. Whereas before, when I used to do this every day, I'd have felt a kinship with this person I didn't even know, I'd have been vaguely impressed by him and would have wondered if he made as much money as I did, now that a couple of years and a shift in priorities have distanced me from the corporate rat race, I feel only pity for him.

I remember, as I stand here, with the lift climbing through the floors, that I once went up, didn't I? Up quite far, actually, and quite fast in my career. But then, one day, I went down. Or, rather, I got sent down with a security guard who had orders to escort me off the premises. I've always thought it interesting how, when they fire you, they manage to make you feel a criminal instead of a victim.

We stop on the eighteenth floor. The doors open. The man puts a hand in his pants' pockets and steps out.

I've often thought you have to be born to the corporate elite. Something has to drive you, beyond the money and the power and the deals. Nobody just kills themselves so they can drive around Vancouver in a brand-new Mercedes. And whatever that gene is, I guess it's missing in me.

Ping. We're at the thirty-third. My heart-rate's up; I hear it pound in my ears. The doors slowly slide open. My hands feel clammy, a sweat breaks out down my back. Then a thought strikes me: If the biggest rush I got from knowing I'd landed this interview was finding a shirt, a jacket, a pair of pants, and a pair of shoes I can barely walk in – a whole 'business' identity that I didn't even come up with on my own, but copied off a girl I'd seen ten minutes previously in a coffee shop – shouldn't that be telling me something?

The scene that appears before my eyes is all too familiar. The elevator doors open out into a vast marble and stainless steel reception, behind which is a designer maze of glass offices filled with exotic plants and exotic people, and furniture that looks too artsy to be comfortable. The women are all good-looking; it's almost unfair that they also have a brain. But they do. They'd have to, to work here. The men are good-looking too, and doubtless highly game-playing. A young guy in jeans and a T-shirt walks past reception, kicking around a football. He's probably trying to come up with the latest big campaign slogan for Honda. Because the creative people in advertising agencies get to dress casually and kick footballs around the office and call it work.

A pretty but semi-witless receptionist smiles at my arrival. She's smiling too keenly, which means she's new. Which means she's there because somebody's told her you have to start at the bottom, that she'll work her way up. But the only 'working your way up' that will get done as far as she's concerned will be by some thinks-he's-a-hotshot creative director who will work his way up her, with promises he would be in the position to keep, but of course he won't. She'll get screwed, used, and then she'll leave. And she'll look in the mirror and she'll think *maybe I should have gone to college*.

Jervais Ladner's logo is blasted across the front of the reception desk.

I want to throw up.

The poor pretty girl who doesn't know what she's got coming smiles at me. I smile back. My heart's hammering so fast I'm sure she must hear it. I reach out a shaky arm and press the 'G' button. The doors slowly close, eventually cutting off our phoney expressions. The elevator pings when we reach the bottom. The concierge smiles at me and says, 'Have a nice day.'

I pass through the revolving doors, out into the fresh air and late afternoon sunshine. I'm shaking. But it's a good shaking.

Have a nice day, he said.

Yeah. I think I will.

20

There are three of us 'new volunteers', and the same number of Team Coordinators, in the tiny, airless, white-walled room on the second floor of the Epilepsy Canada building. There's Kye, a twentysomething Brad Pitt lookalike Physical Education teacher who watched a kid have a seizure after a game of football. 'I stood there with about ten other kids, and watched him thrash around and turn blue,' he tells us, twiddling his pen. 'I thought he was going to die. We all did. A few of his team-mates started crying . . . I didn't know what to do.' He quickly catches my eye, then looks around the table at the rest of the group. 'I think our schools need to know more about epilepsy. I'd like to help in some way.'

Rhonda goes next. Rhonda is a twenty-four-year-old black law student, who says she'd like to get involved in mentoring young people with the disability. 'I had it growing up, but I was lucky cos I grew out of it. But you never forget what it's like living with it . . . Everybody else is fit and healthy, then there's you . . .' Her brows knit together, a perplexed expression on her face. 'I used to have about three grand mals a week. They couldn't control it with meds. My seizures were all everybody focused on, because it was hard not to. Your family . . . your friends . . . you feel like you're not the same as them. That you can't achieve what they will.' She sniggers. 'I was out to prove them all wrong. I said, I'm going to show them.' She shrugs. 'But that's just me. Not every kid with epilepsy is going to be like me, are they?'

Then there's moi. About ten pairs of eyes focus on me when it's my turn to address the room and tell the team, and the other volunteers, why I have come here.

'My name is Angela Chapman,' I start out. 'I don't have epilepsy.'

'Hello Angela Chapman,' one of the older team members says, jokingly. There are a few titters. This brightens me. 'My background is in major advertising agencies, managing brand development for such clients as Kraft Canada and Yves Veggie Cuisine, to name two. But my present role is as Principal of Write Strategies . . .' here goes the bullshit . . . 'a company that provides writing consultancy services to corporate clients in Vancouver . . .' I don't mention that I've just done something either brave or very mad and quit the only crappy bit of employment I had, and am now in fact entirely jobless, given that Write Strategies – this company I'm supposedly the boss of – hasn't earned me a bean, because, really, it doesn't quite exist. But so far, they look like they're buying it. 'I coach business executives of all levels to communicate more effectively on the page – everything from internal emails to reports, speeches and presentations.'

Ahem. Clear throat.

It sounds so cold, after what they've all said. I've told a few white lies, but somehow I have their attention.

'The reason I am here . . .' I take a steadying breath, relieved by how easy it feels to stand up and talk in front of people when I'd imagined I might have lost the knack, '. . . is because two years ago, my husband had an epileptic seizure at the wheel of his car, and was killed.'

I pause to measure reactions. I know from experience what they usually are. Instead of the unqualified sympathy you'd get if you said they'd died any other way, there's often a sharp edge of blame that arrives in the eyes. You can see the thoughts running riot (thoughts that any one of us might have, only because it's them having them and not you, and it's about your husband and not theirs, it immediately puts your back up). The exasperation: *He's lucky he didn't kill somebody! What on earth was he doing driving in the first place?* The fear: *I might be at risk from somebody like that!* And then the blame: *It's your fault. Why did you let him drive?* As though by being wives, we become mothers to our husbands too.

I don't see any of that here, though. Crystal Rae, the well-dressed fiftysomething Executive Team Leader of the society, and one of Vancouver's prominent businesswomen in the telecommunications industry, watches me with a mix of sympathy and expectation.

'The fact is,' I tell them, feeling suddenly confident – I should be; with all the research I've done on epilepsy since Jonathan died, I'm a walking, talking expert – 'We, the great general public, know very little about epilepsy, don't we?' I look at the very hot-looking young PE teacher who is still twiddling with his pen, which distracts me a bit so I try to focus on the others instead. 'Yet a seizure doesn't always mean falling to the ground and thrashing around. My husband had just started having petit mal seizures. Neither one of us knew what they were at the time. Sometimes, I couldn't even tell if he was in one or not, because he would just seem to drift off. They would present themselves as brief, infrequent absences, where it seemed as though the brain just decided it needed a little time-out, and consciousness went away. Just for a few moments. But moments were all it took to cost him his life.'

Crystal nods. Just the other day, she was telling me that one of their members has about two hundred petit mal seizures a day, putting her in an almost permanent state of seizure. Her condition has never responded to medication.

'But I suppose what really brings me here . . . is that shortly after Jonathan died, I heard an ad for Epilepsy Canada on the radio. I realised it was the first ad I'd ever heard about epilepsy, yet I was all too familiar with the ones for the Cancer Society, or Raise the Roof, or Worksafe, or a whole host of other "causes" we've all heard of. Some of their advertisements were really clever; I could remember them for a long while after. Because they'd done something quite smart. They had succeeded in making their cause a brand.'

I pause here, to watch that point sink in. 'But until this day, I'd never seen or heard a Public Service Announcement about epilepsy.' I glance around at all the faces fastened on me. 'I wondered why.'

There's a moment where nobody speaks, and I fear I might have hit them with too much reality. Then Crystal gets up to push open a window. It's a good move; it is warm in here. But the thing seems stuck. 'Here.' Kye, the fit young PE teacher, scrapes back his chair and comes to her rescue. 'Let me.' With a certain manly assurance, he pushes at the frame, and I notice what fit arms he's got, and how tall and lean and striking he is.

Crystal blanches and looks oddly flattered. 'There, that's better,' she says, and quickly glances at me. 'I think we can all breathe now.'

For some reason, a few people laugh.

'Incidentally . . .' Crystal sits back down. 'The ad you did hear on the radio – do you remember what it said?'

I quickly glance at the faces that are all upon me. 'No,' I tell her honestly. 'I don't remember what it said. But then again I only heard it once, and it was quite a long time ago.'

I remember thinking it sucked. But I'm not going to tell them that. Well, not unless I'm really pressed. Then I probably won't use the word 'suck'.

Another twitter of – what? Amusement again? – passes around the advisory board. Rhonda and Kye smile at me, like I've just done a good job.

Progress.

'So what you're leading on to telling us,' Crystal looks at me, her expression a little unreadable, 'is that you think you could be doing far better advertising for us than we're doing ourselves.'

I glance at Kye who is studying me interestedly.

I tap the end of my pen on my notepad. Its sound, and my tension, are swallowed by the distant scream of an ambulance siren coming through the window, along with the nice breeze that I gratefully feel on the back of my neck.

'I think there are two issues here. One is exposure. The other is creative strategy.' I glance at the senior members again.

'Nicely dodged,' Crystal says.

One of the older men on the team either coughs or laughs. It seems this group finds all sorts of unusual things entertaining.

Shit. I probably did come off too strong.

I've not cycled the Stanley Park seawall in over two years. After Jonathan died, I couldn't do it because it was something he and I often did on Sundays. Without him, I couldn't have cycled around that wall any easier than if you'd hacked off my legs.

This Sunday, though, I'm pleased for the chance to get out. The wall's teaming with walkers, dogs, bikers, rollerbladers, runners, and carts and horses full of tourists. At Second Beach, after biking for about forty minutes, Sherrie and I flop onto the grass and devour a Nestlé chocolate ice-cream – which sort of defeats the point of exercising.

The sun beats down on us as the sweat on my back dries. I look at the water twinkling away beyond the pale sand strewn with logs with people sitting on them. Yes, if I didn't live here, I'd miss this feeling of living in the most chilled-out city in the world.

'I'm thinking of leaving my job,' Sherrie tells me suddenly, after we've scoffed our ice-cream.

'Your job?' I look at her hair in its top-knot, pieces of it sticking to her neck. 'You love your job!'

'I did. I mean, I do. It's just that I'm loving it less now as I'm getting older. All the travel . . . it's been the best and yet the worst part of the job.' She sighs hard, looking reflective. 'I mean, hell, Angie, last year there were only two months out of twelve where I didn't have to fly somewhere. And it's not like I even get to go business class! I'm going on long hauls, forced to sit there eating my own kneecaps for eighteen hours . . . I get there and . . .' She flings her hands up in frustration. 'I get off one plane and get on another. Remember when I was in China for a week? I only got to see five buyers! Because I spent most of my time on tiny planes, getting from one middle-of-nowhere cotton mill to the next. It was exhausting.'

'But I thought that's what you lived for . . . all the travelling to exotic places. All the friends you've made around the world.'

'Well, I always vowed that if I was gonna travel a lot, I was gonna have fun and not bitch about having no stability, because I hate people who constantly complain about situations that they can change – a bit like you did for years.' She smiles, looking reflective again. 'In a weird way, I wouldn't have wanted to change it. Not then. But I do now.'

'Really?' Maybe she is serious.

'It was all a big adventure, but now it's become predictable, empty . . . I'm forty-five soon, Angie. I don't wanna be single when I'm fifty, and I'm never gonna have a serious relationship with anybody when I'm never here! When I've got clients or suppliers phoning me across time zones at three in the morning, when I'm always crabby and jet-lagged . . .'

'You're never crabby!'

'Not in front of you. But at home, alone, in front of *me* – whoah, boy! – I'm crabby! It's not that I'm afraid of being old and alone. It's just that I'd like to have somebody to share some stage of my life with. For the longest time, meeting exotic men felt fulfilling and fun, even if they were seven feet three or three feet seven and didn't speak my language, and had strange customs that would never have been accepted in the Western world. I've done single for as long as I know, and it's been a blast, Ange. But I'm ready for a change.' She licks chocolate off her thumb and looks me directly in the eyes. 'Actually,' she grimaces, 'I'm gonna move to Toronto.'

'You're . . . !' I scour her face to see if this is just another of her jokes. 'So you're more than thinking of leaving your job! You've basically decided all this!'

'Basically . . . yeah.'

'But what's in Toronto that's not here?'

'More men. More jobs.'

'But you've got a job. And there's men here!'

'There's not. I've been through them all. There's none left. I can't wait for a whole new crop to be born and grow up. I mean, I've thought about it, but even if I start robbing the cradle, that puts me sexually out of commission at least until their voice breaks. I couldn't do squeaky voices, or wet dreams, or no facial hair!'

'But it feels so drastic, Sher! Packing up and moving to godforsaken Toronto.' (I add that particular adjective for dramatic effect; it's not godforsaken at all, but anything to plant a seed of doubt in her head . . .) 'Why can't you change jobs within the company, get one where you don't have to travel, and stay here?'

'I could. I could switch from being a trader and move into shipping, or some other function. Yee, that's exciting! Shipping! Whoo-ee! My dream job.' She pulls a face. 'Not! No, if I'm changing jobs, I'm changing everything. A whole new start somewhere else.' She nudges me playfully. 'But I've had a cool idea.' She takes my hand between both of hers. 'You could come with me, given that you've just quit your job too. We could have a whole new start together.'

'What?' I laugh, claiming my hand back. 'You're not serious?'

'I'm perfectly serious. I'm gonna sell my condo, buy a small place out there. You could move in with me, don't pay anything until you find a job, and then when you get on your feet again, we'll take it from there.'

Toronto is where Jonathan and I met when I first came to Canada and I didn't have a bean to live on, and I ate macaroni cheese every night and made all my telephone calls from payphones so I didn't have to actually own a phone myself. I can see memories of that first flush of love breaking out all over Toronto – every corner, every crevice, we were there, throwing ourselves at that city, falling in love. Toronto is where Jonathan's family live, who I never particularly got on with, who I rarely hear from any more. How could I move there and not call them? And how could I sit at their dinner table if Jonathan wasn't there? Besides, Toronto is sodding freezing in the winter, and a sauna in the summer. 'I'm not sure Toronto's for me again, Sherrie. It'd feel like a backwards step. It's not where I want to be.'

'Oh, and Vancouver is, right? What have you got here, Ange? Nothing. And if you were in Toronto, if nothing else you'd be five hours closer to your mother.'

I shake my head. 'I could see us becoming like an old married couple. Or a couple of lesbians. All we'd need would be the cat. We'd take turns making dinner. We'd probably even go on holidays together.'

'I'm good at oral sex.'

'Urgh!'

She looks serious for a moment. 'Okay, forget the oral sex. Would it be so bad, you and I sharing a place? Say we never happened to find men and we only had each other. Would that be so terrible?'

I glare at her. 'Yes! Terrible's putting it mildly!'

She laughs. 'I'm going to try real hard not to take that personally.'

I shake my head at her. She can't leave! Not when I love her so much. 'Well, I just want you to know something, Sherrie. If I were going to turn lesbian, it'd be for you, honey, it'd be you all the way.'

'Well, hon, the feeling is mutual.'

She stands up and picks her bike off the ground. 'Let's go, before my ass seizes up and I can't get back on this thing again.' She swings a leg over her seat, looks at me still sitting there on the grass. 'Promise me you'll think about it.'

I get up and dust off my bum and the backs of my legs. 'I'll think,' I tell her.

But I've already thought.

'So?' I say to my mam.

'So, what?'

'You know what. Have you been yet?'

'To the toilet?'

'Not to the bloody toilet! To the doctors!'

'I've been. So there. Are you proud of me? He ran some blood tests. And he increased my Beautiful Pretty pills. And he said that my blue cardigan matched my eyes. Now, can we say no more on this?'

'So what does he think it can be?'

'I think if he knew that he'd have not run tests.'

I tut. 'When will you get the results?'

'In a couple of weeks.'

'A couple of weeks? That's ages! Can't they do it faster? How are you feeling, anyway? Have you had any more dizziness? You haven't felt faint, have you?'

She groans. 'Twaddlesticks! Ring back when you want to talk about the weather.'

She hangs up on me!

Given that I am now effectively unemployed, I take a small and desperate step in the right direction. There's an unpacked box that's marked 'Office' and somewhere inside it, I believe, are my business cards, the ones I had printed for Write Strategies before Jonathan died. All I have to do is find them.

There's also a load of other crap in here too: old CVs, a box of printer paper, an outdated telephone directory, old birthday cards sent to me from Jonathan – I quickly read these, forcing myself not to dwell on his writing or to think that his hands would have touched this card, or to think that the last time I read it, he'd have been alive. Then there's something I don't recognise: a thick, dark grey ring-binder with a black spine. The cover reads:

Write Strategies
A Business Plan
(prepared by Jonathan Chapman, for Angela Chapman)

I fan through the pages and tabulated sections: Background, Overview, Description, Market Analysis, Marketing Plan . . .

He'd told me a million times to get off my backside and write a business plan. He'd obviously given up on me and decided to write one himself. He must have been going to surprise me with it.

When I was packing to move, I must have been so distracted that I didn't even notice it.

I hug the binder to my chest. Is this Jonathan's way of telling me that now I don't have any excuses?

I can't believe we're already into August. I have Jonathan's list of contacts at about one hundred of Vancouver's mid-size to big businesses. Everything from software, which I know nothing about (just like accounting firms, law firms and engineering firms), to marketing firms, which I do have a handle on, and a hot-house tomato-growing company; I'm the first to get excited over a lovely tomato.

I know what my costs will be if I do a direct-mailer. I know how much it is to run quarter-page and full-page ads in leading industry publications like *Marketing* magazine or the Law Society rag. It's a fortune, really, or at least it is for me, but I'm not going to think of the downsides just yet. I know what my call-back strategy is. I've just forked out the fee and joined the Vancouver Board of Trade. I can wear the suit I'm glad I never took back.

And if all fail, U can join me in olive oil business. Georgios writes on MSN Messenger. Georgios and I have emailed a few times now.

U serious? I type furiously.

Very.

Tempting . . . Of course it's not. Not really. Not now that Georgios is getting it on with my ma. Speaking of: I decide to be out with it. *R U in luv with my mother?*

His reply is a little slow. *She not in luv with me.*

How do U know? I bang out.

Again, a pause or two. *Ask Her.*

'I have something to tell you,' Richard looks at me quite seriously across a small, trendy, trattoria table.

'Oh, God, don't tell me you're moving away too!'

I never normally meet Richard for lunch. Today, though, I was in the area where Richard's (and formerly Jonathan's) office is, and thought I'd pop in. I've only been up there once since Jonathan died. I remember how odd it was, at the time, walking into his once cluttered office that was bereft of files and papers. There was only a lone, misshapen paper-clip on the clean surface. Jonathan had a habit of unbending them when he was stressed.

Going up there today was still strange for me. Jonathan's office has been taken over by an articling student fresh out of the University of British Columbia. David is his name. There was a moment's delay in my smile when he walked out of his door to greet me, and held out his hand. I looked past him, thinking maybe Jonathan has been working really, really long hours; that's why he hasn't been home in two years . . . Maybe I'm going to look in there and see him.

Richard fidgets a lot – with the napkin, with a knife; he picks up a bread bun, puts it down, pushes back the flop of auburn hair from his forehead. 'I'm not moving away, exactly. But I am moving out. Or at least, I'm thinking of it.'

I blink. 'Out?'

'I'm leaving Jessica.'

'You're leaving Jessica?' The woman I never saw him with in the first place. Why am I thoroughly shocked and yet not at all surprised?

'I don't know what to say,' I tell him.

'I suppose *why* would be the obvious question . . . And the answer would be because I don't love her. Maybe I never did. Not real love, like the kind I know Jonathan felt for you.' He stops fiddling. 'She doesn't love me, either. I've asked myself, if we were stripped of everything we owned, would she still want to be with me? And the answer I keep coming up with is no.'

'But it can't be about money. She's making her own good money now.'

'Yes, but if you take away all the trappings – it doesn't matter who earned what . . .' He indicates with a sweep of his hand the table, the wine and the plates that held the Cornish game hen and smoked sablefish he made us order, which I thought was a bit lavish for lunch; I almost got the feeling he was celebrating something. What? Surely not this? 'There's nothing there,' he finishes. 'Our marriage was founded on my ability to take care of her.' He shrugs. 'Of course, I always knew that. She always knew she was pretty and she'd never marry a poor man, and she didn't really have passion to stick it in a job. I'm sure she knew she'd go to the highest bidder. Only maybe right when she met me, there weren't all that many bidding, for whatever reason, so somehow I won. She decided she'd do okay with me.'

He sees me smile. 'Sorry,' I tell him. 'It's just odd making it sound like a night out at the casino.'

'Not kind, you mean?'

'I suppose.'

He shrugs. 'She once told me she was lazy, that's why she never wanted to date lots of men; she just couldn't be bothered. And I let her be lazy, certainly when it came to the idea of her working. I even encouraged her to do nothing, even though I suppose I knew that she always looked bored, as though all her free time was a chore. I just thought that was her – she was just too well-off, and too ungrateful.' He looks at me sadly. 'I think we all might have underestimated her.'

'Were you very much in love with her?' He always seemed to be. From the moment I met them, even though they'd already been married a while by then.

'No. I thought I should be. I think that, quite secretly, I wanted to land her. And once I did, I tried to keep the myth alive.'

'I've never heard you talk like this.'

He smiles. 'I never wanted her to have her breasts done, you know.'

'You didn't?' Jonathan and I had plenty to speculate on when the date for her surgery just happened to fall on Richard's birthday.

'I'm more of a legs man. Her breasts were fine as they were.'

'But they look good.' I remember her once telling me, quite seriously, how she'd rather be dead than ugly.

'They irritate me. I don't know why . . .' His eyes very quickly go to my chest, as though he might be about to say something, although I can't imagine what. But instead he says, 'Do you want a coffee? Or we could always go somewhere else and have one?'

'Let's have one here.'

He seems remarkably laid-back. 'Angie, our marriage is like the empty box once the big diamond ring has been taken out of it. There's no substance in it. There's nothing fundamentally there. Just walls, sides, packaging, that keep us together.'

'Does she feel like this too?'

'Oh, I'm sure she does, without saying it. We don't talk. We don't share things with each other any more.'

I wonder if he's worried that now she's making her own money, she might leave him. Does Richard need to be the provider? Her certainly likes to try to take care of me.

He orders two cappuccinos for us, and a vanilla *crème brûlée*.

'What about Emma?' I ask him.

He shakes his head. 'I think without Emma, Jessica and I would have split up after about two years, once I'd got over being flattered that a woman as attractive as her would be interested in a plain guy like me.' He looks off into the distance. 'I mean, for God's sakes, I've got red hair.'

I almost laugh. 'It's not red! It's a sort of burnished chestnut!'

He smiles.

'Sorry, I've made you sound like a description on a hair-colouring kit.'

He smiles again.

'I like it,' I tell him. 'Your hair colour.'

'Do you?'

'Very much.' And I like his hazel eyes. And I like him.

'You know, we can't even sit down and agree on a DVD to rent on a Friday night! That's how polarised our interests are. That's how intense and inflexible we've turned. I think when you're not in love, you blame the other one; you start to get resentful, as though, rather than it being nobody's fault in particular, it's very pointedly theirs.'

Richard is quite a deep person, for a guy, I think. I wonder if he'd have talked to Jonathan like this. Whenever we'd get together as a foursome, he always seemed to gravitate to me for conversation. But then again, he did see Jonathan every day.

We don't speak while the waiter puts our cups and dessert down. 'Have you missed not being in love all these years?' I ask him. I couldn't imagine staying in a loveless marriage. And I'm pretty sure Jonathan would have felt the same. If we'd have fallen out of love, that would have been it: over.

He sits back, stares at the single rosette of cream on top of the *brûlée*. 'Just because I wasn't in love with her doesn't mean I haven't been in love with anybody in all these years.'

I don't want to learn he's had an affair, if this is what he's getting at. For some reason, in spite of everything he's just said, that would disappoint me. 'What are you going to do?' I ask instead.

He shakes his head, looks at me now. When I think he's not going to answer that, he says, 'I'm going to try to make some wrongs right before it's too late for everybody.' He takes a drink of his coffee. 'Does that sound scary?'

I shrug. 'Brave, maybe.'

21

Vancouver's key players in the business community aren't easy to reach. Especially when their secretaries think I'm selling something. Which I suppose I am.

I'm just about to make my twentieth frustrating cold call of the day – I've netted exactly one brief conversation with an actual CEO, who told me he doesn't need my services at this time but he'll keep me on file (well, up his bottom too, as my mother would probably say) – when my phone rings.

'Hi, Angela, it's Crystal Rae.'

It takes me a moment to place the name.

'Epilepsy Canada.'

'Oh! Crystal! Sorry!' How embarrassing for me to forget who she is!

'That's all right,' she says. 'I'm glad I've caught you, anyway. Sorry it's taken a little while to get back to you . . . I was wondering if you'd like to meet with us again to discuss your role with us, and some of your ideas, a little further.'

I grab a notepad, and my diary/calendar, which is empty. I had dreamed that because I'd bought the thing, it might automatically fill itself with appointments. Or that Jonathan, if he could swing it from up there, could land me a few interviews so I might open my appointments page every morning and find that it had magically filled itself up. But not so far. I'm trying hard to get excited at the thought of volunteer work for Epilepsy Canada, but the need for a paycheque is starting to get palpable.

'I'd be thrilled to meet, Crystal! Just tell me when, and I can write up a bit of an agenda and email it to you if you think it might be helpful.' My old habit of over-committing to clients.

'That's great news. How is next Wednesday night for you? Say six thirty? Dinner – or at least a sandwich and pop – will be on us. And an agenda sounds good. Send it through.'

'Sounds good,' I parrot back. 'I'll look forward to it.'

We hang up and I take stock. Okay . . . I'm going to get up to my eyes in work that's probably the most worthwhile thing I've ever done, and will ensure me direct passage into heaven, but I'm doing it for free. I can just see myself – the only homeless person in Vancouver who sits in a doorway typing away marketing plans on their laptop.

Progress.

When I wake up on Sunday morning, I've had a very horny dream. It started out as a dream of Sean. We were in Vancouver and he and I were somehow together but we hadn't yet kissed, and I was anticipating the moment when we would. And then we were kissing. And it was lovely. Only somehow during the kiss, Sean became Richard. I was kissing Richard and enjoying it. It was so nice that my heart was throbbing; my stomach was tightening . . .

I wake up feeling like I literally have just been in a hot snog. I can feel the imprint of another person's mouth on my lips. The tingle is there in my pelvic region . . . yet I'm lying alone in bed, with a racing heart thinking about Richard in a way that I've never thought about him before. I try to go back to sleep, to pick up where I left off, but I can't, so I masturbate. Or try to. Something I've not done in God knows how long. Years. I stop after a few pathetic moments, thinking, *why am I doing this? It's not even feeling good.*

I'm just lying there, staring at the ceiling, when my phone rings.

'It's done. It's up for sale.'

I feel a thud of panic. 'Your condo?' I thought she wouldn't go through with it!

'No. The Telus Building . . . Of course my condo!' My friend lets out a blood-curdling squeal.

'Are you thrilled, or has somebody set you on fire?' I ask her.

'I'm thrilled!' She squeals again.

I wince and move the phone from my ear. 'But your fabulous Coal Harbour condo! You're selling it to move thousands of miles away to a godforsaken city that you don't even know you're going to like!'

'I do like it! I've been there many times on business.' She falls silent for a moment, then her tone changes. 'You're supposed to be my friend and be happy for me, Ange.'

I feel terrible. When I think how good she's been to me . . . 'I *am* happy for you! I'm happy for you being happy. But I'm sad for me. Does that make me a horrible person?' It's the God's honest truth. Even when I thought she was serious, I still didn't think she was *serious*. 'I'm going to miss you! What am I going to do without you?' A part of me is shamefully thinking if I can't pay my rent here any more, moving into her condo can't be my fall-back position if she's sold it. What's wrong with me? Why do I always need a fall-back position?

'But I'm never here to miss as it is, Ange! That's the whole problem. I'm never anywhere half the time. I used to despise roots. But now I realise we need them, because they feed us, don't they? Without them, we'll . . . we're just slowly starving ourselves.'

'That's poetic!'

'I know. I've been working on it.'

When I sold our house, Sherrie offered for me to move in with her. I didn't do it, because I didn't want to be dependent on her, to be sat there waiting for her to come back from her travels to save me from my grief and depression, to make her my replacement Jonathan. But I realise I am dependent on her. We do depend on our friends. We start to put our rights over them ahead of their rights over themselves; we have a strange marriage with them.

But the thing is, and I only realise this now: it's okay. If Sherrie goes, I will miss her desperately. But there are a few other things on my priority list that will take precedence over missing her.

'Have you given any more thought to what you're going to do for work?' I ask her.

'Dunno. May go on the market side. Trade futures. I know some people who've made the move . . . Actually, you won't believe the timing – I got headhunted for Lantic Sugar in Toronto. Just the other day.'

I instantly picture trips to sugar plantations in far-flung exotic corners of Hawaii or the Caribbean. 'That sounds fabulous!'

'No, it's not, though! I don't want to trade sugar. That would just be same shit, different heap.'

'So you turned it down, I take it? God, I wish I had your luxury!'

'I said, sling it, man. Just sling your sugar trading job. Angela, dear girl, I'm very focused on what I want. Or rather, I'm certain of what I *don't* want. A bit like you. You knew the minute your feet walked into that building that you didn't want to work for a top ad agency any more.'

'I'm flattered you think that makes us alike . . . But aren't you apprehensive, even a little bit?'

'Not in the way you mean. Not bad apprehensive. Good apprehensive. You know, the other night I was thinking about myself and my life, and I realised something interesting. I'm a lucky person, because I've never really known what unhappiness is. I've had the best years of my life in this job. If I could have had the exotic job and the husband and family and a base I could feel was truly home . . . Or if I could have had the crazy career and all the fun and not grown a year older, then I could ditch it all, still be the same age, and be able to go out and get the husband and the kid and the house and the dog . . . then it'd have been perfect. But life's not like that, is it? It's only now that I'm starting to feel unhappy with things – or maybe 'frustrated' is a better word. And I don't wanna feel that. I want to move on to new happiness. Just like you're doing.'

'Is that how you see me? As moving on to new happiness?'

She seems to think about this. 'Slowly. But yes, I think you are. And I think that even you yourself probably know it, deep down.'

'I suppose I am, Sherrie. I was thinking the other day that I'm starting to see Jonathan not as somebody I lost, but as somebody I gained . . . Does that make any sense?'

'It makes more than sense,' she says. 'It makes music to my ears, my friend.'

When I hang up, I look around my floor that's got pieces of paper, and lists, and phone directories, and letterheads, and attempted designs for my website all over the place. Argh . . . I put my head back and bite my bottom lip, and try to distance myself from the chaos.

I love what she said about me moving on to new happiness. I wish I could inscribe the very concept on black velvet, put it in a cute little picture frame, and hang it above my bed. Or above the loo: *Angela is moving on to new happiness*.

Am I really, though?

I wish we could all have an inbuilt green light that would come on to show us that the choices we are making are right. But all we have is our hearts, and our hunches.

I suppose I have a good hunch.

*   *   *

'Have you heard anything?' I get up at 6 a.m. to call my mam because she's been on my mind all night.

'Oh, not this again!'

'If you don't want me to give a damn about you, I won't.'

'Can I have that in writing?'

Before I can reply, she says, 'I have had the results, actually. I went this morning.'

I feel a sinking dread. 'Yeah? And?'

'They've found some abnormality. They want to do the tests again.'

I want to press delete, and erase the words. 'What's an abnormality?' I ask, with a choking sensation in my throat.

'Well, it means something's not quite right.'

I tut. 'Yes, I know that! I mean, didn't he say what it was?'

'No.'

'Didn't you ask?' My volume climbs.

'No. He said it was some abnormality with my blood . . .'

The word 'leukaemia' strides through my brain.

'He didn't seem overly concerned,' she says. 'I'm sure it's nothing.'

'How can you be so dismissive?' In that instant I think I'll never be able to live with the idea of my mam having cancer.

'What's the point of being anything else until we know for certain? Anyway, on another topic . . . I've got a bit of a dilemma I could use your input on. Georgios wants to see me again. He wants me to go there again.'

'You can't!'

'Thanks, I'll remember that.'

'Not until you get your test results back.'

'I know. Keep your tresses on. Anyway . . . I'm not going, I don't think, am I?'

'I don't know! Why are you asking me?' I remember what Georgios said I should ask her. 'Mam, tell me something. Are you in love with him?'

'No,' she says, like that didn't take much thinking about.

'Okay.' I didn't expect her to be so blunt. Poor Georgios. 'I think you're mad, if you want my opinion. What's wrong with him?'

'Nothing!'

'Well, if nothing's wrong, then . . . I don't understand.'

She's quiet for a bit. 'There's no future with him, is there?' she eventually says.

'Why not?'

'Because I'm sixty and he's forty-five, Angela.'

'What's wrong with that? He's clearly not bothered. He likes older women.'

'Yes, but will he still like me when I'm eighty and he's only in his mid-sixties?'

I smile. 'He might like you more! Or then again, he might trade you in for a ninety-year-old. Now wouldn't that be an insult?'

'You shouldn't make fun of old age. One day that'll be you, then the shoe will be on the other foot.'

'Oh, Mam! Why don't you just wait until you get your results, then if everything's good, go there, stay for the harvest, pick the olives, have a fantastic time, have a bonk, come home, and if that's it and you don't want to see him again, tell him.'

'Have a *what?*'

'A bonk.'

'Angela!' I hear her smile. 'I don't bonk. I'm too ladylike to bonk.'

'What do you do, then?' I fish. 'I'm curious. Tell me.'

Of course I know she's not going to answer.

*   *   *

In Stanley Park, I'm surprised to run into Richard and Emma. They spot me first. Or, rather, Emma does. I hear the patter of tiny feet approaching ever closer behind me, and when I turn, her little hand is just reaching out to surprise-tap me on the shoulder.

'Emma!' I light up, and look up to see Richard standing there, smiling at me, in a very special way. His face is a little flushed. It crosses my mind that he's blushing. And then so too does the thought. Something I think a part of me has always known: Richard is in love with me.

No sooner does the realisation hit me, than his eyes confirm it. For a moment, neither of us speaks. Then it becomes patently obvious that one of us should say something.

'Hi,' I say.

'Hi,' he says back.

Then the tension becomes so thick you could slice it.

I look at him, trying to see him with new eyes: as a man, not just as Jonathan's best friend. 'Richard . . .' I try to force offhandedness, try to not be bothered by the way he's looking at me.

He seems to snap himself out of it and throws up his hands. 'Of all the parks, in all the world, you had to be walking in this one . . .' He comes and gives my cheek a quick kiss.

It takes me a moment before I notice the tiny black puppy that sets about chomping on the top of my foot, its teeth like razors. 'Ooooh!' I bend down to pet it. 'Is it a he or a she?' I ask Emma.

'She's a he. I mean . . .' She slaps a hand over her giggle. 'She's a she. She's called Spot.'

'Spot?' I laugh as the dog's little wet nose sniffs my hand and then she decides to take a bite out of it too. God, those teeth hurt!

'Because of the marking on her ear,' Emma supplies, just as I register the little white splash that looks like her black ear has been dipped in white paint.

'She's beautiful. How old is she?' I feel Richard's eyes on me intensely.

'Nine weeks.'

'Emma's birthday present,' Richard says, kneeling down and petting the dog, his leg, with its auburn fuzz, not far from mine. I think of the very odd dream I had, Richard's ever steady presence throughout my getting over Jonathan, and then suddenly everything seems to point to one obvious question: has Jonathan sent me Richard? After all, isn't it reasonable to think that Jonathan would want to see me with someone he knew well, trusted and thought highly of? Is this why Richard is leaving Jessica, and I've just realised that Richard has always been in love with me? Is my destiny to be with my husband's best friend slowly unfolding now, right before my eyes?

I snap back to the present. 'Oh, no! Did I miss her birthday?'

'Don't worry,' he says, combing me with his gaze. 'It's next Saturday. Only we had to bring the puppy home yesterday from the shelter, and we realised we really couldn't keep her hidden for a week without Emma finding out she was there. They can only manage those sorts of perfect family moments in the movies.'

Perfect family moments . . . Yes, why would he be bringing a puppy into their home right when they're splitting up? To make it easier for Emma?

'Ten is a very important age,' Emma tells me, and I run a hand over her long, sleek hair, lifting it up off her shoulders, holding it back like a ponytail, thinking, if she were mine, I'd love her to bursting point.

'Walk with us?' Richard asks, looking at my face, steadily.

I hesitate. 'Erm . . . sure.'

We walk in silence for a while, before he says, 'Are you okay? You seem . . .' He doesn't finish.

'I'm fine.' I glance at him but can't meet his eyes, so I bring my attention to the path ahead. Emma and Spot walk on in front, Emma clearly proud by how many ooh's and aah's her new puppy is attracting.

'How are you, though, really? It seems when we went out last week all we did was talk about me.' He asks it in the intimate way of a friend. (Subconsciously, I hear my mam: *Why is it that Canadians always want to know how you are? Do they all have a doctor complex?*)

'Oh, I'm fine. Sometimes I get a bit panicked, thinking maybe I should have hung onto a regular pay-cheque while I had it, but no, generally, I'm okay, I think.'

He studies me closely. Richard's eyes always brim with affection for me; they did from day one. But I always thought that's all it was. I feel guilty for the fact that it might always have been something else.

'I've made some headway with Write Strategies,' I tell him. 'You'd be proud of me. And I'm just trying to contact Kevin. Remember he worked for a design house? I'm hoping he might give me a cheap price for doing a website. I feel that if I can't put 'www' on my letterhead, I'm not real yet; I don't exist. When we're born, we should be given a web address as well as a name, shouldn't we?'

He laughs. 'Are you excited about it?'

Little Spot stops to sniff a black Lab's pee, and Emma pulls her back. 'Gross!' she says.

'I think so. But I'm nervous, too, because I need some money coming in soon.'

He looks uncomfortable, just as uncomfortable as the day he forced me to take nearly eighty thousand dollars from the law firm to help me from going into default on my mortgage. I instantly regret bringing up the word money.

'You know, if it's money you need, Angie—'

'Thanks, Richard, but I'm going to fend for myself this time.'

'Well, you know you can always think of me as your last resort.'

'You're a first-class, five-star resort, Richard, you really are.' I pop a friendly kiss on his cheek.

We walk in silence for a while, Richard keeping a close eye on Emma as the scampering Spot drags her all over the place. The understanding that passed between us earlier seems to linger there, as this sort of thing would. It's all made somehow clearer, and yet more blurred, when he says, 'I'm not leaving her.' He stops walking and holds my gaze. 'Don't misunderstand me. It's not that I no longer want to, or that anything I told you was untrue . . . It's just . . . there's what I want to do, Angie, and there's what I'm going to do . . .' He gestures to Emma's back. 'How can I tell her that there's no real reason why her mother and I are splitting up, we're just wrong for each other, and expect her to understand? And expect her to not hate me?' Emma turns around and looks at us, like she's got some sort of inkling that we're talking about her, so we start walking again.

I think of my mother. If she'd said she was leaving my dad, I think I would have understood. But not at ten. I'd have needed to have my own first taste of demolishing disillusionment before I could have understood somebody else's. 'I guess you can't. She's too young.'

'It was a moment of my imagination running wild,' he says. His arm innocently grazes mine as he moves aside to let some speed-walkers pass. He must feel the contact too, but he doesn't move away. 'I briefly got carried away with hoping for something that might be. Only now, of course, I can see it's very unlikely, if not completely unrealistic.' We stop walking again. He looks at me. Was I just fantasising that Jonathan might have sent me his best friend, because I secretly want

Richard? Or, at least, I want the comfort zone and the safety net of him? Is that why I was kissing him in my dream?

His eyes are studying, regretful, and full of his customary kindness. 'Do you have any idea what I'm talking about?' he asks me.

We know each other too well for lies. 'Yes. I think I do.'

In bed, I talk to Jonathan for the first time in ages: 'You have to make something good happen for me soon.' I don't know what I want or expect him to do any more, only making a general plea can't be a bad thing. He always knew me long before I really knew myself.

Today, I got a bank statement from the machine, and I was shocked to see how anaemic my balance looked without my regular two-week injection of cash. Also, today there were no new messages: not on my email, not on my phone. I've made 'personal' contact – that is, spoken to a real person – with forty-one real companies, all of whom were pleased for me to send them my bio and information, but not one has called back to hire my services. It crosses my mind – for one mad moment – to call David and ask for my old job back. At least sitting on a couch all day listening to him drone on about his past fantasticness isn't so bad if he's paying me to do it.

No, Angie. What sort of a cop-out is that? I imagined Jonathan saying. Sometimes I think Jonathan is driving fire into my brain. Yet I'm lying here asking him to help me, and what sort of response am I getting? None.

The progress of the day is that Kevin is going to do me a fantastic website, and he's not going to charge me. He got evicted from our basement when the new owners moved in, for playing his music too loud. This made me smile. I remember the night Jonathan and I got back from Barbados, the day before he died. We lay in bed trying to sleep, the heavy metal boom of Kevin's sound system downstairs seeming to shake our whole house.

'You wouldn't mind if it was a tune, but it's just noise, isn't it?' Jonathan breathed heavily. 'We may have to kick his ass out, Angie. I mean, it's one thing to have the extra grand a month rent, but I can't go to work on three hours' sleep because some fucker likes to play heavy metal till five in the morning. I think this weekend I'm going to have a small talk with master Kevin.'

I'd seen Jonathan and his small talks. They usually consisted of him pinning somebody to a wall by the skin of their shoulder-blades. I promised him I'd have a word with Kevin instead, even though I knew Jonathan wouldn't really kick him out, because Jonathan knew Kevin didn't have a great deal of money, and Jonathan had a soft heart, even though he'd hate you saying that about him. He'd forgiven Kevin's late rent cheques on more than a couple of occasions. And Kevin knew Jonathan was one of life's good guys.

I never got around to having the talk with Kevin. The next time I spoke to him was to tell him that Jonathan was dead.

'I won't charge you a dime,' Kevin told me when I met him for coffee this morning. 'I think you guys could have thrown me out long ago, but you didn't. I think I owe you.' He smiled at me. 'This one's for Jonathan.'

Argh, but good news is always offset by bad news, isn't it? This morning, when I wake up, after very little sleep from having so much on my mind last night, I pick up the mail from downstairs. In my hand are two envelopes. I rarely get envelopes these days, at least not proper ones. It's mostly junk mail, or direct mail campaigns from charities. (Ooh, something to discuss with Epilepsy on Wednesday: the cost/benefit of a mail drop. *Budget*, I make a mental note. I've got to get them to talk about money, then we know what we've got to work with.)

I look at my two non-junk pieces of correspondence. One is from a law firm whose name I don't recognise. The second is my Royal Bank statement.

I plonk myself down in the chair.

I really don't need to find out how poor I am again today. So I open the law firm envelope first.

22

They've recently put Venetian blinds up at the windows – they weren't there when I came to visit Ms Elmtree before I went to England. I used to have sheer white curtains up. Nets, my mam called them.

'They're not nets!' I remember correcting her. 'They're Thai silk sheer drapes! They cost a damned packet.'

'I could have sent you the same thing from Sunderland for an eighth of the price, including postage.' (Loaded pause where I felt another jab at Canada coming.) 'Do they rip you off EVERYWHERE you go in Canada, Angela? Or do they just have a particular pen-shant for home furnishings?'

I try not to look in their windows, but to focus, instead, on the house opposite: old Ms Elmtree's. The garden's a mess now: dandelions all over the lawn. Jonathan used to mow it for her when he did ours. The grass is dry and long, because since she died nobody's been in to look after it.

I do her trick with the sticky garden gate – lifting and wiggling – walk up the path, and sit on the front step, looking across at the house where Jonathan and I used to live.

The will was quite straightforward, according to the lawyer. Ms Elmtree had no family. The house was to go to me. Whatever little money there was in the bank was to be donated to the Emily Carr Institute of Art and Design.

This house, this place where an old woman lived, across from the place where I lived with my husband, is mine. It takes some sinking in.

I take the key I collected when I went to the lawyer's office to sign the transfer, and go inside. It's strange being in her house without her here. I walk the narrow, creaky hardwood passage into the living room, half expecting to hear her whistling kettle in the kitchen. Because the place still feels lived in – it still feels like she's here. It doesn't feel like death. I feared it would. I feared this place would feel like death and our old house opposite would look like death. But neither of them does. They feel remarkably like . . . life.

I stare at all the paintings on her walls. The Gauguin rip-offs. She obviously really admired him to claim she was related to him. Now they're mine. I can't exactly flog them on eBay. Maybe I can donate them to a community centre or somewhere where they might get displayed for a while.

I've never been upstairs in Ms Elmtree's house. The stairs creak, as much as the main level floors. But it's a wide staircase with a big landing up top, and a skylight from which I see cloudless blue sky. The corridor is surprisingly narrow and uncharming, but it leads off to three bedrooms – one quite large with another skylight above the bed, a spare room, and then a room she had converted into an artist's studio. I go into the master bedroom, wondering whose idea it would have been to put a skylight over a bed: obviously not somebody who needed complete darkness to fall asleep. Someone who liked to connect with heaven? I wonder what it'd be like to lie down every night staring at the sky and the stars.

Maybe it would be very nice.

'I might have to sell,' I tell Richard and Jessica. We're sharing a bottle of wine at my apartment – an invitation that's long overdue. I did consider avoiding Richard for a bit. But he'd know what I was doing, and that would only make matters worse. 'I don't think I can take living there, looking across the street all the time.'

'Ditch it and buy a condo.' Jessica examines her gel-nails as she sits on my sofa. 'You could probably get something brand new downtown with what you'll get for the old house. Imagine brand-new granite countertops. Stainless steel appliances. It'd be small – you're obviously not gonna get a penthouse. But after all, there's only you.'

'Thanks,' I tell her.

Richard and I glance at each other. Jessica is off in a smiling daydream. 'You'd be mortgage free,' she says. 'Imagine that. Everything you earn is yours to spend. Think of all the clothes you could buy . . .'

'Or you could stay,' Richard says, clearly sensing Jessica is saying all the wrong things and I might jump on her and attack her in about two seconds' time. 'You could move in, give it a few nips and tucks to get it looking like it's your place and not her place, and see how you feel then.' He studies my lack of obvious enthusiasm. 'As your self-appointed financial advisor, Angie, I am urging you not to sell. The market's on the upswing. You could be doing yourself out of a nice little profit if you don't hang on to it for a while longer.' He chinks his glass to mine and smiles, only the smile is thin and some sadness seems to lurk behind it.

Sherrie and I sit on Ms Elmtree's front lawn, drinking a bottle of champagne from two polystyrene cups, getting slightly curious looks from people as they pass by: my potential new neighbours.

Sherrie insisted we go round to the house to 'christen' it, even though I told her I'm still not sure I'm keeping it. She wouldn't sit inside, though. 'It reeks of old woman!' she said. She's got a plastic bag with another bottle of champers in it. But this one's to toast her leaving. She's off in two weeks. It's come around so fast.

'We can't drink two bottles,' I tell her. 'We're not a couple of piss-tanks.'

'Speak for yourself!' she says, and tops me up a little too keenly. Golden fizz froths over the poly cup, decadently watering the grass.

'Don't spill it, then! For God's sake . . .' I admonish her. 'Here,' I hold my glass out to her, 'top up what you spilt.'

The garden is an absolute disaster, even worse than when I saw it last, because we just had some relentless rain and then a few days of sunshine. The grass is about two feet long, and weeds are strangling all the once lovely plants in the borders. We talk about everything, including my thought that, if I do decide to keep this place, I could bring my mother here to live with me.

'Do you want to graduate onto the concrete step?' I ask her, when we're almost through our first bottle, and I want to follow the last patch of the evening sun.

So we do. And then we find ourselves with two very sore bums. 'You gotta get better patio furniture than this, hon!' Sherrie says. A pleasant-looking man walks past us with his black Lab, looks across the stone wall, and smiles. Sherrie's gaze follows him down the street.

'Couldn't you handle some nice sex right about now?' she asks me, and lies back, awkwardly settling herself against the step, tilting her face up to the last of the evening rays.

'I haven't thought about it in a while,' I lie, still remembering my confused but horny dream and the very odd business with Richard.

'That's not the answer to the question.'

I glance at her lying back like that with her eyes shut.

'Yes,' I tell her. 'Okay, yes, I could handle it.'

She opens her eyes, turns her head slightly, looks at me. 'So, what are you going to do about it?'

I scowl. 'What *can* I do about it? Call upon Jonathan to send me a lover? I tried that once. It didn't work.'

She sits up, rubs her back and says, 'Man, I'm uncomfortable.'

I titter. 'Me too.'

She sits cross-legged, gripping her champagne cup between her knees. 'Start giving off "available" signals. If a nice man walking a black Labrador looks at you in a certain way, give him it back, hon. Don't look so unapproachable.'

'What? Him? Oh, I'm sure he'll be married with a couple of kids.'

'That's perfect.'

'Give over. No it isn't.'

'If you're scared of falling in love again, Ange, a married man will at least get you back in the sack. And if he doesn't really have feelings for you, but he's bored at home, he'll really go for it. It could be a lotta fun.'

'Seriously, can we . . .'

'Change the subject?' She delves in the plastic bag, pulls out the second bottle. With some deft manoeuvrings, she pops the cork. 'You need lube-ing up,' she tells me. 'Don't worry, we've a bottle to go. Who knows what might be along in the meantime?' She cranes her neck down the street. 'Irish Wolfhound approaching with one tall, dark—'

'Stop it!' I elbow her and we giggle as we thrust out our glasses to catch the drops.

That night, I fall asleep thinking of kindness. Yes, Jonathan was good to Ms Elmtree when he sued the property developer for her. And yes, I used to run to Safeway and get her the odd bag of groceries. I only lived beside her little more than eighteen months, yet looking at her, I saw what my mother could become in twenty-five years. Essentially family-less and left to her own devices. And I hoped that anything I might do for my elderly neighbour might somehow get done for my mother, through some sort of divine karma. I might not believe in promises made by dead husbands any more, but I do believe in karma . . . But still, was our little bit of neighbourly kindness enough to deserve being left a house? I remember the strange way she told me about Jonathan sitting in his car. I wonder if he ever told her about losing all our money; if she knew more than she was letting on. Then again, she knew I was forced to sell our house, so maybe that's why she came to my rescue. But the lawyer told me when the will was written. It was before I sold.

Maybe I'll never truly know how I've come to inherit a house. Maybe sometimes it's best not to wonder too much.

'I don't usually think creatively in the shower,' I tell the room, 'but an idea did come to me the other morning that I think might carry the right mix of message and drama that we are looking for in a campaign approach.'

It's my third meeting with Epilepsy Canada. Our previous two discussed strategy, and now we've moved on to the bit that everybody likes and wants to get their hands on: the fun part, what the campaign's going to look like. My art boards with my terrible attempt at drawing lie face down on the boardroom table, alongside cold coffee and a plate of peanut butter cookies, in this tiny room on a warm late summer evening.

Crystal, Bill, Giles and Kye, the good-looking PE teacher, are present. I notice – again – that Kye has a habit of rotating his pencil. I remember it annoying me in the first meeting. I wonder if it's because I'm boring him. The upshot is, though, it makes me look at his hands. They're evenly tanned, with long, quite artistic fingers and very clean, pink nails. Somehow you could look at those hands in isolation and know that the owner of them would be a very fit, fresh and attractive young fellow in his twenties: a PE teacher, perhaps; maybe of Nordic descent.

'With the limited media that we can afford' – focus, Angela, focus – 'we need a singular, powerful message that will take epilepsy right into the hearts and minds of a broad target base – everyone from young people to old. It's a lot to ask of—'

The pencil comes sailing out of Kye's hand, as though he's flicked it right at me.

'Any single, visual message,' I finish, trying not to react.

'Sorry 'bout that,' he says, and lunges across the table to get his pencil back.

Bill titters.

I've lost my train of thought. 'Erm . . . remembering . . . yeah . . . that . . . the bus shelter ads and the limited print media campaign are there mainly for awareness and to trigger a call to action, I think a powerful creative route would be to go with . . .' I unveil my three feet by three feet whiteboard. . . . 'Ta-da!' I skim their faces, their looks of surprise and engagement.

In the centre of my whiteboard I have drawn an image of the human brain. The brain is all rigged up like a bomb hooked up to a detonator. Underneath, in bold black type, is the simple tagline: Living With Epilepsy.

Kye whistles. Crystal smiles. Bill scowls and wags his pen at the board. 'Don't we need to have more writing to say that living with epilepsy means your brain is essentially a ticking time bomb? Which basically tells them—'

I shake my head. 'The image says that. The line says that. You don't need to explain the obvious. In advertising, less is definitely more. All we need is a line underneath indicating the website, and the 1–800 number – the call to action. Powerful advertising demands – and will get – action.'

'I agree,' says Crystal. 'If you have to explain the joke, then you're assuming the listener is slow.'

'I think it's very good,' Giles says. 'Powerful.'

'It kicks butt,' Kye adds, which makes me smile.

'Let me show you how I see it translating to the website,' I tell them, now that I seem to have them on-side . . .

As I'm packing up my stuff to go, Crystal says, 'Angela, may I talk to you? I've been meaning to call you and ask you how busy you are. I mean, with your work.'

Oh, God, I don't need more things to do that I'm not getting paid for. 'Oh, erm—' I'm crap at making up bullshit on my feet.

'The reason I ask, Angela, is that I'm very interested to talk about how Write Strategies could help me. It seems that half my staff at Zeit can't write as well as they think they can. I would quite like to talk about hiring your consultancy services.'

'You would?' I perk up. I catch Kye looking at me as he slowly puts papers in his bag, the last to leave the room.

'I don't know how it would all fit, but may I have my HR person call you tomorrow for a chat?'

I reach out and offer her my hand, trying to contain my glee behind an air of professionalism. 'I'll look forward to it.'

As I'm about to leave, she says, 'We're very impressed with you here. We're glad you came to us.'

I smile broadly. 'Thank you,' I tell her, and when I get out into the corridor where she can't see me, I dance up and down.

I walk out of the building into the early evening sunshine, still smiling. Kye is sitting on the wall. For a moment, I think he must be waiting for a ride from somebody. I stop a few feet in front of him. 'Sounds like you've got something to celebrate,' he says.

'My first client, possibly,' I beam. 'With a bit of luck.'

'*First* client?' He narrows his eyes at me, looking amused. 'But I thought you were a really successful writing coach.'

I smile again. 'It's called selling yourself. It's in the things you *don't* say.'

'I gotta remember that,' he says. 'You certainly had me convinced.'

'Have a good night,' I tell him, giving him a quick glance over before I start walking.

'Hold up a minute,' he says, after I've gone a few steps. I stop, turn around. 'Would you like to go get some real dinner? Something a bit more substantial than peanut butter cookies?'

When I don't immediately answer, he says, 'Maybe even a beer with it?'

He's hard inside me.

Definitely more substantial than peanut butter cookies.

Different to Jonathan. I'd almost forgotten what variety is like. I can't quite believe how fast I fell into the sack. This might actually be an all-time record. If you don't count Jonathan.

His body is even nicer with his clothes off. We stick and slather, and then he moves away from me to admire my body. His heart isn't into it, of course. I know that. But his body is. I'd forgotten what sex is like without love.

It's good.

He isn't into my feet, doesn't care to kiss my toes, or the backs of my knees, or the inside of my elbows. But he goes a long time, and the rhythm is nice.

'I'm one half German and one half Swedish, actually,' he says when we're finished, answering the question I asked him about an hour ago, just as we stepped inside my apartment after a burger, fries and two beers apiece, and I invited him in for coffee. I didn't know if we were going to have sex. I have a feeling, though, that he knew. Especially when he didn't waste two seconds pulling me against my closed door, and slid his hands up under my T-shirt.

I laugh. I fall off him and flop onto the other side of the bed, and we lie there on our backs, panting and smiling. We lie like this for a few minutes, until we've recovered; it takes me longer than him – I'm obviously out of shape, or out of practice. My eyes skim over his bare chest, the handsome, quite devastatingly sparkling white teeth and blue eyes, as he props himself on an elbow and looks down at me. 'You're quite the surprise,' he says.

'I bet you're quite the PE teacher. I bet you have legions of lovesick teenagers after you.' It feels nice to flirt, to make silly, light conversation. He's so handsome that I almost feel intimidated lying naked beside him.

'Legions,' he jokes. 'No. Not really.' Then he smiles immodestly. 'Well, maybe one or two.' He likes himself. Sure he does. How could he not?

'I hated PE in school,' I tell him.

'Oh, don't tell me you were one of those girls who whines and gets prissy when they have to play soccer?' He shakes his head. 'I hate chicks that wimp out. I get really pissed off when they won't even make an effort, when they come whining with all their lame-ass excuses.'

'You're twenty-six,' I tell him, after a while of studying the healthy face, blond hair, blond eyebrows and lashes.

He strokes the inside of my thigh. 'Is there a reason you have to keep repeating my age?'

His fingers feel fantastic. What am I doing in bed with a twenty-six-year-old? I don't tell him he's the first person since my husband. I don't even mention Jonathan, and he doesn't either.

'So, do you have a girlfriend?' I ask him instead.

He looks the tiniest bit coy, and I don't know whether it's spontaneous or he's putting it on. 'Oh, not sure I want to answer that. Might incriminate me.'

'Go on.' I prod his chest. 'You must have one.'

'Off and on.'

'What's that mean?' I prod him a few more times. 'You mean off and on, as in sometimes you have a girlfriend?'

'I mean there is somebody. We're off and on.'

'What are you at this moment?'

He studies me, pretends to give my body the once-over. 'At this moment? Off. Definitely.' Before I can say any more, he quickly adds, 'Hey, I'm thinking of taking a year off and going to live in Sweden.'

'When?'

'Maybe after Christmas, depending if they'll let me at work.'

'That'll be good for you.'

How nice. He gets to go and bonk lots of Swedish girls . . . He draws circles around my breast now with his middle finger. I tingle again.

'Sooooo,' he says. 'Are we going to do this again?' He runs the finger down the centre of my stomach to my navel, then back up. I notice he doesn't ask much about me. In fact, very little, even over dinner. When we weren't talking about him, or things he wanted to talk about, we just ate in silence.

I push these negatives away. 'Yeah, right now mightn't be a bad plan.'

Sherrie splutters wine all down the front of herself. 'You didn't!'

'I did!' I grin at her across my couch, and point to my bedroom door. 'In there!'

'It makes perfect sense.' Her eyes go from my bedroom, back to me. 'I mean, if you're still nursing that idea that Jonathan's going to send you a lover, then yeah, of course, it all fits that he'd send you a handsome young Phys-Ed teacher who donates his free time to a worthy cause. I mean . . .' She looks up at the ceiling. 'Great job, Jonny baby! I never did like the idea of you sending her that weird Greek, or the married Brit with the wife who felt up a stripper. That sucked. But this one . . . I do believe you got it right this time.'

I stretch my legs out so my feet are on her lap, and dive into my wineglass again. We started off watching a rented DVD but it was lousy, so we packed it in after about twenty minutes and just sat talking instead, and cracked open another bottle of wine.

'What's he like, this Kye who Jonathan's sent you?'

Jonathan wouldn't send me Kye. 'In the sack?'

'No! In the staff-room. Does he clear away his coffee mug? Does he always read the notice-boards? Is he one of these great intellectuals who talk about the brain as an extension of the bicep? Of course in the sack, you turkey!'

'Oh . . . young. And fit. And enthusiastic . . . And quite, quite big,' I tell her, and she just about spills her wine again. 'It's his age, though. That's the real problem.'

'He sounds quite mature . . . volunteering his free time.'

'He is. Well, sort of. But he's into himself, not in an arrogant way, but he knows the girls like him. And he definitely thinks like a single lad. Besides, he's moving to Sweden for a year at Christmas.'

'I thought he said he's only thinking about it?'

'Oh, I bet he'll go. He wants a break from his job and wants to take off and live his life. He's got no commitments. He has an on-off thing with his girlfriend . . . I don't think he's the type to let that stand in his way. No, he's going. I can tell.' I'm as certain of it as I was that Sean wasn't moving to Seattle. 'He'll get there and screw legions of really beautiful *natural* blondes.'

'I bet he didn't have any complaints about you not being a natural blonde!'

I grin again, feeling myself blush thinking how eager I was for him. 'He didn't, actually.'

She chortles. 'I can't believe you were going to sit and watch a movie before you told me this!'

'It's not really that revolutionary though, is it? I mean, sex. We all do it. Okay, some of us haven't done it in a while. But the bigger, better news that you're forgetting is that I have my first client! That's what we should really be talking about – not men. Why do we always talk about men? Isn't the job the best thing that came out of last night?' It should be, but with the thought of Kye on top of me, I'm not so sure.

'To your first client.' She holds up her glass. 'You go, girl!' We toast.

'Who needs men, Ange? You have a home! You have a proper place to live!'

'I do! And I think I'm going to live in it. There's still going to be bills to pay, so I still have to get some income coming in, but I actually think I can live there. I think it's the right thing to do.'

'You have a home, you have a client, and you're getting laid.' She shakes her head and looks at me enigmatically. 'How the heck did all that happen, Ange? How did it all just fall into place?'

'I don't know, Sherrie. I really don't know.'

But in a very weird way, I think I do.

23

On Saturday morning, I ring my mother to see if she's heard anything from the doctor. Also, I wanted to tell her I've downloaded the immigration papers from the Internet and am slowly wading through the forms, to start the process of sponsoring her to come and live with me.

The phone rings and rings. Strange: she's usually home at this time. I'll have to remember to try her again in a couple of hours.

The Salvation Army van comes and gets the furniture belonging to Ms Elmtree that I decide I don't want to keep – her bed, the seat she always sat in by the window that looks grotty now, and a few other things. Then Richard helps me strip the kitchen and living room of the ancient floral wallpaper. We work together comfortably, without talking, with the radio on the classic rock channel: the Rolling Stones' 'Paint it Black' back-to-back with David Bowie's 'Ashes to Ashes', as we pull long and satisfying strips of paper off to reveal a knobbly surface.

'I'm going to do the kitchen in an off-white, and the front room and the stairs in a very pale yellow,' I tell him. 'I thought a richer yellow for the entrance and small corridor might be nice, as well as yellow for my mam's room, and maybe a pale blue for my bedroom, to make my room an extension of the sky . . . Sunny, happy colours.' I've already given my month's notice at the apartment.

Richard looks across at me from atop the stepladder and just smiles.

Yesterday, as I was showing out the man who came to hook up my phone, I met my neighbours – the ones who bought mine and Jonathan's house. I couldn't face meeting them when I sold; I just let the agent handle everything. They're a nice young couple who've just had a baby girl, Chloe. I didn't bother explaining that I used to live in their house. I didn't want to tell them that Jonathan had died, and somehow bring bad karma to a place where a newborn has just arrived. But I like her – Yvonne, the mother. I could see us being friends.

After we're done stripping, Richard perches on the wine-coloured couch. I decided against giving that to charity; it has a certain vintage, decrepit look that somehow says *keep me, I come with the house.* I make us a cup of tea. The other day he was telling me that he thinks Jessica knows he was contemplating leaving her. He said she's been acting 'silently admonishing'.

'You have dust on your nose,' he tells me, affectionately, as I hand him his cup. He points to the end of his own nose. I rub it away, then sit down on one of the boxes Richard helped me move over from the apartment.

'Phew! It's going to be a hell of a job, Richard. What have I taken on?'

'You've got all the time in the world,' he tells me, after a slurp. 'And I'll help you all I can.'

I wonder if Jessica ever resents his involvement with me, if she's sensed his feelings. Did Jonathan know? 'You already have,' I tell him.

He puts his mug down carefully on the floor. 'The thing is . . . I owe you, Angela, more than you realise.' He looks out of the window, then draws a sharp breath and wipes a hand over his mouth.

'What does that mean?' For some weird moment I wonder if he's actually going to admit he loves me.

'Things that weigh on the mind, you know.' He taps his temple, then meets my eye. 'They sit there and you know you're not going to be able to forget them, and that one day it all has to be out in the open. There's no other way.'

'I'm not with you,' I say.

'I should have told you sooner, Ange. I don't know, I think I was nervous about owning up to it . . .' He looks at me quite intensely now.

He's definitely going to tell me he loves me.

'Have you ever wondered why Jonathan ended up losing all that money in the mining venture?'

'Erm . . .' Okay. Maybe he's not. 'No. Well, he made a bad investment, didn't he?'

'Yes, but why did he?' He doesn't wait for my answer. 'Because it was me. I was the one who got him involved in it.'

For some moments I can't react. Then, of course, it all makes sense. Why didn't I sense this before? That there had to be something greater than friendship and affection. This is why Richard is always trying to throw money at me – not because he likes to play the protector, as I briefly thought – but to try to help me keep our house, because he felt responsible for my losing it.

'Oh! Richard! Don't be guilty about that. You've nothing to feel bad about.'

'It was a reliable tip. I wouldn't have gone into it if it hadn't been. I had a vision that we were all going to become instant millionaires.' He rubs a hand over his mouth again. 'The odd thing is, I've never played with my money. I'm always . . . I don't know. Careful. With just about everything.' He looks me right in the eyes. 'Being careful and doing the right thing has always been my downfall. But I had a very strong feeling about this. The odds seemed that we were going to do very well.'

How could I ever blame Richard, who I know would only ever act in Jonathan's and my best interests? 'It wasn't your fault, Richard. How could you ever think I would hold that against you? Jonathan made up his own mind to get into it. You know what he was like.'

'Yes, but I let him put far too much money into it. Far more than I was prepared to put.'

'Yes, but that was Jonathan, always taking risks. You know how it used to drive me mad. Because I'm the complete opposite.' It's back again: anger at him being the way he was.

'That's what I mean. Don't you see? I knew that about him, yet I didn't protect him from himself. And when we lost . . . well, I lost what I could afford to lose and he – you guys – you lost everything.'

'I can't feel pain for money, Richard. Do you understand that? It's old news, now. I've moved on. We all have.'

'Even Jonathan,' he says.

He drinks his tea, stands up, looks across the street to our old house for a long while, then walks to the kitchen with the cup. When he comes back, he stands behind me, so I can't see him unless I turn.

'The thing is . . .' His voice becomes very quiet. I let him talk to my back. 'There's not a day goes by when I don't wonder if the stress of the stock going south is what brought on his seizure that day in the car.'

There it is. Richard is blaming himself for Jonathan's death, just like I've blamed myself. We both think we killed him, yet neither of us did. For a moment I want to get up and put my arms around him, but I know that's the wrong thing to do. I want Richard to go home to his wife, to his life. I want us all to try to forgive ourselves.

'Don't think like that. Stress doesn't cause seizures, Richard,' I lie. In fact, seizures can be triggered by stress, if you're prone to having them. When I turn around, he looks at me. His eyes have tears in them. I know that no amount of reasoning is ever going to remove every last trace of guilt, that always in the darkest corner of his mind – and mine – will be the little question: Could I have stopped it?

I can't bear to see his face, so I look away again.

He continues to stand there for a moment. Then he says in a very flat voice, 'I should go. Jessica will be . . .'

He doesn't finish. We both just stand there awkwardly. 'Let's not talk about this again, shall we not, Richard?'

He closes his eyes, nods.

'Thanks,' I tell him. 'For everything . . .' I touch his face.

He lays his hand on the small of my back, just briefly. Before he moves it away, I feel the firm, short, massage of his fingers.

'Bye,' he whispers, seeming reluctant to move.

When I hear the clunk of the front door, I slowly let my breath out.

I miss Greece. Light, lovely Greece. Georgios, the olive groves, and, to a certain extent, Sean and my day with him. It just comes upon me suddenly, making me dig out the little book with the verse in it. I looked up the poet on the Internet – Iannis Mariatos – but couldn't find anything to suggest he was famous. I read the words over and over, feeling more nostalgic, more optimistic, than sad. I look at my lovely Greek thumb ring that I never take off, even when I sleep, thinking of everything it stands for. Then I get out the camera and start going over all the photos.

One of the first on there is the one of my mam that I took in our bedroom on our first day there. She's standing against the wall, wearing her white mermaid skirt and gold and green Per Una T-shirt, looking strikingly curvaceous and young. I've fired the shutter just in time to catch that look of dignified scathing on her face. She's pretending she finds having her photo taken a big bore, when really she's lapping it up and laying it on thick: her best, most movie star-like pose. I smile.

But then, oh, God! Hang on . . . Somehow, in my mucking about with the buttons, I must have managed to press the video mode. Because all of a sudden, I'm watching a video of my mam, complete with sound. She's lying on the bed in her petticoat and I can hear me prattling on about whether Georgios flirts with all the tourists.

She says it's only us because we're irresistible, and I say, 'My backside,' and she jumps up, bends over and shoves her bum in my face. Then she glances at me over her shoulder. It's a haggard, slightly vacant expression: not the most flattering. She'd hate it. I remember, when I was a kid, how she'd take the scissors to any photo that she didn't like of herself. We've got a shoebox full of photos that have squares cut out of them, where she's lopped off her own head.

'You're a bit disgusting sometimes, for a mother.' I hear myself saying.

Then she smiles. The sort of smile that only a person who loves dearly could give to the object of their adoration.

And then the video cuts out.

I pick up the phone to ring her and tell her, and have a laugh. But it just rings and rings and eventually the answering machine cuts in.

I'm about to put my camera away when I notice that for some reason, the next thing that's come up is a photo of Jonathan. I don't know how it got there – between a video of me and my mother and a photo of a Zante beach – but I recognise it. I took it in Barbados – a close-up of him smiling, looking very unlike Jonathan – peaceful and laid-back. Not looking scathingly at me, not looking impatient, bored, or like he's just told me I shouldn't be so pent up, so scared of everything, so bothered what people think . . . Just smiling like a man who is pretty happy about life.

I stare at it for what feels like an eternity.

*   *   *

Kye has invited me to his house. He's going to cook for us.
My first instinct was to say no, but my body wanted to say
yes. Since I had sex with him a week ago, it's been on my
mind every minute of every day – even more so than my
impending meeting with my first client, which is ridiculous,
really.

Kye lives in White Rock, which is about forty minutes away
by car. It'll be the first time I've driven my Honda Civic in a
good while. I'd thought about selling it, to eliminate expense.
But if I do get clients who are not right downtown, how am I
going to get out to see them, if I don't have a vehicle?

Last night I watched *The Godfather III* on the telly. The last
time I saw it was about four months after Jonathan died.
There's a scene where Al Pacino is coming down the steps of
the opera house after hearing his son's debut performance,
and there's a hail of bullets and his daughter gets shot in the
chest. Al falls to his knees and he tenderly holds her limp
shoulders as he watches her die. Then he screams, only we
don't hear it. It's trapped inside him, overlaid by the music of
Cavalleria rusticana. And then, with his agonised face held
there on the screen, the scream that was trapped inside him
comes out.

I couldn't watch that scene because I'd think of a hail of
shattered windshield glass, a symphony of metal and tyres,
Jonathan having an epileptic seizure at the wheel of his Z4. But
last night when it was on, I felt only Al Pacino's pain, not my
own.

It was the same with the car. There was a while, after the
accident, when I couldn't drive without imagining I was
Jonathan losing control at the wheel. Every hair on my body
would stand up and I'd get a clammy sweat on and a racing
heart. There'd be an awful instant where I'd see myself
suddenly turning the wheel into an oncoming juggernaut.
And I'd hear it, the symphony of metal and tyres. Then I'd

be outside my own body looking down, seeing the shattered windshield glass, seeing me die the way he did.

But tonight I enjoy the drive. It feels liberating being behind the wheel again. Driving south on the Granville Street Bridge, away from Vancouver's dramatic skyline, with the indigo mountains to my right and the ocean looking like a sheet of aquamarine glass in this unreal, fragile stage before sunset, makes me suddenly feel like I have something good ahead of me.

Kye doesn't want me to come over before ten, as he's not going to be home before then. I thought about teasing him about whether he had another date before me, but I didn't. Do I really want to know? Besides, I don't want to start claiming rights to him or it'll take all the fun out of it. Ten's a little late for me for dinner, but I'm hungry, and apprehensive all the same.

The fields and trees out by the highway are still green. And White Rock, the beachy suburb only minutes from the Canada–US border, with its boulevard of trees lit with tiny blue and white lights, is as pretty as I remember it being when I once came with Jonathan and we ate fish and chips on the pier.

His house is small and a total tip. Very much the sort of place you'd expect a young teacher, who doesn't earn much money, to live. Amidst all the rubble of a single man's life, he has an expensive, giant-screen LCD TV. It makes me smile. So does his attempt at making pasta, which consists of chucking a jar of barely warm bottled sauce over some very soggy noodles, which have been on the boil for about half an hour. But he's splurged and bought fresh Parmesan and a bottle of red wine. 'A' for effort. Or maybe B+.

The sex is definitely in my top ten. I tell him this.

He scowls, looking a mite put out. 'Top one would be better.'

It feels like something a young guy would say.

He doesn't quite know how to read me. Because he *is* young. I see it every time I look at him: the absence of hard knocks.

'I've never been to bed with an older woman before,' he says, gazing at me with that impersonal interest you see in young men who know you're only one of a very long string of lovers they're going to have in their lifetime.

'I've never been to bed with a man who's considered me to be an older woman before,' I tell him.

'You're obsessed with age,' he tells me.

'You're the one who brought it up!' I poke him hard in the chest. When we were talking earlier, he said his on-off girl-friend was a few years younger than him. 'So,' I say to him, 'if I'm so obsessed with my age, then, do you like screwing an older woman?'

He pretends to think about this. Or at least, I hope he's pretending! 'Erm. Yes,' he says. 'Yes, I do.'

So we do it again. Just so I can make sure.

I drive home feeling somehow unsettled. Thinking of Kye, thinking of a night and a morning of sex – good sex – thinking of my new client, thinking of my new house, thinking of my mother coming here to live with me, thinking of Richard. Subconsciously thinking of Jonathan.

Everything is good, I tell myself. I've had commitment-free sex with an extremely handsome young guy who I have no intention of getting into a serious relationship with. It was fun. I have everything to be happy about. Never mind that the married best friend of my dead husband might be in love with me, or that for a moment I might have believed that Jonathan had sent me him.

I stab at the radio, searching for songs that might distract me from this dissatisfied feeling I suddenly have; none comes on.

There's a breeze today. Even though it's sunny, it feels like fall, which makes me feel sad and exiled and I don't know why.

For the twenty minutes or so that I am on the highway, I just listen to the burr of my wheels on the road, feeling a strange sort of blah.

As I near where I live, I think how all the trees in my leafy neighbourhood are soon going to lose their leaves and how barren it's all going to look, and how I'm going to be surrounded by family homes, only I'm not going to have a family myself, am I? And then for some reason I think of my mother not answering the phone. It's in that awful, hollow instant that I realise something.

Something has happened to her.

24

I bomb through a 30 km-per-hour zone doing about 90. I bomb right through the four-way stop, wild-eyed, illogical, apoplectic with fear. There is one thought only in my head: I have to hear her voice.

My mother lying passed out on the kitchen floor flashes across my mind. That's why she wasn't answering the phone. Maybe she hit her head.

A whoop comes out of me, like a giant sob that has no beginning and no end, it just rolls around, unable to break free of my throat. I bomb down our street, screech up at my front door. Yvonne is in our old garden and she stops what she's doing to stare, paralysed by the sight of me. I flee inside, almost having to break the garden gate. My hand is trembling so hard I can't get the key in the door. I drop it. Twice. Squeal.

In the living room, fear turns me to stone. The message light on my phone is flashing. I sink onto the sofa, far, far, far too freaked out to play it. I'm still staring at it when it rings. I jump three feet. It's the call. Telling me what I already know. I can't pick up.

It stops. The room goes quiet again, except for the sound of my heartbeat pulsing in my ears. In a spurt of bravery, I pick it up and dial her number. She always gets it before the fourth ring.

One.

Two.

Eight rings.

The recording of her voice tells me that she's not able to come to the phone right now.

I clash the receiver down and curl into a foetal ball. Pictures of her flash before my eyes. Memories, random and senseless, coming at me. Always her and me; my dad in there somewhere too. But always me and my mam. I always wondered what losing her was going to feel like.

The phone rings again. I have to get it this time.

'Angela?' I hear the voice. 'Angela?'

I say the immortal word. 'Mam?'

'Well, who else do you think it is? Joan Collins?'

I start to cry. 'You're not dead!'

There's an odd pause. 'Dead? Are you mocking the afflicted again?'

That pain again, shooting up my nose, filling my head. 'I just phoned . . .' I'm sobbing. 'I thought something had happened. That you'd fainted again. That you were lying there on the kitchen floor . . .'

She laughs now. 'I was on the toilet!'

I want to kill her. 'Why the sodding hell are you laughing? What's funny about it?'

The harder I bawl, the harder she chortles. 'Oh, Angela, you've got to get rid of this business of always thinking people are dying. Nobody wants to think you're looking at them convinced they're going to peg out any minute. It's not nice. It's enough to give them a twitch!'

'But then where the hell have you been? I've been ringing and ringing . . .' Really, when I think about it, it's only been about twice. In my frolicking with a younger man, I'd sort of forgotten about my mother and the blood tests.

'I went to London to meet Georgios!'

'Georgios?'

'He surprised me. Said if I wasn't going there, he was coming here.'

'But . . . but what about the doctor?'

'I'm all right! It's only my thyroid. I mean, not *only*. It's quite a serious thing if it's not looked after. He said it's called Graves' disease. My thyroid's overactive, basically. Which explains a lot of things – why I've been so tired, not sleeping, going to the potty all the time, a few other things. You'd think he'd have checked it when I went up there to see him a few weeks ago. He said he thought it was irritable bowel syndrome when I said I was doing a lot of Barrys . . .'

Despite feeling at the end of my nerves, I have a titter. 'Good God, Mam . . .'

'I've got to go on some pills, which is the bad news. But the good news is the Beautiful Pretty pills must be working, because my blood pressure's gone down.'

'It was high in Greece, when that doctor took it.'

'He was gorgeous. I think he got me worked up.'

I suddenly feel very impatient with her. 'Mam, I've worried myself sick. Didn't you think of ringing me to tell me all this before you swanned off to London to see Georgios?'

'I forgot.'

'You FORGOT?' I do more than despair. 'Your bloody toy boy Georgios never mentioned he was going to London in his emails to me!'

'We'll remember to report to you first, next time we plan anything spontaneous.'

'You both need to grow up and start taking some responsibility! Buggering off to London! I thought you were dead!'

'Stop saying that!' she says, traces of a laugh behind the words.

I feel shattered, like I've been through the mill. 'So, now you're going to run off with him into the sunset, are you? Is that what you're about to tell me?'

'Yes, actually . . . We got married.'

I just about drop with shock. 'Bloody what?'

There's a pause, then she says, 'I'm kidding.'

'You're kidding? You're sick!'

'Yes! Of you!'

'Look . . . can you be serious for a minute and tell me what's really going on?'

'Nothing's going on. I mean, nothing very important. Because, my dear, you might find this hard to believe, but Georgios is not The One. I went to London to give him one more chance, to see if he might be, but it just didn't happen for me.' She sighs, sounding like the very topic is tiresome. 'I'm sorry, but the earth hasn't moved.'

I'm not quite sure what she's getting at, and I don't feel like asking. 'What about him? I think he might be in love with you.'

'Yes, because he thinks I'm playing hard to get. But the thing is, I'm not playing.'

Good God, she's mental. 'Look, can you just think about something, for a minute, before you write him off?'

'Heh?'

'Well, Mam, Georgios *is* a catch. I mean, God, I'd have had him. A lot of women would think you were very lucky.'

'A lot of women would think I was lucky to get your dad. Angela, other people's standards shouldn't make you rethink your own.'

'So Georgios doesn't meet your standards, is that what you're saying?'

'He's just . . . he's just . . . It's not him, Angela. It's me. There's something I'm not feeling. Something I want to feel. I suppose . . . I suppose I'd like to have what you and Jonathan had, if the truth be told.'

Isn't it usually the other way round? The daughter wanting what her parents had?

This softens me, though. 'So would I,' I tell her.

* * *

Today would have been Jonathan's thirty-eighth birthday.

I have not yet learned to rationalise my emotions, and I'm not sure I want to. But I've prepared myself to have a very 'down' day. But, to tell the truth, it feels more like an exercise in faking sadness.

In my new house, I find myself sitting by the window, after breakfast, gazing across the street at our old home. So many memories come to me; but good ones, not sad ones. I realise I don't have to look at the house where he once lived to feel he was ever there. Because he still is here. He's moved over the street with me. He'd have followed me if I'd gone to the moon. That's just the way death is. I don't think I even believe in death any more. All death is, is living once or twice removed.

I go for a bit of a crazy boozy lunch with my new client, a very nice girl who works under Crystal – Sienna is her name. She and I hit it off really well. Next week I'm going to be giving two workshops at Zeit Media. One on a guide to effective report and proposal writing, and the other a grammar refresher. It's all very scary and very exciting. Sienna, though, is excited for another reason. Her boyfriend of just six months proposed, and she's wearing a whopping one-carat diamond from Tiffany. She felt like celebrating, and I am a legitimate excuse for a fancy, expense-account lunch. We don't speak one word of business the whole time. I ask her why they got engaged so quickly. Her answer is, 'We knew. Why wait?' I smile softly, thinking, *lucky her*. It's a lovely lunch. I come away feeling like I've acquired not just a client, but perhaps a new friend.

It strikes me that when I celebrated all of the firsts after Jonathan died, I'd focus on doing anything that would take my mind off what I might have been doing with him. But right now what I want most for his birthday is to do the very thing I'd have done with him if he'd been alive. I'm going to celebrate his life even if he's not here to do it himself. As long as I'm around, Jonathan's always going to have his birthdays.

I call in at the wine store and while I'm perusing the selection, I notice the Marilyn Merlot Napa Valley 2004 with Marilyn Monroe's sexy pout all over the label. Jonathan loved her. He'd have bought it just for the novelty. It surely has to be the perfect choice, then . . .

At home, I crack it open and pour myself a big glass, taking the bottle with me into the back garden. I'm back to thinking about Sienna and her boyfriend, and the idea of them getting engaged so quickly because they knew it was right. I think of my mother knowing that Georgios isn't right. Then I think of me. My Greek meander ring sparkles in the last of the evening sunshine. I move my thumb so that the white gold parts glint in the light, and seem to bring the ring alive. My Greek ring, symbolising the flow of life, eternal life, eternal love.

Just then, the phone rings and I hear Kye's voice. I let the machine take it. I know I won't see Kye again. I didn't know it until about three seconds ago, but now I'm sure of it. I'll see him at the Epilepsy Canada meetings, which is going to be a bit weird, no doubt, especially at first. But I won't see him *that way*. The sex was nice and I'm glad I had it, but it feels good backing off now. I can't see him being too heartbroken. For a brief second, it crosses my mind that Jonathan might have sent me Kye for a quick fling, but more importantly, for me to remember that I'm only going to love the one who is right.

I sit there until it's black dark and I'm chilly, then I go in the house, taking my glass and empty wine bottle.

I've got used to my bedroom, to sleeping under the skylight with the moon shining right in my eyes when I open them. Tonight, though, I'm restless. It's a full moon, and I'm convinced the more I stare at it that I see life up there. It makes me think of Georgios, and his story about Selene, goddess of the moon, and what Georgios and I said that night at the restaurant about how there's always one star that seems to shine brighter than the rest, that seems to twinkle just for us.

Is there really a star that's guiding me? Sometimes I'm sure Jonathan's up there, making something happen, and other times I don't believe in anything other than what I know for a fact – that which can be proven.

'Maybe you just couldn't do it,' I whisper into the dark moonlit room. 'I asked you to send me someone to love, Jonathan, but maybe that was hoping for the impossible.'

The idea that there is something my highly capable husband can't do doesn't make me feel good. I don't want to lose faith in him, or have him diminish in my eyes.

I hold my breath for a few moments, to see if he might say something to reassure me that I'm right in believing he's too stubborn to let death defeat him. To see if he might send me some sort of sign.

A sign, though, when I'm asking for one, wouldn't be Jonathan's style.

25

The newspaper delivery lad – the same lad that used to come when I lived across the street – still has the same lazy habit of flinging the paper onto the lawn instead of the deck, so when it's chucking rain, like it is this morning, I have to get sopping wet, not to mention muddy feet, to go and get my soggy daily news.

I catch him, though, this time. 'Can you just make sure you put it on the deck, please? All the way, if it's not too much trouble.'

He looks at me, recognition flooding his small, fat, freckly face. 'You moved,' he says.

I pull my dressing-gown around me. 'Did I?' I beam at him. 'Maybe you're just losing it.'

'You're the cranky one from across the street!' He looks almost pleased to see me.

'You've definitely got the wrong person,' I tell him.

He walks off, looking over his shoulder at me strangely.

I walk back inside the house, feeling chilly. The weather has changed now, and I wish we could fast-track through winter and months of rain, and have long, warm summer nights again.

The weekend edition is a thick one. I separate sections of the paper, randomly discarding all the ones I don't care to read: Sports, Automotive, Classified . . . I drop them on the floor beside the sofa, keen to find the one I enjoy the most: Arts & Life.

I'm just sitting down in the chair by the window, with my freshly brewed cup of Illy coffee, when the phone rings.

Who would phone at this time on a weekend, if not my mam checking up on me? I pick up. 'Yeah, yeah. What d'you want, this early, Viv?'

I'm expecting her chuckle, but what I get is an, 'Oh. Shit. Sorry to disappoint you. I'm not Viv.'

It doesn't take long for the accent to sink in. The voice.

'Is it really that early there, though?' he says. 'I thought Vancouver and Seattle were in the same time zone?'

'Sean?'

There's another pause, where I feel his pleasure waft through the phone. 'What gave the game away?' he asks, with the sound of a smile in his voice. 'Was it the Irish accent, or the bit about Seattle? I'm dead curious.'

Sean? Can it really be him? 'Oh . . . it was just a wild guess.'

Now I remember him, just as quickly as I'd almost forgotten him. Sean McConnell. The man I sort of fell for, who I left behind on a Greek island, who I thought I'd never hear from again.

'You moved,' I say, nervously playing with my thumb ring. 'I moved.'

'So this means . . . I mean, what does this mean? It means you've left her?' Thoughts of them dancing together seem to pinch me back to reality, and my guard creeps up.

'No, actually. She's sitting right here with me on the settee.'

I'm too astonished to speak.

'She's not,' he says. 'As it happens, I don't know what she's doing and I don't really care. I haven't seen her in nearly two months.'

I stare at my ring, rotating it with a finger, memories of that holiday swimming around me.

Sean McConnell – who left his wife – is here, only two hours away, in Seattle.

'I don't know what I'm supposed to say,' I tell him honestly, because I really don't.

'You're not supposed to say anything. I'm the one that rang you. I'm supposed to say things.'

'Say something, then.'

'Shit. This is harder than I thought it was going to be.'

I smile a bit. 'But . . . I mean, I don't even know how you knew where I am . . . How did you?' Did I give him my phone number? No, I definitely didn't.

'Oh . . . there aren't that many Angela Chapmans in Vancouver who run a company called Write Strategies with a website with a photo on it that looks like you.'

'No,' I say, and grin broadly. 'Just me and that other bitch.'

He laughs. 'But you're much better looking than her.'

'You're making me nervous,' I tell him.

'I have that effect on people,' he says, and then there's a very awkward pause.

'Well, the reason for my call, in case you are wondering – which I reckon you probably are – is that I've found this fabulous little street vendor at the Pike Street Market who makes a mean *gyros*, and I was wondering if you'd like to come down here and have one with me.'

'A *gyros*. Hang on . . . You want me to come all the way to Seattle for a *gyros*?'

'Not just any *gyros*. A bloody big, honking, fantastic pork one, to be precise. With lots of shredded lettuce, thin things of ripe tomato, and tzatziki. Lots of tzatziki slathered all over the place. And don't get me started about the buns.'

'You're very persuasive when you get going.'

'Don't fall over yourself hurrying to answer,' he says. 'The suspense is killing me. How about if I say there's absolutely no strings attached. If you want, you can literally come down here, eat, and leave. I won't be offended. I'll understand what the draw was.'

I can't seem to form a sentence. I'm just about to try to get my tongue around the word 'okay', when something happens. My nervous fiddling with my ring sends it flying right off my thumb. It seems to travel through the air almost in slow motion, and lands with an audible plunk onto the newspaper at my feet. Right onto the front page of the Lower Mainland section. Onto the picture of a man.

It's a face I recognise instantly.

'So, what's it going to be?' Sean says.

EPILOGUE

I take his craggy hand as we walk out of the basilica of Santa Maria in Trastevere, into one of the oldest piazzas in Rome. It's our last of seven nights here, before we move onto the island of Capri tomorrow.

It's the end of May, as yet not quite warm in the evenings, but my shiver vanishes when he puts his arm around me and I burrow into the softness of his navy sweatshirt.

The fountain in the centre of the piazza is floodlit and a throng of people sit on its steps. Two men on giant stilts, painted from head to toe in silver, perform daredevil acrobatics to a cheering crowd. From somewhere, classical music plays, so full and uplifting it feels like it could raise the sky.

We sit at a pricey patio in the square. The restaurant, Sabatini, brims with smart Romans ordering the standard fare – drawn-out courses of antipasti, followed by overpriced pasta, followed by platters of bright-eyed whole fish gleaming here and there with olive oil and lemon, or hunks of roasted lamb on the bone, propped up by a cluster of potatoes. I read about this place in the guidebooks, then completely forgot about it. Yet by chance we've just stumbled upon it, as though we were somehow meant to find it for our last night in this fantastic city. We order two wood oven pizzas, because that's exactly what we fancy, but we splurge on a good bottle of vino.

The pizza is perfect. The wine, a vibrant Chianti whose name I must write down, makes the meal and the moment thoroughly decadent. I get a rush of in-loveness with Rome, and my life – one of those *I could live here with you forever* moments. He sees it. Across the table, his mellow Harveys Bristol Cream eyes twinkle and flare, in response to the tears in my own. I'm too overcome with happiness to speak. He knows this. Even from the very first time we met, this Roger knew things without my having to tell him.

I never went to Seattle. Didn't have to. As soon as my ring landed on that photo of him in my newspaper – Roger Krieger, the controversial city planner opposing some garish new development that's slated to impress the world when the 2010 Winter Olympics is hosted in Whistler – I knew he was the one. I think I always knew from that first disastrous date. Only I wasn't ready then. When I'd gone to bed in my new house knowing I was ready to love again, but with a feeling in my bones that Jonathan had somehow, uncharacteristically, let me down, the fact that Sean phoned right the next morning felt uncanny. But when I saw Roger's face on the page of that newspaper, it felt like fate.

I told Sean I wouldn't be coming to Seattle, that I'd met somebody else. Then I found Roger Krieger's email address. I said that while I knew he probably wouldn't want to touch me with a barge pole after the way I'd behaved the last time we went out, I just wanted to write and tell him that I was feeling much better about myself now, and I was sorry about how our two attempts at dates had turned out. I wrote that any time he wanted to take me to a movie about a kinky widow who went around peeing in bushes while spying on her neighbours having sex, he had only to call. Although I added that I didn't expect he would. I imagined he'd have some other woman in his life by now – it was, after all, almost a year since I'd last seen him.

I got an out-of-office autoreply. He was out of town on business. The following Tuesday, I got a real one.

I hear they're making a sequel.
Roger
PS No other woman, since you asked.

I thought it was a bit short, and I didn't know what to make of it. But then he rang me that night.

'I'd rather do pizza again than the movie,' he said. 'Last time, the waitress felt sorry for me and didn't make me pay. I got to take your pizza home as leftovers. It made a great lunch. Maybe I might get lucky again?'

I smiled down the phone. 'But that assumes I'll walk out on you again.'

'Well, won't you?' he said quietly.

I knew I didn't want to be with Sean. Something about his black and white attitude to his marriage; his inability, it seemed, to forgive. And, Sean aside, I knew I wasn't going to let Roger get away twice.

'No,' I said. 'I'll stick around at least as far as coffee.'

'Can we give everything up and come live here?' I ask him now. He told me I'd love Rome. He was right.

'Yes,' he says, 'if you like.'

'We can? Why do you always give in to me?'

'I don't. I'm humouring you. There's a difference. Besides, I thought it was England you're always wanting to move to. And if we lived here, we'd have nowhere special to go on vacation.' He looks around. 'What could top this?'

I want to be finished with this meal, to walk hand in hand through the tiny, meandering streets of Rome, back to our small but charming B&B, back to our bed where he will hold me, and I'll fall asleep staring out of the window, imagining what we might do tomorrow and listening to the sound of his breathing.

'Nothing could top this,' I tell him.

* * *

We get off the ferry at Marina Grande, Capri's small, chaotic port.

We've somehow acquired a travelling companion: a rather eccentric British woman wearing a white picture hat, who is turning heads wherever we go.

'Has NOBODY in this country heard of the word queue?' she asks, as half the Italian population seem to be pushing on as we are trying to get off. 'You'd love to turn a hosepipe with some pesticide on them, wouldn't you? That'd teach them some manners.' She glares at me. 'We should have gone to Lake Garda.'

Some might call it an odd form of honeymoon, and they might well be right. But I could only afford two weeks off work as Write Strategies has got me quite busy these days, and I couldn't come all the way to Europe and *not* see her. Then I would have spent two weeks moping, and, as Roger said, that would have been a bit of a passion-killer. We have applied to sponsor her to live in Canada, but it could take a long time. So it was actually my husband's idea that we invite her along for our second week: that's the kind of man he is.

'Sophia Loren lives here somewhere,' she tells us, smiling as we cram into the funicular that lifts us high up through the fragrant lemon groves whose branches graze the side of the carriage. Up and up over the massive azure expanse of the Mediterranean, taking us to the island's centre. Her aging hand, with its ever-pink perfect nails clutches the central pole to steady her, her head turning with wonder and curiosity at the glittering view that quickly drops away from us. Roger has his hand around my waist; I feel his thumb rub my bare tummy where my T-shirt doesn't quite meet my skirt. I got my curves back. And my big boobs. I'm a lot like the old me again.

'We'll go looking for her,' he says to my mam.

'Will we?' Her eyes linger on him fondly. My mother loves Roger. 'I'm not sure she's worthy of our efforts, are you? She should come looking for us.' She does that enigmatic posing thing and casts her glance far out of the window; that look that tells me she's more of a star than Sophia ever could be.

Our hotel – Da Fiore – is charm's own self. A private, white, flat-roofed home down a narrow, twisting, bougainvillea-bedecked residential street, perched in a lofty position above this decadently beautiful island – the twinkling Med in sight, and abundant orange and lemon trees drooping over the walls of its small garden, spilling floral fragrance into the air. Da Fiore has a handful of rooms open to tourists who have come to enjoy a non-touristy experience of this moneyed island – and, more importantly, people who want to enjoy its gastronomic flavours, as prepared by Da Fiore's self-styled but quite celebrated chef, Giuseppe, who runs the place along with his son and daughter-in-law. Roger's sister came here several years ago and fell in love with it. A week here was her wedding present to us, which was generous, because it's pretty extortionate.

'*Gracious Ospitality*' reads the handwritten sign at the door. The three of us smile.

'Ow Ospitable of them,' my mother says, and cackles.

Giuseppe, presumably – the man himself – is sitting reading a book on a patio chair in a small, shady vestibule as we come in. He instantly claps his book closed and stands up; when I see it's an Italian translation of a Danielle Steel novel, I instantly start to wonder about the place where we have come to stay.

'Welcome!' he enthuses, in that way I've quickly come to know is sincerely Italian. His gaze falls away from Roger and me, and plasters itself all over my mother.

'We're the honeymooners,' Roger reminds him, right after my husband has taken out a small comb and run it through his hair: his very weird habit. 'Krieger. You have your best room for us.' That's my husband's sneaky way of ensuring he gets what he wants. He sets it up so people can't exactly refuse him. Like when he proposed.

We'd gone for bacon and eggs one Sunday morning at Sophie's Cosmic Café in my neighbourhood. After the waitress had refilled our coffee cups, he asked her if she would ask me if I would marry him.

'Which of the two beautiful ladies is your wife?' asks Giuseppe.

Argh. It's going to be another one of these, is it?

'Less of that dirty grin,' I elbow my mam. Two months ago, my mother went to visit Georgios. She still claims he's not The One, but until The One comes along, Georgios has obviously got something going for him. I, personally, am hoping that she's eventually going to see sense.

Wearing a navy and white checked apron around a stomach that's burgeoning somewhere between well fed and portly, our robust and not unhandsome host with the Kama Sutra eyes flicks through a reservations book, gives up, and searches in the chaos of a desk drawer until he pulls out a wrinkled and not very clean-looking piece of paper.

'*Allora* . . . The reservation was for one room,' he tells us, in adequate English, looking right at Roger. 'See this, here.' He holds out the piece of paper on which somebody has scrawled our last name, and some dates and numbers that could mean anything you wanted them to be, really.

'One room?' I repeat, before Roger can even reply. 'There's obviously been a mistake.'

'There is no mistake, *signora*.' His attention shifts to me. 'One room, and all our other rooms are full. So is take or leave. Is up to you.'

'Come on, it's our honeymoon!' my husband says. 'You must have two rooms.'

Giuseppe taps his pen rhythmically on the countertop,

looking like he's thinking. 'No,' he finally says. 'What we 'ave is a small problem. No?'

My husband sighs heavily through his nose.

'A word in your sweet shell-like.' My mam pulls me aside. 'Why don't you two stay here, as planned, and we just find me a room somewhere else?'

'Is not poss-ible,' Giuseppe butts in. 'Is holiday weekend. Everybody come to Capri. Capri 'otel full. Is waste of your time to try to find room when there is no room. Maybe Tuesday you try, but Saturday, Sunday, Monday, full, full, full.'

Roger sighs again. My husband is a patient man. He will exhaust all other solutions before resorting to fury. 'Maybe we should head to Naples for a few nights, Angela. What do you think?'

'Napoli full,' interrupts Giuseppe.

'Is his name Angela?' Roger says to me, then turns his back on our host. 'Rome, then. How about we head back to Rome?'

'Roma full,' says Giuseppe. 'Italia full. Full, full, full.'

Roger narrows his eyes at him and my mother bursts into a laugh.

Giuseppe's smitten gaze drapes itself all over her like a dust cloth over a good chair.

'There's really nothing funny, Mam! I don't know why you seem to think there is!'

'Isn't there?' she says. 'I think it's hilarious! We come all this way and there's nowhere to stay!'

'Look . . . I 'ave solution,' Giuseppe finally says, then looks for a moment like he's pleased he's got us hanging in suspense. 'I 'ave small house. Is very small, not enough for three,' he indicates with a flourish. 'Certainly not room enough for another man . . .' He gives Roger a disdainful once-over. 'However,' now his gaze is back to my mam, 'this room, it is quite comfortable, for one guest. If it please, the signora may stay there.'

'Done!' my mother fires, and Giuseppe's eyes alight very briefly on her 'buzzum', that does a particularly fetching heave as she speaks.

'Hang on,' I wag a finger at him. 'Where are *you* going to stay, pervert?'

'Angela!' my mother says.

'Don't worry. His English is not that good.'

'Is not your worry,' Giuseppe practically sings. But he's suddenly looking mighty pleased with himself.

'My sentiments exactly,' says my mother. 'Now put a sock in it. It's the best offer we've got. We can't go back to Rome, it's too far, and I can't go back to England, certainly not today.' She looks at me mischievously. 'Who knows? Maybe never.'

'I 'ave a boat,' Giuseppe tells us. 'I sleep on boat. If not on boat, I sleep in garden.' He gestures outside to the splaying lemon groves that make an unbroken green and yellow tent between the earth and the sky. 'If not in garden, I sleep 'ere.' He indicates the patio chair where he was seated, reading his Danielle Steel novel, when we came in. 'I am flatter you should worry about me and where I sleep,' he says to me, looking my mother over. 'But really, you should not.'

I catch them exchanging sneak-in-my-window smiles.

'Come,' Giuseppe says to her, with all the gallantry of a smitten Italian male. 'We go now and I show you.'

'It's what he's going to show you that's got me worried,' I mutter, but she's already sashayed to the door. She sends me one coquettish glance over her shoulder.

'The way things are looking, I'd be more worried for him,' Roger says in my ear.

Giuseppe seems to remember something. '*Aspeta . . .*' He scuttles towards a tiny fridge and pulls out a carafe of wine and two frosty glasses.

'I think you and I need to have a talk,' I say to my mam.

'About protection. In case you . . . in case you get pregnant.' There, I've said it; I'm officially as mad as she is. Her face lights up.

'There's diseases, too, Mam. Some nasty new ones, these days, and I bet he'll have caught a few . . . Maaaam!' I growl. 'I'm being serious.'

But she's already gone.

When Giuseppe sees my worried expression, he pats my arm as he hurries past me, like a man with bigger things on his mind right now, then he slaps Roger's back and flamboyantly indicates the wine waiting for us. 'You are just married. Sit. Drink. Celebrate. All is worked out good, no?'

I look at my new husband, who I realise I can love as much as I loved Jonathan. All is worked out good. I don't know how it happened, but it did. I rub my finger over the back of my ring that I had re-sized and that I've chosen to wear as my wedding band: the Greek meander – the flow of life, eternal life, eternal love. The ring I bought when I said goodbye to Jonathan. Goodbyes are never final things.

THE SECRETS OF MARRIED WOMEN
Carol Mason

Falling in love is easy.
Staying in love is harder . . .

Jill and Rob are happily married – until they discover that Rob can't have kids.

It isn't the end of the world for Jill. She's just happy to have a trustworthy husband, who loves her deeply and presses all the right buttons in the bedroom. But now Rob's gone off sex and refuses to even discuss it. In fact, all communication between them has come to a frustrating halt, and Jill just yearns for a little attention

It wouldn't be so bad if one of her best friends wasn't having the best sex of her entire life (albeit behind her husband's back) while her other friend has a gorgeous husband she's still in lust with.

But are things ever what they seem?

How well do we ever know our husbands, our best friends, or even ourselves?

Jill is about to find out when she faces infidelity and the truth head on . . .

'Full of realistic emotional twists' *Telegraph*